Bernard Cornwell was born in London, raised in Essex, and now lives mainly in the USA, with his wife. He was awarded an OBE in 2006.

As well as the Sharpe series, he is the author of a number of other historical novels including *Azincourt* and his current series on the Making of England.

For more information visit www.bernardcornwell.net

'The same combination of thorough research and narrative drive that distinguished its predecessors. It is a gripping read'
Independent

SHARPE'S REGIMENT

Richard Sharpe and the Invasion
of France, June to November 1813

BERNARD CORNWELL

HARPER

HARPER

An imprint of HarperCollins*Publishers*
77–85 Fulham Palace Road
Hammersmith, London W6 8JB

www.harpercollins.co.uk

This paperback edition 2012
3

Previously published in paperback by Fontana 1987
Reprinted five times

First published in Great Britain by Collins 1986

Copyright © Rifleman Productions Ltd 1986

Bernard Cornwell asserts the moral right to be identified as the author of this work

A catalogue record for this book is available from the British Library

ISBN 978 0 00 745287 3

This novel is a work of fiction.
The incidents and some of the characters portrayed in it,
while based on real historical events and figures, are
the work of the author's imagination.

Typeset in Minion by Palimpsest Book Production Limited,
Falkirk, Stirlingshire

Printed and bound in Great Britain by
Clays Ltd, St Ives plc

MIX
Paper from
responsible sources
FSC **FSC C007454**
www.fsc.org

FSC™ is a non-profit international organisation established to promote
the responsible management of the world's forests. Products carrying the
FSC label are independently certified to assure consumers that they come
from forests that are managed to meet the social, economic and
ecological needs of present and future generations,
and other controlled sources.

Find out more about HarperCollins and the environment at
www.harpercollins.co.uk/green

Sharpe's Regiment
is respectfully dedicated to the men of
The Royal Green Jackets,
Sharpe's successors

'. . . if any 'prentices have severe masters, any children have undutiful parents, if any servants have too little wages, or any husband too much wife, let them repair to the noble Sergeant Kite, at the sign of the Raven in this good town of Shrewsbury, and they shall receive present relief and entertainment. Gentlemen, I don't beat my drum here to ensnare or inveigle any man, for you must know, gentlemen, that I am a man of honour!'

From *The Recruiting Sergeant*
by George Farquhar (1678–1707)

SHARPE'S REGIMENT

PROLOGUE

Spain

JUNE 1813

PROLOGUE

Regimental Sergeant Major MacLaird was a powerful man and the pressure of his fingers, where they gripped Major Richard Sharpe's left hand, was painful. The RSM's eyes opened slowly. 'I'll not cry, sir.'

'No.'

'They'll not say they saw me cry, sir.'

'No.'

A tear rolled down the side of the RSM's face. His shako had fallen. It lay a foot from his head.

Sharpe, leaving his left hand in the Sergeant Major's grip, gently pulled back the red jacket.

'Our Father, which art in heaven.' MacLaird's voice choked suddenly. He lay on the hard flints of the roadway. Some of the dark flints were flecked with his blood. 'Oh, Christ!'

Sharpe was staring into the ruin of the Sergeant Major's belly. MacLaird's filthy shirt had been driven into the wound that welled with gleaming, bright blood. Sharpe let the jacket fall gently onto the horror. There was nothing to be done.

'Sir,' the RSM's voice was weak, 'please sir?' Sharpe was embarrassed. He knew what this hard man, who had bullied and whored and done his duty, wanted. Sharpe saw the struggle on the strong man's face not to show weakness in death and he gripped MacLaird's hand as if he could help this last

3

moment of a soldier's pride. MacLaird stared at the officer. 'Sir?'

'Our Father, which art in heaven, hallowed be thy name,' the words came uncertainly to Sharpe's lips. He did not know if he could remember the whole prayer. 'Thy kingdom come, thy will be done on earth as it is in heaven.' Sharpe had no belief, but perhaps when he died then he too would want the comfort of old phrases. 'Give us this day our daily bread, and forgive us our trespasses, as we forgive those who trespass against us.' One pound of twice-baked bread a day and it had been the bastard French who had trespassed. What were the next words? The flints dug into his knee where he knelt. 'Lead us not into temptation, but deliver us from evil, for Thine is the kingdom, the power, and the glory, Amen.' He thought he had remembered it all, but it did not matter now. MacLaird was dead, killed by a piece of stone the size of a bayonet that had been driven from a rock by the strike of a French cannon-ball. The blood had stopped flowing and there was no pulse in his neck.

Slowly Sharpe uncurled the fingers. He laid the hand on the breast, wiped the tears from the face, then stood. 'Captain Thomas?'

'Sir?'

'RSM's dead. Take him for burial. Captain d'Alembord!'

'Sir?'

'Push those picquets fifty yards further up the hill, this isn't a god-damn field-training day! Move!' The picquets were perfectly positioned, and everyone knew it, but Sharpe was venting an anger where he could.

The ground was wet, soaked by overnight rain. There were puddles on the track, some discoloured with blood. To Sharpe's left, where the hillside fell away, a party of men hacked at the thin soil to make graves. Ten bodies, stripped of their jackets and boots that were too valuable to be buried, waited beside the shallow trench. 'Lieutenant Andrews!'

'Sir?'

'Two Sergeants! Twenty men! Collect rocks!'

'Rocks, sir?'

'Do it!' Sharpe turned and bellowed the order. In this mood men were foolish who crossed the tall, dark-haired officer who had risen from the ranks. His face, always savage, was tight with anger.

He walked to the sheltered place by the big rocks where the wounded were sheltered from wind's knife-edge. Sharpe's scabbard, which held the big, Heavy Cavalry blade that he wielded with the force of an axe, clanged on the ground as he crouched. 'Dan?'

Daniel Hagman, Rifleman and ex-poacher, grinned at him. 'I ain't bad, sir.' His left shoulder was bandaged, his jacket and shirt draped over the bound wound like cloaks. 'I just can't fill my pipe, sir.'

'Here.' Sharpe took the short clay stump, fished in Hagman's ammunition pouch for the plug of dark, greasy tobacco, and bit a lump free that he crumbled and pushed into the bowl. 'What happened?'

'Bloody skirmisher. I thought the bastard was dead, sir.' Hagman was the oldest man in the Battalion; perhaps he was over fifty, no one really knew. He was also the best marksman in the Regiment. He took the pipe from Sharpe and watched as the officer brought out a tinder-box. 'I shot the bugger, sir. Went forward, and he cracks me. Bastard.' He sucked on the pipe, blew smoke, and sucked again. 'Angel got him. Knifed the bastard proper.' He shook his head. 'I'm sorry, sir.'

'Don't be a fool, Dan. Not your fault. You'll be back.'

'We beat the buggers, sir.' Hagman, like Sharpe, was a Rifleman; one of a Company who, like flotsam in this ocean

5

of war, had ended up in the red-jacketed ranks of the South Essex. Yet, out of cussedness and pride, they still wore their green jackets. They were Riflemen. They were the best. 'We always beat the buggers, sir.'

'Yes.' Sharpe smiled, and the sardonic, mocking look that his face wore because of the scar on his left cheek suddenly disappeared. 'We beat the bastards, Dan.' They had, too. The South Essex, a Battalion under half its full strength, worn down by war the way a bayonet is thinned by use and sharpening, had beaten the bastards. Sharpe thought of Leroy, the American who had been the Battalion's commanding officer. Leroy would have been proud of them today.

But Leroy was dead, killed last week at Vitoria, and soon, Sharpe knew, there would be a new Lieutenant Colonel, new officers, new men. Those new men were coming from England and Sharpe would give up his temporary command of this shrunken force that should not even have fought a battle this day.

They had been marching to Pasajes, ordered there in the wake of the great victory at Vitoria, when orders had come, brought on a sweating, galloped horse, that asked the South Essex to block this track from the mountains. The staff officer had not known what was happening, had only given a panicked account of a French force erupting from the frontier, and the South Essex, by chance, were closest to the threat. They had left their women and baggage on the main road and gone north to stop the French.

They succeeded. They had lined the track and their muskets had cracked in the deadly rhythm of platoon fire, flaying the northern approach, shredding the blue-jacketed enemy ranks.

The South Essex had not given ground. Their wounded had crawled to shelter or bled where they fell. Even when the enemy mountain gun had opened its fire, hurling back whole files in bloody shambles, they had not stepped back. They had fought the bastards to a standstill and seen them off, and now Major Richard Sharpe, the taste of tobacco still sour in his mouth, could see what price he had paid.

Eleven dead, and more would yet die of their wounds. At least twelve of the wounded would never return to the ranks. Another dozen, like Hagman, should live to fight again, unless their wounds turned filthy, and that fevered, slow death did not bear thinking about.

Sharpe spat. He had no water, for an enemy bullet had smashed his canteen open. 'Sergeant Harper!'

'Sir?' The huge Irishman walked towards him. Perhaps alone in the Battalion this Rifleman would not fear Richard Sharpe's anger, for Harper had fought beside Sharpe in every battle of this long war. They had marched the length of Spain until, in this summer of 1813, they were close to the French frontier itself. 'How's Dan, sir?'

'He'll live. Do you have any water?'

'I did, but someone worked a miracle on it.' Harper, who illicitly had red wine in his canteen, offered it to Sharpe. The Major drank, then pushed the cork home.

'Thank you, Patrick.'

'Plenty more if you need it, sir.'

'Not for that. For being here.' Harper had married just two days before and Sharpe had ordered the huge Irishman to stay with his new Spanish wife when the order to fight had come, but Harper had refused. Now Harper stared northwards at the empty horizon. 'What were the buggers doing here?'

'They were lost.' Sharpe could think of no other explanation. He knew that a number of French units, cut off by the defeat of Joseph Bonaparte at Vitoria, were straggling back to France. This one had outnumbered Sharpe, and he had been puzzled why they had broken off the fight when they did. The only explanation he could find was that the enemy must have suddenly realised that the South Essex did not bar the way to France and thus there was no need to go on fighting. The French had been lost, they had blundered into a useless fight, and they had gone. 'Bastards.' Sharpe said it with anger, for his men had died for nothing.

Harper, who at six feet four inches, was taller even than Sharpe, frowned. 'Terrible about the RSM, sir.'

'Yes.' Sharpe was looking at the sky, wondering whether more rain was coming. This summer had been the worst in Spanish memory. 'You've got his job.'

'Sir?'

'You heard.' Sharpe, while he commanded the Battalion, could at least give it the best Regimental Sergeant Major it would ever have. The new Colonel would be in no position to change the appointment. Sharpe turned away. 'Lieutenant Andrews!'

'Sir?' The Lieutenant was leading a morose party of men who staggered under the weight of small boulders.

'Put them on the graves!' The stones would stop animals scrabbling down to the shallowly buried flesh.

'All the graves, sir?'

'Just ours.' Sharpe did not care if the foxes and ravens gorged themselves on rotting French flesh, but his own men could lie in peace for whatever it was worth. 'Sergeant Major?'

'Sir?' Harper was half grinning, half unsure whether a grin was acceptable at this moment. 'Yes, sir?'

'We'll need a god-damned cart for our wounded. Ask a mounted officer to fetch one from the baggage. Then perhaps we can get on with this damned march.'

'Yes, sir.'

That night rain fell on the pass where the South Essex had stood and suffered, and where their dead lay, and from which place the living had long gone. The night's rain washed the scanty soil from the French dead who had not been buried but just covered with soil. The teeming water exposed white, hard flesh, and in the morning the scavengers came for the carrion. The pass had no name.

Pasajes was a port on the northern coast of Spain, close to where the shoreline bent north to France. It was a deep passage cleft in the rocks, leading to a safe, sheltered harbour that was crammed with shipping from Britain. The stores that fed Wellington's army came to Pasajes now, no longer going to Lisbon to be carried by ox-carts over the mountains. At Pasajes the army gathered the stores that would let it invade France, but the South Essex who, even before the fight in the nameless pass had been considered too shrunken by war to take its place in the battle line, had been ordered to Pasajes instead. Their job, until their reinforcements arrived, was to guard the wharves and warehouses against thieves. They were fighting soldiers, and they had become Charlies, watchmen.

'Bloody country. Bloody stench. Bloody people.' Major General Nairn punctuated each remark by tossing an orange out of the window. He paused, waiting hopefully for a cry of pain or protest from beneath, but there was only the sound of the fruit thumping onto the cobbles. 'You must be bloody disappointed, Sharpe.'

Sharpe shrugged. He knew that Nairn referred to the task of guarding the storehouses. 'Someone has to do it, sir.'

Nairn scoffed at Sharpe's meekness. 'All you can do here is stop the bloody Spanish from pissing in our broth. I'm disappointed for you!' He lumbered to his feet and crossed to the window. He watched two high-booted Spanish Customs officers slowly pace the wharves. 'You know what those bastards are doing to us?'

'No, sir.'

'We liberate their bloody country and now they want to charge us bloody Customs duty on every barrel of powder we bring to Spain! It's like saving a man's wife from rape, then being asked to pay for the privilege! Foreigners! God knows why God made foreigners. They aren't any bloody use to anyone.' He glared at the two Customs men, debating whether to shy his last orange at them, then turned back to Sharpe. 'What's your strength?'

'Two hundred and thirty-four effectives. Ninety-six in various hospitals.'

'Jesus!' Nairn stared incredulously at Sharpe. He had first met the Rifleman at Christmas and the two men had liked each other from the first. Now Nairn had ridden to Pasajes from the army headquarters in search of Sharpe. The Major General grunted and went back to his chair. He had white, straggly eyebrows that grew startlingly upwards to meet his shock of white hair. 'Two hundred and thirty-four effectives?'

'Yes, sir.'

'I suppose you lost some the other day?'

'A good few.' Three more men had already died of the wounds they received in the pass. 'But we've got replacements coming.'

Major General Nairn closed his eyes. 'He's got replacements coming. From where, pray?'

'From the Second Battalion, sir.' The South Essex, for much of the war, had only possessed one Battalion, but now, in their English depot at Chelmsford, a second Battalion had been raised. Most regiments had two Battalions, the first to do the fighting, the second to recruit men, train them, then send them as needed to the First Battalion.

10

Nairn opened his eyes. 'You have a problem, that's what you've got. You know how to deal with problems?'

'Sir?' Sharpe felt the fear of uncertainty.

'You dilute them with alcohol, that's what you do. Thank God I stole some of the Peer's brandy. Here, man.' Nairn had pulled the bottle from his sabretache and poured generous tots into two dirty glasses he found on the table. 'Tell me about your bloody replacements.'

There was not much to tell. Lieutenant Colonel Leroy, before he died, had conducted a lively correspondence with the Chelmsford depot. The letters from England, during the previous winter, told of eight recruiting parties on the roads, of crowded barracks and enthusiastic training. Nairn listened. 'You asked for men to be sent?'

'Of course!'

'So where are they?'

Sharpe shrugged. He had been wondering exactly that, and had been consoling himself that the replacements could easily have been entangled in the chaos that had resulted from moving the army's supply base from Lisbon to Pasajes. The new men could be at Lisbon, or at sea, or marching through Spain, or, worst of all, still waiting in England. 'We asked for them in February. It's June now; they must be coming.'

'They've been saying that about Christ for eighteen hundred years,' Nairn grunted. 'You heard for certain they were being sent?'

'No,' Sharpe shrugged. 'But they have to be!'

Nairn stared into his brandy as though it was a fortuneteller's bauble. 'Tell me, Sharpe, have you ever heard of a man called Lord Fenner? Lord Simon Fenner?'

'No, sir.'

'Bastard politician, Sharpe. Bloody bastard politician. I've always hated politicians. One moment they're grovelling all over you, tongues hanging out, wanting your vote, the next minute they're too bloody pompous to even see you. Insolent bastard jackanapes! Hate them! Hope you hate politicians, Sharpe. Not fit to lick your jakes out.'

'Lord Fenner, sir?' Sharpe knew bad news was coming. He knew that Major Generals, however friendly, did not ride long distances to share brandy with Majors.

'Foul little pompous bastard, he is.' Nairn spat the insult out. 'Secretary of State at War, works to the Secretary of State of War, and probably neither would know what a war was even if it stuck itself in their back passages. So he wrote to us.' Nairn took a piece of paper from his sabretache. 'Or rather one of his poxed clerks wrote to us.' He was staring at Sharpe rather than the letter. 'He claims, Sharpe, that there are no reinforcements available to the South Essex. That none have been sent, and none are going to be sent. None. There.' He handed the letter to Sharpe.

Sharpe could not believe it. He took the letter, fearing it, to find that it was a long list, sent by the War Office via the Horse Guards, of the replacements that could be expected in the next few weeks. At the end of the list was the South Essex, against whose name was written; '2nd Batt now Hold'g Batt. No Draft available.' That was all and, if it was true, it meant that the South Essex's Second Battalion had become a mere Holding Battalion; a place where boys of thirteen and fourteen, too young to fight, waited for their birthdays, or where men in transit or wounded men were put to wait for new postings. A rag-tag Battalion, without pride and of small purpose.

'It can't be true! There are recruits! We had eight recruiting parties!'

Nairn grunted. 'In a covering letter, Sharpe, dictated by His bloody Lordship himself, but which I won't offend you by showing to you, he recommends that your Battalion be broken up.'

For a few seconds Sharpe thought he had misheard Nairn. A Spanish muleteer shouted outside the window, from the harbour came the cranking sound of a windlass, and in Sharpe's head echoed the words 'broken up'.

'Broken up, sir?' Sharpe felt a chill in this warm room.

'Lord Fenner suggests, Sharpe, that your men be given to other Battalions, that your Colours be sent home, that your officers either exchange into other regiments, sell their commissions, or make themselves available for our disposal.'

Sharpe was incredulous. 'They can't do it!'

Nairn gave a sour laugh. 'Sharpe! They're politicians! You can't expect sense from the bastards!' He leaned forward. 'We're going to need all the experienced units we can scrape together; all of them, but don't expect Lord Fenner to understand that! He's the Secretary of State at War and he wouldn't know a bayonet from a ramrod. He's a civilian! He controls the army's money, which is why there isn't any.'

Sharpe said nothing. He was thinking of the Battalion's Colours laid up in some English church, hanging high in a dusty chancel while the men who had fought for them were scattered in penny-packets around the army. He was feeling anger, bitter anger, that his men, who had fought for those flags, who had suffered, whose comrades were in unmarked graves on a dozen battlefields would be broken up, disbanded. He was thinking of a Battalion that, like a family, had its quarrels and laughter, its warmth and pride, all to be sacrificed!

'Breaking you up.' Nairn said it brutally. 'Bloody shame. Busaco, Talavera, Fuentes d'Onoro, Ciudad Rodrigo, Badajoz, Salamanca, Vitoria, hell of a way to finish! Like sending a pack of hounds to the shambles, eh?'

'But we had eight recruiting sergeants out!'

'It's no good telling me, Sharpe, I'm just a dogsbody.' Nairn sniffed. 'And even if we make you into a provisional Battalion

13

you'll go on losing men. You need a draft of replacements!' It was true. If the South Essex was joined to another Battalion they would still take casualties, until the joint Battalion was shrunken and diluted again. Instead of being broken up, the South Essex would simply wither and die, its Colours forgotten, its morale wasted.

'No!' Sharpe almost howled the word in agonised protest. 'They can't do it!'

'Let us hope not,' Nairn smiled. 'The Peer is not happy. He is damned crusty about it, Sharpe.' Nairn spoke of Wellington. 'He has this strange idea that the South Essex could be useful to him in France.' The compliment was truthful. A veteran Battalion like the South Essex, even if its ranks were half-filled with raw replacements, had a morale and knowledge that doubled its fighting value. The South Essex had become a killing machine that could be guaranteed to face anything the French threw against it, while a fresh Battalion, however well trained in England, could take months to reach the same efficiency. Nairn splashed more brandy into the two glasses. 'The Peer, Sharpe, does not trust those bastards in London. War Office! Horse Guards! Foreign Office! Ordnance Department! We've got more damned offices running this damned war than we've got Battalions! They've made a mess of it, they've lost their paperwork, they've got their breeches round their ankles and they can't find mother to pull them up. Who's in charge at Chelmsford?'

Sharpe had to think. His brain was in a turmoil of anger and astonishment that his Battalion could be broken up! 'In Chelmsford, sir? Man called Girdwood. Lieutenant Colonel Girdwood.'

'Ever met him?'

'Never set eyes on him.'

'He's got men! He just doesn't want to lose them! Happens

14

all the time, Sharpe! Man has a Second Battalion, trains them, makes them into toy soldiers, and he can't bear sending them abroad where the First Battalion will make them dirty! So go and see this Girdwood.' Nairn said the name with mocking relish. 'Persuade Girdwood to give you some men from this so-called Holding Battalion! Lick Girdwood's boots! Get Girdwood drunk! Offer to pleasure Girdwood's wife! You'll find some men in Chelmsford!' Nairn laughed at Sharpe's expression, then tossed a sealed packet of orders to him. 'Authorisation for you and three others to go to England to select replacements. Be back by October. That gives you nearly four months.'

Sharpe stared at the Scotsman. 'Go to England?'

'I know it's a grim thought, Sharpe,' Nairn grinned, 'but nothing's going to happen here, nothing! Boody politicians won't let us invade France until Prussia makes up its mind whether to join the dance again. All we're going to do is take San Sebastian and Pamplona then sit on our backsides doing nothing! You might as well go home, you'll miss nothing. Go to Chelmsford.'

'I can't go home!' He meant he could not leave his men.

'You bloody well have to! You want the South Essex to die? You want to be a storekeeper?' Nairn drank his brandy. 'The Peer doesn't want to break you up. He'll make you into a Provisional Battalion if he must, but he'd rather you brought yourself up to strength. Go to Chelmsford, find men! If there are none there, then find other men!'

'And if there aren't any men?'

The Scotsman drew his finger across his throat. 'Death of a regiment. Damned shame.'

And now of all times? Now, when the army gathered its strength at the edge of Napoleon's heartland, on the border of France? Soon, perhaps this autumn or next spring, the men who had first landed at Lisbon would march into France and the South Essex should march with them. They had earned that privilege. On the day when the enemy's empire was finally brought down, the flags of the South Essex should be flying in victory. Sharpe gestured at Lord Fenner's letter. 'How do I oppose that?'

Nairn shook his head. 'It's a mistake, Sharpe! Has to be! But you can't put mistakes right by sending letters! We've written to the useless bastards, but letters to the Horse Guards are put in a drawer marked Urgent Business to be Ignored. But they can't ignore you. You're a hero!' He said it with friendly mockery. 'Go to Chelmsford, find your men, and bring them back. It will take half the time of doing it by letter.'

'Yes, sir.' Sharpe sounded dazed. Go to England?

'And bring me back some whisky, that is a direct order! There's a shop on Cornhill that gets the stuff from Scotland.'

'Yes, sir.' Sharpe spoke distractedly. Going home? England? He did not want to go, but if the alternative was to watch a Battalion die that had earned its right to tramp the roads of France, then he would go through hell itself. For his Regiment, and for its Colours that had flown through the cannon smoke of half a continent, he would go to England so that he could march into France. He would go home.

PART ONE

England

JULY – AUGUST 1813

CHAPTER ONE

Sharpe, arriving in Chelmsford, could not remember the way to the South Essex's depot. He had only visited the barracks once, a brief visit in '09, and he was forced to ask directions from a vicar who was watering his horse at a public trough. The vicar looked askance at Sharpe's unkempt uniform, then thought of a happy explanation for the soldier's vagabond appearance. 'You're back from Spain?'

'Yes, sir.'

'Well done! Well done! First class!' The vicar pointed eastwards, directing the soldiers out into the open country. 'And God bless you!'

The four men walked eastwards. Sharpe and Harper earned odd glances, just as they had in London, for they looked as if they had come straight from a Spanish battlefield and still expected, even in this county town's quiet streets, to meet a French patrol. Captain d'Alembord was dressed more elegantly than Sharpe or Harper, yet even his uniform, like Lieutenant Price's, showed the ravages of battle. 'It ought to work wonders with the ladies.' D'Alembord fingered a rent in his scarlet jacket, made by a French bayonet at Vitoria.

'Speaking of which,' Lieutenant Harry Price had drawn his sword as they left the town behind and now slashed with the blade at the cow-parsley that grew thick in the lane, 'are you going to give us some leave, sir?'

'You don't want leave, Harry. You'll only get into trouble.'

'All those girls in London!' Price said wistfully. 'Most of them haven't met a hero like me! Back from the wars and what are you smiling at, Sergeant?'

Harper grinned broadly. 'Just having a grand day, sir.'

Sharpe laughed. He was beginning to think that this journey was entirely unnecessary. He was convinced now that Lord Fenner's letter was a mistake, and that there were, indeed, replacements waiting in Chelmsford. In London Sharpe had visited the Horse Guards, reporting his presence to the authorities, and the clerk in the dusty, impatient office had confirmed that the Second Battalion was indeed at Chelmsford. The man could offer no explanation as to why it was now called a Holding Battalion, suggesting wearily to Sharpe that it was, perhaps, merely an administrative convenience, but he could confirm that it was drawing rations and pay for seven hundred men.

Seven hundred! That figure gave Sharpe hope. He was certain now that the First Battalion was saved, that within weeks, even days, he would lead the replacements south to Pasajes. He walked towards the barracks with high hopes, his optimism made yet more buoyant by the splendour of this summer countryside.

It seemed like a dream. Sharpe knew that England was as heavy with beggars and slums and horror as any city in Spain, yet after the plains of Leon or the mountains of Galicia, this landscape seemed like a foretaste of heaven.

They walked through an England heavy with food and soft with foliage, a country of ponds and rivers and streams and lakes. A country of pink-cheeked women and fat men, of children who were not wary of soldiers or strangers. It was unnatural to see chickens pecking the road-verges undisturbed, their necks not wrung by soldiers; to see cows and sheep that were in no danger from the Commissary officers, to see barns unguarded, and cottage doors and windows not broken apart for firewood, nor marked with the chalk hieroglyphs of the billeting sergeants. Sharpe still found himself judging every hill, every wood, every turn in the road as a place to fight. That hedgerow, with its sunken lane behind, would be a deathtrap to cavalry, while an open meadow, bright with buttercups and rising towards a fat farm on a gentle hill, would be a place to avoid like the plague if French cuirassiers were in the area. England seemed to Sharpe to be a plump country, lavish and soft. Yet if he found it strange it was nothing to the reaction of Harper's wife.

Harper had asked that Isabella should come with them. She was pregnant, and the big Irishman did not want her following the army into strange, hostile France. He had a cousin who lived in Southwark, and there Isabella had been deposited until the war should end. 'A man doesn't need his wife on his coat-tails,' Harper had declared with all the authority of a man married less than a month.

'You didn't mind her there before you were married,' Sharpe had said.

'That's different!' Harper said indignantly. 'The army's no place for a married woman, nor is it.'

'Will she be happy in England?' Sharpe asked.

'Of course she'll be happy!' Harper was astonished at the question. Happiness to him was being alive and fed, and the thought that Isabella might be fearful of life in a strange country did not seem to have occurred to him.

And, to Isabella, England seemed most strange. On the journey from Portsmouth to London she had shyly whispered questions to her husband. Where were the olive trees? Were there no oranges? No vines? No Catholic churches? She could not believe how full and plentiful were the rivers, how carelessly the villagers spilt water, how green, thick and tangled was the vegetation, how fat were the cows.

And even three days later, walking out of Chelmsford, it still seemed unreal to Sharpe that a country could be so plump. They passed ripening orchards, grain fields bright with poppies, and pigs running free that could have fed an army corps for a week. The sun shone, the land was warmed and fragrant, and Sharpe felt the careless joy of a man who knew that a task he had thought difficult or even impossible was suddenly proving so simple.

His optimism was dashed at the barracks. It was dashed as suddenly as if Napoleon's Imperial Guard had appeared in Chelmsford's marketplace. He had come here in hope, expecting to find seven hundred men, and the depot seemed deserted.

There was not even a guard on the gate. The wind stirred the dust, weeds grew between the paving stones, and a door creaked back and forth on ungreased hinges. 'Guard!' Sharpe's voice bellowed angrily and was met by silence.

The four soldiers walked into the archway's shadow. The depot was not entirely abandoned for, on the far side of the wide parade ground, a file of cavalrymen walked their horses. Sharpe pushed open the creaking door and looked into an empty guardroom. For a few seconds he wondered if the Battalion had been shipped to Spain, if somewhere on the wind-fretted ocean he had crossed their path on this useless mission, but surely the Horse Guards would have known if the Battalion had moved?

'Someone's home,' d'Alembord said. He nodded towards the Union flag that stirred weakly from a flagpole in front of an elegant, brick-built building which, Sharpe remembered, housed the officers' Mess and the regiment's offices. Beside the flagpole, its shafts empty, stood an open carriage.

Harper pulled his shako over his forehead. 'What in hell's name are cavalry doing here?'

'Christ knows.' Sharpe's voice was grim. 'Dally?'

'Sir?' d'Alembord was brushing the dust from his boots.

'Take the Sergeant Major. Go round this place and roust the bastards out.'

'If there's anyone to roust out,' d'Alembord said gloomily.

'Harry! With me.'

Sharpe and Price walked towards the headquarters building. Sharpe's face, Price saw, boded ill for whoever had left the guardroom empty and the depot unguarded.

Sharpe climbed the steps of the elegant house and, as at the main gate, there was no sentry at the door. He led Price into a long, cool hallway that was hung with pictures of red-coated men in battle array. From somewhere in the house came the tinkle of music and the sound of laughter.

Sharpe opened a white-painted door to find an empty office. A fly buzzed at the unwashed window above the dead bodies of other flies. The papers on the desk were thick with dust. A small, black-cased clock on the mantel had stopped with both its hands hanging down to the six.

Sharpe pushed open a second door on the far side of the hall. He stared into an elegantly appointed dining room, empty as the office, with a great, varnished table on which stood silver statuettes. A half-empty decanter of wine held a slowly drowning wasp. Sharpe closed the door.

The hallway was carpeted, its furniture heavy and expensive, and its paintings new. Above a curving staircase was a huge chandelier, its gilded brackets thick with wax. Sharpe put his shako on a table and frowned as the laughter swelled. He heard a girl's voice distinct above the trilling of the spinet. Lieutenant Price grinned at the sound. 'Sounds like a brothel, sir.'

'It does, too.' Sharpe's voice hid the anger that was thick in him, an anger at an unguarded barracks where women's laughter mingled with tinkling music.

He went to the last door in the hallway, the one that he remembered opened into the Mess and from which came the laughter. He pushed the door slowly open, stood in the dark shadows of the hallway, and watched.

Three officers, all wearing the yellow facings and chained-eagle badge of the South Essex, were in the room. Two girls were with them, one sitting at the spinet, the other blindfolded in the centre of the room.

They were playing blind-man's bluff.

The officers laughed, they dodged the lunges of the blindfolded girl. One of them stood guard so that she should not stumble into a low table that carried a tea of thin sandwiches, small pastries, and delicate porcelain cups. That officer, a Captain, was the first to see Sharpe.

The Captain made a mistake. It was a common enough error. In Spain men often mistook Sharpe for a private soldier for the Rifleman wore no badges of rank on his shoulders, and his red, whip-tasselled officer's sash had long been lost. He wore an officer's weapon, a sword, but in the hall's shadow the Captain did not see it. He only saw the rifle on Sharpe's shoulder and he assumed, naturally enough, that only a private would carry a long-arm. Harry Price, whose uniform was more conventional, was hidden behind Sharpe.

The Captain frowned. He was a young man with a sharp-featured, thin-lipped face beneath carefully waved blond hair. The smile he had worn for the game was suddenly replaced by irritation. 'Who the devil are you?' His voice was confident, the voice of the young master in his little domain, and it stopped the blindfolded girl in her tracks.

The other two officers were Lieutenants. One of them frowned at Sharpe. 'Go away! Wrong place! Go!'

The other Lieutenant giggled. 'About-turn! Quick march! One-two, one-two!' He thought he had made a fine joke and laughed again. The girl at the spinet laughed with him.

'Who are you? Well? Speak up, man!' The Captain's voice snapped petulantly at Sharpe, then suddenly died away as the Rifleman stepped out of the shadows.

The realisation that they might have made a mistake came to all three young officers at the same moment. They were suddenly silent and scared as they saw a tall man, black haired, with a face darkened by a foreign sun and scarred by a foreign blade, a strong face that was given a mocking look by the scarred left cheek. That mocking expression vanished when Sharpe smiled, but he was not smiling as he stalked into the Mess. He might have worn no badges of rank, but there was something about his face, about the sword at his side and about the battered hilt of the rifle slung on his shoulder that spoke of something far beyond their understanding. The girl in the room's centre took off her blindfold and gasped at Sharpe's sudden, startling appearance.

The room was well lit by tall southern windows. The carpet was thick. Sharpe came slowly forward and the Captain put his feet together as if at attention and stared at the faded jacket and tried to convince himself that the dark stains on the green cloth were not blood.

Harry Price, seeing that one of the two girls was pretty, leaned nonchalantly against the door jamb with what he considered a suitably heroic expression. Sharpe stopped. 'Whose carriage is outside?'

No one spoke, but one of the girls made a hesitant gesture towards her companion. Sharpe turned. 'Harry?'

'Sir?'

'You will arrange for the coach outside to be harnessed.' He looked at the two girls. 'Ladies. What is about to happen here is not for your ears or eyes. You will oblige me by going to your carriage with Lieutenant Price.'

Price, delighted with the orders, bowed to the girls, while one of the two Lieutenants, the young man who had laughed at his own jest and who looked hardly more than seventeen, frowned. 'I say, sir . . .'

'Quiet!' It was a voice that sent orders across the chaos of battlefields and the snap of it made the girls squeal and stunned the three officers into shocked silence. Sharpe looked again at the girls. 'Ladies? You will please leave.'

They fled, snatching scarves and reticules, abandoning music sheets, uneaten cakes, cups of tea, and a bowl of chocolate confections. Sharpe closed the door behind them.

He turned. He took the rifle from his shoulder and slammed it onto a varnished, delicate table. The sound made the three officers shiver. Sharpe looked at the Captain beside the spinet. 'Who are you?'

'Carline, sir.'

'Who's officer of the day?'

Carline swallowed nervously. 'I am, sir.'

Sharpe looked at the Lieutenant who had told him to go away. 'You?'

The Lieutenant forced his voice to sound unafraid. 'Merrill, sir.'

'And you?'

'Pierce, sir.'

'What Battalion are you?' He looked back to Carline.

Carline, scarcely older than the two Lieutenants, tried to match the dignity of his higher rank with an unruffled face, but his voice came out as a frightened squeak. 'South Essex, sir.' He cleared his throat. 'First Battalion.'

'Who's the senior officer in the depot?'

'I am, sir,' Carline said. He could not, Sharpe thought, have been more than twenty-two or three.

'Where's Lieutenant Colonel Girdwood?'

There was silence. A fly battered uselessly against a window. Sharpe repeated the question.

Captain Carline licked his lips. 'Don't know, sir.'

Sharpe walked to a massive sideboard that was heavy with decanters and ornaments. In the very centre of the display was a silver replica of a French Eagle which he picked up. On its base was a plaque. 'This Memento of the French Eagle, Captured at Talavera by the South Essex under the Command of Colonel Sir Henry Simmerson, was Proudly Presented by Him to the Officers of the Regiment in Memory of the Gallant Feat.' Sharpe grimaced. Sir Henry Simmerson had been relieved of the command before Sharpe and Harper had captured the Eagle. He turned to the three officers, the Eagle held in his hands as though it were a weapon. 'My name is Major Richard Sharpe.'

Sharpe would have needed a soul of stone not to enjoy their reaction. They had been frightened of him from the moment he had walked from the hall shadows, but their fear was almost palpable now. A man they had thought a thousand miles away had come to this plump, soft, lavish place, and each of the three men felt a terrible, quivering fear. Pierce, who had laughed as he ordered Sharpe to about-turn, visibly shook. Sharpe let the fear settle into them before speaking in a low voice. 'You've heard of me?'

'Yes, sir,' Carline answered.

These officers, Sharpe knew, were the rump of the First Battalion, the men who kept its home records and who were supposed to despatch replacements to Spain. Except there were no recruits, there were no replacements, because the depot was dead and empty, and its officers were entertaining young ladies.

Sharpe looked at the two Lieutenants, seeing fleshy, spoilt faces above rich uniforms that, well cut though they were, could not hide the spreading waists and fat thighs. Merrill and Pierce, in turn, stared back at the tall, battle-hardened Rifleman as though he was a visitor from some strange, undiscovered island of savages.

Sharpe put the Eagle back on the sideboard. 'Why was there no guard detail on the gate?'

'Don't know, sir.' Carline, Sharpe saw, was wearing glossy dancing shoes buttoned over silk stockings.

'What in Christ's name do you mean? You're officer of the day, aren't you?' The sudden loudness of Sharpe's voice startled them.

'Should have been, sir.' Carline said it helplessly.

Sharpe looked through the window as the file of horsemen, dressed in fatigues, trotted past. 'Who the hell are they?'

'Militia, sir. They use the stables here.'

The three young men, standing rigidly at attention, watched Sharpe as he moved about the room, examining ornaments, picking up a newspaper, once pressing a key of the spinet and letting the plucked note die into ominous silence before he again spoke softly. 'How many men of the First Battalion are here, Carline?'

'Forty-eight, sir.'

'Detail them!'

Carline did. There was himself, three Lieutenants, four sergeants, and the rest were all storekeepers or clerks. Sharpe's face showed nothing, yet he was seething with frustration and anger within. Forty-eight men to revive a wounded First Battalion, and no sign of the Second Battalion!

He stopped by the window and looked at each man in turn. 'You god-damn bloody astonish me! No guard mounted,

28

but you've got time to play blind-man's buff and have a little teaparty. What do you do when you exert yourselves, arrange flowers?' All three kept a judicious, embarrassed silence, avoiding his eyes as he looked at them again in turn. 'Starting at six this evening, and thereafter on the hour, every hour, day and night till I'm bored with you, you will report in full regimentals to Sergeant Major Harper, who, you will be glad to hear, has returned from Spain with me. You!' Sharpe pointed at Merrill, whose face showed utter horror at the thought of parading in front of an inferior, 'and you!' The finger moved to Pierce. 'You will find Captain d'Alembord outside. You will request him to parade the men and tell him I am making an inspection in ten minutes, and once I have done that I shall inspect the barracks. Move!'

They moved like hares out of a coursing trap, running out of the room, leaving Carline alone with Sharpe.

Sharpe ate a sandwich. He let the silence stretch. The walls of this comfortable room were bright with hunting pictures, red-coated horsemen in full cry across grass. Sharpe's sudden question made Carline jump. 'Where's Lieutenant Colonel Girdwood?'

'Don't know, sir.' Captain Carline now sounded plaintive, like a small boy hauled up in front of a fearsome headmaster.

Sharpe stared with distaste at the thin, petulant man. 'Colonel Girdwood does command the Second Battalion?'

'Yes, sir.'

'So where the hell is he? And where in Christ's name is the Second Battalion?'

'I don't know, sir.'

Sharpe stepped close to him, close enough to smell the tea on Carline's breath and the pomade in his carefully waved hair. 'Captain.' Sharpe, taller than Carline, looked down into the pale eyes and made his voice conversational. 'You've heard men speak, presumably, of Regimental Sergeant Major MacLaird?'

Carline gave the smallest nod. 'I've heard the name, sir.'

'Less than one month ago, Carline, I saw his guts in blood. His belly was slit open. It was not a pretty sight, Captain. It would have spoilt your tea. But I'll show it to you, Captain Carline. I'll rip your bloody guts out with my own hands unless you answer me some god-damned questions! I'll pull your spine out of your throat! You hear me?'

Carline looked as if he might faint. 'Sir?'

'Where is the Second Battalion?'

'I don't know, sir.' He said it pleadingly, with naked fear in his eyes, and Sharpe believed him.

'Then what the hell do you know, Captain Carline?'

Slowly, haltingly, Carline told his story. The Second Battalion, he said, had been stood down six months before, converted into a Holding Battalion. All recruiting had been stopped. Then, abruptly, the Second Battalion had marched away.

'Just like that?' Sharpe snarled the question. 'They simply vanished?'

'Yes, sir.' Carline said it plaintively.

'No explanations?'

Carline shrugged. 'Colonel Girdwood said they were going to other units, sir.' He paused. 'He said the war's coming to an end, sir, and the army was being pruned. We were to send our last draft out to the First Battalion and then just keep the depot tidy.' He shrugged again, a gesture of helplessness.

'The French are pruning the bloody army, Carline, and we need recruits! Are you recruiting for the First Battalion?'

'No, sir. We were ordered not to!'

Sharpe saw Patrick Harper dressing a feeble Company into

30

ranks on the parade ground. He turned back to Carline. 'Colonel Girdwood said the men were being taken to other units?'

'Yes, sir.'

'Would it surprise you, Carline, to know that the Second Battalion still draws pay and rations for seven hundred men?'

Carline said nothing. He was doubtless thinking what Sharpe was thinking, that the seven hundred were non-existent and their pay was being appropriated by Lieutenant Colonel Girdwood. It was a scandal as old as the army; drawing the pay of men who did not exist. Sharpe, in a gesture of irritation, swatted a fly with his hand and ground it into the carpet with his boot. 'So what do you do with the Second Battalion's mail? Its paperwork? I presume some of it still comes here?'

'We send it on to the War Office, sir.'

'The War Office!' Sharpe's astonishment made his voice suddenly loud. The War Office was supposed to conduct war, and Sharpe would have expected the paperwork to go to the Horse Guards that administered the army.

'To Lord Fenner's secretary, sir.' Carline spoke with more confidence, as if the mention of the politician's name would awe Sharp.

It did. Lord Fenner, the Secretary of State at War, had suggested in his despatch to Wellington that the First Battalion be broken up and now, it seemed, he was the man responsible for the disappearance of the Second Battalion, a disappearance that must obviously have the highest official backing. Or else, and it seemed unthinkable, Lord Fenner was an accomplice with Lieutenant Colonel Girdwood in peculation; stealing money through a forged payroll.

Footsteps were loud in the hallway, and Patrick Harper

loomed huge in the doorway of the Mess. He slammed to attention. 'Men on parade, sir. What there are of them.'

Sharpe turned. 'Regimental Sergeant Major Harper? This is Captain Carline.'

'Sir!' Harper looked at Carline rather as a tiger would look at a goat. Carline, in his dancing shoes and with one hand on the spinet, seemed incapable of speaking. To think of himself as a soldier in the presence of these two tall, implacable men was ridiculous.

'Sergeant Major,' Sharpe's voice was conversational, 'do you think the war has addled my wits?'

There was a flicker of temptation on the broad face, then a respectful, 'No, sir!'

'Then listen to this story, RSM. The South Essex raises a Second Battalion whose job is to find men, train men, then send them to our First Battalion in Spain. Is that correct, Captain Carline?'

'Yes, sir.'

'So it recruits. It did recruit, Captain?'

'Yes, sir.'

'And six months ago, RSM,' Sharpe swung back, 'it is made into a Holding Battalion. No more recruiting, of course, it is merely a convenient dung heap for the army's refuse.' He stared at Carline. 'No one knows why. We poor bastards are dying in Spain, but some clodpole decides we don't need recruits.' He looked back at Harper. 'I am told, RSM, that the Holding Battalion has been broken up, it has disappeared, it has vanished! Its mail goes to the War Office, yet it still draws rations for seven hundred men. Sergeant Major Harper?'

'Sir?'

'What do you think of that story?'

Harper frowned. 'It's a real bastard, sir, so it is.' He smiled.

'Perhaps if we break some heads, sir, some bastards will stop lying.'

'I like that thought, Sergeant Major.' Sharpe stared at Carline, and his voice was conversational no longer. 'If you've lied to me, Captain, I'll tear you to tatters.'

'I haven't lied, sir.'

Sharpe believed him, but it made no difference. He was in a fog of deception, and the hopelessness of it made him furious as he went into the sunlight to inspect the few men who had been assembled by d'Alembord. Either there were no men in the Second Battalion, in which case there would be no trained replacements for the invasion of France, or, if they did exist, Sharpe would have to find them through Lord Fenner who would, doubtless, not take kindly to an interfering visit from a mere Major.

He stalked through the sleeping huts, wondering how he was to approach the Secretary of State at War, then went to inspect the armoury. The armoury sergeant, a veteran with one leg, was grinning hopefully at him. 'You remember me, sir?'

Sharpe looked at the leathery, scarred face, and he cursed himself because he could not put a name to it, then Patrick Harper, standing behind him, laughed aloud. 'Ted Carew!'

'Carew!' Sharpe said the name as if he had just remembered it himself. 'Talavera?'

'That's right, sir. Lost the old peg there.' Carew slapped his right leg that ended in a wooden stump. 'Good to see you, sir!'

It was good to see Sergeant Carew for, alone in the Chelmsford depot, he knew his job and was doing it well. The weapons were cared for, the armoury tidy, the paperwork exact and depressing. Depressing because, when Lieutenant Colonel Girdwood had marched the Second Battalion away, the records revealed that he had left all their new weapons behind. Those brand-new muskets, greased and muzzle-stoppered, were racked beneath oiled and scabbarded bayonets. That fact suggested that the men had been sent to other Battalions who could be expected to provide weapons from their own armouries. 'He didn't take any muskets?' Sharpe asked.

'Four hundred old ones, sir.' Sergeant Carew turned the oil-stained pages of his ledger. 'There, sir.' He sniffed. 'Didn't take no new uniforms neither, sir.'

Non-existent men, Sharpe thought, needed neither weapons nor uniforms, but, just as he was deciding that this quest was hopeless because the Second Battalion had been broken up and scattered throughout the army, Sergeant Carew gave him sudden, extraordinary hope. 'It's a funny bloody thing, sir.' The Sergeant lurched up and down on his wooden leg as he turned to look behind him, fearful that they would be overheard.

'What's funny?'

'We was told, sir, that the Second's just a holding Battalion. No more recruits? That's what they said, sir, but three weeks ago, as I live and breathe, sir, I saw one of our parties with a clutch of recruits! Sergeant Havercamp, it was, Horatio Havercamp, and he was marching 'em this way. I said "hello", I did, and he tells me to bugger off and mind my own business. Me!' Carew stared indignantly at Sharpe. 'So I talks to the Captain here and I asks him what's happening? I mean the recruits never got here, sir, not a one of them. Haven't seen a lad in six months!'

Sharpe stared at the Sergeant, and the import of what Carew was saying dawned slowly on him. Holding Battalions did not recruit. If there were recruits then there was a Second Battalion, and the seven hundred men did exist, and the Regiment could yet march into France. 'You saw a recruiting party?'

'With me own eyes, sir! I told the Captain too!'

'What did he say?'

'Told me I was drunk, sir. Told me there were no more recruiting parties, nothing! Told me I was imagining things, but I wasn't drunk, sir, and sure as you're standing there and me here I'm telling you I saw Horatio Havercamp with a party of recruits. Now why would they not come here, sir? Can you tell me that?'

'No, Sergeant, I can't.' But he would find out, by God he would find out. 'You're certain of what you saw, Sergeant?'

'I'm certain, sir.'

'This Sergeant Havercamp wasn't recruiting for another regiment?'

Carew laughed. 'Wore our badge, sir! Drummer boys had your eagle on the drums. No, sir. Something funny happening, that's what I think.' He was stumping towards the door, his keys jangling on their iron ring. 'But no one listens to me, sir, not any more. I mean I was a real soldier, sir, smelled the bloody guns, but they don't want to know. Too high and bloody mighty.' Carew swung the massive iron door shut, then turned again to make sure none of the depot officers were near. 'I've been in the bloody army since I was a nipper, sir, and I know when things are wrong.' He looked eagerly up at Sharpe. 'Do you believe me, sir?'

'Yes, Ted.' Sharpe stood in the slanting evening light, and almost wished he did not believe the Sergeant, for, if Ted Carew was right, then a Battalion was not just missing, but deliberately hidden. He went to inspect the stables.

A missing Battalion? Hidden? It sounded to Sharpe like a madman's fantasy, yet nothing in Chelmsford offered a rational explanation. By noon the next day Sharpe and d'Alembord had searched the paperwork of the depot and found nothing that told them where Lieutenant Colonel Girdwood had gone, or whether the Second Battalion truly existed. Yet Sharpe believed Carew. The Battalion did exist, it was recruiting still, and Sharpe knew he must return to London, though he dreaded the thought.

He dreaded it because he would have to seek an interview with Lord Fenner, and Sharpe did not feel at home among such exalted reaches of society. He suspected, too, that His Lordship would refuse to answer his questions, telling Sharpe, perhaps rightly, that it was none of his business.

Yet to have come this far to fail? He walked onto the parade ground and saw Carline, Merrill and Pierce standing indignantly to attention as Patrick Harper minutely inspected their uniforms. All three officers had shadowed, red-rimmed eyes because they had been up all night. Harper, used to broken nights of war, looked keen and fresh.

'Halt!' The sentry at the gate, eager to impress Major Sharpe, bellowed the challenge.

Sharpe turned.

A mounted officer appeared in the archway, glorious and splendid on a superb horse, dazzling in the red, blue and gold uniform of the 1st Life Guards, an officer utterly out of place in this remote, dull barracks square.

'Bit hard to find, aren't you?' The officer laughed as he dismounted close to Sharpe. 'It is Major Sharpe, yes?'

'Yes.'

The Captain saluted. 'Lord John Rossendale, sir! Honoured to meet you!' Lord John was a tall young man, thin as a reed, with a humorous, handsome face and a lazy, friendly voice. 'First time I've been here. I'm told there's a decent little pack of hounds up the road?' He pronounced the word hounds as 'hinds'.

'I wouldn't know.' Sharpe said it ungraciously. 'You're looking for me?'

'Rather,' Rossendale beamed happily. 'Got something for you, sir. Or I did.' He dug into his sabretache, failed to find whatever he had brought, clicked his fingers, cursed himself for foolishness, then, with a happy and enlightened burst of memory, found what he was looking for in his saddlebag. 'There you are, sir! Safely delivered.' He handed Sharpe a thick piece of folded paper, richly sealed. 'Can I get luncheon here, sir? Your Mess does a decent bite, does it, or would you recommend the town?'

Sharpe did not answer. He had torn the paper open and was reading the ornate script. 'Is this a joke?'

'Lord, no!' Lord John laughed anyway. 'Bit of a privilege really, yes? He's always wanted to meet you! He was happy as a drunken bat when the Horse Guards said you'd come home! We heard you'd died this summer, but here you are, eh? Fit as a fiddle? Splendid, eh? Should be quite jolly, really!'

'Jolly?'

'Rather!' Lord John gave Sharpe his friendliest, most charming smile. 'Best flummery and all that?'

'Flummery?'

'Uniform, sir. Get your chap to polish it all up, put on a bit of glitter, yes?' He glanced at Sharpe's jacket and laughed. 'You can't really wear that one, eh? They'd think you'd come to scour the chimneys.' He laughed again to show he meant no offence.

Sharpe stared at the invitation, and knew that his luck had turned. A moment ago he had been apprehensive, rightly so, about seeing Lord Fenner, for what mere Major could demand answers of a Secretary of State at War? Now, suddenly, the answer had been delivered by this elegant, smiling messenger who had brought an invitation, a command, for Sharpe to go to London and there meet a man who, within the last year, had insisted that Sharpe was promoted, and a man whom even Lord Fenner dared not offend. The Prince of Wales, Prince Regent of England, demanded Major Richard Sharpe's attendance at court, and Sharpe, if he was clever enough, would let that eminent Royal gentleman demand to know where the Second Battalion had been hidden. Sharpe laughed aloud. He would go over Lord Fenner's head, and, with Royalty's help, would march the Colours of his regiment into France.

CHAPTER TWO

'There is a yellow line on the carpet. Observe it.'

'Yes,' said Major Richard Sharpe.

'It is there that you stop.' The chamberlain gave a small, fanciful gesture with his white-gloved fingers as if illustrating how to come to a halt. 'You bow.' Another curlicue of the fingers. 'You answer briefly, addressing His Royal Highness as "Your Royal Highness". You then bow again.'

Sharpe had been watching people approach the throne for ten tedious minutes. He doubted that, after seeing so many examples, he needed to be given such minute instructions, but the courtier insisted on saying it all again. Every elaborate gesture of the man's white-gloved hand wafted perfume to Sharpe's nose.

'And when you have bowed the second time, Major, you back away. Do it slowly. You may cease the backward motion when you reach the lion's tail.' He pointed with his staff at the rampant lion embroidered onto the lavish red carpet. The courtier, with eyes that seemed to be made of ice, looked Sharpe up and down. 'Some of our military gentlemen, Major Sharpe, become entangled with their swords during the backwards progression. Might I suggest you hold the scabbard away from your body?'

'Thank you.'

A group of musicians, lavishly dressed in court uniform, with powdered wigs, plucked eyebrows, and intent, busy expressions, played violins, cellos, and flutes. The tunes meant nothing to Sharpe, not one of them a stirring, heart-thumping march that could take a man into battle. These tunes were frivolous and tinkling; mincing, delicate things suitable for a Royal Court. He felt foolish. He was grateful that none of his men could see him now; d'Alembord and Price were safely in Chelmsford, putting some snap into the half-deserted depot, while Harper, though in London, was with Isabella in Southwark.

Above Sharpe was a ceiling painted with supercilious gods who stared down with apparent boredom on the huge room. A great chandelier, its crystal drops breaking the candlelight into a million shards of light, hung at the room's centre. A fire, an unnecessary luxury this warm night, burned in a vast grate, adding to an already overheated room that stank of women's powder, sweat, and the cigar smoke that drifted in from the next chamber.

An Admiral was being presented. There was a spatter of light, bored applause from the courtiers who crowded about the dais. The Admiral bowed for a second time, backed away, and Sharpe saw how the man held his slim sword away from his body as he bobbingly reversed over the snarling lion.

'Lord Pearson, your Royal Highness!' said the overdressed flunkey who announced the names.

Lord Pearson, attired in court dress, strode confidently forward, bowed, and Sharpe felt his heart beating nervously when he thought that, in a few moments, he would have to follow the man up the long carpet. It was all nonsense, of course, ridiculous nonsense, but he was still nervous. He wished he was not here, he wished he was anywhere but in this stinking, overheated room. He watched Lord Pearson say his few words and thought, with a sense of doom, how impossible it would be to bring up the subject of the missing Battalion in those few, scaring seconds of conversation.

'It is best,' the courtier murmured in his ear, 'to say as little as possible. "Yes, your Royal Highness" or "No, your Royal Highness" are both quite acceptable.'

'Yes,' Sharpe said.

There were fifty people being presented this evening. Most had brought their wives who laughed sycophantically whenever the courtiers on the dais laughed. None could hear the witticism that had provoked the laughter, but they laughed just the same.

The men were resplendent in uniform or court dress, their coats heavy with jewelled orders and bright sashes. Sharpe wore no decorations, unless the faded cloth badge that showed a wreath counted as a decoration. He had received that for going into a defended breach, being the first man to climb the broken, blood-slick stones at Badajoz, but it was a paltry thing beside the dazzling jewelled enamels of the great stars that shone from the other uniforms.

He had taken the wreath badge from his old jacket and insisted that the tailor sew it onto his brand-new uniform. It felt odd to be dressed so finely, his waist circled by a tasselled red sash and his shoulder-wings bright with the stars of his rank. Sharpe reckoned the evening had cost him fifty guineas already, most of it to the tailor who had despaired of making the new uniform in time. Sharpe had growled that he would go to the Royal Court in his old uniform and give the tailor's name as the man responsible, and, as he had expected, the work had been done.

His uniform might be new, but Sharpe still wore his comfortable old boots. Sharpe had obstinately refused to spend money on the black leather shoes proper to his uniform, and the Royal Equerry who had greeted Sharpe in the Entrance Hall of Carlton

House had frowned at the knee-high boots. Polish them as he might, Sharpe could not rid them of the scuff marks, or disguise the stitches that closed the rent slashed in the left boot by an enemy's knife. The Equerry, whose own buckled shoes shone like a mirror, wondered whether Major Sharpe would like to borrow proper footwear.

'What's wrong with the boots?' Sharpe had asked.

'They're not regulation issue, Major.'

'They're regulation issue to colonels of Napoleon's Imperial Guard. I killed one of those bastards to get these boots, and I'm damned if I'm taking them off for you.'

The Equerry had sighed. 'Very good, Major. If you so wish.'

By Sharpe's side, in its battered scabbard, hung his cheap Heavy Cavalry sword. At Messrs Hopkinsons of St Albans Street, the army agents who were part bankers, part post office and part moneylenders to officers, he had a presentation sword from the Patriotic Fund, given to him as a reward for capturing the French Eagle at Talavera, but he felt uncomfortable with such a flimsy, over-decorated blade. He was a soldier, and he would come to this court with his own sword. But by God, he thought, he would rather be back in Spain. He would rather face a battalion of French veterans than face this ordeal.

'A pace forward, Major?'

He obeyed, and the step took him closer to the edge of the crowd so that he could see better. He did not like what he saw; plump, self-satisfied people crammed into rich, elegant clothes. Their laughter tinkled as emptily as the music. Those who looked at Sharpe seemed to show a mixture of surprise and pity at his dowdiness, as though a bedraggled fighting cock had somehow found its way into a peacock's pen.

The women were mostly dressed in white, their dresses tightly bound beneath their breasts to fall sheer to the carpet. Their necklines were low, their throats circled by stones and gold, their faces fanned by busy, delicate spreads of ivory and feathers. A woman standing next to Sharpe, craning to see over the shoulder of a man in front of her, showed a cleavage in which sweat trickled to make small channels through the powder on her breasts.

'You had a good voyage, Major?' the courtier asked in a tone which suggested he did not care one way or the other.

'Yes, very good, thank you.'

'Another pace forward, I think.'

He shuffled the obedient step. He was to be the last person presented to His Royal Highness. From another room in this huge house came a tinkle of glasses and a burst of laughter. The musicians still sawed at their instruments. The faces of the crowd that lined the long carpet glistened in the candlelight. Everyone, with the exception of Sharpe, wore white gloves, even the men. He knew no one here, while everyone else seemed to know everybody else, and he felt foolish and unwelcome. The air that he breathed seemed heavy, warm and damp, not with the humidity of a summer day, but with strong scent and sweat and powder that he thought would choke in his gullet.

A woman caught his eye and held it. For a second he thought she would smile at him to acknowledge the moment when their eyes locked, but she did not smile, nor look away, but instead she stared at him with an expression of disdainful curiosity. Sharpe had noticed her earlier, for in this overheated, crowded room she stood out like a jewel amongst offal. She was tall, slim, with dark red hair piled high above her thin, startling face. Her eyes were green, as green as Sharpe's jacket, and they stared at him now with a kind of defiance.

Sharpe looked away from her. He was beginning to feel sullen and rebellious, angry at this charade, wondering what would happen to him if he simply turned and walked away from this place. But he was here for a purpose, to use the

43

privilege of this presentation to ask a favour, and he told himself that he did this thing for the men who waited at Pasajes.

'Remember, Major, to hold the sword away as you leave the presence.' The courtier, a head shorter than Sharpe's six foot, gave his delicate smile. 'I shall see you afterwards, perhaps?' He did not sound overjoyed at the prospect.

The moment had come. He was at the front of the crowd, facing the vast carpet, and he could see the eyes staring at him and then the overdressed servant at the foot of the dais looked at him and nodded.

He walked forward. Christ! he thought, but he would trip over or faint. His boots suddenly felt as heavy as pig-iron, his scabbard seemed to swing malevolently between his knees, then he frowned because, to his right, applause had begun and the applause grew and someone, a woman, shouted 'bravo!'

He was blushing. The applause made him angrier. It was his own god-damned fault. He should have ignored the Royal command, but instead he was walking up this damned carpet, the faces were smiling at him and he was sure that he would become entangled with the huge sword that clanked in its metal scabbard by his side.

The woman who had stared at him, the woman with green eyes, watched him walk to the yellow line. She clapped politely, but without enthusiasm. A dangerous-looking man, she thought, and far more handsome than she expected. She had been told only that he came from the gutter, a bastard son of a peasant whore. 'You won't want to bed him, Anne.' She remembered those words, and the mocking tone of the voice that spoke them. 'Talk to him, though. Find out what he knows.'

'Maybe he won't want to talk to me.'

'Don't be a fool. A peasant like that will be flattered to speak to a lady.'

Now she watched the bastard son of a common whore bow,

and it was plain that Major Richard Sharpe was not accustomed to bowing. She felt a small surge of excitement that surprised her.

The courtier waited for Sharpe's clumsy bow to be made. 'Major Richard Sharpe, your Royal Highness, attached to His Majesty's South Essex Regiment!'

And the courtier's words provoked more applause which the man sitting in the gilded, red-velvet cushioned throne encouraged by lightly tapping his white gloved fingers into his palm. No one else had received such applause, no one; and Sharpe blushed like a child as he stared into the glaucous eyes and fat face of the Prince of Wales, who, this night, was encased in the full uniform of a British general; a uniform that bulged on his thighs and over his full belly.

The applause died. The Prince of Wales seemed to gobble with delighted laughter. He stared at Sharpe as if the Rifleman was some delicious confection brought for his delight, then he spoke in a fruity, rich voice that was full of surprise. 'You are dressed as a Rifleman, eh?'

'Yes, your Majesty.' Oh Christ, Sharpe thought. He should have called him 'Your Royal Highness'.

'But you're with the South Essex, yes?'

'Yes, your Royal Highness.' Then Sharpe remembered that after the first answer he was supposed to call him 'sir'. 'Sir,' he added.

'Yes?'

Sharpe thought he was going to faint because the fat, middle-aged man was leaning forward in the belief that Sharpe wished to say something. Sharpe's right hand fidgeted, wanting to cross his body and hold the sword handle. 'Very honoured, your Majesty.' Sharpe was sure he was going to faint. The room was a thick, indistinct whirl of powder, white faces, music and heat.

'No, no, no, no! I'm honoured. Yes, indeed! The honour is

entirely mine, Major Sharpe!' The Prince of Wales snapped his fingers, smiled at Sharpe, and the small orchestra abruptly stopped playing the delicate melody that had accompanied Sharpe's lonely walk up the carpet and, instead, started to play a military tune. The music was accompanied by gasps from the audience, gasps that were followed by more applause that grew and was swelled by cheers that forced the musicians to play even louder.

'Look!' The Prince of Wales gestured to Sharpe's right. 'Look!'

The clapping continued. Sharpe turned. A passage had been made in the applauding crowd and, through it, marching in the old-fashioned goose-step that Sharpe had not seen in nearly twenty years, were three soldiers in uniforms of such pristine perfection that they must have been sewn onto their upright bodies. They had old-fashioned powdered hair, high stocks, but it was not the three soldiers, impressive and impractical though they were, that had started the new applause.

'Bravo!' The shouts were louder as Sharpe stared at what the central soldier carried in his hands.

Sharpe had seen that object before, on a hot day in a valley filled with smoke and foul with the stench of roasting flesh. The wounded, he remembered, had been unable to escape the grass-fires and so they had burned where they lay on the battle-field, the flames exploding their ammunition pouches and spreading the fire further.

He had seen it before, but not like this. Tonight the staff was oiled and polished, and the gilt ornament shone in the candlelight. Before, on that hot day when the musket wads had burned and the wounded had screamed for Jesus or their mothers, Sharpe had held the battered, bloody staff, and he had scythed it like a halberd, cutting down the enemy, while beside him, screaming in his wild Irish tongue, Sergeant Harper

46

had slaughtered the standard-bearers and Sharpe had taken this Eagle, this first French Eagle to be captured by His Majesty's forces.

Now it was polished. About the base of the Eagle was a laurel wreath. It seemed unfitting. Once those proud eyes and hooked beak and half-spread wings had been on a battlefield, and it still belonged there, not here, not with these fat, sweating, applauding people who stared and smiled and nodded at him as the staff was thrust towards him.

'Take it! Take it!' the Prince Regent said.

Sharpe felt like a circus animal. He took it. He lowered the staff and he stared at the Eagle, no bigger than a dinner plate, and he saw the one bent wingtip where he had struck a man's skull with the standard, and he felt oddly sorry for the Eagle. Like him it was out of place here. It belonged in the smoke of battle. The men who had defended it had been brave, they had fought as well as men could fight, and it was not right that these gloating fools should applaud this humbled trophy.

'You must remind me of everything that happened! Just exactly!' The Prince was struggling from the dais, coming towards Sharpe. 'I insist on everything, everything! Over supper!' To Sharpe's horror the Prince, who, during his father's madness, was the Regent and acting monarch of England, put an arm about his shoulders and led him across the carpet. 'Every single small detail, Major Sharpe, in utter detail. To supper! Bring your bird! Oh yes, it's not every day we heroes meet. Come! Come!'

Sharpe went to supper with a Prince.

There were twenty-eight courses in the supper, most of them lukewarm because the distance from the kitchens was so great. There was champagne, wine, and more champagne. The musicians still played.

The Prince of Wales was extraordinarily solicitous of Sharpe. He fed Sharpe's plate with morsels, encouraged his stories, chided when he thought Sharpe was being modest, and finally asked the Rifleman why he had come to England.

Sharpe took a breath and told him. He felt a small moment of pleasure, for he was doing what he had come to do; saving a Regiment. He saw some frowns about the table when he spoke of the missing Battalion, as if the subject was unfitting for such an evening, but the Prince was delighted. 'Some of my men are missing, eh? That won't do? Is Fenner here? Fenner? Find Fenner!' Sharpe suddenly felt that blaze of victory, like the moment in battle when the enemy's rear ranks are going back and the front was about to crumple. Here, in the Chinese Dining Room of Carlton House, Sharpe had persuaded the Prince Regent himself to put the question which Sharpe himself had so dreaded taking to Lord Fenner. 'Ah! Fenner!'

A courtier was conducting the Secretary of State at War towards the Prince's table.

Lord Fenner was a tall man, in court dress, with a thin, pale face dominated by a prominent, hooked nose. There was, Sharpe thought, a worried expression on Lord Fenner's face that seemed perpetual, as though he solemnly carried the nation's burdens on his thin shoulders. He was, Sharpe guessed, in his early fifties. His voice, when he spoke to the Prince, was high and nasal; a voice of effortless aristocracy.

The Prince demanded to know why Lord Fenner wanted to abolish the South Essex. 'Out with it, man!'

Fenner glanced at Sharpe, the glance of a man measuring an enemy. 'It's not our wish, sir, rather the Regiment's own.'

The Prince turned surprised eyes on Sharpe, then looked again to Lord Fenner. 'Their own wish?'

'A paucity of recruits, sir.'

48

'There were plenty of recruits!' Sharpe said.

Lord Fenner smiled a pitying smile. 'Under-age, undernourished, and unsuitable.'

The Prince was beginning to regret his sally on Sharpe's behalf, but he gallantly persisted with the attack. 'And the Second Battalion's missing, eh? Tell me about that, Fenner!'

'Missing, sir?' Lord Fenner glanced at Sharpe, then back to the Prince. 'Not missing, sir. Gone.'

'Gone? Gone! Vanished into thin air, yes?'

Fenner gave a smile that subtly mixed boredom with sycophancy. 'It exists on paper, sir.' He made the subject sound trivial. 'It's a normal bureaucratic procedure. It enables us to assign stray men who would not otherwise be paid until they can be found a proper billet. I'm sure if Major Sharpe is fascinated by our paperwork I can arrange for a clerk to explain it to him. Or indeed to your Royal Highness.' The last statement verged on rudeness, hinting that the Prince Regent, despite being Britain's monarch while his father was ill, had no authority over the army or War Office.

No authority, but influence. The Prince's brother, the Duke of York, commanded the army, while the War Office was run by politicians. The Prince Regent commanded nothing, though he had the massive power of patronage. Sharpe had tried, indeed had succeeded, in harnessing that influence, but Lord Fenner seemed untroubled by it. He smiled. 'Your brother, sir, would doubtless welcome your interest?'

'Oh Lord!' the Prince laughed. Everyone knew of the bad blood that existed between the Prince and the Duke of York, the army Commander in Chief. 'Freddie thinks the army belongs to him!' The prospect of speaking to his brother was obviously hateful. 'So, Fenner, there's no missing Battalion, eh?'

'I fear not, sir.'

The Prince turned his face that, extraordinarily, was thick

with cream and powder, towards Sharpe. 'You hear that, Major? Lost in a welter of paperwork, eh?'

Lord Fenner was watching Sharpe. He gave a smile so thin-lipped that it seemed like a threat. 'Of course, sir, we shall do all we can to find Major Sharpe a new Regiment.'

'Of course!' The Prince beamed at Sharpe, then at Fenner. 'And quickly, Fenner! Sharply, even!'

Fenner smiled politely at the jest. 'You are in London, Major?'

'At the Rose Tavern.'

'You will receive fresh orders tomorrow.' Major Sharpe had tried to outflank Lord Fenner and had failed. The Prince of Wales would not be allowed to interfere with the War Office or Horse Guards, and Lord Fenner's tone suggested that the orders would be a harsh revenge for Sharpe's temerity.

'Send him to Spain, you hear me!' The Prince waved peremptorily at Fenner, gobbled delightedly as a servant poured more wine, then put a fat hand on Sharpe's arm. 'A vain journey, eh Major? But it gives us a chance to meet again, yes?' Sharpe was startled by the word 'again', but a warning look from Lord John Rossendale, who sat across the table, made him give a non-committal answer.

'Indeed, sir.'

'Tell me, Major, was it not hot on the day we took the Eagle?'

Lord John was making furious signs at Sharpe not to protest the word 'we'. Sharpe nodded. 'Very hot, sir.'

'I do believe I remember it! Indeed, yes! Very hot!' The Prince nodded at his companions. 'Very hot!'

Sharpe wondered if the man, like his father, had lost his wits. He was speaking as if he had been there, in that valley of the Portina where the wounded sobbed for mercy. There had been small black snakes, Sharpe remembered, wriggling away from the grass-fires. His mind seemed a whirl of black snakes, memories, and sudden shock because his journey had been useless. Lord Fenner would order him away tomorrow; there would be no replacements for the South Essex, and a Regiment would die.

The Prince nudged Sharpe and smiled again. 'We shocked them, Major, yes?'

'Yes, sir.'

'What a day, what a day!' The Prince shook his head, sifting white powder from his hair into Sharpe's wine. 'Ah! A syllabub! Splendid! Serve the Major some. We have a French chef, Major. Did you know that?'

It was four in the morning before Sharpe escaped. He had been invited to play whist, refused on the grounds that he did not know how, and he only managed to leave the Prince's company by promising to attend a levée in two days' time.

He stood in the entrance of Carlton House in a mood of angry self-mockery. He had endured the flummery, the foolery, and he had failed. Lord Fenner, even faced with the Prince's demand, had flicked the questions away as though they were flies. Fenner, Sharpe was sure, had also lied. Either that or Sergeant Carew, at Chelmsford, had not seen the recruiting party, but Sharpe believed Carew, he did not believe Fenner.

Sharpe had come to England for nothing. He stood, dressed in a uniform he had not wanted to buy, his head thick with the fumes of cigar smoke, and he reflected that, far from winning the victory he had anticipated at the moment when the Prince summoned Lord Fenner, he had been effortlessly beaten.

He went down the steps, acknowledging the salutes of the sentries, and out into Pall Mall where, to the amazement of Europe, gas lights flared and hissed in the night. It was warm still, the eastern sky just lightening into dawn over the haze of London's smoke. He walked towards the dawn, his boot-heels making echoes in the empty street.

51

But not quite empty, for a carriage rattled behind him. He heard the hooves, the chains, the wheels, but he did not turn round. He supposed it was another of the Prince's guests going home in the dawn.

The carriage slowed as it reached him. The coachman, high on his tasselled box, pulled on the reins to stop the vehicle, and Sharpe, annoyed by the intrusion, hurried. The coachman let the horses go faster until the carriage was beside the walking Rifleman and the door suddenly opened to flood yellow lantern-light onto the pavement.

'Major Sharpe?'

He turned. The interior of the carriage was upholstered in dark blue and in its plushness, like a jewel in a padded box, was the slim woman with the startling green eyes. She was alone.

He touched the peak of his shako. 'Ma'am.'

'Perhaps I can help you home?'

'I've a long way to go, Ma'am.'

'I don't.' She gestured at the seat opposite her.

He paused, astonished at her boldness, then thought that such a simple conquest would be a fitting consolation on this night of failure. He climbed into the carriage, and went into the London night.

Much later, after the sun had risen and the morning was half gone, long after the time when Sharpe had told Harper to meet him at the Rose Tavern, she rolled onto him. Her red hair was tousled about her mocking face. 'You're Prinny's latest toy. And mine.' She said it bitterly, as though she hated herself for being in bed with him. She had made love as though she had not made love in a decade; she had been feverish, clawing, hungry, yet afterwards, even though stark naked, she had somehow managed to imply that she did Sharpe a great favour and that he did her a small one. She had not smiled since they reached her bedroom, nor did she smile now. 'I suppose you'll boast about this with your soldier friends?'

'No.' He stroked the skin of her back, his hands gentle in the deep, slim curve of her waist. She was, he thought, a beautiful, embittered woman, no more than his own age. She had not given him her name, refusing to answer the question.

She dug her fingernails into his shoulders. 'You'll tell them you bedded one of Prinny's ladies, won't you?'

'Are you?'

She gave a gesture of disdain. 'Prinny only likes grandmothers, Major. The older the better. He likes them rancid and ancient.' She traced the scar on his face with one of her sharp nails. 'So what did you think of Lord Fenner?'

'He's a lying bastard.'

For the first time she laughed. She searched his face with her green eyes. 'You're accurate, Major. He's also a politician. He'd eat dung for money or power. How do you know he's lying?'

He still stroked her, running his hands from her shoulder-blades to her thighs. 'He said my Second Battalion was disbanded, a paper convenience. It isn't.'

'How do you know?' She said it with the trace of a sneer, as if a simple soldier back from the wars would know nothing.

'Because they're still recruiting. Disbanded regiments don't recruit.'

'So what will you do?'

'Look for them.'

She stared at him, then, in a gesture that was surprisingly gentle, pushed his dark hair away from his face. 'Don't.'

'Don't?'

She seemed to sneer again, then hooked her legs round his.

'Stay in London, Major. Prinny's court is full of little whores. Enjoy yourself. Didn't Fenner say he'd help you find another regiment? Let him.'

'Why?'

'Turn over.' Her hands were pulling at him, her nails tearing at his skin. He felt as scarred as if he had fought a major battle.

She would not give him her name, she would only give her lean, hungry body. She was like a cat, he thought, a green-eyed, lithe cat who, when he dressed, lay naked on the silk sheets and stared at him with her mysterious, disdainful eyes. 'Shall I give you some advice, Major Sharpe?'

He had pulled on his boots. 'Yes.'

'Don't look for that Battalion, Major.'

'So it does exist?'

'If you say so.' She pulled the sheets over her body. 'Stay in London. Let Prinny slobber all over you, but don't make an enemy of Lord Fenner.'

He smiled. 'What can he do to me?'

'Kill you. Don't look for it, Major.'

He leaned down to kiss her, but she turned her face away. He straightened up. 'I came to England to find it.'

'Go away, Major.' She watched him buckle on his sword. 'There are stairs at the back, no one will see you leave. Go back to Spain!'

Sharpe stared at her from the open door. The house beyond this bedroom seemed vacant. 'There are men in Spain who need me, who trust me.' She stared at him, saying nothing, and he felt that his words were inadequate. 'They're not special men, they wouldn't look very well in Carlton House, but they are fighting for all of you. That's why I'm here.'

She mocked his appeal with a sneer. 'Go away.'

'If you know something about my Battalion, tell me.'

'I'm telling you to go away.' She said it savagely, as though she despised herself for having taken him to her bed. 'Go!'

'I'm at the Rose Tavern in Drury Lane. A letter there will reach me. I don't need to know who you are. The Rose Tavern.'

She turned away from him again, not replying, and Sharpe, walking out into the back alley and blinking at the sudden sunlight, wished he were truly at home; in Spain, with his men, at the place where the war was being fought. This city of luxury, lies, and deceit seemed suddenly foul. He had come to London, he had achieved nothing, and he walked slowly back to Drury Lane.

CHAPTER THREE

The British soldiers, red coats bright and muskets tipped with bayonets, went into the smoke. They cheered. They charged. A drummer beat them on.

The French ran. They scrambled desperately at the hillside while, behind them, the redcoats came from the smoke to fire a single volley. Two of the French, their blue jackets unmarked, turned and fell. One gushed blood from his mouth. His arms went up. He span slowly, screaming foully, to collapse at the feet of the advancing British infantry whose boots gleamed with unnatural brilliance. A French officer, his wig awry, knelt in quivering fear and held clasped hands towards the victorious British soldiers.

'And then, my Lords, Ladies and Gentlemen. The cavalry!'

The orchestra went into a brazen, jaunty piece of music as four mounted men, wooden sabres in their hands, rode onto the wide stage. The audience cheered them.

The ten defeated Frenchmen, needed again, formed a line at the bottom of the plaster hill, levelled their muskets, and the four cavalrymen lined knee to knee. The limelights glared on their spurs and scabbard chains.

'Across Vitoria's proud plain, Ladies and Gentlemen, the thunder of their hooves was loud!' The drums rolled menacingly. 'Their swords were lifted to shine in the bright sunshine of that great day!' The four sabres raggedly lifted. 'And then, my Lords, Ladies and Gentlemen, the pride of France was humbled, the troops of the Ogre brought down, and the world watched in awe the terrible prowess of our British Cavalry!'

The pit orchestra worked itself into a cacophonous frenzy and the four horsemen trotted over the stage, screaming and waving their sabres. The wooden blades hacked down on the ten men who, once again, squeezed their bags of false blood and strewed themselves artistically about the stage's apron.

Sergeant Patrick Harper watched enthralled. He shook his head in admiration. 'That's just grand, sir.'

The drums were rolling again, louder and louder, drowning the screams of the dying actors and the excited shouts of the audience.

The back of the stage was opening up. It was, Sharpe admitted, impressive. Where, just a moment before, there had been a field of grass with some carefully arranged rock hills, all mysterious with the smoke from the small pots, now there was a magnificent castle, that, as it leaved outwards, pushed the hills and smoke aside.

The bass drum began a thunderous rhythm, a rhythm that made the audience clap with it and cheer in anticipation. The cymbals shivered the theatre, and the narrator, high on a pulpit beside the stage, raised his hands for silence.

'My Lords! Ladies! Gentlemen! Pray silence for His Majesty, his unutterable Majesty, his foul, proud, Napoleonic Majesty, King Joseph!'

An actor, mounted on a black horse, carrying a sword and wearing on his face a scowl of utmost ferocity, pranced onto the stage and, pretending to notice the audience for the first time, stared haughtily at the packed theatre.

The stalls booed him. He spat at them, waved his sword, and the boos became louder. The horse staled.

'King Joseph!' the narrator cried above the threatre's din. 'Brother to the Ogre himself, a Bonaparte! Made King of Spain by his brother, tyrant to the proud nation of Spain, hated wherever liberty is loved!'

The audience jeered louder. Isabella, fetched from the house in Southwark, leaned on the plush cushion at the front of the box and stared in awe. She had never been inside a theatre before, and thought it was magical.

King Joseph shouted orders to the ragged file of resurrected French soldiers. 'Kill the English! Slaughter them!'

The audience cat-called. A cannon was wheeled from the castle gateway, pointed at the audience, and a shower of sparks and smoke gushed from its muzzle.

Isabella gasped. Patrick Harper was wide-eyed with wonder at the spectacle.

The token for this box had been given to Sharpe by the landlord of the Rose Tavern. 'You should go, Major,' the man had said confidingly. 'You was there, sir, it'll bring it all back! And free oysters and champagne on the house, sir?'

Sharpe had not wanted to go, but Harper and Isabella had been desperate to see the 'Victory at Vitoria Enacted' and eager for Sharpe to share the delight. He had agreed for Harper's sake and now, as the pageant neared its end, Sharpe found himself enjoying the antics far more than he had expected. The effects, he thought, were clever, while some of the girls, conveniently introduced as persecuted peasants or grieving widows into the stage's carnage, were luminously beautiful. There were worse ways, Sharpe thought, of spending an evening.

The audience screamed in delight as King Joseph began a panicked flight about the stage. British troops, come from the wings, chased him, and he successively shed his sword, his hat, his boots, his gilded coat, his waistcoat, his shirt, and finally, to the delighted shrieks of the women in the audience, his breeches. All that was left to him was a tiny French tricolour about his arse. He stood shivering on top of the cannon, clutching the flag. The drums rolled. A British soldier reached for the small flag, the drum-roll grew louder, louder, the audience shouted for the soldier to pull the flag away, there was a clash of cymbals, and Isabella screamed in shock and delight as the flag was snatched away at the very instant that the curtain fell.

The audience chanted for more, the orchestra swelled to fill the tiers of boxes with triumphal music, and the curtain, after a brief pause, lifted again to show the whole cast, King Joseph cloaked now, facing the audience with linked hands to sing 'Proud Britons'. A great Union flag was lowered above their heads.

Sharpe was thinking of a sinuous, hungry, beautiful woman who had clawed at him and told him to go back to Spain. Sharpe wanted nothing more, but he knew that Lord Fenner had lied, that the Second Battalion existed, and, sitting here watching the flummery on stage he had suddenly dreamed up the perfect way to find them. Actors and costumes had put the thought into his head, and he told himself that he was foolish to think of meddling with things he did not understand. The mysterious, green-eyed woman had said that Lord Fenner would kill him, and though that threat did not worry Sharpe, nevertheless he sensed that there were enemies in this, his homeland, every bit as deadly as Napoleon's blue-jacketed troops.

Isabella gasped and clapped. From either wing of the stage, sitting on trapezes slung on wires, two women dressed as Goddesses of Victory were swooping over the heads of the actors. The Goddesses were scantily clad, the gauze fluttering over their bare legs as they swung above the linked actors and dropped laurel wreaths at their feet. The men in the audience cheered whenever the motion of the two trapezes peeled the gauze away from the Goddesses' legs.

The Goddesses of Victory were hoisted off stage when 'Proud Britons' was finished, and the orchestra went into a spirited 'Rule Britannia' which, though hardly appropriate for a soldier's victory, had the advantage that the audience knew its words. The cast stood upright and solemn, singing with the audience, and when the song was done, and the audience beginning its applause, the narrator held up his hands once more for silence. Some of the young men in the pit were shouting for the half-naked Goddesses to be fetched back, but the narrator hushed them.

A drum was rolling softly, getting louder. 'My Lords! Ladies and Gentlemen!' A louder riffle of the drums, then soft again. 'Tonight you have seen, presented through our humble skill, that great victory gained by noble Britons over the foul forces of the Corsican Ogre!' There were boos for Napoleon. The drums rolled louder, then softer. The narrator silenced the audience. 'Brave men they were, my Lords, Ladies and Gentlemen! Brave as the brave! Our gallant men, through shot and shell, through sabre and blade, through blood and fire, gained the day!' Another drum-roll and another cheer.

The door to the box opened. Sharpe turned, but it was merely one of the women who looked after the patrons and he presumed that, as the pageant was ending, so the boxes were being opened onto the staircase.

'Yet! My Lords, my Ladies and Gentlemen! Of all the brave, of all the gallant, of all the valorous men on that bloody field, there was none more brave, none more ardent, none more resolute, none more lion-hearted than . . . !' He did not finish the sentence, instead he waved his hand towards the boxes and, to Sharpe's horror, lanterns were coming into his box, bright lanterns, and in front of them were the two Goddesses of

Victory, each with a laurel wreath, and the audience was standing and clapping, defying the cymbals that clashed to demand silence.

'My Lords, Ladies and Gentlemen. You see in our humble midst the men who took the Eagle at Talavera, who braved the bloody breach at Badajoz, who humbled the Proud Tyrant at Vitoria. Major Richard Sharpe and his Sergeant Harper ...' and whatever else the narrator wanted to say was drowned by the cheers.

'Stand up, love,' whispered a Goddess of Victory in Sharpe's ear. He stood, and to his utter mortification, she put the laurel wreath on his head.

'For Christ's sake, Patrick, let's get out ...' But Harper, Sharpe saw, was loving it. The Irishman raised his clasped hands to the audience, the cheers were louder, and truly, in the small box, the giant Irish Sergeant looked huge enough to take on a whole French army by himself.

'Wave to them, love,' said the Goddess of Victory. 'They paid good money.'

Sharpe waved half-heartedly and the audience doubled its noise again. The Goddess pulled at his sword. 'Show it to them, dear.'

'Leave it alone!'

'Pardon me for living.' She smiled at the audience, gesturing with her hand at Sharpe as though he was a dog walking on its back legs, and she his trainer. Her face was as thickly caked with paint and powder as the Prince Regent's.

The drums called for silence, the narrator waved his hands and slowly the noise subsided. The faces, a great smear of them, still stared up at the two soldiers. Sharpe reached up to take the laurel wreath from his black hair, but the Goddess of Victory snatched his hand and held it.

'My Lords, Ladies and Gentlemen! The gallant heroes you

61

see before you are, this very night, residing at the Rose Tavern next to this theatre, where, I am most reliably assured, they will, this night, regale you with the stories of their exploits, lubricated, no doubt, by your kind offerings of good British ale!'

The audience cheered again, and Sharpe cursed because he had allowed himself to be gulled into being an advertisement for a sleazy inn, famous for its whores and actresses. He pulled his hand from the Goddess's, snatched the laurel wreath from his head, and flung it towards the stage. The audience loved it, thinking it a gesture for them, and the cheering became louder.

'Sergeant Harper!'

'Sir?'

'Let's get the god-damned hell out of here.'

Sergeant Patrick Harper knew that growl well enough. He gave one last, huge wave to the audience, tossed his own laurel wreath into the maelstrom, then followed his officer onto the stairs. Isabella, terrified of the Goddesses and lanternbearers, hurried after them.

'Of all the god-damned bloody nonsense in this god-damned bloody world!' Sharpe flung open the theatre door and stormed into Drury Lane. 'God in his heaven!'

'They didn't mean harm, sir.'

'Making a bloody monkey out of me!' Last night it had been the Royal Court, stinking like a whore's armpit, and now this! 'There wasn't a bloody castle at Vitoria!' Sharpe said irrelevantly. 'Let's get the hell out of here!' The audience was coming into the light of the lanterns hung beneath the theatre's canopy and some were clapping the two soldiers.

'Sir!' Harper shouted at Sharpe who had plunged into an alleyway. 'You're going the wrong way!'

'I'm not going near the bloody tavern!'

Harper smiled. Sharpe in a temper was a fearsome thing, but the huge Irishman had been long enough with the officer not to be worried. 'Sir.' He said it patiently, as though he spoke to a fool.

'What?'

'They're not meaning any harm, sir. It's a few free drinks, eh?' He said the last as if it was an irrefutable argument.

Sharpe stared at him belligerently. Isabella clung to the big Sergeant, her dark eyes staring fearfully at Sharpe. He cleared his throat, growled, and shrugged. 'You go.'

'Sir! They'll want to see you.'

'I'll be there later. One hour!'

Harper nodded, knowing he would do no better. 'One hour, sir.'

'Maybe.' Sharpe crammed his shako onto his head, hitched his sword into place, and walked into the alley.

'Where's he going?' Isabella asked.

'Christ knows.' The big Sergeant shrugged. 'Back to the woman he was with last night, I suppose.'

'He said he was walking!' Isabella said indignantly.

Harper laughed. He turned to the crowd, bowed to them and, like a monstrous pied piper, led his public towards the taproom where they could buy him drink and listen to the tales, the loving, long, splendidly told tales of an Irish soldier.

Anne, the Dowager Countess Camoynes, listened for a few moments to the orchestra playing in the great marbled hall where, this evening, an Earl entertained a few close friends. The friends, numbering some four or five hundred, were vastly impressed by the Earl's largesse. He had built, in his garden, a mock waterfall that led to a plethora of small pools in which, lit by paper lanterns, jewels gleamed. The guests could fish for the jewels with small, ivory handled nets. The Prince Regent, who had fished for half an hour, had declared the entertainment to be capital.

Lady Camoynes, sheathed in purple silk, fanned her face with a lace fan. She smiled at acquaintances, then went to the open air to stand on the garden steps. More than most guests here she needed to fish in the fake pools for the emeralds and rubies that glinted beneath the small golden fish, but she dared not do it for fear of the hidden laughter. All society knew of her debts, and all wondered how she clung onto the perquisites of her rank like the carriage and liveried servants. It was rumoured, in the fashionable houses of the quality, that she must be exchanging her slim body for a bare income, and she could do nothing to fight the rumours for she was too poor to afford that pride and, besides, there was truth in the sniggering whispers.

She sipped from a glass of champagne and watched the Prince Regent make his stately progress about the tables set on the lawn's edge. He was dressed this night in a coat of silver cloth, edged with gold lace. Lady Camoynes thought with malicious delight of the people of England who, in their good sense, hated this Royal family with its mad King and fat, gaudy, wastrel Princes.

'My dear Anne.' She turned. Lord Fenner stood behind her on the steps of the house. He watched the Prince, then put a pinch of snuff on the back of his hand. 'I have to thank you.'

'For what, Simon?'

Lord Fenner stepped down to her level. He sniffed the powdered tobacco into his hooked nose, arched his eyebrows as he fought the sneeze, then snapped the box shut. 'For your little tête-à-tête with Major Sharpe. I trust it was as satisfying to you as it was to me.' He smiled maliciously. Lady Camoynes said nothing. Her green eyes looked at the waterfall, ignoring

Lord Fenner, who laughed. 'I trust you didn't bed him.' She was amused at his jealousy. Lord Fenner had once asked Anne Camoynes to marry him, she had refused, and he had retaliated by buying her dead husband's debts. Still she had refused to be his wife, even though his hold over her forced her to his bed. Now familiarity had bred contempt in Fenner. He no longer wanted her in marriage, just in thrall. 'Well, Anne? Did you bed your peasant hero?'

'Don't be absurd.'

'I just worry what strange pox he might have fetched from Spain. I think you owe me an answer, Anne. Is he poxed?'

'I would have no way of knowing.' She stared at the laughing people who dipped their nets into the jewelled pools.

'If I find I need a physician's services I shall charge it to your account.' Fenner laughed and pushed the snuffbox into a pocket of his waistcoat. 'But thank you for your note.'

Lady Camoynes had written, in the early afternoon, that Sharpe intended to search for the Second Battalion. She sensed how important this matter was to Fenner and she suddenly wondered how she could turn that concern to her own profit. She looked at Fenner. 'What are you going to do with Major Sharpe, Simon?'

'Do? Nothing! My Lord!' He bowed to a man who climbed the steps, then glanced into Lady Camoynes' startling green eyes. 'I've sent him orders that will pack him off to Spain. Tomorrow.'

'That's all?'

He stared at her speculatively. 'Would it concern you if there was more? Would you warn him, Anne?' There was a shriek of laughter at the end of the garden as a choice ruby was fished up from a pool. Lord Fenner stared at the man who had found the ruby and who now placed it, to much laughter, in the cleavage of a young woman who was one of the actresses so loved by the Prince and his circle. 'Would it worry you, Anne, if I said that Major Sharpe will be dead by morning?'

'Will he?'

He looked at her, his eyes shamelessly staring at her body beneath its sheath of silk. 'Did you know, Anne, that there was a report that he was hanged this summer?'

'Hanged?'

'It turned out to be false. So his death is overdue. Does it worry you? Did you like him?'

'I talked to him, that was all.'

'And no doubt he was flattered.' Fenner stared into her eyes. 'Don't try and warn him, Anne. Not unless you want me to foreclose on the Gloucester estate.' He smiled, knowing he had his victory over her, then dropped a bag at her feet. 'I'll let you stoop for that, Anne. It's your payment for talking to the peasant.' He gave her the merest hint of a bow. 'If both my lanterns are lit when you go home, do come to see me.' He walked away from her, going towards the revellers about the waterfall.

Anne, Dowager Countess Camoynes, moved so that the hem of her dress hid the bag, then, when no one seemed to be watching, she bent quickly and picked it up. It was damp. It must, she thought, contain jewels from the garden pools, jewels that would help her pay off the debt that her husband's death had bequeathed to her and which she paid in Fenner's bed. She paid so that her only son, away at school, could inherit his father's estates. She hated Fenner and she despised herself, and she could see no escape from the trap that her dead husband's profligacy had made for her. No man would marry her, despite her beauty, for her widow's jointure was the monstrous, hateful debt.

She turned back into the house, unable to watch the jewels fetched from the water any longer, and she thought of the

Rifleman. She had not meant to take Sharpe to her bed, she had not wanted to show any weakness to the gutter-bred soldier, yet she had been astonished by the sudden need to hold onto a man. She had hated Sharpe last night because she could not possess him for ever, because she wanted him, because he was gentle. He was also, she suddenly thought, Fenner's enemy, and any man who was Lord Fenner's enemy must be her friend.

Tonight, if Fenner was right, Sharpe would die. Lady Camoynes paused, the damp bag of stones in her hand, and dreamed suddenly of revenge. If Sharpe survived this night, if he proved he could win this one battle over her enemy, then perhaps he would be a worthy ally for total victory. She turned to stare into the garden and her embittered, thin face smiled. She would have an ally, a soldier, a hero, so she would take the risk and have her vengeance if only, on this night of laughter and luxury, her soldier lived.

Richard Sharpe walked into a bad place. He did it knowingly, deliberately, and without fear.

It was called a rookery, one of many in London, but this was as foul a rookery as any the city could boast. The houses were tiny, crammed together, and built so flimsily that sometimes, without any apparent cause, they slumped into the alleyways in a thunderous cascade of timber, bricks and tiles that killed the people who lived a dozen to a room. This was a place of disease, poverty, hunger, and filth beyond reason. It was Sharpe's home.

He had lived in this rookery as a child. He had learned his first skills here, how to pick locks and open barred shutters. Here he had coupled with his first woman and killed his first man, and both before he was thirteen.

He walked slowly. It was a dark place, lit intermittently

by the flaring torches of the gin shops. The alleys were crowded, the people had suspicious eyes that were sunk in thin, starved, vicious faces. They wore rags. Children cried. Somewhere a woman screamed and a man bellowed at her. There was no privacy in a place such as this, a whole life was lived open to the gaze of predatory neighbours.

'Sir?' A thin hand wavered at a doorway. He shook his head at the girl, walked on, then suddenly turned back. The girl, her head wrapped in a scarf, stood above a stinking, legless man who held a knife. The man jerked his head. 'You can go in the alley with her.'

Sharpe stooped to the man. 'Where do I find Maggie Joyce?'

'Who are you?'

'Where do I find Maggie Joyce?' He did not raise his voice, but the crippled pimp heard the savagery, the threat, and he covered the knife blade with his left hand to show he meant no harm. 'You know Bennet's place?'

'I know it.'

'She runs it.'

The news confirmed what Sharpe had learned from a beggar outside the Rose Tavern and, in thanks, he gave the girl a coin. She would be dead, probably, before she was eighteen.

The place stank worse than he remembered. All the filth of these lives was poured into the streets, the dung, urine, and dead mixed with the scum in the gutters. He found, that by not even thinking about it, he could still thread the labyrinth into which criminals disappeared with such ease.

No one dared chase a man into these alleys, not unless he had friends to help him inside. It would have taken an army to flush out these dark, chill places. Here the poor, who had nothing, were lords. This was their miserable kingdom, and their pride was in their reputation for savagery, and their protection lay in the fact that no one, unless he was a fool, would dare walk these passages. Here poverty ruled, and crime was its servant, and every night there were murders, and rapes, and thefts, and maimings, and not one criminal would ever be betrayed because the strictest code of the rookery was silence.

Men watched Sharpe pass. They eyed his boots, his sword, his sash, and the cloth of his jacket. Any one of those things could be sold for a shilling or more, and a shilling in St Giles was a treasure worth killing for. They eyed the big leather bag that he carried, a bag that, except during the skirmish at Tolosa when it had been guarded by Isabella, had not left either Sharpe or Harper's side. The men of the rookery also saw Sharpe's eyes, his scars, the size of him, and though some men spat close to his boots as he walked slowly through the dark, damp alleys, none raised a hand against him.

He came to a torch that flared in an old, rusted bracket above a brief flight of steps. Women sat on the steps. They had gin bottles in one hand, babies in the other. One had lost an eye, another was bleeding from her scalp, while two clasped sucking children to their bare breasts as Sharpe climbed the stairs and pushed open a much-mended wooden door.

The room he entered was lit by tallow candles that drooped from iron hooks in the ceiling. It was crowded with men and women, children too, all drinking the gin that was the cheapest escape from the rookery. They fell silent as he entered. Their faces were hostile.

He pushed through them. He kept one hand firmly on his pouch in which were a few coins and his other hand gripped the neck of the stiff leather bag which was the reason for his visit to this place. He growled once, when a man refused to move, and when the customers saw that the tall, well-dressed soldier was not afraid of them, they moved reluctantly to let him pass. He went towards the back of the room, pressing through a stink equal to the stench of Carlton House, towards a table, well lit by candles, on which were ranked rows of gin bottles either side of an ale barrel. Two men, with scarred, implacable faces, guarded the table. One carried a bell-mouthed horse-pistol, the other a cudgel. Some of the customers were jeering Sharpe now, shouting at him to get out.

A woman sat behind the table, a massive woman with a face like stone and arms like twisted ropes. She had red hair, going grey, that was twisted back into a bun. Beside her, against the wall, was a second, iron-tipped cudgel. She stared at him with hostility. 'What do you want, soldier?' she sneered at him. Officers did not come here to mock the poverty of a rookery with their tailor-made clothes.

'Maggie?'

She looked at him suspiciously. Knowing her name meant nothing, everyone in the rookery knew Maggie Joyce; gin goddess, midwife, procuress, and eight times a widow. She had grown fat, Sharpe saw, fat as a barrel, but he guessed that the bulk was hard muscle and not soft flesh. Her hair was going white, her face was lined and hard, yet he knew she was no more than three years older than himself. She jerked her head at one of her two guards, making him step closer to the soldier, then glared at Sharpe. 'Who are you?'

Sharpe smiled. 'Where's Tom?'

'Who are you?' Her voice was hard as steel.

He took his shako off and smiled chidingly at her. 'Maggie!' He said it as if she had wounded him by her forgetfulness.

She frowned at him. She looked at the officer's sash, the leather bag, the sword, up to his high, black-collared neck and to his scarred, hard face, and suddenly, almost alarmingly, she wept. 'Dear Christ, it's yourself?' She had never lost the accent of Kilkenny, the only legacy her parents had given to her, besides a quick wit and an indomitable strength. 'Dick?' She said it with utter disbelief.

70

'It's myself.' He did not know whether to laugh or cry.

She reached over the table, clasped him, and the astonished gin-drinkers watched in awed surprise as the officer held her back. She shook her head. 'Dear God, look at the man! You an officer?'

'Yes.'

'Dear Christ on the cross! They'll make me into the bloody Pope next! You'll take some gin.'

'I'll take some gin.' He put his shako on the table. 'Tom?'

'He's dead, darling. Dead these ten winters. Christ, look at yourself! Will you be wanting a bed?'

He smiled. 'I'm at the Rose.'

She wiped her eyes. 'There was a time, Dick Sharpe, when my bed was all you ever wanted. Come round here. Leave those sinners to gawp at you.'

He sat beside her on the bench. He put the bag on the floor, stretched his long legs under the crude counter, and Maggie Joyce stared at him in astonishment. 'Oh Christ! But you look good in yourself!' She laughed at him, and he let his hand rest in hers. Maggie Joyce had been a mother to him once, rescuing him when he ran away from the foundling home, and he had known her when she had first gone onto the streets. Later, when he had become skilled at opening locked doors, she would come back in the dawn and climb into his bed and teach him the ways of the world. She had been lithe then, as sharp a whip as any in the rookery.

She had tears in her eyes. 'Christ, and I thought you were long gone to hell!'

'No.' He laughed.

They both laughed, perhaps for what had been and what might have been, and while they laughed, and while she took the small coins from her customers and poured gin into their tin cups, the two men who had followed Richard Sharpe from

Drury Lane stood unnoticed at the back wall and watched him. Two men, one swathed in a greatcoat despite the warm night, the other a native of this rookery. Both men had weapons, the skill to use them, and much, much patience. They waited.

CHAPTER FOUR

The two men, by not ambushing Sharpe on his way to Maggie Joyce's, had lost a fortune.

In Maggie's back room Sharpe unlaced the leather bag and spilt, onto her table, a king's ransom in diamonds. She stared at it, poking at the gems with a finger, as if she could not believe what she saw, 'Christ in his heaven, Dick! Real?'

'Real.'

'Mary, Mother of God!' She picked up a necklace of filigreed gold, hung with pearls and diamonds. 'Clean?'

'Clean.'

Which was not utterly true, yet the owners of the jewellery had no claim on it now. This was part of the plunder of Vitoria, the treasure of an empire that had been abandoned by the French in their panic to escape Wellington's victory. Men had become rich that day, and none richer than Sharpe and Harper who had taken these diamonds from a field of gold and pearls, silks and silver. Maggie Joyce delved into the heap of treasure that had once dazzled the aristocracy of the Spanish court. 'You're a rich man, Dick Sharpe. You know that?'

He laughed. This was a soldier's luck and that, he knew only too well, could turn sour in the flash of a musket's pan. 'Can you sell them for me?'

'Sure and I can!' She held a ring to the light of a candle. 'Would you remember Cross-Eyed Moses?'

'Green coat and a big stick?'

'That's him. His son, now, he's your man. I'll have him do it for you. You'll get a better price if you're patient.' She was pushing the jewels back into the bag.

'Take as long as you like.'

Sharpe could have let Messrs Hopkinsons, his army agents, handle the jewels, but he did not trust them to give him full value, any more than he would have trusted the fashionable jewellers of West London. Maggie Joyce, a queen in this kingdom of crime, was one of his own people and it was unthinkable that she would cheat him. She would take her commission on the sale, and that he expected, but rather her than the supercilious merchants who would see the Rifleman as a sheep to be fleeced.

She pushed the bag into a cupboard that seemed filled with rags. 'Would you be wanting money now, Dick?'

'No.' There had been gold at Vitoria too, so much gold that the coins had spilt into the mud to be reddened by the setting sun. He had put a year's salary of French gold into the army agent's safe, money that he would live on while in England and which would gather interest when he returned to Spain. He wrote down Messrs Hopkinsons' address for Maggie Joyce. 'That's where you put the money, Maggie. In my name.' He and Harper would split the proceeds later.

She laughed. 'Christ, Dick, but you always were a lucky bastard! When I first saw you I didn't know whether to drown you or eat you, you were that skinny, but the good Lord told me to be kind to you. Ah, Christ, and He was right! Now, are you going to get drunk with me?'

He was, and he did; splendidly, laughingly drunk, and even the problems of a lying Lord Fenner disappeared in the haze of gin and half-forgotten stories that were embroidered by Maggie's Irish skill into great sagas of youthful lawlessness.

He left her late. The city bells were ringing a quarter to three, and his head was spinning with too much gin and too much smoke in a small room. Even the stinking alleyway smelt good to him. 'You take care of yourself!' she called after him. 'And bring yourself back soon!'

It was dark as sin in the alleys. There was a moon, but small light got past the high, narrow houses that seemed to lean together at their tops.

Sharpe was drunk, and he knew it. He was happy, too, made sentimental by a visit to a past he had half forgotten. He crossed a small court, went under an archway, and it seemed to him now that the rookery, instead of being a foul place of poverty and disease, was a warm, intricate warren of friendly, caring people. He laughed aloud. God damn all Lords! Especially lying bastards of politicians. He decided he hated no one, no single evil soul in all the whole mad world, as much as he hated bloody politicians.

The two men who followed him were sensibly cautious, but not apprehensive. They had been astonished when the officer had come into the rookery, for one of them was a killer hired from these very alleyways, and their victim had been foolish enough to come into the one place where his death would be easy and unquestioned. No Bow Street Runner dared enter the St Giles Rookery.

The two men knew who their victim was, but the knowledge did not worry them. These men did not fear a soldier, not even a famous soldier, and certainly not a drunken one. No man, however fast and skilled with weapons, could resist an ambush. Sharpe would be dead before he even knew that he was in danger.

Sharpe was unaware of them. Instead of their footsteps he

listened to the crying children. That was a memory that came swamping back. The rookery was always full of children crying, small children, for once they had reached four or five they had learned not to cry. The sound made him think of his own daughter, orphaned in Spain, and that thought was maudlin. He rested against a wall.

There were few people about. The rookery, he knew, was alive and watching, but only a few whores were in the alleys, either against walls or coming home from Drury Lane. Their men, the hard masters who took their pence, stood in small groups where a torch lit a patch of mud and brick.

He took a deep breath. The last time he had been as drunk as this was in Burgos Castle, the night before the explosion, and the war in Spain suddenly seemed a long, long way off, as though it belonged to another man's life. He walked on, crossing one of the open ditches that ran with sludge thick as blood in the darkness.

He heard feet running behind him and he turned, always knowing to face a strange sound, and he saw a girl come from under the archway, stop, turn, and then walk awkwardly towards him. She had a scarf wrapped about a thin face that was bright-eyed with consumption. It was odd, he thought, how the dying consumptives went through a period of lucent beauty before their lungs coughed up the bloody lumps and they died in racking agony.

She crossed the ditch, raising her skirts, then clumsily swayed her hips as she came close to him. The smile she gave him was nervous. 'Lonely?'

'No.' He smiled back. He assumed she had seen him pass and had been sent to take some coins from the rich-looking officer to make up her night's earnings.

To his surprise she put her thin arms up to his neck, her cheek on his cheek, and pressed her body against his. 'Maggie sent me. Two men followed you and they're behind you.' She said it in a garbled rush.

He held her. To his right there was a gateway. He remembered it opened into an entranceway that ran between two houses. At its far end was a stairway that climbed to an old garret. A Jew had lived there, it was odd how the memories came back, a Jew who had worn his hair in long ringlets and had walked about with his nose deep into books. The rookery had left the old man alone, knowing him to be harmless, but after his death it was rumoured that a thousand gold guineas had been found in his room. The rookery was always full of such rumours. 'Come with me.'

He took her hand. He laughed aloud as if he was carelessly drunk, but the girl's message had sobered him as fast as a French twelve-pounder shot smashing the air close to him. He took her through the gate, into the alley, and into the deep shadows by the wooden stairway.

'Here.' The girl was hoisting her skirts.

'I don't need that, love.' He grinned.

'You want this.' At her waist was a belt and, hanging from the leather, a hook. It was an old device for hiding stolen goods, but now the girl had the huge horse-pistol hooked by its trigger guard. It was a fearful weapon with a splayed brass muzzle that, like a blunderbuss, would spray its charge of metal fragments in a widening fan. An ideal weapon, Sharpe supposed, with which the guard cowed Maggie Joyce's gin rooms. The barrel, Sharpe saw, was stuffed with rags to keep the missiles in place, and he pulled them out, then tapped the butt on the ground to tamp the stones and nails back onto the charge. He thumbed the heavy cock back. It was stiff, but clicked into place.

'Who are they?'

'One's called Jem Lippett, she doesn't know the other. Jemmy's a topper.' She gave the news that one of the men was a professional killer without any tone of alarm. This was a rookery.

Sharpe drew his long battle-sword. 'Get behind me.'

She crouched low. Sharpe guessed she was fifteen, perhaps fourteen, and he supposed she whored for her living. Few girls escaped the rookery, unless they were startlingly beautiful, and then their men would hawk them further west where the prices were higher. 'How do you know Maggie?' He spoke softly, not worrying about silence, because the men, if they were following him, would expect to hear voices from the entranceway.

'I work for her.'

'She was beautiful once.'

'Yes?' The girl sounded disinterested. 'She says you grew up here.'

'Yes.'

'Born here?'

'No.' He was watching the dark shape of the gate. His sword was beside him on the ground. 'Born in Cat Lane. I came here from a foundling home.'

'Maggie said you killed a man?'

'Yes.' He turned to look at her thin face. 'What's your name?'

'Belle.'

He was silent. He had killed a man who was beating the living daylights out of Maggie. Sharpe had cut the man's throat, and the blood had soaked into Maggie's hair and she had laughed and cuffed Sharpe round the head for messing her up. She had sent Sharpe out of the rookery, knowing that the murdered man's friends would look for revenge, for Sharpe had killed one of the kings of St Giles, one of the leaders of the criminals who lived in such safe squalor in the dark maze. Maggie had saved Sharpe's life then, and she was doing it again now, even though she could have left him unwarned, hoped for his death, and kept the jewels of Vitoria for herself.

Or perhaps she was not saving his life, for he could neither see nor hear anything untoward. Somewhere a dog barked, fierce and urgent, and then there was a yelp as it was silenced with a blow. A voice sang in an alleyway, there was laughter from a gin shop, and always the cries of babies and the shouts of anger and the screaming of men and women who lived and fought together in the tight filth of the small rooms where two families could share one room with a third in the hallway outside.

The girl coughed, a racking, hollow, dreadful sawing that would kill her before two winters had passed, and Sharpe knew the sound would bring the men into the alley if, indeed, they looked for him.

A bottle broke nearby. The gate of the entranceway creaked open an inch, stopped, and creaked again.

The girl's hands were on his back as if his nearness gave her comfort. He held the gun with both hands, its butt on the ground, its muzzle facing upwards so that the loose charge of killing fragments would not trickle down the barrel. He waited. The gate had opened only a few inches.

The gate was the only entrance into this place. It did not move again. Sharpe wondered if the two men waited for him to come out, preferring to ambush him as he came through the gateway rather than come themselves into the dark cul-de-sac where he might be waiting. He knew he must tempt them inside, make them think he was defenceless here, and he felt the crawling excitement that he had thought he would only get on a battlefield where he faced the French. At this moment, just as he did on a battlefield, he must dictate the enemy's move for them. He smiled. The two men who pursued him, if indeed they came to kill him, had found themselves an enemy. 'Belle?' He spoke in a whisper.

'What?'

'Make a noise!'

She knew what he meant. She began to moan, to give small gasps, and her hands rubbed up and down his back as the noises grew louder. 'Come on,' she said. 'Come on, my love, come on!' The two men obeyed her.

Two men, and moving so swiftly and silently that at first Sharpe was hardly aware that they had slunk past the door, then he saw the gleam of a knife and he pressed back with his spine to keep Belle moaning and the noise drew the two men towards the dark space beside the stairs.

Sharpe pulled the trigger. He half expected the old gun not to work, but the priming flashed; he had already closed one eye to keep his night vision; and the huge pistol bucked in his hands as the charge exploded and the barrel tried to leap upwards.

It was a nasty weapon. Its effect, in the tight entranceway, was as if a canister had been fired from a field gun. The scraps of stone and metal sprayed out from the stubby, splayed barrel and ricocheted from the walls to throw the two men backwards in blood and smoke and, even as they fell, Sharpe was moving. He dropped the empty gun, picked up the long, heavy, killing sword, and shouted the war-shout that put fear into his enemies.

One of the men, the one dressed in the greatcoat and in whose hand was a pistol, was dead. Half his head was missing, smeared in blood that fanned up the alley's wall, but the second man, cursing and sobbing, was trying to stand and in his right hand was a long knife.

The sword knocked the knife out of the bloodstained hand and Sharpe dropped his knee onto the wounded man's belly. He put the huge sword against the man's throat. 'Who are you?'

The man's answer was short.

Sharpe drew the sword an inch to one side and the man,

struck in the shoulder, waist, and thigh by the horse-pistol's scraps, gasped as the edge cut into his throat.

'Who are you?'

'Jemmy Lippett!'

'Who sent you?' Sharpe let the sword slip another fraction.

'No one sent me. I came with him!' Lippett's eyes, their whites bright in the gloom, looked towards the dead man. The smoke from the pistol still lingered in the entranceway. Sharpe heard the girl move behind him. He pushed the blade down, making the man gasp.

'Who was he?'

'I don't know!'

'Who wanted me dead?'

'Don't know!'

Sharpe drew the blade another half inch. 'Who?'

'I don't know!' The man felt the pressure of the steel and he whimpered. 'Just a bleeding soldier! Honest! He knew my da!'

Sharpe jerked his head towards the dead man. 'He's a soldier?'

'Yes!' Lippett's eyes, staring up at Sharpe's face, suddenly moved. Belle had come to Sharpe's shoulder, was looking down at Lippett, and the recognition in his eyes was his death warrant. If he lived he might call for revenge on the girl, even on her mistress, and besides, if he lived he would be able to say that Sharpe lived too.

Sharpe jerked his knee. 'Listen!'

'I'm listening!'

'You tell your da . . .' But there were no more words to be said because the sword, with sudden skill, had sliced down into the man's throat, driven by Sharpe's right hand on the handle and his left hand on the backblade, so now the man could not betray Maggie. His blood spurted up, striking Sharpe in the face, but the Rifleman kept the blade moving until it hit bone.

Sharpe had long known one thing, that if a man's death is sought, then it is good for that man to pretend to be dead. Earlier this very summer he had fooled the French because they believed him hanged, and now he would do the same to whoever had sought his death. No one would come into this rookery to search for bodies. By morning both the dead men would be stripped of their clothes, and their naked corpses would be tipped into an open sewer. By killing both men, Sharpe had guaranteed a mystery of his own.

Nor would he go back to Spain, at least not yet. If nothing had happened tonight, if he had gone back to the tavern, slept, and woken with a hangover, then perhaps he might have decided that discretion was the better part of valour. But not now, for someone had declared war on Sharpe, someone wanted him dead, and Sharpe did not run from his enemies.

'Christ!' Belle was running swift hands over the first dead man, searching for coins. 'Look!'

She had pulled open the dark greatcoat. Beneath it was a uniform; a red uniform with yellow facings, and with buttons that bore the badge of a chained eagle. Sharpe had killed a man of the South Essex, and he pulled the greatcoat away from the bloody uniform and saw on the man's sleeve the chevrons of a Sergeant.

'He's a bloody soldier!' Belle said.

Sharpe retrieved the rag that had stopped the pistol muzzle, wiped his face with it, then his sword blade. The blade scraped as he pushed it into the scabbard. He picked up the gun and gave it to the girl who hoisted her skirts and hung it on the hook, then she knelt awkwardly down to rummage through the clothes of the second dead man. She found some coins and smiled.

Sharpe peered out of the alley. No one waited for him, no one came to see why a shot had been fired. Instead, as always in the rookery, there was a strange silence while people waited to hear if the trouble was coming their way. He picked up the pistol that had been carried by the soldier and pushed it into his belt, then took two golden coins from his pouch. 'Belle?'

'Christ!' She stared at them.

'Those are for Maggie, these are for you.' He gave her two more. 'You've seen nothing, heard nothing, know nothing.'

She ran, one hand holding the gun through her skirts, and Sharpe waited till the sound of her bare feet faded to nothing, then, in the odd silence, he walked back to Drury Lane.

'You've seen nothing, nor have you, until you've seen it!' Even at half past three in the morning the huge Ulsterman was talking happily. 'More men than the Lord God killed in Sodom and Gomorrah. They cover the earth like locusts, and at their centre, at the very heart of them, there are the drummers.' Harper began to bang his palms on the table. 'A great, solid mass of men! They're coming and the very earth is shaking, so it is, and they're coming at you!' His hands still beat the table, rattling the bottles that he had made good use of.

A crowd listened.

'And the guns! The guns. I tell you. If you can imagine it, if you can imagine all the powder in all the earth crammed into the barrels, and the gunners working themselves into a slather, and the sound of it is like the end of the world! The drums, the guns, and the Frenchies with their bayonets, and there's just you and a few comrades. Not many, but you're there! You're waiting, so you are, and every mother's son of you knows that the bastards are coming for you, just you!'

Sharpe stood at the door, the dead Sergeant's civilian great-coat covering his uniform. He grinned, then whistled a few, brief, apparently tuneless notes.

Patrick Harper held his hands up as though he was pushing on a great door. 'They're coming towards you, so they are, and you can't see the sky for the smoke itself, and you can't hear a thing but the guns and the screams, and you're thinking that it's a long wee step from Donegal to Sallymanker, and you're wondering if you'll ever see your mother again!' He shook his head dramatically.

Sharpe whistled the notes once more, a Rifleman's battlefield call that meant 'close on me'. He repeated it.

The Sergeant looked about the faces. 'You'll not go away?'

More than a dozen people were left, listening enthralled, and Sharpe almost wished they had come here to recruit, for he and Harper could have walked out of the taproom with a dozen prime youngsters.

The Sergeant pushed his chair away from the table and grinned at his audience. 'Time for a dribble, lads. Just you wait!' He came to the door, took in the dark coat and the blood that was still on Sharpe's face. 'Sir?'

'Get my rifle, all my kit, everything! And yours! Fetch Isabella. We're going. Back alley in ten minutes.'

'Aye, sir.'

Sharpe went outside. No one had seen him, no landlord or tavern servant would be able to say that he had seen Major Sharpe alive. Now he and Harper must take Isabella back to the Southwark house and then, with the inspiration he had gained from watching the actors, they would go to find the Second Battalion of the South Essex.

It was dawn before Isabella was safely restored to the Southwark house. She accepted the sudden panic gracefully, though even she was curious as Sharpe and Harper stripped

84

themselves of their uniforms and gave their weapons to Harper's cousin. 'You keep them for us!' Harper said.

'They'll be safe.'

Mrs Reilly brought them old, ragged clothes, and Sharpe exchanged his comfortable French boots for a pair of broken, gaping shoes. Each man hid a few coins in their rags.

'How do I look?' Harper asked, laughing.

'Awful,' Sharpe laughed with him.

When Harper had come from the Rose Tavern, gripping Isabella in one hand and Sharpe's belongings in the other, he had brought orders that had been delivered to the tavern during the evening. Sharpe had read them. Lord Fenner ordered him to report instantly to the Chatham depot for transport to Spain. If Lord Fenner had also been behind the murder attempt then these orders, Sharpe surmised, were merely a disguise, or perhaps a precaution against Sharpe's survival.

The Reillys had a pen, some ink and old, yellowed paper. Sharpe wrote his own orders on the paper, addressed to d'Alembord, which told that officer and Lieutenant Price to make themselves scarce, to get out of Chelmsford, and to hide in London. 'Wait for messages at the Rose Tavern. Do not wear your uniforms and do not report to the Horse Guards.' They would be mystified, but they would obey. Sharpe, thinking ahead, knew he would need d'Alembord and Price, and he dared not run the risk that Lord Fenner would order those two officers, like himself, back to Spain. Sharpe would post the letter express this morning, paying the extra for it to be carried by a horseman.

The mail office would think it strange that such a vagabond should pay such a sum for a letter, for Sharpe, like Harper, was in rags and for a purpose. Somewhere in Britain there was a hidden Battalion, and Sharpe did not know how to find it. Yet the Battalion was recruiting, and that meant its recruiting sergeants were on the roads of Britain, and those sergeants, Sharpe knew, would take their men back to wherever the Battalion was concealed.

Sharpe could not find the Battalion, but the Battalion could find him. Major Richard Sharpe and Sergeant Major Patrick Harper, who only the night before had been crowned by the Goddesses of Victory, were going to become recruits again. They had donned the costumes of tramps and must act the parts of the desperate men whose last recourse was to join the ranks. Sharpe and Harper would join the army.

CHAPTER FIVE

They walked north from London into a countryside that was heavy with summer and lush with flowers, a countryside that, compared to Spain, gave easy living. No gamekeeper in England could compete with a Spanish peasant at protecting his land, and the two Riflemen lived well.

There was only one problem in their first days on the road, and that a real one, which was Harper's inability to drop the word 'sir'. 'It's not natural, sir!'

'What isn't?'

'Calling you . . .' he shrugged.

'Dick?'

'I can't!' The big Irishman was blushing.

'You've bloody well got to!'

They slept in the open. They trapped their food, stole it, or, despite the money hidden in their rags, begged in village streets. Four times in the first week they were chased out of parishes that did not want such stout looking troublemakers in their boundaries. They looked villainous, for neither man shaved. Sharpe wanted them to appear to be old soldiers, discharged legally, who had failed to find jobs or homes outside the army. Patrick Harper, who accepted this turn in his fate philosophically, nevertheless worried at the problem of why the Second Battalion was hidden and secret. He constantly thought of the

Sergeant who had tried to ambush Sharpe in the rookery. 'Why would the bugger want to kill you, sir?'

'Don't call me . . .'

'I didn't mean it! But why?'

'I don't know.'

Whatever secret was hidden with the Second Battalion stayed hidden, for in those first days they did not see any recruiting parties, let alone one from the South Essex. They stayed clear of the coast, fearing to be scooped up by a naval press-gang, and they wandered from town to town, always hoping to find one of the summer hiring fairs that were such good hunting grounds for a recruiter. They worked one day, hedging along the Great North Road, hoping that a recruiting party would pass. They were paid a shilling apiece, poor wages for country labouring, but suitable pay for a soldier or vagabond. Harper rough-hewed the hedge and Sharpe, coming behind, shaped it. At midday the farmer gave them a can of ale and stopped to talk about the weather and the harvest. Sharpe, eating the bread and cheese the farmer had brought, wondered aloud what was happening in Spain.

The farmer laughed, perhaps to hear such a question from a tramp. 'Don't fash yourself over that, man. Best place for the army, abroad.' He stood and arched his back. 'You're doing well, lads. You'll work another day?'

But the traffic on the road was small and their one day's work had been less enjoyable than their wandering, so they refused. And, indeed, Sharpe enjoyed it all. To be so free, suddenly, of responsibility, to walk apparently aimlessly beneath the warm skies of summer, along hedgerows thick with flowers and berries, to fish country streams and steal from orchards, to poach plump estates and wake each morning without needing to check rifle and sword; all this was oddly pleasant. They went slowly north, indulging their curiosity to leave their track to explore villages or gawp at old, ancient houses where the ivy lay warm on stone walls. Somewhere beyond Grantham they came to a flat, black-drained country, and they hurried their pace across the fens as though eager to discover what lay beyond the seemingly limitless horizon.

'Perhaps Ted Carew was wrong, sir,' Harper said.

'Don't call me "sir"!'

'We'll look a pair of bloody idiots if he's wrong!'

The thought had occurred to Sharpe, but he stubbornly clung to the old armoury sergeant's belief that the Second Battalion, which was supposed to exist only on paper, was still looking for recruits. And at Sleaford Sharpe found what he was searching for.

He found a real, booming, busy hiring fair, crammed with people from the nearby countryside; a recruiting sergeant's prayer. There was a giant on display, properly hidden behind a canvas screen, and the giant's keeper offered Harper a full crown in silver money if he would agree to become the giant's brother. There were Siamese twins, brought, the barker shouted, at great expense from the mysterious kingdom of Siam. There was a two-headed sheep, a dog that could count, a monkey that drilled like a soldier, and the bearded lady without whom no country fair would be complete. There were whores in the inns, gaitered farmers in the public rooms, and noisy Methodists preaching their gospel in the marketplace. There was a recruiting party from a cavalry regiment, and another from the artillery. There were jugglers, stilt-walkers, faith-healers, a dancing bear and, close to a Methodist preacher, but giving a different sermon, there was Sergeant Horatio Havercamp.

Sharpe and Harper saw him over the heads of the crowd and, slowly, they worked their way towards him. He was a big-bellied, red-faced, smiling man, with mutton-chop whiskers and twinkling eyes. He was being heckled by a good-natured crowd, but Sergeant Horatio Havercamp was equal to any heckler. He stood on a mounting block and was flanked by two small drummer boys.

'You, lad!' He pointed to a thin, tall country boy dressed in an embroidered smock. 'Where are you sleeping tonight?'

The boy, embarrassed to be picked out, merely blushed.

'Where, lad? Home, I'll be bound! Home, eh? All alone, yes? Or are you keeping a milkmaid warm, are you doing that now?'

The crowd laughed at the boy, whose face was now scarlet.

Sergeant Havercamp grinned at the boy. 'You'll never sleep alone again in the army, lad. The women? They'll be dropping off the trees for you! Now look at me, would you call me a handsome man?' He got the answer he deserved and wanted from the crowd. He raised his hands. 'Of course not. No one ever called Horatio Havercamp a handsome man, but, lad, let me tell you, there's many a lass been through these hands, and why? Because of this! This!' He plucked at his red jacket with its bright yellow facings. 'A uniform! A soldier's uniform!' The drummer boys rattled a quick tattoo with their sticks.

The embarrassed farm boy had wormed his way out of the crowd and now wandered towards the Methodists who offered joys of a different sort. Sergeant Havercamp did not mind. He had the attention of enough young men in the crowd and he looked about for another butt. He could hardly miss Patrick Harper, a full head and shoulders taller than most of the people who pressed towards the inn where the Sergeant had his pitch. 'Look at him!' Sergeant Havercamp cried. 'He could win the war single-handed. You ever thought of being a soldier?'

Harper said nothing. His sandy hair made him look younger than his twenty-eight years. Sergeant Havercamp rubbed his hands in glee. 'How much money have you got, lad?'

Harper shook his head as though too embarrassed to say anything.

'Nothing, I'll be bound! Look at me, now!' Sergeant Havercamp produced two golden guineas from his pocket and dexterously rolled them between his fingers so that the gold glittered mesmerically as he skilfully wove the two coins in and out of his knuckles. 'Money! Soldier's money! You heard of the battle at Vitoria, lad? We took treasure there, we took gold, we took jewels, we took more money than you'll dream of in a lifetime of dreams!'

Harper, who had fought at Vitoria, and taken a king's ransom from that battlefield, gaped convincingly.

Sergeant Havercamp juggled the two coins with one hand, tossing one up, then catching the other while the first twinkled beside his whiskers. 'Rich! That's what you can be as a soldier! Rich! Women, glory, money, and victory, lads!' The two drummer boys performed another obedient drum-roll, and the young men in the crowd stared bewitched at the gold coins.

'You'll never be hungry again! You'll never be without a woman! You'll never be poor again! You can walk with your head up and never fear again, because you will be a soldier!'

The drum-roll again, and still the gold coins went up and down beside Sergeant Havercamp's smiling, confiding, friendly face.

'You've heard of us, lads! You know of us! We're the South Essex. We're the lads who tweaked Bonaparte's nose! That monkey loses sleep because of us. The South Essex! We've put fear into the heart of an Emperor, and you can belong to us! Yes! We'll even pay you!'

The drum-roll once more. The coins stopped in Havercamp's raised right hand. He took off his shako, revealing red hair, and, holding the inverted shako in his left hand, as the drummer boys struck one sharp blow on their skins, he tossed one of the golden guineas into the hat. A second drumbeat marked the second guinea joining the first and, still without saying a word,

Sergeant Havercamp produced more guineas from his pouch and tossed them, one by one, into the shako.

'Three!' A small, weasel-faced man who had wriggled his way close to Sharpe and Harper shouted, 'Four! Five!' Another man took up the count and, as the guineas mounted, the crowd called the numbers aloud to drown the thin hymn singing of the Methodists.

'Fifteen! Sixteen! Seventeen! Eighteen! Nineteen! Twenty! Twenty-one! Twenty-two!'

The count stopped. Sergeant Havercamp grinned at them. He put his hand into his pouch and brought out a half-guinea, held it up to the crowd, then tossed it into the hat. The drummers beat their skins. The Sergeant followed the half-guinea with a quick shower of shillings and pence, raised the hat, then shook it to let the crowd hear the heavy sound of the money inside.

'Twenty-three pounds, seventeen shillings, and sixpence! That's what we'll pay you! Twenty-three pounds, seventeen shillings, and sixpence! Just to join the army! We'll pay you!' He shook the hat again. 'Now, lads, I was young once!' He held up a hand to check the good-natured jeers. 'True! Even I, Sergeant Horatio Havercamp was young once, and let me tell you something! He paused dramatically, looking from face to face in the crowd. 'I never did meet, nor ever will, a pretty girl who could resist the sound of money! Now, lads! If they'll kiss you for a shilling, what will they do for a guinea, eh?' He raised one finger, licked it, and laughed. 'Twenty-three pounds, seventeen shillings, and sixpence!'

'I'll marry you for that!' a woman called out, provoking laughter, but the young men in the crowd were remembering the golden stream of coins that added up to more than six months' wages for most of them. Six months' wages! All at once, and just for signing up!

Sergeant Havercamp shook his head sadly. 'I know what you're thinking, lads! I know! You've heard stories! You've heard the lies they put about!' He shook his head again in silent sadness at the sinfulness of a world that could tell lies about the army. 'They say the army's a harsh place! They say there's disease and worse but, oh, my lads! Oh, my lads! My own mother begged me. She did! She said "Horatio! Don't you go for a soldier, don't you go!" She threatened never to talk to me again. But I did! Ah, I'll admit I was young and I was headstrong and I was too tempted by the girls and the glory and the money; and my old mother, God bless her grey hairs, she said I'd broken her heart! Broken her very heart!' He let the enormity of this sink into them, then slowly smiled. 'But, my friends, my dear mother today lives in her own cottage and with every breath she takes, my friends, she blesses the name of Horatio Havercamp! And why? Why?' He paused dramatically. 'Because, my friends, it was I who bought her the cottage and I who planted her wallflowers and I who have given her the rest she so richly deserves.'

He smiled modestly. 'Only the other day the General passes by her garden gate. "Mother Havercamp," he said, "I sees your son Horatio has done you bravely!" "He has," she says, "and all because he went for a soldier."'

Horatio Havercamp opened his pouch and tipped the money glintingly inside. He put his shako on his head, tapped it down, and drew himself up to his considerable height. 'Well, lads! The chance is yours! Money! Glory! Riches! Fame! Women! I won't be here long! There's a war that has to be fought and there are women that wait for us and if you don't come to us today then perhaps your chance will never come! You'll grow old and you'll rue the day that you let Horatio Havercamp go out of your life! Now, lads, I've spoken long enough and I've a thirst like a dry dog in a smithy, so I'm spending some of that money the army gives me on some pots of ale in the Green Man! So come and see me! No persuasion, lads, just some free froth on your lips and a wee chat!'

The drummers gave a last, loud roll, and Sergeant Havercamp jumped down to the roadway.

The small, weasel-faced man who had led the chanting as the guineas were thrown, looked up at Patrick Harper. 'Are you going with him?'

Sharpe guessed the man was a corporal, one of Havercamp's assistants salted into the crowd to snare the likeliest recruits. He wore a corduroy coat over a moleskin waistcoat, but his grey trousers looked suspiciously like standard issue.

Harper shrugged. 'Who wants to be a soldier?'

'You're Irish?' The small man said it delightedly as though, all his life, he had nurtured a love for the Irish and had never, before this moment, had a chance to display it. 'Come on! You must be thirsty!'

'The ale's free?'

'He said so, didn't he? Besides, what can he do to us?'

Harper looked at Sharpe. 'You want to go, Dick?' He blushed like an eight year old as he used Sharpe's name.

The small, sharp-featured man looked at Sharpe. The scar, and Sharpe's older face, made him pause, then he grinned. 'Three of us, eh? We can always walk away if we don't take to the fellow! You're called Dick?'

Sharpe nodded. The man looked up at the huge Irishman. 'You?'

'Patrick.'

'I'm Terry. Come on, eh, Paddy? Dick?'

Sharpe scratched the thick, stiff bristles of his unshaven chin. 'Why not? I could drink a bloody barrel.'

Sharpe and Harper went to join the army.

* * *

Sergeant Horatio Havercamp had been wonderfully successful. Five lads, other than Sharpe and Harper, were in the Green Man's snug where the good Sergeant ordered quarts of ale and glasses of rum to chase the beer down. A window opened onto the street and the Sergeant sat close by it so he could shout pleasantries to any likely-looking young man who wandered towards the fair's attractions. He had also, Sharpe noted, positioned himself close enough to the door so that he could cut off the retreat of any of his prospective recruits.

The Sergeant made a great show of giving Harper two quarts of beer. 'So you're Irish, Paddy?'

'Yes, sir.'

'You don't call me "sir"! Lord love you, boy! Call me Horatio, just like my mother does! You're a big lad, Paddy! What's your other name?'

'O'Keefe.'

'A great name, eh?' Sergeant Havercamp paused to shout for more beer, then glanced suspiciously at Sharpe who had sat himself in the darkest corner of the room. Havercamp was wise to the men who drank free beer and tried to escape at evening's end, and he jerked his head in a tiny, almost imperceptible motion that made Terry move his pot of ale and sit at Sharpe's side. Then Havercamp smiled confidingly at Harper. 'It's a great regiment for the Irish, you know!'

'The South Essex?'

'Aye, lad.' Sergeant Havercamp lowered most of his quart pot, wiped his moustache, and patted his belly. 'You've heard of Sergeant Harper?'

Harper choked, blowing the froth off the ale into the table, then, with sheer amazement on his broad, good-natured face, he gaped at Horatio Havercamp. 'Aye, I've heard of him.'

'Took an Eagle, lad! A hero, that's what he is, a hero. No

95

one minds him being Irish, not in the South Essex. Home from home, you'll find it!'

Harper drank his first quart in one go. He looked at the smiling Sergeant. 'Would you be knowing Sergeant Harper yourself, sir?'

'Don't call me "sir"!' Havercamp chuckled. 'Would I be knowing him, you ask! Would I just! Like that, we are!' He crossed two of his fingers, nodded, and an expression of regret for the good times that were in his past flickered over his face. 'Many's a night I've sat with him, within earshot of the enemy, lad, just talking. "Horatio," he'd say to me, "we've been through a lot together." Aye, lad, I know him well.'

'He's big, I hear?'

Havercamp laughed. 'Big! He'd give you six inches, Paddy, and you're not a shrimp, eh?' He watched with approval as Harper downed the second quart. Havercamp pushed the rum towards him. 'Get yourself on the outside of that, Paddy, and I'll buy you some more ale.'

Harper listened wide-eyed as the wonders of the army were unfolded before him. Havercamp seemed to embrace all of his potential recruits as he expanded on the future that waited for them. They would be Sergeants, he said, before the snow fell, and as likely as not, they would all be officers within the year. Havercamp laughed. 'I'll have to salute you, yes?' He threw a salute to a bony, hungry boy who drank his beer as though he had not taken sustenance in a week. 'Sir!' The boy laughed. Havercamp saluted Harper. 'Sir!'

'Sounds grand,' Harper said wistfully. 'An officer?'

'I can see it in you now, Paddy.' Havercamp slapped the rump of the girl who had brought a tray of ale pots. He distributed them around the table and ordered more. 'Now you've all heard of our Major Sharpe, haven't you?'

Two or three of the boys nodded. Havercamp blew at the

froth on his pot, sipped, then leaned back. 'Started in the ranks, he did. I remember him like it was yesterday. I said to him, I said, "Richard," I said, "you'll be an officer soon." "Will I, sarge?" he says.' Havercamp laughed. 'He didn't believe me! But there he is! Major Sharpe!'

'You know him?' Harper asked.

The fingers twined again. 'Like that, Paddy. Like that. I call him "sir" and he says, "Horatio, there's no call for a 'sir' to me. You taught me half I know. You call me Richard!"'

The potential recruits stared in awe at the Sergeant. The drinks came fast. Three of the boys were farmers' lads, dressed in smocks, all of them, Sharpe judged, likely to become good, solid men if only Horatio could persuade them to take the shilling. One of the farm boys had a bright, lively face and a small terrier that shared his ale. The dog, he said, was called Buttons. Buttons' owner was named Charlie Weller. Horatio Havercamp ordered a bowl of ale specially for Buttons.

'Can I bring my dog?' Charlie Weller asked.

'Of course you can, lad!' Havercamp smiled. Weller, Sharpe guessed, was seventeen. He was sturdy, cheerful, and any Battalion would be pleased to have him.

'Will we fight?' Weller asked.

'You want to, lad?'

'Aye!' Weller grinned. 'I want to go to Spain!'

'You will! You will!'

The hungry boy, called Tom, was half-witted. His eyes flicked about the small room as though he expected at any moment to be hit. The last of the five was a sad-faced, frowning man of twenty-three or -four, dressed in a faded coat of broadcloth with a decent but shabby shirt beneath. This last man, whose face and hands suggested he had never worked in the open air, hardly spoke. Sharpe guessed that he had already made up his mind to join and that this drinking and japery were not to his taste.

Tom, the half-wit, Sharpe judged, would join simply so as not to be hungry. He would fatten up in the army and could be taught to stand in the musket line and perform his duty. Havercamp, Sharpe could see, was worried about Harper and the three farm lads. They were the ones he wanted, the ones he wanted to see drunk, the ones he wanted to snare before sobriety drove sense into their head.

Sharpe himself, sitting in the corner, was ignored. It was not till dusk, when the drink had already made the three farm boys unsteady and silly, that Sergeant Havercamp came over to Sharpe's corner.

The Sergeant sat down. Sharpe was about to lift the pot of ale to his mouth when Havercamp's big hand came across the table and pushed Sharpe's down.

The Sergeant's face, hidden from his other victims, was suddenly knowing and unfriendly. He kept his hand on Sharpe's wrist. 'What's your bloody game?'

'Nothing.'

'Don't blind me, you bastard! You've served, haven't you?'

Sharpe stared into the small, blue eyes. At this distance he could see the broken veins in Havercamp's skin, the knowing lines about his eyes. Sharpe nodded. 'Thirty-third.'

'Discharged?'

'Wounded, Sarge. India.'

'Or you bloody ran.'

Sharpe smiled. 'I'd hardly be here, Sarge, if I was a scrambler, would I?'

Sergeant Havercamp stared at Sharpe suspiciously as though he might have discovered a deserter. His fingers tightened on Sharpe's wrist. 'So you're not a scrambler, eh? A jumper?'

'No, Sarge.'

'You'd better not be, lad, or else I'll tear your bloody eyes out and shove them up your arse.' Havercamp feared this might be a man who signed up, took that part of the bounty which was given first, then absconded to repeat the trick with another recruiting sergeant.

'No, Sarge, I'm not a jumper.'

'No, Sarge, I'm not a jumper.' Havercamp mimicked him cruelly. 'So why are you here?'

Sharpe shrugged. 'No work.'

'When did you leave?'

'Year back, maybe more.'

Havercamp stared at him. Finally he let go of Sharpe's wrist and let him lift the ale to his lips. The Sergeant watched him as though he begrudged every sip Sharpe took. 'What's your name?'

'Dick Vaughn.'

'Read and write?'

Sharpe laughed. 'No.'

'Got a clean back?'

Sharpe shrugged, then shook his head. 'No.' He had been flogged years before, in India.

'I'm watching you, Dick Vaughn. I'm watching you every bleeding step to the bleeding depot, you understand? You queer my pitch, lad, and I'll have the rest of the skin off your bloody back. You know what I mean.'

'Yes, Sarge.'

Sergeant Havercamp reached into his pocket and took out a shilling piece. His expression, as he held the coin out, mocked Sharpe's failure to survive outside the army. His voice was jeering. 'Take it.'

Sharpe nodded. Reluctantly, as though this was an act of desperation, as though every movement was an acknowledgement of his failure, he took the shilling.

'There, lads!' Havercamp turned round. 'Dick here has joined up! Well done, Dick!'

The farm boys cheered him. 'Well done, Dick!' Buttons, half drunk and excited by the cheers, barked.

The half-wit was next, grabbing the shilling eagerly, and laughing as he bit it and pushed it into his rags. The young man in the broadcloth coat took his without any fuss, resigned to it, taking it as though he was bored.

'Now, Paddy! What about you?'

Harper laughed. 'You think I'm a fool, eh? Just because I'm Irish?'

One of the drummer boys, sitting on his drum, snored in a corner. Sergeant Havercamp watched as his two corporals, both of whom had taken their shillings obediently as they still pretended to be recruits, poured rum for the three boys in their smocks. He looked up at the big Irishman. 'What's the problem, Paddy. Tell me, eh?'

Harper traced patterns on the wooden table with spilt beer. 'It's nothing.'

'Come on, tell me!'

'Nothing!'

Havercamp rolled a shilling into the spilt beer. It fell onto its side. 'Tell me why you won't take it?'

Harper frowned. He bit his lip, shrugged, and looked at the Sergeant. 'Do I get a bed?'

'What?'

'A bed? Do I get one? A bed?'

Havercamp stared at him, saw the intensity on the big face, and nodded. 'Fit for a King, Paddy. You'll get a bed with satin sheets and pillows big as bloody cows!'

'That's grand!' Harper picked up the shilling. 'I'm all yours!'

Sergeant Havercamp failed with the three farm boys. Charlie Weller was desperate to join up, but would not take the

100

shilling unless his two friends joined with him, and they were reluctant. Sharpe watched Havercamp try all the tricks, even the old one of slipping the shillings into their beer so they would pick them out of the dregs in astonishment, but the three lads were wise to that one. They became drunker and drunker, so drunk that Sharpe was sure that one of them would take the proferred, glittering coin, yet at the very moment when it seemed that Charlie Weller would take his anyway, even without his friends, the door to the snug banged open and a woman stood there, screaming in rage, shouting at Havercamp and hitting with her fist at Charlie. 'You little bastard!'

'Ma!' he shouted. 'Ma! Stop it!'

'Out! And you, Horace and James! Out! Disgrace, you are, disgrace to your families! Playing at soldiers! You think I brought you into this world to see you throw yourself away?' She cuffed Charlie Weller about the ears. 'Only a fool joins the army, you fool!'

'Aye, you're right,' Harper said drunkenly.

Havercamp surrendered the three boys gracefully. He had, to console his loss, twenty-eight men in a barn outside town, he had scooped up four today, and he had high hopes of the whores who were working the inns for him. He would have a tidy enough number to take back to Lieutenant Colonel Girdwood. He smiled reassuringly at his recruits as Mrs Weller left, drained his last ale, and ordered them to their feet.

They had taken the King's Shilling, but they were not quite yet the King's men. Sharpe lay that night in the broken-down stable behind the Green Man and he stared at the stars through the gaping thatch. He smiled. Six weeks before, in the nights after the battle of Vitoria, he had slept in a great bedroom with the whore of gold, the Marquesa, the woman who was a spy and who had been his lover. He had lain with an aristocrat

101

and now he lay in old, filthy straw. What would she think if she could see him now?

The other recruits snored. In the next stable a horse whinnied softly. Beside Sharpe the straw rustled.

'You awake?' Harper whispered.

'Yes.'

'What are you thinking of?'

'Women. Helene.'

'They come and go, eh?' Harper chuckled, then pointed at the broken roof. 'We could go now. Bugger off, eh?'

'I know.'

But they did not. They were in England, recruited, and going to battle.

CHAPTER SIX

In the morning Sergeant Horatio Havercamp had thirty-four men, the last few brought in by the whores whom he had brought from London and who were paid to dazzle young men with unfamiliar spirits and flesh. Twenty-eight of his men were guarded in the barn outside of town, while the nine new recruits were in the Green Man's stable.

'On your feet, lads! On your feet!' Sergeant Havercamp was still genial, for none of these nine recruits were in the bag yet, even though they did have the King's Shilling. 'Come on, lads! Up!'

A man in a long, brown, woollen coat and with a tall, brown hat stood next to the Sergeant. His nose dripped. He coughed with a cavernous, retching cough that, each time it exploded in his chest, made him groan afterwards with a hopeless, dying moan. He went round the stable, peering at each man, sometimes asking them to lift up a leg. It was the quickest medical inspection Sharpe had ever seen, and when it was done the doctor was given a handful of coins. Sergeant Havercamp clapped his hands as the doctor left. 'Right, lads! Follow me! Breakfast!'

The two corporals, magically transformed into redcoats with tall, black shakos, helped hustle the nine men towards the inn. It was not fully light yet. A cock crowed in the yard and a maid carried a clanking pail from the pump.

'In here, lads!'

It was not for breakfast. Instead, a magistrate waited in the public room, a grey-haired, savage-faced, irascible man with pinched cheeks and a red nose. A clerk sat next to him with a stack of papers, a pot of ink, a quill, and a pile of bank notes.

'Right! Let's see you lively!' Sergeant Havercamp whisked them forward one by one, chivvied them to the table, and stood over them as they were sworn in. Only three of the recruits, one of them the quiet young man in his broadcloth coat, could write. The others, like Sharpe and Harper, made crosses on the paper. Sharpe noticed that the doctor had already signed the forms, presumably before he came out to the stable to glance at the recruits. He noticed, too, that no one offered the recruits the chance of a seven-year engagement; it was simply not mentioned. The form, that he pretended he could not read, was headed 'Unlimited Service'.

He put his cross in the place the clerk showed him. 'I, *Dick Vaughn*,' the paper read, 'do make Oath that I am or have been —————', Sharpe declared no occupation and the clerk left it a blank, 'and to the best of my Knowledge and Belief was born in the Parish of *Shoreditch* in the Country of *Middlesex* and that I am the age of 32 Years'. Sharpe decided he would take four years off his age. 'That I do not belong to the Militia, or to any other Regiment, or to His Majesty's Navy or Marines, and that I will serve His Majesty, until I shall be legally discharged. Witness my Hand. *X. Dick Vaughn, his mark.*

The magistrate took the paper and scribbled his own name on it. 'I, *Charles Meredith Harvey*, one of His Majesty's Justices of the Peace of *the borough of Sleaford*, do hereby certify that *Dick Vaughn* appeared to be 32 years old, *six* feet – inches high, *Dark* Complexion, *Blue* Eyes, *Black* Hair, came before me at *Sleaford* on the *Fourth* Day of *August* One thousand Eight Hundred and *Thirteen* and stated himself to be of the Age of

Thirty-Two years, and that he had no Rupture, and was not troubled with Fits, and was no ways disabled by Lameness, Deafness, or otherwise, but had the perfect Use of his Limbs and Hearing, and was not an Apprentice; and acknowledged that he had voluntarily enlisted himself, for the Bounty of *Twenty-Three pounds Seventeen shillings and Sixpence* to serve His Majesty King George III, in the ———— Regiment of ———— commanded by ———— until he should be legally discharged.'

Sharpe noticed that, although the clerk filled in the personal details of each man as they stood at the table, and though the magistrate's blanks were all filled, strangely the South Essex's name did not appear in its proper place. At the end of the document there was an attestation that he had received one guinea of his bounty which was pressed into his hand by the clerk. 'Next!'

He was in. Sworn in. He had taken the King's Shilling, and accepted a new-fangled, scruffy pound note to make it into a guinea, and he watched silently as the other men went forward. More money, he saw, passed hands as the magistrate left, presumably so that worthy official would ignore the absence of any regiment noted down on the attestation form, then Sergeant Havercamp was bawling at them to get outside, into the inn yard, and there each man was given a chance to drink at the pump and half a loaf of stale bread was pushed into their hands.

The two corporals, grinning in their red jackets, helped push the nine men into two crude ranks. The drummer boys, yawning and sticky-eyed, banged their drums and, before the sun was risen properly, they were marching through the detritus of the hiring fair. The young man in broadcloth, who had given his name to the clerk as Giles Marriott, walked in front of Sharpe. He did not speak a word to his neighbour, the half-wit, Tom. Sharpe noticed, as they crossed the marketplace in the grey dawn, how Marriott stared at a fine, brick-built house.

'Move it! Come on!' Corporal Terence Clissot pushed Marriott. 'Get a bloody move on!'.

Yet still Marriott stared back, half-tripping as he walked, and Sharpe turned to look at the house, wondering what it was that made the young, good-looking man stare so fixedly at it. The drums still rattled and it was, perhaps, their sound that made one of the shutters open on the upper floor.

A girl stared out. Sharpe saw her, looked at Marriott, and thought there was a glistening in the man's eye. Marriott lifted a hand half-heartedly, then seemed to decide that the small gesture was futile in the face of this huge gesture he had just made to spite the girl who had jilted him. He dropped his hand and walked on. Yet the half-gesture, so feebly made and so quickly retracted, had not escaped Sergeant Havercamp. He saw the girl, looked at Marriott, and laughed.

They marched south. The hedgerows were thick with dew. The drums, now they were out of the town, fell silent. None of the nine men spoke.

A dog barked. Nothing unusual in a country dawn, except this dog was chasing after them and Sergeant Havercamp turned, snarled, raised his boot to kick at it, then checked his foot.

It was Buttons. Behind the dog, running just as hard, smock flapping and with a bundle on his shoulder, was Charlie Weller. 'Wait for me! Wait for me!'

Havercamp laughed. 'Come on, lad!'

Weller looked behind, as if to make sure that his mother was not following him, but the lane was clear. 'Can I join, Sergeant?'

'You're welcome, lad! Into line! We'll swear you in at the next town!'

Weller grinned at Sharpe, pushed in beside him, and the boy's face showed all the excitement proper at the beginning of a great adventure. They collected the other recruits and their guards from the barn, then headed south for a soldier's life.

At Grantham, where they were locked into the yard of the Magistrate's Court, Sharpe watched Sergeant Havercamp strike a deal. Twelve prisoners were released to him, manacled men who were pushed into the back of the line. More bread was given to them and Sharpe watched young Tom, the half-wit, thrust the loaf at his mouth and gnaw at it. The boy grinned constantly, always watching for a cuff, a curse or a kick. If he was spoken to he giggled and smiled.

That night three men ran, two successfully getting away, almost certainly to find another recruiting party and gull another guinea from the King. The third was caught, brought to the yard where they had slept, and beaten by Corporal Clissot and Sergeant Havercamp. When the beating was over, and the man was lying bleeding and bruised on the yard's cobbles, Sergeant Havercamp retrieved the King's guinea, then kicked the man out into the road. There was small future in taking a jumper back to the Battalion for the man would doubtless only try to desert again.

Giles Marriott had stared in awe at the beating, flinching when the Corporal's boots slammed into the man's ribs. Marriott was pale by the time the punishment was given. He looked at Sharpe. 'Are they allowed to do that?'

Sharpe was astonished that Marriott had spoken, the young man had hardly opened his mouth since he had come to the inn to get his shilling. 'No,' Sharpe shrugged. 'But it's quicker than turning him over to a magistrate.'

'You've been in before?'

'Yes.'

'What's it like?'

'You'll be all right.' Sharpe smiled and drank the mug of tea that was their breakfast. 'You can read and write. You'll become a clerk.'

Charlie Weller was petting his dog. 'I want to fight!'

Marriott still stared at Havercamp, who was shutting the yard gate on the bruised, bleeding man. 'They shouldn't behave like that.'

Sharpe wanted to laugh aloud at the hurt words, but instead he looked sympathetically at the frightened young man. 'Listen! Havercamp's not bad. You're going to meet much worse than him. Just remember a few rules and they can't touch you.'

'What?'

'Never step out of line, never complain, never look into a sergeant's or an officer's eyes, and never say anything except yes or no. Got it?'

'I don't understand.'

'You will,' Harper said. He had come back from the pump in the yard under which he had dunked his head so that the water now streamed down his face and soaked his thin, torn shirt. 'By God you will, lad.'

'You! Paddy!' It was Sergeant Havercamp's voice, booming over the yard. 'Turn round!'

Harper obeyed. The water had soaked the thin shirt to his hugely muscled back and showed, through its thin weave, the scars that lay over his spine. Sergeant Havercamp grinned beneath his red moustache. 'Paddy, Paddy, Paddy! Why didn't you tell me?'

'Tell you what, Sarge?'

'You served, didn't you? You're an old soldier, Paddy!'

'You never asked me!' Harper said indignantly.

'What regiment?'

'Fourth Dragoon Guards.'

108

Havercamp stared at him. 'Now you didn't scamper, did you, Paddy?'

'No, Sarge.'

Havercamp stepped a pace closer. 'And you're not going to give me any trouble, are you, Paddy?' Havercamp, wary of the huge man, was nevertheless resentful of all the beer he had poured into Harper's throat in an attempt to make him join an army that, obviously, the big Irishman had wanted to rejoin all along.

'No, Sarge.'

''Cos I'm bleeding watching you.'

Harper smiled, waited until Havercamp was a pace away, then spoke. 'Bastard!' He said it just loud enough for Havercamp to hear, and just softly enough for the Sergeant to pretend that he had not. Harper laughed and looked at Marriott. 'I'll tell you one other thing, lad.'

'What?' Marriott's face was pale with worry.

'Just remember that all the officers and a good few of the sergeants are bloody terrified of you.'

'All the officers?' Sharpe said indignantly.

'Well, almost all,' Harper laughed. He was enjoying himself. He picked Buttons up, fondled the dog, and grinned at Sharpe. 'Isn't that right, Dick?'

'You're full of bloody Irish wind, you are, Paddy.'

Harper laughed. 'It's the English air.'

'On your feet!' Sergeant Havercamp shouted. 'Come on, you bastards! Get on your plates of meat! Move!'

Sharpe was wondering whether he and Harper would have to jump. It could be done, he knew, simply by overpowering the slack guard that watched them each night. He feared it would be necessary because every southwards step seemed to be taking

them towards Chelmsford and he could not imagine the igno-
miny of being delivered to Captain Carline and his plump
Lieutenants. Sharpe had embarked on this deception in the
belief that they would be taken to wherever the Second Battalion
was hidden, yet Sergeant Havercamp was inexorably leading
them towards the Chelmsford barracks.

Then, at a large village called Witham, and to Sharpe's relief,
Sergeant Havercamp took them off the Chelmsford road. The
Sergeant was in high spirits. He made them march in step,
putting Sharpe and Harper at the front and the corporals at
the back. 'I'll teach you buggers to be soldiers. Left! Left!' One
of the drummer boys tapped the pace with his stick.

They spent their last night of travel in a half-empty barn.
Havercamp had them up early, and they marched in the dawn
into a landscape like none Sharpe had seen before in England.

It was a country of intricate rivers, streams, marshes, a
country loud with the cry of gulls telling Sharpe they were close
to the sea. There was a smell of salt in the air. The grass was
coarse. Once, far off to his left, he saw the wind whipping a
grey sea white towards a great expanse of mud, then the view
disappeared as Sergeant Havercamp turned them inland once
more.

They marched through flat farmlands where the few trees
had been bent westwards by the wind from the sea. They crossed
the fords of sluggish rivers that ran in wide, muddy beds to
meet the salt tide. The houses, low and squat, had weather-
boards painted a malevolent black, while the churches were
visible far over the flat land.

'Where are we?' Harper asked. He and Sharpe still led the
small procession as Havercamp turned them eastwards again,
into the wind with its smell of salt and its lonely sounds of
seabirds.

'Somewhere in Essex.' Sharpe shrugged. No milestones

marked the road they now walked, and no fingerboards pointed to a village or town. The only landmark now was a great house, brick-built, with spreading, elegant wings on either side of its three-storeyed main block. On the house's roof was an intricate weathervane. The house was two miles away, a lonely place, and Sharpe wondered, as they marched along the deserted road towards the great, isolated building, whether the house was their destination.

'Fall out! Fast now! Fall out!' Sergeant Havercamp was suddenly bawling from the back of the line. 'Into the ditch! Come on! Hurry, hurry, hurry, you bastards! Into the ditch! Fall out!'

Corporal Clissot pushed Sharpe, who stumbled into Harper so that both of them fell into the ditch that was stinking with green slime. They sat up to their waists in the foul water, and watched as a carriage and four came towards them. Giles Marriott, who had shown in the last two days a distressing urge to stand up for what he saw as his rights, protested at having to stand in the ditch, but Havercamp unceremoniously kicked him into the foul sludge, then jumped the obstacle, turned smartly in a turnip field, and stood to attention with his right hand saluting the carriage.

Two coachmen sat on the carriage's box, and three passengers sat within its cushioned interior. The leather hoods had been folded back, and one of the passengers, a girl, held a parasol against the sun.

'Christ!' Harper said.

'Quiet!' Sharpe put a hand on the Irishman's arm.

Sir Henry Simmerson, riding in the open carriage, raised a fat hand towards Sergeant Havercamp, while his small, angry eyes flicked over the muddy, gawping recruits in the ditch. Sharpe saw the jug ears, the porcine face, then he stared down at the green scum on the water so that Sir Henry would not notice him.

'That's . . .' Harper began.

'I know who the hell it is!' Sharpe hissed.

And next to Sir Henry Simmerson, opposite a stern, grey-haired woman, and beneath a parasol of white lace, was a girl whom Sharpe had last seen in a parish church four years before. Jane Gibbons, Simmerson's niece, and the sister of the man who had tried to kill Sharpe at Talavera.

'On your feet! Hurry! Come on!'

The dust from the carriage wheels was gritty in the air as Sharpe and Harper climbed from the ditch and dripped water onto the dry road. 'Form up! In twos!'

Sharpe stared at the receding carriage. He could see the passengers sitting stiffly apart and he tried to tell himself that Jane Gibbons was hating to be beside her uncle.

'By the front! Quick march!'

Sharpe had held the Eagle in Carlton House before the admiring gaze of the courtiers, and now another remembrance of that far-off day had come back. Sir Henry Simmerson had been the first Lieutenant Colonel of the South Essex, an angry, arrogant fool who had believed the battle lost and had taken the Battalion from the battle line in panic. He had been relieved of his command, and the South Essex, who had been shamed by his leadership, recovered their honour that day by capturing the French standard.

And afterwards, when Sharpe and Harper had been alone in the battle-smoke, amidst the litter of death and victory, Lieutenant Christian Gibbons, Sir Henry's nephew, had tried to take the Eagle from them.

Gibbons had died, stabbed by Harper with a French bayonet, yet the inscription on his marble memorial, undoubtedly composed by Sir Henry, claimed that he had died taking the Eagle. And on Sharpe's last visit to England, in a small parish church which must, he knew now, be close to this flat, marshy place, he had met Jane Gibbons.

In all the years since, on battlefields and in foul, smoky, flea-ridden billets, in the palaces of Spain where he had met La Marquesa, in his own marriage bed, he had not forgotten her. Sharpe's wife, before she died, had laughed because he carried a locket with Jane Gibbons' picture inside, a locket Sharpe had taken from her dead brother. The locket was lost now, yet he had not forgotten her.

Perhaps because she was the image of the England that soldiers remembered when they fought in a harsh, hot country. She had golden hair, soft cheeks, and eyes the same colour as the bright blue gowns that draped the Virgins of all Spanish churches. Sharpe had lied to her, telling her that her brother had died a hero's death, and he had been nervous before her grateful smile. She had seemed to him, in that cool, dark church, where she had come to place a pot of gilliflowers beneath her brother's memorial, to be a creature of another world; gentle, with a vein of quick life, too beautiful and precious for his harsh hands or battle-scarred face.

She must, he thought as they followed the carriage's tracks, be married by now. Even in an England where, as Captain d'Alembord often said, there were not enough well-washed men for well-born girls, surely such a beautiful, smiling creature would not be left unwed. And seeing her again, this suddenly, on this desolate track in the marshes at the edge of England, he felt the old attraction, the old, hopeless attraction for a girl so lovely. He felt, too, the old temptation to believe that no girl, come from so foul and treacherous a family, could be worthy of love.

'Pick your bloody feet up! Move!' Sergeant Havercamp slashed with his cane at his recruits. 'Put your shoulders back, Marriott! You're in the bloody army, not in a bloody dance! March!'

The carriage turned off the road ahead and Sharpe saw it

go towards the large, elegant, brick house, with its white painted window frames and its weathervane which, as the small band of recruits got closer, Sharpe saw to be in the shape of a French Eagle. That bird, he thought, was coming back to haunt him. That one act on a battlefield, that first capture of a vaunted enemy standard, had made the South Essex's reputation, had saved Sharpe's career, and now, he feared, it was a symbol of the men who had tried to kill him in London, and who would certainly try again if they discovered his identity.

'If that bugger sees us . . .' Harper did not finish the sentence.

'I know.' And how fitting it would be, Sharpe thought, if Sir Henry was among his enemies.

'Shut your faces! March!' Sergeant Havercamp cracked his cane on Sharpe's back.'Pick your bloody feet up! You know how!'

They did not go to Sir Henry's house, for the eagle on the weathervane had convinced Sharpe that the big place was indeed Sir Henry's, but instead turned southwards onto an even smaller track. They filed along a bank beside a drainage ditch, waded a deep ford that was sticky with mud, and, when Sir Henry's house was far on the horizon, turned left again onto a larger road rutted by cart tracks.

A bridge was ahead of them, a wooden bridge guarded by soldiers. 'Break step! That means walk, you bastards, or else you'll break the bloody bridge!'

A dozen men in the South Essex's yellow facings guarded the crossing. A sergeant called cheerfully to Havercamp as the recruits straggled over the echoing bridge that crossed a deep, mud-banked creek of the sea.

'Left! Left!' The drum tap gave them the beat by which they could regain proper marching step, they were off the bridge, past the picquet, and ahead of them Sharpe saw the place he had come to find.

He did not know where he was, except that this was a lost, empty part of the Essex coast, but ahead of him, in a wet, marshy land, he saw an army camp. There were huts, tents, two brick buildings, and, on a higher swell of land, a great parade ground that was thick with marching men. Buttons, as if as eager as his master to get into the army, ran excitedly ahead.

Sharpe felt the same excitement. He had found the Second Battalion of the South Essex, he had found the men he would lead to France. All that was left to do now was to find out why Lord Fenner had lied and then to take these men, against all his enemies here and in London, out of this hidden place and to the war against the French.

CHAPTER SEVEN

On the mornings of the second and fourth Monday of each month, at eleven o'clock precisely, Lieutenant Colonel Bartholomew Girdwood's servant brought a small pot of boiling pitch to his master. Then, carefully, he put a thick cloth over the Colonel's mouth, other cloths on his cheeks and nostrils, and, with a spatula borrowed from the Battalion surgeon, he smeared the boiling tar into the Colonel's moustache. He worked it in, forcing the thick, steaming mess deep into the wiry hairs, and, though sometimes the Colonel's face would flicker as a boiling drop reached the skin of his lip, he would stay utterly silent until the servant had finished the task. The cloths would be removed, there would be a pause while the tar set solid, then the servant, with scissors, file and heated spatula, shaped and polished the moustache so that, for another two weeks, it would need no further attention.

'Thank you, Briggs!' The Colonel tapped his moustache. It sounded like a nail rapping on ivory. 'Excellent!'

'Thank you, sir.'

Lieutenant Colonel Girdwood stared into the mirror. He liked what he saw. Tarred moustaches had been a fashion for officers of Frederick the Great's army, a fashion which forced a man's face into an unsmiling, martial expression that suited Lieutenant Colonel Girdwood's unsmiling, martial character.

He fancied himself a harsh man. He was unfortunately smaller than he wished, but his thick-soled boots and high shako made up for the lack of inches. He was thin, muscled, and his face could have belonged to no one but a soldier. It was a hard face, clean-shaven but for the moustache, with harsh black eyes and black hair trimmed short. He was a man of rigorous routine, his meals taken to the minute, his days governed by a strict timetable that was meticulously charted on the wall of his office.

'Sword!'

Briggs held out the sword. Lieutenant Colonel Girdwood drew a few inches of the blade from the scabbard, saw that it had been polished, then handed it back to his servant who, with deferential hands, buckled it about his master's waist.

'Shako!'

That too was inspected. Girdwood levered the brass plate that bore the badge of the chained eagle away from the black cloth stovepipe of the shako's crown and saw, to his pleasure, that Briggs had polished the back as well as the front of the badge. He put it on his head, checking in the mirror to see that it was perfectly straight, then buckled the chin strap.

Lieutenant Colonel Girdwood held his head high. He had no choice. He favoured the stiff leather four-inch stock that dug into the skin of a man's chin. The new recruits, forced into the collar, would be unable to turn their heads because of the rigid leather, and within hours their skin would have been rubbed sore, even bleeding. Girdwood knew that the fighting Battalions had abandoned the stock, and he understood the wisdom of that, for the lack of it allowed a man to aim a musket more efficiently, but for a fresh recruit there was nothing like a good, stiff, neck-abrading stock. It made them keep their heads up, it made them look like soldiers, and should the bastards dare to run away, then the two red weals under their chin were as good as any brand to identify them.

'Cane!'

Briggs gave the Colonel his polished cane, its silver head brilliant, and Girdwood gave it an experimental cut and heard the satisfying swish as it split the air.

'Door!'

Briggs opened the door smartly, holding it at a right angle to the wall, and outside, exactly on the stroke of half past eleven as he should be, stood Captain Smith, one of Girdwood's officers.

The Captain's right boot slammed next to his left, he saluted. 'Come in, Smith.'

'Sir!' Smith, who would accompany the Colonel on his noon inspection, reported that Sergeant Havercamp had returned from his Midlands foray. 'Very successful, sir! Very! Forty-four men!'

'Good.' Girdwood's face did not betray his elation at the good news. Twelve recruits was reckoned a good number for a Sergeant to bring back, but Horatio Havercamp had always been his best man. 'You've seen them?'

'Indeed, sir.' Smith still stood at a rigid attention as Lieutenant Colonel Girdwood demanded.

Girdwood tucked his cane under his left arm. He leaned forward from the waist, and into his dark, small eyes came a look of almost feverish intensity. 'Any Irish, Smith?'

'One, sir.' Smith's voice, a trifle apologetic, managed to convey that the news was not entirely bad. 'Just the one, sir.'

Girdwood growled. It was an odd noise that was intended to convey a threat. 'We shall give them,' he said slowly, and with some relish, 'to Sergeant Lynch.'

'Very good, sir.'

'And I will inspect them in twenty-three minutes.'

118

'Very good, sir.'

'Follow me.'

The sentries slammed to attention, saluted, and the sun glinted on the polished, gleaming moustache as Lieutenant Colonel Bartholomew Girdwood set out, with officers and clerks in attendance, on his noonday inspection.

'You'll say goodbye to me, lads.' Sergeant Horatio Havercamp walked slowly down the line of his recruits. Each man was dressed in fatigues now; grey trousers, boots, and a short, thin, pale blue jacket. Havercamp brushed at his moustache. 'But I shall be back, lads, come to see you when you're soldiers.' He stopped opposite Charlie Weller. 'Keep the bleeding dog out the way, Charlie. The Colonel don't like dogs.'

Weller, at whose side Buttons wagged his tail, looked worried. 'Out the way, Sarge?'

'I'll have a word with the kitchens, lad. Can he rat?'

'Yes, Sarge.'

Havercamp walked on down the line, stopping at Giles Marriott. 'You, lad. Keep your bleeding mouth shut.' He said it in a kindly enough way. He disliked Marriott with the irrational dislike that some people engendered simply by their looks and manner, but, now that Havercamp was leaving the squad, he gave the lovesick clerk the same advice that Sharpe had given him. 'Just keep your bloody nose clean.'

'Yes, Sarge.'

Havercamp punched Harper lightly in the belly. 'You didn't give me no trouble at all, did you?'

''Course not, Sarge.'

'Good luck, Paddy. Luck to you all, lads!'

And oddly it was sad to see him walk away, going for more recruits, leaving them in this strange place where everyone, except themselves, seemed to understand what happened and what was expected of them.

'Left turn!' a corporal shouted. 'Let's have you bastards! Move!'

Their clothes had been taken, labelled in sacks, they had been given their fatigues, and now they were issued with what the army called their Necessaries: gaiters, spare shoes, stockings, shirts, mittens, shoe-brush, foraging cap, and knapsack. Then, loaded down with the kit, they were taken, one by one, into a clerk's hut and peremptorily told to sign a piece of paper that was thrust at each man.

Sharpe made his cross. Giles Marriott, inevitably, complained.

Harper, standing outside, heard the whining voice and groaned. 'Stupid bastard!'

'I protest!' Marriott was shouting at the clerk. 'It's not fair!'

Nor was it. They had each been promised a bounty of twenty-three pounds, seventeen shillings and sixpence. Sergeant Havercamp had dazzled the recruits with his cascade of gold in Sleaford, and the guinea they had each received at their attestation had compounded the promise, but now came the reality.

The paper they signed confirmed that there was no bounty, or rather, that each recruit was deemed to have already spent it.

The army had charged them for their Necessaries. It had charged them for the food they had eaten on their journey, and for the ale and rum they had drunk in Sergeant Havercamp's generous company. It charged them for the laundry they had not had washed, for the army hospitals at Chelsea and Kilmainham that most had never heard of and, by one deduction after another, it was proved to them that, far from the army owing them the balance of their bounty, the recruits all owed money which would be deducted from their pay.

Of course it was not fair, but the army would have no recruits unless it made the extravagant promise, and no money to fight the war if it kept it. Nevertheless, Sharpe had never known so much to be stripped from the bounty. Someone, he reflected as Marriott's shrill protest continued, was making a fine profit from each recruit.

'Filth!' The voice came from behind them, startling them, making them turn to see a small, immaculately uniformed Sergeant pacing towards them with a face of such concentrated fury and hatred that the recruits instinctively shrank back, letting the small, dark-faced man stride into the clerk's hut.

There was a shriek from inside, followed by a yelp of protest, then Marriott came backwards from the door, tripped, fell, and the Sergeant followed, slashed him about the head with his cane and kicked him in the shins with his gleaming boots.

'Up, filth! Up!'

Marriott, shaking, stood. He was a head taller than the Sergeant who, once Marriott was standing, punched him in the belly. 'You've got a complaint, filth?'

'They promised us . . .'

The Sergeant punched him again, harder. 'You've got a complaint, filth?'

'No, Sergeant.'

'I can't hear you, filth!'

'No, Sergeant!' There were tears on Marriott's cheeks.

The Sergeant snapped his head round to look at the other recruits, then past them to where Lieutenant Colonel Girdwood approached with his retinue. 'Filth!' He shouted at them all. 'Fall in!'

Lieutenant Colonel Bartholomew Girdwood was a man soured by life, a man mistreated by life, a man that few understood.

He was a soldier, he regarded himself as a great soldier, but he had never, not once, been allowed to go into battle. The closest he had come to war had been in Ireland, but he despised fighting against peasants; and even when the peasants had decimated his troops and run him ragged round the damp countryside, he had still despised them. Those he caught, he hanged, those he did not catch, he ignored. He dreamed only of fighting the French, and could not understand an army that had not allowed him to go to Spain.

'Filth!' The Sergeant screamed the word. 'Shun!'

The recruits shuffled to attention. Lieutenant Colonel Girdwood, with his eye for military punctilio, noticed the two men who did it properly, whose thumbs were against the seams of their ragged trousers and whose heads and shoulders were back and whose feet were angled at a precise thirty degrees. Two old soldiers, two men easy to train, and two men who, because they knew all the tricks, he must watch like a hawk. He watched them now, seeing the scarred face of the older man and the hugeness of the younger, and he made the strange, snarling noise in his throat that was supposed to be a warning to them. He glared at the scarred man. 'What regiment were you?'

Sharpe, who knew better than to stare into an officer's face, was nevertheless fascinated by the rock hard, gleaming black moustache that contrasted so oddly with the white, scraped skin of Girdwood's face. 'Thirty-third, sir!'

'Discharged?'

'Sir!'

Girdwood glanced at the huge man, instinctively disliking Harper because he was so tall. 'You?'

'Fourth Dragoon Guards, sir!'

Sharpe, who was amused that Harper had chosen such an elegant regiment for his supposed past, sensed that Lieutenant

Colonel Girdwood's hostility had been increased by the big man's answer. Girdwood made the odd, snarling noise in his throat once more, then tapped his left palm with the silver-topped cane. 'The Royal Irish!' He said it slowly, with savage dislike. 'Then listen to me, soldier, this is not an Irish regiment. I'll have none of your damned insolence here, do you understand me?'

'Sir!'

'None of it!' Girdwood's voice was a harsh shriek that startled the other recruits whom he glared at, staring at them one by one as if, by the sheer force of his dark, harsh gaze, he could fill them with fear and respect.

He seemed to stare at them for a long, long time, saying nothing, but in his head the angry thoughts uncoiled. Peasants, he thought, nothing but peasants! Scum, filth. Horrid, stinking, foul, stupid, lax, undisciplined scum. Civilians!

His gaze came back to Harper's stolid, expressionless face. 'Who's the King of Ireland?'

'King George, sir!'

Girdwood's polished black moustache was level with the second button of Harper's fatigue jacket. The Colonel glared up at the huge man. 'And what are the rebels?'

Harper paused. Sharpe, standing next to him, prayed that the Irishman would lie. Harper, if an accident of hunger and fate had not driven him into the British army, would doubtless have been one of the rebels who had fought so hopelessly against the British in Ireland. Harper, who liked his job, and who fought the French as enthusiastically as any man, had never lost his love for Ireland, any more than had most of the Irishmen who made up a third of Wellington's army in Spain.

'Well?' Girdwood asked.

Harper chose dumb stupidity as his best tactic. 'Don't know, sir!'

'Scum! Pig-shit! Bastards! Irish! That's what they are! Sergeant Lynch!'

'Sir!' The small Sergeant who had so effectively silenced Giles Marriott took one pace forward. He looked as if he could have been Girdwood's twin; they were two moustached, small, black-haired, manikins.

Girdwood pointed with his cane at Harper. 'You'll note this man, Sergeant Lynch?'

'I'll do that, sir!'

'I'll not have Irish tricks, by Christ I will not!'

'No, sir!'

Sharpe, who was feeling relief that the Colonel had not demanded that Harper repeat his litany against the Irish rebels, now saw that the Colonel was staring with apparent shock towards the end of the line of recruits. Girdwood raised his cane. It was shaking. 'Sergeant Lynch! Sergeant Lynch!'

Lynch turned. He too froze. When he spoke, in seemingly equal shock, his voice had a sudden touch of the Irish accent that he had worked so hard to lose. 'A dog, sir? One of the filth has a dog, sir!'

Buttons, sensing the sudden interest in him, wagged his muddy tail, ducked his head, and started forward to be petted by these new men who stared at him.

Girdwood stepped back. 'Get it away from me!' His voice betrayed true panic.

Sergeant Lynch darted forward. Charlie Weller stepped forward too, but a corporal tripped him just as Sergeant Lynch kicked the dog, a brutal, rib-breaking kick that forced a yelp out of the animal and lifted it into the air to fly, screaming as it went, a full five yards away. Charlie Weller, his face aghast, tried to stand up, but the corporal kicked him in the head, and kicked again to keep the boy down.

Buttons, his ribs broken, came whimpering and limping

124

back towards his master. He flinched away from Sergeant Lynch, but the Sergeant stood over the dog, lifted his heel and smashed it down onto the dog's skull. Buttons shrieked again, the heel was forced slowly, grindingly down, and the recruits stood in horror as the dog slowly died.

It seemed to take a long time. No one spoke. The corporal pulled Weller upright, blood on the boy's face, and pushed him, too stunned to resist, back into the line.

Sergeant Lynch smiled as the small dog stopped moving and Lieutenant Colonel Girdwood breathed a sigh of relief. Girdwood hated dogs. They were undisciplined, messy, and savage. He had been bitten as a child, after throwing a half-brick at a mastiff, and the terror had never gone. 'Thank you, Sergeant!'

There was blood on Lynch's right boot. 'Only my duty, sir!'

The death of the dog had lifted Lieutenant Colonel Girdwood's spirits from the depression caused by hearing Harper's accent. Depression, for Lieutenant Colonel Girdwood had cause to hate Ireland, for it was in that country, as a Captain, that he had been reprimanded by a Court of Enquiry held in Dublin Castle. Not just reprimanded, but dismissed from the Dublin garrison.

It had not been his fault! He had been ambushed! By God, it was not his fault! If His Majesty's troops could not march in decent close order down an Irish highway, where could they march? They had been traitorous peasants, the men who shot from behind hedges and who had tumbled his men in blood on the sunken road while Captain Girdwood, screaming in anger, had ordered his redcoats to form line and fix bayonets, but by the time he had imposed decent order on his Company, the Irish bastards had gone. Gone! Run away! In other words, as he had told the Court, he had defeated them! 'I was left master of the field,' he had said, and was it not true?

The Court had thought not. They had passed him over for promotion, dismissed him from the garrison, reprimanded him, and recommended that Captain Bartholomew Girdwood be no longer employed in the service of His Majesty's army.

He had taken his reprimand to Sir Henry Simmerson, Member of Parliament, Commissioner of the Excise, a man known to be a scourge of the lax discipline that was creeping into the army. And from that fortuitous meeting, in which their two minds were of such sweet accord, had come promotion and this opportunity. Sir Henry, with his friend, Lord Fenner, had purchased a Majority for Girdwood, then promoted him to Lieutenant Colonel, and presented him with a Battalion and with a chance to become wealthy. There was more to come. The war, Girdwood was assured by both Sir Henry and Lord Fenner, was ending, and he could look forward, thanks to their generosity and patronage, to a peacetime career of eminence and comfort. He would be married to Sir Henry's niece; he would become rich, powerful, and, until then, he would continue to do the job that he believed he did better than any man alive; the job of turning undisciplined, lax civilians into soldiers. He shivered as he remembered the shock of seeing a dog, then smiled at his rescuer, Sergeant Lynch. 'Carry on, Sergeant, and well done!'

One man in this camp hated the Irish more than the Colonel, and that was Sergeant John Lynch. He had been christened Sean, but, just as he tried to lose the accent of his native Kerry, so he had lost his native name.

He modelled himself on Girdwood, seeing in the Lieutenant Colonel the quality of rigid discipline that had made Britain's army victorious over the Irish rebels. Sergeant John Lynch wanted to be with the winners, and not just with them, but of them. Instead of being an Irish peasant forced to show unwilling respect to the English, he wished to be a man to whom that respect was shown. He had turned against his country with all the passion of a convert, exactly as he had abandoned his parents' faith to become an Anglican. There could have been no man better suited to attract Patrick Harper's hatred, or, indeed, the hatred of every man in the squad, for Sergeant John Lynch was a most harsh trainer of troops. Yet, as Sharpe grudgingly allowed, an effective one.

The training was done the old-fashioned way, by brutal discipline, punishment, and unrelenting hard work. Girdwood believed that what made a man stand in the musket line and fight outnumbering enemies was not pride, nor loyalty, nor patriotism, but fear of the alternative. He made soldiers, and, it was apparent, he made money too.

Indeed, within three days, it seemed to Sharpe that perhaps money was the reason for the camp's secrecy. It was not just the way that Lieutenant Colonel Girdwood's men had stolen the bounty from each recruit, but the way that, day after day, the debts piled up. At every inspection Sergeant Lynch would find a fault with a man's Necessaries; a torn knapsack strap, a holed sock, and each fault would be noted and the cost of the item deducted against future pay. Sharpe guessed that no man at the camp received pay, that all of it was channelled into the hands of Girdwood. Such raids on men's pay were quite normal in the army; half of every man's wages was deducted for food alone; yet Sharpe had never seen it done on such a scale or with such enthusiastic rapacity.

Only the training was pursued with more enthusiasm, and Sharpe had not seen any camp in which recruits were worked so hard. They drilled from morning till sundown. The grammar of soldiering was hammered into them until the clumsiest recruit, after one week, could perform all the manoeuvres of

Company drill. Only Tom, the half-wit, was considered untrainable and he was given to the Sergeants' Mess as a cleaner.

The object of their life, from the cold mornings when they were roused before dawn until the sun was set and the bugle called the lights-out, was to avoid punishment. Even after the bugle there was still danger, for it was a maxim with Lieutenant Colonel Girdwood that mutinies were plotted at night. He made the Sergeants and officers patrol the tent lines, listening for voices, and it was rumoured that Girdwood himself had been seen, on hands and knees, threading his body between the tent guy ropes to put an ear close to the canvas.

The punishments were as varied as the crimes that occasioned them. A whole squad or tent could fetch a normal fatigue duty; digging latrines, clearing one of the many drainage channels that ran to the mudflats, or mending, with stiff twine and a leatherworker's needle, the stiff canvas of the tents. Sergeant Lynch favoured a swift beating, and sometimes used a knapsack filled with bricks as his instrument of punishment, either worn for extra drill, or else held at arm's length while he stood behind ready to cut with his cane at the first quiver of fatigue in the outstretched arms.

There were beatings and floggings and, savage though they were, they could all be avoided by the simple expedient of obedience and anonymity. Most of the recruits learned fast. Even when it rained, and it seemed impossible to keep the mud from their uniforms, or from the tarpaulins that formed the groundsheets of their tents, they learned to scrape and wash the mud entirely away, and even though the cleaning water, that was blessedly abundant in the low, marshy land, soaked their thin straw palliasses, it was better to sleep shivering and damp than to incur the wrath of Lieutenant Colonel Girdwood's inspection.

Yet Giles Marriott, who had joined the army in a mood of

self-destruction because his girl had jilted him for a richer man, earned punishment after punishment. Morning after morning, at the dawn inspection, Sergeant Lynch would find a speck of mud on Marriott's pipeclay and the Sergeant's voice would snap at the terrified man. 'Strip!'

Marriott would strip. He would stand shivering.

'Run!'

He would run the tent lines, stumbling in the mud, jeered on his way by sergeants and corporals who would slash at his bare buttocks with their canes or steel-tipped pacing sticks. 'Faster! Faster!' He would come back to Sergeant Lynch with tears in his eyes and his pale flesh scarred by the welts of the blows.

'Just keep your bloody mouth shut,' Harper told him.

'We're not animals. We're men.'

'No you're not. You're a bloody soldier now. Never look the bugger in the eyes, never argue, and never complain.'

Marriott listened, but did not hear. The other recruits did both, for in only a few hours Sharpe had become their unofficial leader and guide within the army. On their very first day Sharpe had calmed Charlie Weller down, gripping the boy's shoulders till it hurt. 'You do nothing, Charlie!'

'He killed him!'

'You do nothing! You bloody endure, that's all. It gets better, lad.'

'I'll kill him!' Weller, with all the passion of his seventeen years, could not hold back the tears caused by Buttons' death.

'After Patrick's torn his head off, maybe,' Sharpe grinned. He liked Weller. The boy was one of those rare recruits who had joined the army, not out of desperation, but because he wanted to serve his country. Weller, given time, would rise in the army, but Sharpe knew that first the seventeen year old must survive this place.

A place where, to his astonishment, he discovered that there were more than seven hundred men in training. Some were close to finishing, almost ready to take their place in the ranks that must fight the French, others, like his own squad, still learned the basic grammar of the trade. Yet there were more than enough men here to save the First Battalion in Pasajes and to form the core of a properly constituted Second as well.

He discovered too where the camp was. On a rainy, drizzling day he was ordered to the kitchens where he unloaded a cart of half-rotted cabbages. A Mess-corporal, leaning in the doorway and staring at the low cloud to the south, grumbled what a god-awful bloody place it was.

'What place?' Sharpe asked.

The corporal lit a pipe and, when it was drawing to his satisfaction, spat into the mud. 'End of the bleeding world. Called Foulness.'

'Foulness?'

'Bloody foul too, yes?' The corporal laughed. 'Christ knows why they sent us here. Chelmsford was all right, but the buggers want us here.'

The corporal was happy to talk. Foulness, he said, was an island, joined by the wooden bridge to the mainland, and on the island there was a single, small, poor village and this army camp. To the south, the corporal said, was the Thames estuary. At low tide it was a great desert of mud. To the east was the North Sea and to the north and west were the tangling tidal creeks and rivers of the Essex coast.

'It's like a prison,' Sharpe said.

The corporal laughed. 'You won't be here long. Six weeks and they ship you out! You should feel sorry for me. Stuck out here!'

Sharpe had guessed already that the corporal, like the two senior Companies in the camp that, alone on Foulness, were dressed in red jackets, was one of the men who were here to guard the recruits against escape. It truly was like a prison, with water as its walls and troops as its jailers. Sharpe chopped a cabbage in half. 'Where do they ship us to?'

'Wherever the buggers want you. You know that, you're an old soldier.'

And being an old soldier was to Sharpe's advantage, for it kept him out of trouble and spared him the punishments that racked the less experienced men. No sergeant wanted to punish Sharpe or Harper, for the simple reason that both men gave the appearance of being able to take any punishment that was handed to them. Instead it was Marriott, always Marriott, who, with his tuppence worth of education, was unable to rid himself of the idea that he was superior to the illiterate men who were his fellow recruits. He argued stubbornly, wept when he was punished, and even at night, in the stillness of the tent lines, when the soft tread of the patrolling sergeants and officers listening for mutiny could be heard outside, Marriott cried.

Harper's view was simple. 'It's his own bloody fault.'

'He thinks he's too clever to be sensible.' Sharpe was the only man to whom Marriott would listen, but even Sharpe could not drive into the ex-clerk's head that the only route to survival lay in acceptance and submission.

'I'm going to get out. I'll run!' Marriott had told him. He had only been in the army a week.

'Don't be a fool.' There was a snap in Sharpe's voice that made Marriott's head jerk up, the snap of an officer. 'You're not running away!'

'They can't do this to people!'

That night, before the bugle called the lights-out, Sharpe told Harper that Marriott wanted to run. Harper shrugged. 'What about us?'

'Us?'

'Bugger Marriott, it's time we got the hell out of here.'

'We don't even know what they're doing here.' Sharpe knew that the camp did not exist solely to steal the men's pay. If that was its sole purpose, why were they trained so hard?

'Still time we got out.' Harper said it stubbornly.

'Give it another week, Patrick. Just one more week.'

The huge Irishman nodded. 'But promise me one thing?'

'What?'

The big, flat face grinned slowly. 'I'd like to come here as RSM for just one day. Just one day. And one hour with that bastard Lynch.'

Sharpe laughed. Above his head, beautiful and crisp against the darkening sky, a skein of geese glided towards the eastern mudflats. 'It's a promise, Sergeant.'

A promise he would keep. But first he would discover just why this hidden Battalion of the South Essex trained so hard and were punished so savagely in the lost, wet, secret marshland camp called Foulness.

CHAPTER EIGHT

'Say it, filth!'

Patrick Harper, staring stolidly over Sergeant Lynch's shako, bawled out the words that he was required to say at every single parade. 'God save the King!'

'Again, filth!'

'God save the King!'

Sergeant Lynch, in the eight days since he had taken over this squad, had not found fault with Harper once; with Marriott a thousand times, but with the big Irishman, not once. Sergeant Lynch had decided that the big man was broken. He had assured as much to Lieutenant Colonel Girdwood. 'He's just a big, stupid boar, sir. No trouble at all.' Indeed, Sergeant Lynch was glad to have Privates O'Keefe and Vaughn in his squad, for the presence of two trained men hastened the training of the other recruits.

'Again, filth!'

'God save the King!'

It was a beautiful morning. The sun was drying the mudflats and a small breeze brought the smell of salt to the parade ground. Sergeant Lynch, whose moustached face seemed unhappy this splendid day, stepped back from Harper to face his three ranks. 'Filth! Stocks off!'

It was an extraordinary relief to unhook the thick, stiff,

leather collars that they were then ordered to hand down the ranks to the men in the right file who, in turn, handed them to a corporal. Sergeant Lynch stared at them with his habitual expression of dislike. 'Filth. You have work to do! Ditching work! If just one of you bastards gives me trouble, just one! I'll damage you! I'll damage you!' It was evident he disapproved of the fatigue duty, preferring the close order drill in which every mistake was obvious and easily punished. 'Left turn! Quick march!'

Each of the squad was issued with either a rake, a billhook, or a shovel. Sharpe assumed that they were to attack another of the island's drainage channels, but, instead, Sergeant Lynch ordered them onto the embanked road which led off the island.

The Sergeant, like his two corporals, was armed with a musket. If this was a prison, then now the squad was under armed guard as they left Foulness. Sharpe noted again the strength of the picquet that stood sentry duty at the wooden bridge. More than a dozen men watched the squad pass, while the presence of a tethered horse beside the wooden guard hut suggested to Sharpe that an officer was on duty there as well.

Sergeant Lynch took them back along the road they had come when they had first arrived at Foulness, then north on the track which led to the big brick house with its eagle weather-vane, and Sharpe prayed that they were not being marched to Sir Henry Simmerson's home. They splashed through the ford, climbed to the track on the bank, then, before reaching Sir Henry's house, they turned right onto a narrow path that led, ever more narrowly, into the reeds of the sea-marsh.

It seemed to Sharpe that they must be skirting Sir Henry's estate. They worked their way east, then north, and Sharpe was glad to see a creek between themselves and the house of the one man who might recognise him in this corner of Essex.

Nevertheless his worry increased as, pace by pace, Sergeant Lynch led them closer and closer to the big, splendid house.

It looked peaceful on this bright summer's day. The morning sun caught the gleaming white paint of the window and door frames that faced east. Before the east facade was a terrace that sloped down to a wide, close-cut lawn that ended with a brick retaining wall. The top of the wall was level with the lawn, while at its base was the muddy channel of the creek.

The channel was silted and choked, the mud banked and overgrown with plants. Sergeant Lynch, stopping by a belt of sea-rushes, ordered the men to halt. 'Listen, filth!' His voice was softer than usual, perhaps because he did not want to offend the ears of the English gentry beyond the silted creek. 'You are going to clear out this bloody channel! Start there!' He gestured with his pacing stick to the end of the garden wall, 'And you will work it down to that marker!' He pointed behind him and Sharpe saw, some two hundred yards away, a wooden pole that leaned in the marsh. 'You will work in silence! Corporal Mason!'

'Sergeant!'

'Take the odd-numbered men and start at the marker!'

'Sir!'

Sharpe and Harper, because they paraded beside each other, had consecutive numbers, so that Harper, who as the tallest man in the squad was number one, was taken with the corporal to the far marker. Sharpe, as number two, went with the second corporal through the rushes and down into the channel beside Sir Henry's wall. Sergeant Lynch, impeccable in his regimentals, decided to stay on the dry bank.

It was hard, messy work. The mud was overgrown with rice grass that had to be tugged up, its spreading, linked roots hard to drag out of the slime, then the men with shovels, working behind, deepened the channel so that the slimy water, stinking of old vegetation, gurgled and seeped about their shins. Sharpe was sweating quickly, though oddly he found the work enjoyable, perhaps because it was so mindless and because there was a strange pleasure working in the sucking, thick cool mud.

It was clear that Sir Henry Simmerson had requested the channel cleared, not just so that his east lawn should be edged with water as if by a moat, but because, halfway down the brick, moss-grown wall, there was an archway that led into a boathouse. A barred gate, rusted and padlocked, faced the creek, while behind the bars Sharpe could see three old punts that would need this channel excavated if they were ever again to float. Beyond the punts Sharpe could see a stone stairway that must lead up to the garden.

'You! You, filth!' Sergeant Lynch was pointing at Sharpe. 'Vaughn!'

'Sergeant?'

'Wait there, filth!'

It seemed to Sharpe that he had been singled out for punishment, though for what he could not think, but instead he saw, through the bars of the water gate, a man descend into the boathouse. He felt a second's panic, fearing that it was Sir Henry himself, but instead it was a servant who, stooping along a brick walk built at one side of the tunnel that formed the arched dock, came and unlocked the padlock. The key took a deal of turning, so stiff was the lock, but finally it was undone and the gate creaked open.

The man sniffed, as though it was beneath his dignity to talk to a mere muddy soldier. 'It has to be cleared out.' He gestured at the boathouse. 'Deep enough for the craft to float at high tide. Do you comprehend me?' He frowned, as if Sharpe was an animal who might not understand English.

'Yes.'

Sergeant Lynch sent Marriott to help Sharpe, and first they

had to lift the punts out of the tunnel and put them on the bank of the creek. Next there was a mess of tarpaulins, poles, fishing lines, paddles and awning hoops to drag out of the dark, dank tunnel, and only then could they begin to dig at the stinking, clinging mud.

Marriott attacked the mud like a maniac, flinging it with his shovel out into the creek. Sharpe protested, telling him to slow down.

'Slow down?'

'They can't see us in here! We take our bloody time.' It was strange, Sharpe thought, how he slipped back into the ways of the ranks. As a Major his job was to make men work, but now, at the bottom of the army's heap, he found himself looking for ways to avoid undue exertion.

Marriott did not argue, but instead slowed to such a dawdling pace that it would have taken them a full two days to dig the mud out from the boathouse. Sharpe approved. They were out of Sergeant Lynch's sight, while the corporal in charge of this half of the squad was more concerned about keeping the mud from his shoes and trousers than how hard his men worked.

'They shouldn't do this to us,' Marriott said.

'Better than bloody drill.' Sharpe was sitting on the brick walkway, wondering if he dared try and steal a few moments' sleep.

'Labourer's work, this.'

'We are bloody labourers,' Sharpe yawned. A butterfly came down the garden steps, hovered bright in the boathouse entrance, then flew away. 'We're soldiers, lad. Our job is to clear up the bloody mess the politicians make. We're the buggers no one wants until the politicians make their mistakes, then everyone's grateful to us.' He was surprised to hear himself say it, not because it was untrue, but because it did not tally with the character he had adopted in this squad. He pretended to be nothing more than a disappointed old soldier, unthinking and obedient, wise to the army's ways and uncritical of its behaviour.

Marriott stared at him. 'You know? You're cleverer than you think.' He said it patronisingly.

'Bugger off,' Sharpe said.

'I'm going to. I shouldn't be here.' Marriott's face was feverish. 'I had this letter, see?'

'A letter?' Sharpe could not keep the astonishment out of his voice, an astonishment that made Marriott look curiously at him.

'A letter, yes.'

'How did they know where to send it?'

'The depot at Chelmsford, of course.' Marriott seemed as astonished as Sharpe that the matter should be worthy of surprise. 'That's where they told us letters should be sent.'

'I can't write, you see,' Sharpe said, as if that explained his astonishment. It seemed obvious now that Girdwood, to prevent discovery of this camp, would order those men who wanted to send letters to use the Chelmsford address, their replies to be forwarded from there to some London clerk of Lord Fenner's who, in turn, despatched the mail to Foulness.

'It was from my girl.' Marriott said it eagerly, wanting to share his good news with someone.

'And?' Sharpe was only half listening. He had heard a shout from the direction of the house.

'She says she was wrong. She wants me to go back!'

The desperation in Marriott's voice made Sharpe turn to him. 'Listen. You're in the bloody army. If you run, they'll catch you. If they catch you, they'll flog you. There are other girls, you know! Christ!' He stared at the unhappy Marriott. 'You're bright, lad! You could be a bloody Sergeant in a year!'

'I shouldn't be in the bloody army.'

Sharpe laughed grimly. 'Lad, you're too bloody late.' He turned away. He had heard a shout, but not just any shout. This was a bark of command, an order to quick march, and now, from the lawn above him, he could hear the voice shouting crisp drill orders and he wondered what on earth was happening in that wide, spacious garden of Sir Henry's. 'Where's the corporal?'

Marriott peered out of the archway. 'Twenty yards away.'

'Watch him for me.'

Sharpe crept up the steps as slowly, as carefully as if he expected to find a French picquet at their top. He was hidden by the bulk of the boathouse from Sergeant Lynch beyond the creek, but there was precious little cover at the head of the steps to hide him from the house; nothing but a stone flowerpot in which grew bright red geraniums.

Yet he did not need to climb to the very top. From a few inches below the level of the upper step he could see what he wanted to see.

On the north lawn, two Companies of infantry were being drilled. They were dressed in fatigues, carried muskets and bayonets, and were commanded in their drill by Sergeant Major Brightwell of the Foulness camp. Brightwell, a great bull of a man, did not concern himself with the lowly squads of new recruits, only with the Companies, like these two on the lawn, that were close to finishing their training.

They seemed to be giving a display of drill to a group of seated officers who sipped drinks as they watched the two Companies. Behind the officers, standing stiffly at ease, was a line of sergeants.

Sharpe watched for ten whole minutes, watching a comprehensive display of Company drill that finished with some crisp musket movements. The officers, sitting in wrought-iron chairs, clapped politely. A servant brought more drinks on a silver tray.

Sergeant Major Brightwell ordered the parade to attention, to open order, to order arms, then there was silence.

The officers stood. Sharpe, his face half hidden by the geranium pot, saw Lieutenant Colonel Girdwood walk forward and, next to him, the unmistakeable figure of Sir Henry Simmerson who was, this fine summer's day, dressed in his old uniform. Somehow there was no surprise in this proof that Sir Henry was allied to Girdwood. The two men, followed by the other officers, strolled up and down the paraded ranks.

'What are you doing?' Marriott whispered.

'Shut up!'

Sergeant Major Brightwell ordered a half-dozen men out of the ranks. They seemed to have been selected at random by the officers and the six were lined at the bottom of the garden, facing north, and the Sergeant Major took cartridges from his pouch and handed them to the men. Sharpe watched as the six, with reasonable proficiency, fired two small volleys into the empty marshland. The muskets sounded flat in this wide, damp landscape. The smoke, in small white clouds, drifted over the scythed lawn. Two of the visiting officers turned back to the house. Both were laughing, both holding drinks in their hand, and Sharpe saw that both had buff facings on their red jackets. He had not seen many officers at Foulness, but whoever these men were, they were not of the South Essex.

Two more officers turned back towards the house. One had white facings, the other red, and suddenly Sharpe understood why officers from other regiments were brought to this remote place. He understood, and the realisation made him slide back down the steps so he was hidden, and he wondered if he could be right, yet knew that he was, and part of him was filled with admiration for such a clever, profitable scheme. Sir Henry Simmerson and Lieutenant Colonel Girdwood were nothing but crimpers, god-damned bloody crimpers! And what was more, Lord Fenner was with them.

Crimping was not an honourable trade. The army was chronically short of recruits. In 1812, Sharpe knew, it had lost more than twenty-five thousand men through disease or war, and fewer than five thousand had come forward in Britain to take their place. A good regiment, like the Rifles, was never short of volunteers, but for most regiments of foot there was always a shortage that was combated with extravagant promises of lavish bounty, promises that were never sufficient to fill the ranks who fought in India, in Spain and in America, and who garrisoned forts from the Far East to the Fever Islands. The army was short of recruits, and crimping was one answer to that simple, eternal fact.

A crimp was a contractor, a man paid so much a head for recruits, and Lieutenant Colonel Girdwood and Sir Henry Simmerson had turned the Second Battalion of the South Essex into just such a contractor! Sharpe knew he was right. They were raising the recruits, using the achievements of the First Battalion as a lure, training the men, then selling them to those unfashionable, unsuccessful regiments who could not attract their own recruits. What Sharpe had just seen on this lawn was the end of the process, the display of the goods, and now, he supposed, in Sir Henry's drawing room, the money would be paid over. Seven years before, Sharpe knew, a crimper could fetch twenty-five pounds for a man. The price must have doubled since then!

He guessed there were close to two hundred men on the north lawn. If each man fetched fifty pounds then there was a profit this day alone of ten thousand pounds! Enough to keep a man in solid comfort for two lifetimes! Add to that the stolen bounty and the other peculations of the Foulness Camp and it seemed to Sharpe that Sir Henry and Lieutenant Colonel

Girdwood could be making a profit of close to seventy pounds a man.

Crimping was not illegal. The army often contracted with a businessman to raise recruits, but crimping by a regiment was definitely outside the law. It was clever, it was profitable, and it was starving the South Essex to death. Sharpe felt a sudden, fierce exultation because he had solved the problem, he knew it, and just as he felt that soaring pulse of success, he felt fear too.

He felt fear because a dog, a tiny, white, fierce little handful of a dog, came scampering down the steps from the lawn, saw him, and began barking at him in a shrill yelp.

'Shut up!' he hissed. 'Bugger off!'

'Rascal!' It was a girl's voice. 'You know the Colonel hates you! Rascal! Come here!'

Sharpe, sitting on the stone steps, slithered urgently towards the cover of the boathouse's tunnel, but suddenly there was a shadow on the stone and a voice above him. 'It's all right, he won't hurt you. It's just that the Colonel's terrified of dogs.' She laughed.

He knew he should not have looked. He should have muttered an acknowledgement then, like some creature of the earth, skulked back into the dark, wet tunnel.

But the voice was that of a young woman of whom he had dreamed impossible dreams, prompted by a single, brief meeting in a dark, cool church before her brother's memorial stone.

He did what he knew he should not do. He looked up at her. He reasoned that she would not recognise him, and he wanted, after these four years, to see if she was as truly lovely as his memory of her.

She was stooping, petting the dog, and she smiled again. 'He sounds very fierce, but he isn't. He's a coward, really, though he frightens Lieutenant Colonels, don't you, Rascal?' Her voice faded.

Jane Gibbons was staring at him.

She saw a man smeared with mud, yet she recognised him.

He wondered how, in all creation, it was possible for her to recognise him, yet she did. She stared, her mouth open, the dog forgotten, and Sharpe stared back.

He had remembered her as beautiful, but the image of her that he had carried in his head was entirely wrong. He had thought of her as a kind of doll, a creature manufactured in his dreams to be all that he wanted her to be, while now, staring at each other in silent amazement, she seemed to Sharpe to be suddenly so alive and there was the double shock, of seeing her face as he had seen it once before, and of seeing someone so independently alive, not captive in his dreams.

She opened her lips, as if about to speak, but no sound came from her. Her face, shadowed by the straw bonnet that softened the strong lines of her mouth and cheekbones, had the clear, fresh skin that came of England's climate and that Sharpe so rarely saw in Spain. Her hair, pale as sun-drenched gold, was looped beneath her ears. She had been a sister to one of Sharpe's enemies and was niece to another. Jane Gibbons.

She stared, and for a moment he thought she was going to call out, but then, suddenly, with an impulsive vivacity, she sat on the top step and shook her head. 'It's you!' She spoke in amazement. 'It is you?'

He did not know what to say. To confirm it was to risk that she would call out, to deny it was to lose this chance of speaking with her, and Sharpe was silent, struck dumb by her loveliness and he thought how he had devalued this beauty in his memory of her, then he felt panic as she turned from him to look towards her uncle.

She did not call out. Instead she looked back to Sharpe, her eyes shining with a kind of quick mischief. 'It is you?'

'Yes.'

'He said you were dead!' She looked once more towards her uncle and it struck Sharpe that she feared Sir Henry as much as he at this moment did. She looked to Sharpe again. 'What are you doing here?' She had grabbed the small dog and now cuddled it in her lap. 'What are you doing?' She repeated the question with almost breathless astonishment, mixed with pleasure, and Sharpe, who had only met her once, was startled by her quick vivacity, by the secret delight she took in this meeting. She was beautiful, and there was a streak of mischief in her that gave quickness to that beauty.

Sergeant Major Brightwell's voice boomed loud over Sharpe's head. 'Companies! Close order! March!'

Instinctively Sharpe shrank back, fearing discovery, and to his astonishment Jans Gibbons gathered her skirts up, clutching the dog with her other hand, and, with one more backward glance towards her uncle, came down the steps until she was hidden from the lawn. She sat close to Sharpe. 'What are you doing here?'

Giles Marriott gaped at them. 'Dick?'

'Go away! Leave us!' Sharpe hissed it. 'Go and clear the entrance! Go on!'

Marriott backed into the darkness of the boathouse tunnel. Jane Gibbons laughed nervously. 'I can't believe it! It is you! What are you doing?'

'I came to find the Second Battalion.' He made a gesture of impatience, not with her, but with himself as if he was uncertain how to explain the long story of his presence, but she understood immediately.

'They hide them here and sell them off. They auction them.'

'Auction?' It was Sharpe's turn to sound astonished.

144

Somehow auctioning seemed to make the crimping worse. 'That's what they're doing up there?'

She nodded. 'They make their bids over lunch. My uncle said it was legal, but it isn't, is it?'

He almost smiled, so solemnly had she asked the question. 'No, it isn't.'

'He said you were dead!'

'Someone tried to kill me.'

She shuddered, staring at him with her astonished, huge eyes. 'But you're still an officer?' It was a natural enough question, seeing him smeared to the waist with mud.

'Yes. A Major.'

She bit her lower lip, smiled, and looked to the top of the steps as if fearing her uncle's approach. Her dog wriggled in her arms and she quieted it. 'I saw your name in *The Times*. After Salamanca. A place with a funny name?'

'Garcia Hernandez.'

'I think so. They said you were very heroic.'

'No. I was in a cavalry charge. I couldn't stop the horse.'

She laughed. Both were uncertain. Sharpe had dreamed so often of seeing her again, of talking with her, yet now he seemed struck dumb. He stared into her face as though he would try to remember it for ever. Her skin looked so soft. Her hair was gold. 'I . . .' he began to say, but at the very same moment she said, 'Will . . .' and they both stopped, embarrassed and smiling.

'Go on,' he said.

'Will they try and kill you again?'

'If they know who I am. They don't. I'm calling myself Dick Vaughn.'

'What will you do?'

'I have to get away. Me and a friend. You remember Sergeant Harper? The big fellow?'

She nodded, but her face was suddenly worried. 'You have to escape?'

'Tonight.' He had made up his mind. He knew now what happened here, that Girdwood, Simmerson, and Lord Fenner were crimping on a grand scale. He had no more business as Private Dick Vaughn, just vengeance as Major Richard Sharpe. 'After dark tonight.'

She glanced back up the steps, then to Sharpe again. 'They guard the camp.' Her voice was an earnest, sibilant warning. 'They have militia patrolling from here to Wickford. There are cockle boats on the sands, off the shore, and they even watch those. If they catch men deserting they get a reward.'

'The fishermen?'

'And the militia. I've heard shooting in the night.' Above them, Sergeant Major Brightwell ordered the Companies to turn left. Jane bit her lip and held her dog tight. 'You could take one of our punts. Cross the river. They don't guard the north bank.' Her voice was only a whisper.

He smiled, suddenly delighted that she had become a conspirator. She could have betrayed him, she could have screamed at the sight of him, but instead she had come into this hiding place and plotted with him. She had taken his sudden presence as coolly as a veteran soldier would have taken an ambush, she had not screamed, nor shouted, just made her decision and talked with him. He admired her for it, and, looking into her eyes, he suddenly knew that his own heart was beating like a frightened recruit facing the French for the first time. 'Can you leave us some food? Money?'

'Two guineas?'

'That would be plenty. In the boathouse? Tonight?'

She nodded, her eyes suddenly bright with mischievous delight. 'And you'll stop the auctions?'

'I'll stop them. With your help.' He smiled at her, and it

seemed like a miracle that their heads were so close. He could smell her scent, like a clean thing in a foul land.

She looked at the dog in her lap. She seemed embarrassed suddenly, then her big eyes came back to Sharpe and she hesitated. 'I want ...' But whatever she was to say could not be said, for there was a sudden yelping coming from the lawn.

'Jane!' It was the petulant, peremptory voice that had haunted Sharpe through the summer before Talavera. 'Where are you, girl? Jane!' Anger flecked Sir Henry's voice. Sharpe imagined him, portly and red-faced, striding over the lawn. 'Jane!'

She scrambled backwards up the steps. 'I was looking for Rascal, uncle. He got out of the house!' She was at the top of the steps now, and Sharpe was shrinking back into the tunnel. Sir Henry's voice was desperately close.

'Lock him up, for God's sake, girl! You know Colonel Girdwood doesn't like dogs! Now hurry!'

'I'm coming, uncle!'

She turned, walked away without a backward glance, and Sharpe, muddy and undiscovered in the boathouse, wanted to shout his luck aloud. His heart was still beating in extraordinary, tremulous excitement and he was filled with a crazy, idiotic happiness that made him want to laugh out loud, to shout his good news across these lonely marshes, to forget that he was trapped in this crimping business of Lieutenant Colonel Girdwood's Battalion.

She remembered him! He had thought so often of her. Even when he was married, and the dreams had seemed unworthy, he had thought of her and tried to convince himself that her behaviour to him in that small, cool church where they had met so briefly had shown that she liked him. And now this!

She remembered him, she trusted him! She would help him! She had given him the key to escape. He knew, from their first

147

meeting, that her parents were dead, that she lived with her aunt and uncle, and he had assumed that she would be long married, but he had seen no ring on her finger. Instead he had seen delight on her face as she, surely, must have seen it on his.

The happiness was on him, the foolish, crazy, insane happiness of a man who believes himself, despite the lack of evidence, to be in love, and the happiness made him laugh aloud as he leaned down to pick up his shovel and as he wondered how he and Harper would escape from Foulness this night.

Then the happiness went.

He had not noticed it till this moment, so bound up was he by her sudden appearance and by the shock of her words on all his hopes, but Giles Marriott, whom Sharpe had ordered to go away, had obeyed. He had gone.

CHAPTER NINE

Sharpe shifted responsibility from himself by claiming that Marriott had left to talk with the corporal.

'Filth!' Sergeant Lynch glared at Sharpe. 'You're lying, filth!'

'Sarge! He said he wanted to talk to the corporal!'

Sergeant Lynch stalked around Sharpe, but the Rifleman stood, rigid and unblinking, the very image of a soldier who might know what his superior wants to know, but who will never lose his attitude of dumb, outraged innocence. It was a pose Sergeant Lynch knew well, and it convinced him of the futility of pursuing the charge of complicity. 'So when did you miss him, filth?'

Sharpe blinked and frowned. 'Twenty minutes, Sarge? No more.'

'And you said nothing!' Lynch screamed the words:

'He said he'd gone to the corporal!' The two men stood by the entrance of the boathouse. The rest of the squad, terrified, stood in the flooding mud of the incoming tide. Corporal Mason, in whose party Harper worked, watched nervously from further down the creek bed.

'Sergeant Lynch?' It was Lieutenant Colonel Girdwood's voice, coming from the top of the wall that raised Sir Henry's garden above the level of the marsh. 'What the devil's this noise about?'

'Deserter, sir!' Sergeant Lynch's fox-like face was tight with embarrassment and anger. 'One of the filth scrambled, sir!'

'How? For God's sake, how, man?' Sharpe heard the note of alarm in Girdwood's voice, and he understood it. Girdwood might sell men to other regiments, but there they came under the discipline of men who, by attending the auctions, were thus implicated in the crime and had an interest in keeping its details hidden. A deserter, though, loose in England, might just tell a strange story to the wrong ears. Sharpe kept his back to the wall, hoping that Sir Henry would not come and investigate the sudden alarm. Girdwood did not wait for Lynch to answer his question, instead he ordered the Sergeant to form his work-party into a cordon that should search the marshland eastwards as far as the River Roach. 'You know what to do with the scum, Sergeant Lynch!'

'Yes, sir!'

The search was intense. Men of the two Companies who were the permanent guards at Foulness were fetched from the camp and formed into a second cordon well to the west of Sir Henry's house. There were also men from the militia cavalry searching; horsemen who rode into the marshland beside the River Crouch and who combed the small yards and barns of the inland farms. Sharpe, looking back from the eastern bogland, could see a group of men armed with telescopes on the leads of Sir Henry's house beneath the proud eagle weather-vane. It occurred to Sharpe that this was a practised manoeuvre, a well-rehearsed specific against the danger of men deserting from Foulness.

Sergeant Lynch's squad struggled eastwards across the marshland towards the North Sea, and to Sharpe it seemed an unlikely direction for Marriott to have taken. It was possible, Sharpe supposed, that the young clerk did not know the lie of the land, or that, in the desperation of his lovelorn unhappiness, he had fled into the emptiness of the marsh in search of any refuge, but capture, in this direction, seemed certain. The marsh was waterlocked, the going was treacherous, and the boy would have been forced to stay clear of the few tussocky patches of higher ground where the footing was firm, but from which he could have been seen for miles over the flat land.

Sergeant Lynch's squad straggled over the glutinous, sucking ground and through the intricate, shallow creeks that mazed the wetland. A corporal was at either end of the line, while Sergeant Lynch was in its centre, all three men with loaded muskets. Every man, even Sergeant Lynch, was smeared filthy with mud and green slime. The sun backed the squad and seemed to make the smell of the marsh gasses, when they were disturbed by trampling feet, even more noxious than usual.

There was no sign of Marriott. As the afternoon wore on, and as they worked their way even deeper into the marshland, Sharpe guessed their search was pointless. He supposed that Marriott, sensibly, must have gone west towards the firmer, higher ground that lay inland and Sharpe found himself, for the first time ever, wishing a deserter well. He had found Marriott insufferable and pompous, but not even on Marriott would he wish Lieutenant Colonel Girdwood's vengeance.

They came, in the early afternoon, to a deeper, faster running stream that flowed north into the wider Crouch. The water of this small river, that spread itself across the marshland at its banks, was turbulent where the freshwater current met the incoming tide. The clash of waters made swirls of muddy violence and even, as the wind gusted from the north, small explosions of spray as sea fought river. It was the end of their search for, on the far bank, Sharpe could see uniformed men across the marshes and he realised that he stared into Foulness itself. Two miles away he could see the white tents of the camp, and then he saw Marriott.

The fool had fled east. He had crossed this river, presumably when the tide was low, only to find himself on the island from which he had wanted to escape. Now he was clinging to the stark, dark ribs of a boat's skeleton that was grounded on the mud where the smaller River Roach met the larger Crouch.

As Sharpe saw him, so did Sergeant Lynch. The Sergeant fired his musket into the air, startling waterfowl up with flapping, loud wings, and the hammering shot, ranging far over the flat land, brought the attention of the men on the island.

Lynch held the musket above his head, pointing with it, and the corporal at the northern end of the search line, to add urgency to the signal, fired his own musket into the air and the second shot seemed to spur Marriott from his paltry refuge.

He ran.

He did not run further east, perhaps realising at last that only the sea lay in that direction. Instead, half ducking to let the sea-rushes hide him from the men on the island, he ran down the far bank of the River Roach. He was running in front of Sergeant Lynch's squad, trying to escape south.

The river was too deep, and the flowing tide made it too fast for any man to cross. A good swimmer, stripped of his clothes, might have crossed the small channel, but neither Sergeant Lynch, nor his two corporals, attempted it. Instead the Sergeant shouted at the fugitive. 'Stand still, you bastard! Stand still!'

Marriott ignored the command. The squad watched him in silence. He was thirty yards from them, running down the far bank towards a bend in the channel that would take him out of their sight. Sergeant Lynch ran opposite him, bellowing at him, splashing through the shallow river margin, screaming at him to halt, yet still Marriott ran.

'Your musket!' Lynch shouted to the second corporal, standing beside Harper, and the corporal held out his unfired gun. 'Stop, you bastard!' Lynch, with a quick, practised motion, brought the musket into his shoulder, cocked it, and Sharpe, at the far end of the line from Sergeant Lynch, supposed that the Sergeant intended only to put a shot in front of Marriott that would check the deserter's panicked flight.

Sharpe was wrong. He realised it as he saw Lynch leading the musket on the target, he opened his mouth as if he was an officer shouting at a man to hold his fire, but before he could utter a sound, Lynch fired.

The range was forty yards, a long shot for a smooth-bore musket, but the ball went perilously close to Marriott. It must, Sharpe guessed, have missed the small of the boy's back by inches, for he saw the flicker of the rushes beyond as the ball crashed home. It would have been murder, nothing less, for Marriott was already trapped by Girdwood's converging forces.

Lynch swore when he missed, threw the fired musket at the corporal, and shouted at his squad to follow the fugitive. They ran, stumbling in the marsh at the river's edge, and Sharpe saw that the sound of the three shots had attracted horsemen from the direction of Sir Henry's house and he prayed that Sir Henry was not among them.

'The wee bastard tried to kill him!' Harper had waited for Sharpe to catch up with him, and his voice was incredulous.

'I saw it.'

'God help him one day.' Harper said it with relish.

Marriott's day of reckoning, if not Sergeant Lynch's, was close. The officer of the bridge guard had sent a squad of men north and they were ahead of Marriott. He saw them, knew that he was blocked in front and from both flanks, but he was panicked, his eyes wide and wild, and, though he was cornered, he refused to abandon his hopeless quest for freedom. He turned again.

He ran north, then saw that other men, advancing along the low sea wall that dyked Foulness against the tides, had headed him off. He stopped. Sergeant Lynch and his corporals were reloading their muskets. Marriott saw the ramrods thrusting down and, in panic and desperation, threw himself into the Roach and splashed out as though he would swim, not just to the opposite bank where Sergeant Lynch waited, but clean out to the wide, wind-fretted, tide-treacherous waters of the Crouch estuary.

And he floundered. He choked. His arms flayed the water and he called out desperately, flailed with his hands, and Sharpe, who had learned to swim in India, kicked off his mud-heavy shoes and plunged into the river, struggling through the muddy shallows towards the dark whorls of the seething deeper channel where, his footing gone, he splashed clumsily towards the drowning man.

He clutched Marriott. He had never tried to bring a drowning man out of water before, nor had he dreamed it could be so difficult. He thought that Marriott would pull him down, so viciously did the young man thrash and fight, and Sharpe, gulping great mouthfuls of salt-tainted river water, fought back to suppress Marriott's struggles.

'Let me go!' Marriott wailed at Sharpe. He kicked, hit, and Sharpe flinched from one blow, then let go his hold in desperation as the boy's fingers clawed at his eyes. Sharpe was swallowing water, choking, but suddenly, from the bank, he heard Harper's voice raised in a shout of anger as though, instead of Private O'Keefe, he was once again Sergeant Major Patrick Harper and on a battlefield.

'Hold your fire! Don't shoot!'

Harper was stumbling through the shallow river margin,

shouting his order again at Sergeant Lynch. Harper had shouted because he had seen Lynch bring his reloaded musket into his shoulder, and the musket, Harper knew, could just as easily strike Sharpe as Marriott. 'Hold your fire!'

Lynch glanced at the huge man, ignored him for the moment, then looked back down the length of the musket's browned barrel.

Sharpe had let go of Marriott and a whorl of the clashing currents had swept the boy away from him, carrying Marriott close to the western bank where, shin deep in the muddy water, Sergeant Lynch waited.

'Don't fire!' Harper was still shouting, still too far from the Sergeant to do anything but shout, and the obstinate river current brought Marriott closer still to the bank. The boy thrust with his feet on the river bed, pushing himself towards the wider Crouch and, as Harper shouted his futile order yet once more, Lynch fired.

The bullet smashed Marriott's skull. Blood spurted eighteen inches into the air, fell to redden the river, spurted again, then mercifully the head rolled the wound beneath the water to hide the obscene, heart-pumped fountain. Marriott's hands splashed once, as if, from beneath the water, he tried to haul himself from its grasp, then he was still, floating calm in a great swirl of blood that drifted with the muddy water towards the sea. Charlie Weller, who had seen much blood on his father's farm, had never seen a man shot. He vomited, and Lynch laughed as he splashed back from the shallows.

Harper had checked at the shot. His temper, slow to rouse, but dreadful once it had been goaded, made his voice loud and terrible. 'You murderous bastard! You traitorous, murderous bastard!' He moved towards the Sergeant, the other recruits shrinking back as Lynch reversed the musket to strike at the huge man, when a new voice made them all turn.

'Sergeant!' It was Lieutenant Colonel Girdwood. He was spurring his horse over the marsh, picking his way carefully. 'You got him, Sergeant?' Sir Henry Simmerson was close behind, his horse following Girdwood's path.

Sharpe was hauling the body to the bank. He thought he tasted Marriott's blood in the water, then huge hands reached for him, hands that pulled the weight of Marriott from him. Harper, turning away from Lynch, had plunged to his waist in the river and now dragged both Sharpe and the corpse to the bank. Sharpe, spitting water and blood, did not see the horsemen.

'Mud.' Harper hissed it. Sharpe did not seem to understand. 'Sir!' The Irishman hoped that word would attract Sharpe's attention, but still Sharpe had not seen Sir Henry, so Harper, in desperation, scooped up a handful of the sticky, black mud and, his action hidden from Lynch and the officers by his body, slapped it onto Sharpe's face. He smeared more on his own.

'Well done!' a voice said. Sharpe knew that voice. As his vision cleared he saw two horses ahead of him and on one of them, the closer one, he saw Sir Henry Simmerson. Sir Henry glanced at Sharpe, then peered down at the body. 'Well done, Sergeant! A head shot!'

'Thank you, sir.' Lynch was reloading the musket.

Sir Henry barked at Sharpe. 'Stand back, man! Let me look!'

'Stand back, filth!' Lynch echoed. Sharpe stepped back, keeping his head low, but Sergeant Lynch shouted again. 'Look smart now, there's an officer present! Head up, man! Attention!'

Sharpe obeyed, hoping that Harper's quick thinking with the mud would suffice. He found Sir Henry staring at him.

Sharpe had won battles by letting the enemy see what they expected to see, by lulling them to false security. He had once

156

hoisted old rags onto two bare staffs and, because the enemy expected to see a full Battalion with Colours flying, they saw in the ragged symbols of Sharpe's rain-obscured garments evidence of an overpowering force instead of the ammunition-less half-Battalion which, in reality, was all that barred their escape. He had once let his Riflemen lie in the open, without support, close to an overwhelming enemy, but, because the French expected to see dead men where the crumpled bodies lay, they gave the Riflemen no thought until the bullets tore their gun-team apart and gave the victory to Sharpe.

Men see what they expect to see, and though his niece had recognised Sharpe, Sir Henry did not. The mud clung to Sharpe's face, he let his mouth loll open and Sir Henry, who had spent a whole summer locked into a mutual dislike with Sharpe, and who now stared with distaste at his old enemy, saw only what he expected to see; a muddy, gawping recruit. Jane Gibbons, perhaps because she had thought of Sharpe as frequently as he of her, had recognised him instantly, while Sir Henry, who had been assured by Lord Fenner that Major Sharpe had been killed in London and thus prevented from carrying on with his inconvenient search for replacements, did not expect to see Sharpe and so did not. 'You're filthy, man. Clean yourself up!'

Sir Henry tugged at his reins and, as he turned away, Sharpe heard him complain querulously to Lieutenant Colonel Girdwood that this business had delayed his journey to London. 'Still, it's over! Bury him, Girdwood! Where he is!'

Girdwood wished Sir Henry a safe journey then, when Simmerson was on his way back to the house and out of earshot, he looked down on Sergeant Lynch. 'How in God's name did it happen, Sergeant?'

Sergeant Lynch was standing rigid, his trousers muddied to his thighs. 'My belief is that he had help, sir. O'Keefe!' The

157

mention of the Irish name was sufficient to cause Girdwood to make the odd, growling sound in his throat.

'Help, Sergeant?'

'O'Keefe tried to stop me apprehending the filth, sir! Tried to hit me, sir!'

'Hit you?' Girdwood repeated the words with disbelief.

Lynch smiled with satisfaction. 'Tried to strike me, sir. Assault, sir.' He stared at Harper, knowing that he had said enough to ensure a terrible revenge for Harper's defiance.

Lieutenant Colonel Girdwood urged his horse closer to Harper. He looked down with hatred, staring at the huge, drenched man as if he saw a foul beast that had lurched up from the mud of the river bank. 'You thought to hit a Sergeant, did you, filth?'

'Because he's a murdering bastard, sir.' Harper, all caution gone to the wind, said it scornfully. 'A murdering, traitorous bastard!'

For a second Sharpe thought that Girdwood would strike Harper with the cane, and he feared that Harper would strike back, and Sharpe was planning how to seize the musket from Corporal Mason before Harper was shot. The other recruits stood in frozen fear, the wind lifting their hair and stirring the pale grasses about Marriott's still body. Girdwood stared down at the huge Irishman, and perhaps it was Harper's size, or perhaps it was the implacable look of dangerous ferocity on the huge man's face that made the Lieutenant Colonel tuck the silver-topped cane into his armpit. 'This filth is under arrest, Sergeant Lynch.'

'Yes, sir.'

'And bury that scum!' Girdwood tugged at his reins, gave one last malevolent glance at Harper, then spurred his horse after the far figure of Sir Henry Simmerson.

They buried Marriott in the marsh, using the tools with

which the squad had half cleared Sir Henry's creek, burying him without benefit of prayer or clergy, as though he was a criminal. Doubtless, Sharpe thought as they forced the body into the wet, gurgling hole in which Marriott floated obscenely until they had forced mud onto his corpse, Girdwood would claim in his records that the boy had drowned and been swept to sea. No one knew of the Foulness Camp, no one cared what happened here. No one ever would care unless Sharpe and Harper managed to escape from this place to take their story to the authorities.

Yet escape, that Sharpe had planned for tonight, seemed hopeless now. Harper was under arrest, guarded first by Lynch and his two corporals, and soon by a further squad of redcoats who took the huge Irishman back to the camp where, locked in a foul small building that had once been a pigsty, the Irishman waited for the justice that ruled in Foulness and which had already killed one man this summer's day.

'They killed him!' Charlie Weller still seemed unable to believe that Marriott was dead.

'Served him right.' Jenkinson, one of the convicts freed to Sergeant Havercamp by Grantham's magistrates, was scrubbing at the mud on his trousers. The evening inspection was imminent. 'He was a whining bastard.'

'He would have made a good soldier.' Sharpe said it mildly. Oddly, it was true. If Marriott had been in the Rifles, where the discipline was expected to come from within a man rather than without, the boy might have made a fine skirmisher.

Jenkinson said nothing. He was wary of Sharpe, as he had been of Harper, for the two had early stopped the bullying tactics of the released convicts, who, thinking themselves to have found easy victims in the other recruits, had tried to make them into servants.

Weller slapped at the dried mud on his fatigue jacket. 'What will they do to Paddy?'

'Flog him.' Sharpe looked to the east where, black against the pale dusk, the geese coasted down to the mudflats. He was wondering how, this night, he was to both rescue Harper and escape. If Jane Gibbons – and the thought of her made his heart give a strange, small leap of warmth – put the food and money he needed into the boathouse then it was unlikely, he conceded, that it would remain hidden all the next day. Tonight. He must escape tonight, not just to save Harper from punishment, but because, with the secret of the Foulness camp uncovered, he was impatient to end Girdwood's crime and return to Spain.

The bugle sounded for inspection. The squad lined up in front of the tent and listened to the shouts of the sergeants and corporals. 'Christ!' Charlie Weller muttered. 'It's the bloody Colonel tonight.' Girdwood's inspections were always more burdensome than those of the other officers.

'Silence!' Corporal Mason shouted from behind.

Sharpe stood to attention. He had noticed, as he fetched cleaning water, how a whole block of the tents was empty this evening and he presumed that the two Companies whose auction he had seen on Sir Henry's lawn had already marched to their new regiments. The thought of his own men, left in Pasajes, being thus denied the reinforcements they needed, made him suddenly angry as Lieutenant Colonel Girdwood paced in front of Sergeant Lynch's squad.

The Colonel looked each man up and down. There had not been time to clean all the mud from their uniforms and Girdwood's eyes showed his disgust. 'Filthy! Filthy! You're supposed to be soldiers, not pigs! What's that?' He pointed with his cane at a forlorn pile of kit that lay at the tent door.

Sergeant Lynch, immaculate once more, stiffened. 'Private Marriott's Necessaries, sir!'

'Marriott?' Girdwood frowned. 'Who's Marriott?'

'The deserter, sir!' Lynch's eyes flickered towards the kit, then back to the Colonel. 'Being returned to stores tonight, sir!'

'You can add the Irishman's too.' Girdwood said it with a smile, as though the thought had suddenly cheered him.

'Sir! Private Vaughn! Fetch the Irish filth's Necessaries!'

Sharpe frowned, as though not understanding. 'Sergeant?'

Lynch took one crisp pace forward and pushed his moustached face up to Sharpe's. 'Fetch O'Keefe's kit, Vaughn, and do it now!'

Sharpe obeyed, rolling Harper's few spare clothes into the blanket, then carrying them outside.

'Put them there, filth!' Lynch pointed with his pacing stick at Marriott's pile. 'Smartly!'

Sharpe knew he should say nothing, but the thought that Harper might be, like Marriott, dead, or might be dead before the night was done, was too much to keep him silent. He dropped the blanket roll, stood to attention, and looked respectfully towards the Lieutenant Colonel. 'Is he not coming back, sir?'

Girdwood straightened. He had been rapping the guy ropes of the tent, ensuring they were taut, for in Foulness no guy ropes were allowed to be slack, even in rain. It meant broken tents, but ensured the neatness that Girdwood loved. The Colonel looked towards Sergeant Lynch. 'Did the filth speak, Sergeant?'

'He spoke, sir!'

Girdwood stood in front of Sharpe. 'You spoke?'

Sharpe looked into the white face. The Colonel's moustache was breaking through its mould of tar; small hairs struggling free between the cracked pitch. Sharpe made his voice as military and toneless as he could. 'Private O'Keefe, sir. I wondered if he'd gone, sir.'

'Does it matter?' Girdwood smiled.

'Friend, sir!' Sharpe was staring now at the brilliantly polished badge on Girdwood's shako, a badge which showed the chained Eagle that Sharpe and Harper had captured.

'You do not, filth, speak unless you are spoken to. You do not, filth, address yourself to an officer!' Girdwood's voice was rising, the only sound in the great camp. 'You do not, filth, concern yourself with matters beyond your competence. You are insolent!' This last was almost screamed. It was followed by a silence in which Girdwood, who could not remember a man daring to ask him a question during an inspection, drew back his cane. 'Filth!' The cane whistled savagely, striking Sharpe's left cheek. 'Filth!' Girdwood back-handed the weapon, drawing blood on Sharpe's right cheek. 'What are you?'

Sharpe could feel the blood on his face. He dropped his eyes to Girdwood's, meeting the Colonel's gaze. He was tempted to smile, to show that the blows had not hurt, but this was not a time to mire himself in further difficulties. 'Filth, sir. Sorry, sir.'

Girdwood stepped back, his eyes fascinated by the blood that was trickling down to Sharpe's jawbone. He gained a strange pleasure from so hurting and humiliating a taller, stronger man whose sudden, dark gaze had given him a second's alarm. 'You will watch this man, Sergeant Lynch!'

'I always do, sir!'

The blows seemed to have vented an anger in the Colonel so that he did not care, suddenly, that the squad's uniforms still showed the effects of their day in the marsh. He straightened his shoulders, tucked the cane beneath his arm, returned Lynch's salute, and walked on to the next squad.

'Stand still!' Sergeant Lynch shouted as he saw the infinitesimal slackening of shoulders as the Colonel left. Sharpe obeyed, his back erect, his gaze going through the tents to the darkening east where, pale still in the dying sunlight, a great moon hung low on the horizon. He waited for the night, an inconveniently bright moonlit night, but a night in which he would run this place ragged and show these little men, these petty, moustachioed fools, these murderous, bullying bastards, what real soldiers were and how they fought.

CHAPTER TEN

Twelve sergeants and four officers were ready for the night's sport. They had taken precautions against the prisoner escaping by sending a patrol to the northern sea-wall, a patrol that had orders to herd the fugitive, should he try to flee into the estuary's mudflats, back towards the hunters in the island's marsh.

Lieutenant Colonel Girdwood called for attention. 'You know the rules, gentlemen! Sabres or swords only! You hunt in pairs! Firearms will be used only to head the man off or in self-defence!' All of the officers and four of the sergeants were on horseback and had cavalry carbines sheathed in their saddle holsters. The other sergeants carried muskets, but their job this night was merely to beat the prey towards the hunters. Girdwood spoke to his mounted men. 'I want to see clean cuts, gentlemen, approved strokes!' He meant that he wanted to see his men wielding their sabres and swords according to the diagrams in the cavalry training manuals. The officers and sergeants knew, too, that it was tactful to leave the killing stroke to the Colonel who was proud of his sabre-work. They might draw blood, but Girdwood liked to finish the sport. The Lieutenant Colonel smiled at them. 'He's an old soldier, so keep your wits! Don't lose him!' He pulled a great turnip watch from his pocket as Sergeant Lynch pushed the prisoner onto the embanked road north of the camp. 'Thank you, Sergeant!'

Girdwood could have flogged Harper, but Sergeant Lynch had tactfully pointed out that the huge man had been flogged before. 'Incorrigible, sir!' It was a word Lynch had learned from Girdwood and used frequently of his fellow countrymen.

'How true.' Girdwood had sat in his office, turning over in his head the options of punishment.

'The Navy?' Captain Smith had asked. Often the camp had rid itself of hardened troublemakers by sending them under escort to the North Sea fleet that was ever grateful for men. Girdwood gave a brief smile.

'I doubt our sea-going brethren would be grateful for this one. He's scum, Hamish, scum. I know them, you forget that!'

Captain Hamish Smith, who, like all Girdwood's officers, had been growing old, seeing himself passed over for promotion and getting ever deeper into debt until the Colonel offered him this chance of redemption and wealth, said nothing. He guessed what the outcome would be, for he had seen before, and with some shame, how the boredom and brutality of Foulness increasingly encouraged its officers and sergeants to the foulest licence that even encompassed murder. This camp was secret, protected by the powerful, and looked only to Girdwood for its laws and justice.

Sergeant Major Brightwell, a great bull of a man with small, hard eyes and a face like pounded steak, grunted his opinion. 'We could exercise ourselves, sir? Hunt the bastard.'

'A hunt.' Girdwood said it slowly, as though he had not been thinking of just that idea. 'A hunt!'

It was not the first time that, on a moonlit night, the officers and sergeants had hunted a man through the waste that was the northern half of Foulness. The marsh offered little cover, except the ditches, and it was easily surrounded so that the victim could not escape. Girdwood had drunkenly claimed one night that such an exercise sharpened their military skills as if that excuse, in some obscure way, justified the enjoyment. Now, in the pale moonlight, the hunt was about to begin. Girdwood's voice was crisp and sure, as though this night's excitement was a normal military exercise.

'Prepare him, Sergeant Major!'

Brightwell swung himself from his borrowed horse. The prisoner did not need much preparation, for he wore nothing but shoes, trousers and shirt, and the purpose of Brightwell's attentions was only to ensure that the victim carried nothing that could be used as a weapon. The Sergeant Major saw the glint of metal at Harper's neck and tore the shirt aside.

'Sir?' Brightwell had seized the chain, pulled so that it broke, and now handed the crucifix to Girdwood.

Harper wore the crucifix because, like many another married man, his wife was eager that he should show more devotion to his faith. A better reason, in Harper's eyes, was that the symbol convinced Spanish villagers that its wearer was a true Catholic, not a heathen Protestant, thus persuading them to more generosity with food, tobacco or wine.

To Lieutenant Colonel Girdwood, an officer of a country that still denied public office to Catholics, the crucifix added a patriotic spice to the night's events. He looked at the symbol, sneered, and tossed it into the ditch beside the road. He urged his horse forward and Harper, in the brilliant moonlight that was silvering the marsh, could see every detail of the Colonel's uniform and weapons. Girdwood looked down on the Irishman.

'I'm giving you a sporting chance. More than you deserve. You see that post?' He pointed to a stake that was thrust into the far side of the marsh. 'You have twenty minutes to reach its safety. If you do it successfully I shall overlook your mutiny of today. If not? I shall punish you. You have two minutes' lead over us and I wish you good luck.' The mounted men smiled at the lie. Girdwood snapped the watch-lid open. 'Go!'

For a second Harper did not move, so astonished was he by the turn the night had taken. He had expected a formal charge, a military court, and then, almost certainly, a beating. Instead he was to be hunted in the wetland. Then, knowing that every second counted, he ran northwards.

Girdwood watched him. 'Going straight for the mark. They always do.' He spoke to Captain Finch, the second Captain at Foulness, who was Girdwood's partner for the hunt. Captain Smith, as officer of the day, was not with the hunters. This was not a sport Smith relished, though to protest was to open himself to Girdwood's scorn or worse.

Corporals stood on the embanked road that was raised two feet above the lowland. Their job was to cut off the southwards escape of the fugitive as well as to watch his every movement. Harper was dressed in a white shirt and light grey trousers which, though filthy, showed easily in the bright moonlight.

'One minute!' Girdwood called out. Next to him Captain Finch drew his sword, the steel scraping on the scabbard's throat with a soft, sinister hiss.

In the marsh Harper ran desperately, stumbling on the soft patches, tripping on tussocks, going towards the tall pole that was his mark. He had counted sixteen hunters, could see, far off on the island's northern rim, the shapes of more men, but already, as a good Rifleman should, he was planning his battle. He ran as fast as he could, needing space in which to manoeuvre, but watching the ditches and tussocks like a hawk. He jumped the water clumsily, stumbled on a soft patch, then looked behind to see if his pursuers yet moved.

Lieutenant Colonel Girdwood laughed when the big man stumbled. 'He won't put up much of a fight, Finch.'

'We can hope, sir.' Finch, of an age with Girdwood, had the face of a drunkard. There was rum on his breath, but most of the men who would hunt the marsh this night carried liquor in their canteens.

'No.' Girdwood was in high spirits. 'I know the Irish, Finch. They're cowards. They're happy to brawl, but they can't fight.' Girdwood looked at his watch, snapped the lid shut, and thrust it into a pocket. 'Time, gentlemen! Good hunting!' The horsemen whooped and spurred forward, while the Sergeants on foot, muskets loaded, went in a line to the west of the marsh. The hunt had started.

Harper heard the cries of the hunters and broke to his left. He knew he would not be friendless this night, but he knew, too, that his survival did not depend on Sharpe. Nor did Harper believe that, if he should reach the stake in the marsh, his life would be spared. These men smelt of death, but he grinned as he thought that they fought a Rifleman from Donegal. The bastards would suffer.

He saw the horsemen making a line to the east, the sergeants on foot going west, and he saw how they would make a great rectangle in the marsh, its other two sides formed by the guards to north and south. He turned abruptly back, aiming at a place he had spotted a moment before, and, reaching it, he fell flat.

'Mark him!' Girdwood shouted. The big Irishman, three hundred yards from his nearest pursuers, had disappeared in the deep, moon-cast shadows. 'Watch that place! Drive him! Drive him!'

The shout was to the sergeants who, on foot, must now flush the fugitive from his hiding place towards the horsemen. The sergeants stared at the place where Harper had disappeared, hurried to flank it, then, in pairs for protection and with their muskets held ready, they cautiously advanced.

'It was near here.' Sergeant Bennet spoke to Lynch as both men stepped over one of the smaller ditches.

'Careful now. He's a big bugger.'

Two larger ditches met here, forming a V in the wetland that almost, but not quite, pierced to the smaller ditch and was separated from it by a gleaming patch of bare mud on which the two sergeants now stood. The water of the angled ditches was slickly silvered beneath the high grasses at their banks. The sergeants stared at the ground inch by inch, knowing that it was just yards beyond the V's apex that the big man had gone to cover, but they could see no sign of him.

'Come on! Hurry!' Girdwood's petulant voice carried far over the flatland.

Lynch, in charge of the beaters this night, licked his lips. Extraordinarily he could see no sign of the big man. The marsh, lit silver and black by the moon in the cloudless night, seemed empty and innocent.

'You have him?' Girdwood shouted impatiently.

'Bugger's gone!' Bennet said.

'Charlie! John! Flush him out!' Lynch shouted. 'You too, Bill.'

Sergeant Bennet, like the other two sergeants, aimed his musket into a patch of shadow. He fired. Normally such a volley would startle a man from his paltry cover even though the bullets went nowhere near him, but this time the shots died into silence and the smoke drifted over a marsh that still revealed no fugitive. 'He's bloody gone!'

'Don't be a fool!' Lynch snarled, but, unbidden and unwelcome, he was remembering his mother's stories of the magicians and ghosts of Ireland's great bogs. He even had an instinct to cross himself that he fiercely thrust back. 'Forward now! Gently!' He probed with his bayonet-tipped musket at a patch of shadow then, keeping to the higher tussocks, went slowly forward. He saw nothing. Behind him Bennet reloaded the musket.

'Sergeant Major?' Girdwood said impatiently. 'See what they're doing.'

'Sir!' Brightwell spurred forward. A horseman's greater height gave him an advantage in this bleak landscape of low tangled shadows, yet when, minutes later, he reached the line of sergeants, he could see no sign of the Irishman. 'Jesus Christ!' Brightwell, suddenly fearing the worst, looked westward. 'The bastard's gone!'

'He can't!' Lynch protested.

'Then find him!' Brightwell snarled and turned his horse. 'Sir?' He stood in his saddle to shout. 'Bastard's gone, sir!'

Girdwood heard and did not believe, but he had been schooled well in one thing by Sir Henry, and that was to apprehend any man who might escape from the island. He could not credit that the huge prisoner had truly evaded the searchers, but he would take no chances. He swore. 'Lieutenant Mattingley!'

'Sir?'

'Alert the bridge! And Sir Henry's household! Tell Captain Prior!'

'Sir!' Mattingley spurred towards the road. What Girdwood had done was put into motion the elaborate, careful procedure that would trap a deserter. The only dry way from the island was by the bridge, which was now alert to the danger, while Captain Prior's militia cavalry, billeted on the mainland, would guard the banks of the waterways. The precautions, Girdwood reflected, were almost certainly unnecessary, but essential and, the order given, he spurred forward. 'Come on! Hunt him! Find him!'

Harper, just yards to the west of the line of sergeants, listened. He had dropped into one of the larger ditches, knowing that he had two or three precious minutes before the hunters reached the place where he had disappeared and, once in the shadow of the tall grasses of the banks, he had, like a berserk child, smeared himself in the slime of the ditch bed, covering his face, hands, shirt and trousers with the slippery, slick mud that was dark as night. He had stuffed handfuls of uprooted marsh grass into his waist and collar, hiding his shape, doing the things that any Rifleman, isolated in a skirmish line and closer to the French than to his own lines, would have done. Then, keeping low, and like some massive, dark, killing beast of the wetlands, he had slithered west.

The danger, he had known, was the patch of mud between the larger and smaller ditches, but his trained eye had seen that it was inches lower than the land about it, and with his clothes now the colour of the marsh he pulled himself over it, head low so that his nose scraped in the mud, slithering by pulling with his hands so that, undetected, he slid, head first, into the stinking slime of the smaller ditch. Then, completely hidden again, and twelve yards from the place he had dropped out of sight, he pulled himself through the smaller ditch, gaining yet more precious yards, not freezing into immobility until he heard the first squelching footsteps come close. Then he had drawn himself into a tight ball and hunched his body against the ditch's side. The sergeants did not look at him once. They began their search to the east of him, not guessing for a second that their prey was already beyond their cordon, a prey that crouched in a wet, stinking ditch and listened to them.

Harper waited, scarcely breathing, his head tucked low so that his nostrils were almost touching the foul water. He wished the bastards would move further east, but instead, uncertain and beginning to panic, they clung stubbornly to the place where they were certain he had disappeared. Then, to Harper's annoyance, he heard Girdwood's voice and the chink of curb chains and the thump of hooves. He was undetected, but all the hunters were close, and he stayed still, utterly still, eyes closed, ears alert to the smallest night sound of the marsh, and prayed that Sharpe would strike soon.

Sharpe had waited till he could hear no footsteps of the men who patrolled the tent lines against Girdwood's fear of mutiny. He had waited, too, until the canvas of the tent was as dark as it would become, yet still it was treacherously light. Then he moved.

'What are you doing, Dick?' It was Charlie Weller.

'You stay here!' Jenkinson growled the words, fearing punishment if one man of the squad broke the rules, but Sharpe ignored him, went to the back of the tent and pulled the canvas up from its small pegs. He was staring west, across twenty yards of open ground towards the closest drainage ditch.

'Dick?' Weller asked again.

'Quiet. All of you!' He rolled under the canvas, the tent throwing a shadow over him, and he stared north and south, seeing no one, then stood carefully between the taut guy ropes of the tent.

He waited. He could hear no patrols, yet he knew that if one was close then they would be hidden by the tent's bulk. He listened, ignoring the snores and the sound of the wind on the silvered grass, then ran.

He dropped at the drainage ditch, rolling himself in the mud to fall into the water. Like Harper, he was seeking to hide in the mud with the help of the mud. He paused when he had fallen, feeling the ripples beat back from the ditch's side against his body, and listened.

No one called out, no patrol ran towards him.

He worked his way northwards, hidden by the ditch that stank because it drained the officers' latrines. Its smell haunted the tents each night, but now, as he crawled north towards the

172

buildings of the camp's administration, it was thickly foul in his face.

He saw a group of men standing on the embanked road. They stared further northwards, towards the empty marsh, and he thought nothing of it except to be grateful that they did not look back towards the ditch where, ten yards from the kitchens, he climbed into the moonlight and, like a great predator, slipped into the shadows of the buildings.

There were guards in the compound between the stables and offices and they too, Sharpe saw, stared northwards. Then, from that direction, he heard three shots, close together, their sounds flattened by the night, and the sound alarmed him. Had they taken Harper into the marsh to shoot him like a dog?

He crossed the space between the kitchens and the stores. He made himself ignore his fears, for to hurry was to court defeat, and to be defeated was to deny the South Essex their victory in this war. He flattened himself against the store wall, on its dark side, and waited.

He had chosen to make his ambush here for it was a favoured place with the men who wore the redcoats and guarded the camp. He waited, hearing indistinct shouts from the northern marsh, then, much closer, he heard what he wanted to hear.

The footsteps came close and stopped just round the corner from Sharpe. There was the rustle of cloth as buttons were undone, a grunt, then the sound of liquid falling onto the ground.

Sharpe moved with the speed of a man who has fought in wars for close to twenty years, a man who knew that speed in a fight was the prelude to victory, and the edge of his right hand, travelling upwards as he cleared the corner, caught the soldier beneath the chin and Sharpe's left hand, following the first blow, thumped onto the sentry's chest to knock the breath from him and fill his heart with pain, and, before the man could call out or bring his hands up in defence, his collar was grabbed and he was hauled savagely into the shadows around the corner. The man grunted, then a knee dropped into his belly and two fingers, rigid and jabbing, pressed into the base of his eyeballs. 'Where's the big Irishman?'

'Stop!' The man's eyes were hurting. Sharpe pressed harder. 'Where is he?'

'They're hunting him!' The man spoke in panic. 'The marsh!'

'How many of them?'

The man told him what he knew, which was not much, and, when Sharpe was certain there was no more to be had from his captive, he slowly, leaving the eyes undamaged, drew back his hand. He hit the frightened man, once, twice, and again, until he was sure the man was unconscious.

He stood, retrieving the soldier's fallen shako, then, with difficulty, stripped the man of his jacket and weapons. Sharpe wiped the mud from his face, pulled the jacket on and strapped the bayonet and ammunition pouch about his waist. He slung the musket, checked that the man was still insensible, then walked boldly out into the moonlit compound between the Battalion's buildings.

No one noticed anything strange as a sentry strolled from the makeshift latrine towards the stables. No officer or sergeant challenged Sharpe as he went into the darkness beyond the stable door. 'Hello!'

No one answered. There was only a single horse left in the stable, and no saddle that Sharpe could see, but he did find an old bridle hanging on the wall. He put it onto the horse, his movements clumsy, but the beast seemed used to such unskilled treatment in this camp of infantrymen. Sharpe tied the reins to a hook by the door, then crouched down beside the straw of an empty stall.

He lifted the musket's pan lid and found, as he had feared,

that the weapon was loaded. He did not want to fire a shot at this moment, drawing attention to himself, and he cursed softly, for what he must do now would render the musket useless for the rest of the night, but time was passing and the problems that were to come would have to be faced without a weapon.

He took one cartridge from the captured pouch, bit the bullet free and spat it away. He tore the stiff wax-paper cylinder open and laid it carefully beside him on the stable floor.

He lifted the musket, raised the frizzen again, turned the weapon over and shook its priming onto the ground. If the flint fell now there was no powder to spark the charge in the barrel.

He needed the spark of the flint and the flare of the pan, but he had to stop the musket firing. He pinched a lump of earth from the stable entrance into his palm, spat on it, then worked it into a small ball of mud. He pressed the mud into the touch-hole of the musket, blocking it, then, with powder from the opened cartridge, he re-primed the pan. He spat onto the powder to retard its explosion, then, carefully, he twisted the rest of the cartridge into a paper spill that was filled with gunpowder.

He prayed that the mud would stop up the touch-hole, held the paper of the torn cartridge in his right hand, and pulled the trigger with his left.

The flint snapped down, struck sparks from the steel, but the powder did not catch. He swore, wondering if he had moistened the powder overmuch, and cocked the gun again. He pulled the trigger a second time and again it did not catch. He did it yet again, and this time, fizzing and sparking, the powder flared and Sharpe held the paper spill in the sudden seething fire and willed the flame to catch. For a second he thought it would not, then the powder wrapped in his paper caught the flame and burst brightly upwards. The horse, seeing the sudden fire, whinnied and shuffled sideways. Sharpe clicked his tongue, then pushed the burning paper deep into the straw of the stall. He stood, slinging the musket on his shoulder. It was useless as a firearm until its touch-hole was cleared, but he might yet need it as a club.

He had planned a fire whatever might happen tonight; a diversion to draw men away from Harper. The straw was smoking, small flames creeping up the stems, and to help it he broke apart and scattered more cartridges on the fire. Then, satisfied that the stable was doomed, he climbed clumsily onto the horse's back, leaned forward to unloop the reins, and almost fell from the bareback horse as it started forward under the stable door. Sharpe ducked beneath the lintel, clung to the horse's mane, and snatched at the slung musket as it fell down to his elbow.

God, but it was hard to ride bareback! He slipped left, corrected his balance, and almost fell from the horse's right side. He wrenched the reins, driving it north between two buildings, and he heard the first shout of alarm as a man saw the leaping, fierce flames that now spread among the dry summer straw. No man thought it strange that a uniformed man should ride towards the marsh this night, nor was any man willing to challenge Sharpe, for, in an infantry Battalion, the men who rode horses were usually officers. Sharpe, unmolested and with the chaos about to begin, rode to join the hunt.

'Quiet!' Lieutenant Colonel Girdwood called for silence. The hunters were gathered in a perplexed knot where the two ditches met. 'Sergeant Lynch?'

'Sir!'

'You're sure it was here?'

'Certain, sir.'

Girdwood sent the eight dismounted sergeants westward. 'Form a line there! We'll drive him towards you. Gentlemen!' He beckoned at his horsemen. 'Five yards apart! Go slowly!'

It took a few moments for Girdwood to be satisfied with the alignment of his men, then, dropping his sabre as if he gave a signal on a battlefield, he walked his horsemen forward. 'Search every shadow!'

Captain Finch was the southernmost horseman, the one closest to the camp, and the man whose advance would bring him directly to Harper's hiding place. Finch held his carbine with the reins in his left hand and the sword in his right. He probed with the long blade into every deep shadow and fingered the carbine's trigger in case his sword should roust the fugitive out of hiding.

Harper, when the hunters had gathered to hear Girdwood's orders, had slid a few feet further down the ditch. He waited now, knowing that the line was coming towards him, and knowing, too, that the swords and sabres that stabbed down were his danger. Thirty yards behind Harper, muskets loaded and primed, the sergeants waited.

Captain Finch spurred over a bare patch of grass and sliced his sword down into a shadow. As he did it, the shadow seemed to flicker and disappear, a new light challenged the moon, and he looked southwards and saw, to his horror, that the stables were exploding into flame. 'Fire!'

Sergeant Bennet almost obeyed, his finger tightening convulsively on the trigger before he saw that the horsemen were staring at the camp and at the roiling smoke that billowed up from the burning wooden stables.

Lieutenant Colonel Girdwood, whose evening pleasure was already nightmarish enough, was trapped between his need to find the Irishman and his desperation to extinguish the sudden

177

fire before it spread to the other buildings of his command. 'Stay here, Finch! Come with me, Sergeant Major!'

Finch stared, appalled. He saw a horseman come out of the camp and trot towards the hunters, then the Colonel and Brightwell passed Finch, goading their horses into a canter on the treacherous ground. Finch, at the very edge of a small ditch that his sword would explore next, turned to shout orders to the remaining huntsmen when, inexplicably, his horse reared.

Finch leaned forward to soothe the horse, but still it rose, screaming in terror, then lurched sideways. The captain caught a glimpse of a man, black as the night, dripping and huge, who had erupted from the ditch to seize one of the horse's forelegs and now, with massive strength, was tipping the beast over. Finch tried to hit the man with his carbine, but his hand was seized and he was pulled with dreadful force to fall at his attacker's feet, while his frightened horse, released by Harper, skittered away.

'Don't move!' Harper, stinking and filthy from the ditch, shouted at the sergeants. 'I'll kill him!' They froze. The huge Irishman, dripping wet, had pulled the sword from Finch's right hand and now held it at the officer's throat.

Harper stripped the carbine from Finch, then pulled the ammunition pouch from the officer's belt, breaking it free with a massive tug as if the two leather loops that held it were no stronger than rotted cotton. He looked up at the sergeants. 'Step back! Step back!' Then, from behind him, came the shout he had waited for.

'Patrick! Patrick!'

Harper dropped the sword and dragged Finch backwards. He stumbled over the ditch, still watching the sergeants who, in turn, stared appalled as their prey, who had appeared from nowhere like an embodied shadow, dragged his hostage towards the lone horseman who came over the marsh.

Girdwood checked and turned his horse. He saw the Irishman dragging Finch backwards. He saw, too, the horseman who approached Harper's rear and the Colonel supposed that the rider must be one of his own men. 'Kill him! Kill him!' But instead the rider dismounted beside the huge Irishman and Girdwood, frozen in indecision between the calamities on either hand, called out to his sergeants. 'Kill them!'

One of the sergeants raised his musket, but Harper hauled Finch to his feet and held the sword at the officer's throat. 'One bullet and he's a dead man! Now step back!'

Sharpe jumped down from the horse. He knew that Harper, who had been reared to ride the wild ponies of the Donegal Moors, was a much better horseman than himself. 'You take the horse, Patrick! Hold onto that bastard!' Sharpe threw away the useless musket and took the carbine from Harper. He checked that the carbine was of the Heavy Dragoon pattern that took the same calibre bullet as those in his captured pouch, then, seeing that Harper was mounted with the unfortunate Finch draped over the horse in front of him, he started westwards.

Girdwood watched in horror. 'Fire!' He shouted it to the sergeants who were closest to Sharpe and Harper, but none dared fire for fear of hitting Captain Finch. Girdwood stood in his stirrups. 'Stop them!'

Yet not one of Girdwood's men wanted to be a hero this night, not in such an ignoble cause and not when they knew that the two fugitives merely fled towards the waiting picquet at the bridge. Beyond the bridge the militia cavalry waited, and so Girdwood's men, happy that others should rescue Captain Finch and apprehend the armed deserters, followed the fugitives without enthusiasm. Girdwood spurred his horse towards the laggard sergeants. 'Go on! Go on! Go on!'

Sharpe heard the shout, turned, and brought the carbine

into his shoulder. Girdwood could just spur these men into action and Sharpe knew they must be discouraged. He aimed at Girdwood's horse, closed his eye against the flash of powder, and fired.

Girdwood's horse swerved away, startled by the bullet, and Sharpe heard the sergeants swear. He reloaded, his hands swift in the old actions, and he astonished his pursuers by sending a second bullet to flutter the air just seconds after the first. He turned and sprinted after Harper and heard a single musket fire in reply. The ball went wide. No one now, not Girdwood, not his officers, and not one of the sergeants, wanted to hurry the pursuit into the face of such deadly skill. They let Sharpe and Harper stretch their lead and were confident that the militia or the picquet at the bridge would end this nonsense.

Sharpe caught up with Harper. 'All well?'

'Bastard's quiet, sir!' Harper had found a pistol in Finch's belt and had rapped the captain on the skull with its butt. 'Where to?'

'This way!' Sharpe, running hard, turned off the road and led Harper back to the marsh. They were still on Foulness, still pursued, and there were enemies ahead, but they were Riflemen, hardened by war, and they would use their skills in this night of moonshine and madness. They would fight.

CHAPTER ELEVEN

That morning, when Sergeant Lynch had marched them off
the island, Sharpe had noted a drainage ditch that angled north-
west from the road and pointed, like a straight line on a map,
towards Sir Henry's house. It was beside that ditch that he and
Harper now went. 'We're going to the creek! You go ahead!'
Sharpe reloaded the carbine, watching to see if the pursuers
pressed close, but his earlier shots had taken what small courage
they had and destroyed it. He felt a moment's shame that these
men wore the uniform of the South Essex, then turned and
ran after Harper.

The Sergeant had stopped beside the creek which edged the
island. 'Can we lose this bastard, sir?' He plucked at Finch's
jacket tails.

'Drop him!' The pursuit was too far behind for them to
need a hostage now, and Harper hit Finch again, to keep him
quiet, then tipped the officer into the mud. He coaxed the
horse forward to the water. 'Give me the gun, sir!'

Sharpe handed up the carbine and his belt with its ammunition pouch. The tide was low, the water scarcely up to his knees,
but if he tripped and soaked the cartridges they would be
defenceless. The horse, nervous in the water, eagerly climbed
up to the great reed bed that banked the creek. Sharpe followed,
his shoes sticking in the thick mud.

'Another river, sir!' Harper called out and Sharpe, to his consternation, saw that they had succeeded in leaving Foulness only to gain the dubious refuge of this smaller island, scarcely more than a great stand of reeds among the water. This next crossing was wider and looked deeper, the moon-sheened water swirling menacingly as it swept seawards. 'Take the bridle for me, sir!'

Sharpe led the horse into the deeper water and the current snatched at him. He supposed this must be the Roach, where Marriott had so nearly drowned him, and then he was half swimming, half being dragged by the panicked horse, until, with relief, he felt the beast heaving itself up the far bank and dragging him with it. He let go of the bridle, shook the water from his hair, then saw Sir Henry's house and, running straight towards it, the path on the sea wall that they had trodden that morning.

'Sir!'

'What is it?'

'Cavalry.' It was odd, suddenly, but it felt like Spain. Harper slid from the horse, his right hand feeling in the carbine pan to check that it was loaded. 'Skirmish line of the bastards, sir. Half a mile.' He pointed west. 'Haven't seen us yet, but they will if we're mounted.'

'Moving?'

'No.' Harper grinned in the moonlight. 'Dozy bastards.'

It was a fine decision that had to be made. If Sharpe or Harper rode the horse, and the other ran alongside grasping the stirrup to keep up, they would be seen in this flat land by the searching cavalry. Their journey would be faster, but the militia, unencumbered by double-mounting or stirruping, would be faster still. If they went on foot they would be hidden, but the journey from here to the creek would take twice as long; twice as much time in which they might be found. It was visibility and speed against deception. Sharpe looked back the way they had come, but he could see no one and hear nothing. Finch must still be stunned by the blow Harper had given him.

Sharpe took the gun and ammunition. 'Hobble the horse. We walk.'

'We bloody run.' Harper was unbuckling the bridle. He tied the horse's front feet together. It whinnied nervously, and the Irishman soothed it. 'I'm ready.'

They crouched low. The embankment, on which the path ran so clear and straight towards Sir Henry's house, gave them cover. They were bent over, tripping sometimes on the tussocks, cursing as they stumbled, but always pushing on in the bank's shadow. Sharpe stopped only once to peer through the grass at the embankment's top. He could see the moonlight shining on the sabres and helmets of the cavalry, who, strung in a long line, searched the shadows and reed beds a quarter-mile away. Sharpe caught Harper up. 'The buggers are closer, but they won't catch us.'

'Where are we going anyway?'

'We're stealing one of Sir Henry's punts. We'll cross the river.' He stopped, crouching by nettles that bordered the road before Sir Henry's house. The road was white in the moonlight, as was the pointing of the bricks in the high wall that fronted the garden. Sharpe tapped Harper's shoulder. 'You first.'

The big Irishman slithered over the road, showing the scarcest profile, and moved fast into the ditch at the far side. No cavalry trumpet sounded, no shout echoed on the flat land. 'Patrick!'

Sharpe threw the carbine across the road, then the ammunition. He looked behind once, saw the cavalry still far away, then half ran, half rolled over the dry road into the ditch. 'Come on!'

It was simple now to slip into the shadows of the half-cleared creek bed. The three duck-shooting punts, that Sharpe and Marriott had hauled onto the eastern bank just that morning, still lay in their tangle of awnings and hoops. 'Break the bottoms of two of them, Patrick, get paddles, take the third to the river. I'll join you.'

'Sir!'

Mercifully the barred gate of the boathouse was still unlocked. If Jane Gibbons had left the food and money then it could only take an instant to find them, and Sharpe groped along the brick ledge that ran the length of the tunnel. It was pitch black under the arched roof. His hands explored the empty walkway, finding nothing. There was no bundle, no food, no money. He heard the splinter of boards behind him as Harper pushed his foot through the bottom of one of the punts.

'Major Sharpe?'

He jumped, scared by the sudden voice, and then a cloth bundle was pushed at him and he saw, dim in the darkness, a hooded sharpe. 'Miss Gibbons? Is that you?'

'Yes! I have to talk to you!'

Sharpe climbed onto the ledge. He saw Harper look nervously southwards as he stove in the second punt. Sharpe was holding the bundle while Jane Gibbons' gloved hand, in an unconscious gesture of nervousness, rested on his arm. She was silent now, staring past Sharpe at the huge man who wrestled to turn the third punt over.

He smiled. 'Thank you for this.'

She shook her head. 'I wanted to help. Are the militia out?'

'Yes.'

'They'll come here. They always warn us.' She took her hand from his arm. She was standing on the platform that was built at the end of the tunnel, the stage from which someone could step down into the boats. 'You are going to stop them?'

'The actions? Yes.'

'What happens to my uncle?'

Somehow the question surprised him; he had thought of her as an ally, a conspirator, but suddenly he saw what he had not seen all day, that the disgrace of her uncle would reflect upon this household. 'I don't know.' It was a feeble answer. He was tempted to tell her of the men who waited in Pasajes. of the disgrace they would suffer if their pride was to be laid up and they were to be denied a victory for which they had suffered and endured these long years.

'And Colonel Girdwood? Will he be finished?'

There was a hollow knocking of wood as Harper tossed two paddles into the punt, then began to drag it towards the far marker that showed where this creek joined the River Crouch. Sharpe nodded. 'He'll be finished. Disgraced.'

'Good!' She hissed the word, revelling in it. For a moment she was silent. The boathouse was in shadow, but her eyes glistened with the pale reflection of moonlight. She stared at Sharpe almost defiantly. 'They want me to marry him.'

It was like the moment when, on a clear day, a twelve-pounder enemy shot thumps the air close by, astonishing and sudden, threatening and unexpected. Sharpe only gaped. 'They what?'

'We're supposed to marry!'

'Him?'

'My uncle demands it,' she paused, her eyes bright in her shadowed face, 'but if he's in disgrace . . .'

'He'll be finished.' Sharpe heard a clinking sound, the fall of a hoof on the road. At the same moment came the call of a nightjar, soft and insistent. 'Cu-ick, cu-ick, cu-ick.' Sharpe had never heard a nightjar in marshland. It was Harper sounding a warning. 'I have to go!' For a second, a mad second, he wanted to take her with him. 'I shall come back. You understand?'

She nodded, then there was a sudden braying of a trumpet,

a whoop like that of a huntsman, and he pulled away from her. 'I'll come back!' The first carbine shots cracked down the creek bed.

The militia was like a second British army, but a privileged one. A man who joined the militia could never be asked to serve abroad and his wife, unlike the wife of a regular soldier, received an allowance while he was away from home. It was a pampered, soft, well-trained, and useless army. It had been raised to resist an invasion that had never come, while now, nine years later, it starved the regular army of good men. Some militia men transferred to the regulars, attracted by the bounty and wanting, after their training, to do some real fighting, but most preferred to avoid the dangers of real soldiering.

The militia cavalry of South Essex, whose honorary Colonel was Sir Henry Simmerson, kept a troop quartered close to Foulness. Their task was to patrol the creeks against smuggling, guard the Foulness Camp, and protect Sir Henry's big brick house. When a man ran from Foulness, the militia cavalry went eagerly into a practised routine, because they had been offered a bounty should they ever succeed in stopping a deserter. Now, like a gift from heaven, the troops saw the big man who hauled the punt north towards the Crouch. Their first bullets drove him into the cover of the reeds.

Sharpe ran from the boathouse, gun, ammunition and bundle all held in his arms, and his shoes slipped in the treacherous mud as he turned towards Harper. A man shouted behind, a bullet cracked and whined off the brickwork to Sharpe's left while another drove a fountain of bright water up to his right. He heard the militia officer order his men forward. Some had dismounted to come down into the creek bed, others spurred their horses to its far bank.

She was to marry Girdwood? She was to be put with that tar-faced fool? A bullet crackled in the reeds to Sharpe's right, he slipped again as yet another shot thumped wetly into a rill of mud by his feet, then he was by the punt. 'Here!' He threw the carbine to Harper, then the ammunition pouch, and tossed Jane's bundle into the punt. 'I'll drag it! You hold the bastards off! And Patrick!'

'Sir?' Harper was finding cover as Sharpe hauled the punt on towards the river.

'Don't kill any of them. They're on our side, remember?'

'I don't think they know that, sir.' Harper grinned. If anything he was fractionally faster than Sharpe with a gun. British infantry could fire four shots a minute, while the best of the French could only manage three, yet Sharpe and Harper could both fire five shots in a minute from a clean musket on a dry day. Harper grinned and buckled on the belt with its ammunition pouch. The militia were about to discover what it was to fight against the best.

Sharpe dragged the heavy punt, struggling and cursing, forcing his tired legs to push through the mud, water and clinging roots. A bullet clattered through the reeds beside him, another struck the punt with a thump that ran up Sharpe's arm, then, mercifully, the creek turned, hiding him from his pursuers, and there was enough water in the half-cleared bed to ease the punt's progress. Sharpe wondered, with a sudden, terrible fear, whether a stray bullet might have ricocheted into the boathouse. Marry Girdwood? By God he would break that vicious fool!

Patrick Harper knelt at the bend in the creek. He thumbed the cock of Captain Finch's carbine back, saw that the dismounted cavalrymen were closer than their mounted comrades, and fired.

He rolled to one side, clearing his own smoke, and took a cartridge from the captured pouch. He was doing his job now, albeit with a short carbine instead of a rifle, and his second shot hammered down the creek bed within twelve seconds of his first and he saw the cavalrymen, who had never faced an enemy who fired real bullets, dive into cover.

He reloaded again. He saw a mass of men dark in the reeds to the left of the creek and he put a bullet into the ground ahead of them, and then a horseman on the bank was bellowing orders for the dismounted cavalry to spread out, to fire back, and Harper lay down as the volley cut into the reeds about him. 'Forward!' The cavalry officer shouted. 'Forward!' And there was something in that arrogant voice that touched a nerve in Harper. He knelt up, his face grim, and he put a bullet into the man who led the rush up the creek's wet bed. 'That's from Ireland.' He said it under his breath, and already the next cartridge was in his hand, the bullet in his mouth, and the wounded cavalryman was screaming and thrashing and his comrades were stunned because real blood had come into this night, their blood, and Harper was already moving right to snap off his next shot.

He was enjoying himself. It was only an officer like Sharpe, he decided, who would give an Irishman a chance like this, and though his first shots had been aimed only to warn and to wound, and though Sharpe had told him not to kill, the militia officer's voice, and the proximity of the last volley, had got his Irish blood roused. He was talking to himself, muttering in Gaelic, watching for the officer who had stayed safely on the bank and shouted at his men to hurry into danger. 'Forward!' The man shouted. 'Spread left! Hurry now!'

Harper had the gun at his shoulder. He saw the officer waving his sword, urging his muddy troops on, but not dirtying himself with the pursuit, and Harper knew where the bullet would go. He knew precisely where it would go. He smiled, tightened his finger, fired, and saw the officer fall back with the bullet exactly where Harper had aimed it. One dead, one wounded, and he was reloading again, and the militia, who had never seen how Wellington's men fought, were getting a taste of it in this Essex marsh.

'Patrick!'

Grinning, letting them off his hook, Harper slid backwards to the shallow water, turned, and with the carbine and ramrod held in separate hands, ran towards Sharpe. The punt was afloat in a pool among the reeds, and Sharpe gestured at him to get in.

The Irishman's weight momentarily grounded the punt, but Sharpe heaved with a paddle in the mud, and they headed towards the open river that flowed past the marker pole. A bullet snickered through the rushes to their right, another splashed overhead, and Sharpe grabbed a handful of the tough plants at the channel's edge and dragged the punt forward until the bow was suddenly snatched eastwards by the violent current, he gave the boat one last heave with the paddle, and they were out in the wide River Crouch and being swept towards the sea that must be, Sharpe knew, some two miles eastwards.

'Paddle!' Both men, kneeling in the flat craft, dug their blades into the water and drove the punt towards the northern bank.

There was a shout behind them, a yell of anger, and Harper muttered the prayer that all sailors and soldiers said before the enemy fired. 'For what we are about to receive, may the Lord make us truly grateful.'

The volley made the water dance about them, small spouts of white that rose and fell, and the two men pumped their arms and drove the punt through the ripples of the gunshots, out into midstream, and Sharpe heard the rattle of ramrods behind him.

'They're slow,' Harper said scornfully. 'We'd have had two shots off by now.'

'They can still kill us. Paddle!'

Harper paddled, his strength driving his side of the punt

faster than Sharpe's. Water splashed cold on them from their clumsy strokes. 'I'm afraid I killed one of the buggers, sir!'

'You what?'

'I killed one, sir! It was an accident, of course. Didn't mean to.'

Sharpe did not seem to care. 'Bugger them. They shouldn't try and kill us.' He said it angrily and dug his paddle in the water just as the second volley came from the southern bank.

The second volley was more ragged, the splashes wider spaced because the punt was now more than a hundred paces away from the shore, but one bullet struck a thwart, drove splinters up, then whined into the darkness. Harper laughed. 'Lucky bloody shot.'

'Paddle!'

They had been carried down river and were now opposite Foulness, and Sharpe could see, dark on the southern bank, the shapes of men and a single horseman. He saw, too, the sudden sparkle of muskets, muzzle flashes that were reflected in long, shimmering lights on the water, but again the volley went wide, fired at hopeless range, then the bow of the punt bumped on the northern shore and Harper, carbine in his hand, jumped onto the bank and hauled the boat up.

Sharpe, carrying the bundle, followed and found Harper kneeling on the sea-dyke, aiming the carbine.

'Don't waste the shot,' Sharpe said.

'This one won't be wasted, sir!' Harper aimed at a horseman on the southern bank, and pulled the trigger. The bullet whipped away over the Crouch, then Harper, standing to his full height, filled his lungs and gave a yell that filled the night above the moon-silvered river and marsh. 'That's from Ireland, you bugger!'

There was a yelp from Lieutenant Colonel Girdwood, though

whether from wounded pride or flesh, Sharpe could not tell. Then, laughing because of Harper's challenge, he turned and led the big Sergeant inland.

They had escaped Foulness, but not Colonel Girdwood's pursuit. Sharpe knew that even now horsemen would be riding towards the first ford or bridge over the Crouch and that he and Harper must move and move fast.

They went north in the moon-drenched night. They slanted westwards to where they could see hills and trees, the cover sought by all infantrymen in trouble. They walked fast, pushing away from the Crouch, away from the country that an enraged militia would search in the dawn. Always they watched the west, looking for horsemen, looking for the flash of moonlight on a sabre or badge, but they seemed to be alone in a rich, deep-planted country of sleeping farms, gentle hills, wide pastures, and dark woods.

Dawn ended the exhilaration of their escape. They had reached a hill that showed them the view northwards and it was depressing; worse, it could mean defeat, for, stretching from west to east, bright in the rising sun, was another river. It was a river far wider and deeper than the Crouch. This was a great, shining barrier that blocked their northern escape, just as the sea and the River Crouch blocked them to the east and south. They could only go west and there, Sharpe knew, the cavalry would be waiting. By dawn that cordon of cavalry would start combing this land between the rivers.

He unwrapped the bundle that Jane Gibbons had given him. She was to marry Girdwood? The thought stunned him. Sir Henry would marry her off to that posturing idiot? He remembered her hand on his arm, the sheen of moonlight on her eyes, and he wished, against all his better judgment, that she could share this journey of danger. It would take her from the fate that she feared, which offended Sharpe so horribly and deeply, because he had plans of his own, ridiculous, unfounded plans, marriage plans.

A shabby black cloak wrapped the bundle. Inside was a package of waxed paper that held a great chunk of pale and crumbling cheese, a half-cut loaf and, wrapped in more waxed paper, a strange piece of jellied meat.

'What is it?' Harper stared at the meat.

'Don't know.' Sharpe sliced it with the bayonet he had taken from the sentry in Foulness, then ate some. 'Bloody delicious!'

Beside the cheese was a leather purse that he opened to find, God bless the girl, three guineas in gold.

Harper helped himself to some of the meat. 'Would you mind me asking you a question, sir?'

'What?'

'Did you persuade Sir Henry to leave this for us?' he grinned.

'He's gone to London.' Sharpe remembered Sir Henry saying as much over Marriott's body. He cut the cheese. 'You remember that bugger you killed at Talavera? Christian Gibbons?'

'Aye?'

'Remember his sister?'

Harper had met Jane Gibbons in the porch of the church on that day, nearly four years before, when Sharpe had spoken to her by her brother's memorial. Harper stared at Sharpe with suspicion and amusement. 'She left this for us?'

'Yes.' Sharpe said it as though it was the most normal thing in the world for young ladies to help men desert from army camps. 'Good cheese, isn't it?'

'Grand.' Harper still stared at him. 'I seem to remember, sir, that she was a pretty wee thing?'

'I seem to remember that, too,' Sharpe said. Harper laughed, as if unsure what to say, then shook his head as though there was nothing to say. He whistled instead, a sound as insolent as it was amused, and Sharpe laughed. 'Shall we now forget Miss Gibbons, Sergeant Major?'

'I will, sir.'

'And how the devil do we get out of here?'

'There,' Harper was pointing north, down to the bank of the wide river, and Sharpe saw, by a huddle of small houses, a line of great barges that lifted their masts high over the shingle roofs of the small village. 'One of them must be going somewhere, sir.'

'Let's find out.'

They walked the mile to the river's bank, going gently and cautiously, watching always for the cavalrymen who Sharpe knew must come from the west. No horsemen had appeared yet. Dogs barked as they approached the small hamlet, and Sharpe gestured Harper into the cover of a ditch and gave him the carbine and bayonet. 'Wait for my signal.'

Sharpe walked on into the tiny village. A dog snapped at him and, outside a shuttered inn, a woman grabbed a child and held it against her skirts until the mud-smeared vagabond had passed. He went down to a small, wooden pier that jutted into the wide river, a pier to which the huge, tall-masted barges were moored.

The barges were loaded with hay, great cargoes that were netted and roped down beneath heavy booms wrapped in swathes of red sail. The bargemen looked suspiciously at him. One told him to make himself scarce, but Sharpe tossed one of his three guineas into the air, caught it again, and the sight of the gold quieted them. He picked one man who looked less surly than the others. 'Where are you going?'

The man said nothing at first. He stared Sharpe up and down before, slowly and reluctantly, giving an answer. 'London.'

'You take passengers?'

'Don't like vagrants.' He had the broad Essex accent that Sharpe had heard so often in the battle line of his regiment.

Sharpe tossed the guinea in his hand. 'Do you take passengers?'

'How many?'

Behind Sharpe, a cock challenged the morning. He was listening for hooves, but he dared not show any fear to this man. 'Two of us.'

'One each.' It was sheer robbery, but the man, recognising the tattered fatigue jacket beneath the mud, must have guessed at Sharpe's desperation.

Sharpe gave him the guinea and showed him a second. 'It's yours when we get there.'

The man nodded towards the boats. 'It's the *Amelia*. I'm casting off in five minutes.'

Sharpe put two fingers into his mouth, whistled, and the vast figure of Harper with his gun came into sight. The man watched them in silence as they went aboard, then, with only a boy to help him, and eschewing any assistance from the two soldiers, he hoisted three huge red sails. The barge crept away from the jetty, into the river that he said was called the Blackwater, and they glided, with a gentle land breeze, out towards the sea.

A half hour later, as they cleared the land and headed out to make the wide turn about the sandbanks of the Essex coast, Harper nodded back towards the shore. The bargeman looked and saw nothing, but Sharpe, whose life and health in Spain depended on spotting cavalry at a distance, saw the horsemen on one of the low hills.

They leaned back on the small deck beside the cargo. Before they reached London Sharpe knew he must throw the carbine and bayonet overboard, but for now the weapons were a small insurance against the temptation for the bargeman to turn them in as deserters. The water slapped and ran down the boat's side, the wind bellied the sails, the sun was hot, and Harper slept. Sharpe dozed, the carbine on his knees, and dreamed of a shadowed, hooded girl who had been waiting for him in a damp tunnel. Thanks to Jane Gibbons, they had escaped Foulness, but she, engaged on her uncle's orders, was still trapped in the marshland. He day-dreamed of revenge, and let the boat carry him towards safety.

CHAPTER TWELVE

The next morning Sharpe saw posters being pasted onto walls throughout London. The printing was thick and black, with a gaudy red Royal coat of arms emblazoned at the top. He paused, on his way from Southwark where he had spent the night, and read one of the posters on Old London Bridge.

A GRAND REVIEW
In the Presence
and by the Gracious Command of

HIS ROYAL HIGHNESS THE PRINCE OF WALES

On the Forenoon of Saturday 21st August, in Hyde Park, His Majesty's Cavalry, Artillery, and Infantry, with their Bands, Colours and Appurtenances, will Parade before His Royal Highness, the Prince of Wales, the Prince Regent, and before His Royal Highness, the Duke of York, together with the Trophies and Artillery pieces captured in the Present Wars against the French now being fought in Spain.
And, by His Royal Highness's Gracious Command and Pleasure, the troops will enact, with Precision and

196

Verisimilitude, the Recent Great Victory Gained over the
forces of the Corsican Tyrant at Vitoria.

GOD SAVE THE KING!

The battle of Vitoria, Sharpe thought, was being milked for
all it was worth, presumably to take the minds of Londoners
away from the rising price of food and the ever-increasing taxes
that fuelled the war.

He was dressed in the uniform he had bought to attend
Carlton House, his old boots polished, his scabbard shining,
only the crusts of blood on his cheeks remaining of his time
at Foulness. He had left Harper in Southwark, eating a huge
breakfast and regaling Isabella and his relatives with stories of
the chase over the marshland. The Sergeant, as soon as breakfast
was done, was taking a message to the Rose Tavern for
d'Alembord and Price. Sharpe fervently hoped that those two
officers had stayed safely out of Lord Fenner's notice.

Sharpe stopped in St Alban's Street and, from Mr Hopkinson,
took thirty guineas of the gold he had left with the army agent.
He had money again, he wore a proper uniform, and he was
ready for battle against Girdwood, Simmerson, and all the men
who made their profits from the camp at Foulness.

He had thought long, as the Thames barge lumbered towards
London on an incoming tide, just how he should fight the
battle. Harper had been all for an immediate descent on the
camp, both men in uniform, but, tempting as the prospect was,
Sharpe had decided against it. Instead, with some trepidation,
he would go to the authorities. He would turn the bureaucracy,
behind which Simmerson and Girdwood hid, against them. He
would return to Foulness, but in his own time, and on different
business; the business of a golden-haired girl who had helped
him escape.

He crossed Whitehall, stepped round a pile of horse-dung that was being swept from the Horse Guards' courtyard, returned the salute of the sentries, and nodded at the porter who opened the door to him. Another porter, resplendent in his uniform, eyed Sharpe suspiciously as he came to the long table where he must state his business. 'Your name, sir?'

'Major Richard Sharpe. South Essex.'

'Of course, sir. You was here a few days back.' The man, as big as Harper, had lost one eye. He was an old soldier, discharged wounded from the war, and, because Sharpe was a fighting man and not a uniformed administrator, he unbent enough to give the Rifleman a smile. 'And what can we do for you today, sir?'

'I've come to see the Duke of York.'

The smile went. 'At what time, sir?' The question was polite, but there was an undoubted warning in the words.

'I don't have an appointment.'

The porter, rocking slowly up and down on the balls of his feet, stared with his one good eye at the Rifleman. 'You don't have an appointment, sir?' He said each word very slowly and distinctly.

'No.'

'His Royal Highness, the Duke of York,' the porter said as though the King's second son was on intimate terms with him, 'will see no one without an appointment, sir. If you'd like to write your business, sir.' He waved an imperious hand towards a writing desk that was set beneath the windows which opened onto Whitehall.

'I shall wait,' Sharpe said.

He refused to be dissuaded, just as he refused to put on paper the nature of his business. He insisted that he would wait until the Commander in Chief would see him, sat in a leather armchair beside an empty grate and turned a deaf ear to all the porter's entreaties.

Men came and went in the hallway. Some looked curiously at the Rifle officer; others, sensing that he was being importunate, looked hurriedly away. Sharpe himself, as the great clock by the stairway ticked heavily through the morning, gazed up at a great oil painting above the fireplace. It showed the battle of Blenheim, and Sharpe stared at it for so long that it almost seemed as if the red lines of British infantry were moving before his eyes. Not much had changed, he thought, in a hundred years. The infantry lines were thinner now, but battlefields looked much the same. He yawned.

'Major Sharpe?'

A staff officer, perfectly uniformed, smiled at him.

'Yes.'

'Captain Christopher Messines. Most honoured, sir. Would you like to step this way?'

The porter gave Sharpe a look that seemed to say 'I told you so,' as Sharpe followed Messines through a doorway. They went down a hallway hung with paintings, and into a small reception room that looked out to the parade ground. Messines gestured to a chair. 'Coffee, Major? Tea, perhaps? Sherry, even?'

'Coffee.'

Messines went to a sideboard where silver pots waited and, into two tiny, fragile cups decorated with blue flowers, poured coffee. 'You wanted to see His Royal Highness? Do please sit, Major. No need for ceremony. A water-biscuit, perhaps? The weather really is splendid, isn't it? Quite wonderful!' Messines seemed fascinated by the two crusts of blood on Sharpe's cheeks, but was far too well bred to think of asking how they had come to be there.

Messines was charming. He regretted that His Royal Highness

was consumed with work, and that, even as they spoke, His Royal Highness's carriage was waiting outside, and the Lord alone knew when he would be back, but if Major Sharpe cared to tell Captain Messines the nature of his business?

Major Sharpe would not.

Captain Messines blinked as though Sharpe must have misunderstood, then gave his most winning smile. 'Isn't it splendid coffee? I believe the beans for this brew were captured at Vitoria. You were there, of course?'

'Yes.'

Messines sighed. 'His Royal Highness really will not see random visitors, Major. I do hope you understand.'

Sharpe drained the small cup. 'You're telling me it's hopeless to wait?'

'Quite hopeless.' Messines gave his engaging smile to soften the bad news.

Sharpe stood. He pulled the great sword straight in its slings. 'I'm sure the Prince of Wales would be fascinated by my news.'

It was a shot at random, but it must have struck home, for Messines raised both hands in a gesture of placation. 'My dear Major Sharpe! Please! Sit down, I beg you!'

Sharpe guessed that there was little love lost between the pleasure-loving Prince of Wales and his sterner brother, the Duke of York. The Duke, whose ineptness as a General had given currency to a mocking little rhyme that described how, in his Flanders campaign, he had marched ten thousand men to the top of a hill and marched them down again, had nevertheless proved an efficient, meticulous, and mostly honest administrator. There had only been one scandal, when his mistress had been found selling commissions, and Sharpe's words suggested, rightly, that the Prince would relish another scandal that would sully his younger brother's stern reputation.

Messines smiled. 'If you could just tell me what it's about, Major?'

'No.' Sharpe had decided that his words should be only for the Duke, for the Commander in Chief. There were other men in this building, important men, but he did not know which of them were involved, like Fenner, in the Foulness business. It had even occurred to him that perhaps there were other camps doing the same crimping trade.

Messines sighed again. He steepled his fingers and stared at a print of cavalrymen that hung on one wall, then shrugged at Sharpe. 'You may be in for a very long wait, sir.'

'I don't mind.'

Messines gave up. He invited Sharpe to stay in the small room, even fetching a copy of that morning's *Times* for him.

The newspaper shocked Sharpe. It printed a report from San Sebastian on Spain's northern coast and it appeared, though this was not the burden of the report, that at least one assault on the town had failed and the British army, however optimistic the newspaper sounded, was baulked and taking casualties. It was what followed that shocked Sharpe. The newspaper was reporting a victory, though its report was confusing, and Sharpe, who had been told by Major General Nairn that the rest of this summer would see a lull in the war, now read that a French thrust over the Pyrenees had been repulsed after grim fighting. There was a list of casualties on an inside page and Sharpe read it intently. There was no mention of any man from the shrunken South Essex, so perhaps, he thought, they still guarded the Pasajes wharves.

He stared into the parade ground. Men were fighting and dying in Spain and he was here! It struck him as a bitter fate. His place was not here where men drank their coffee from small, exquisite cups.

A clock in the passage struck eleven.

He read the rest of the paper. There was no other news from Spain. There had been riots because of the high price of bread in Leicestershire and the militia had been called out and found it necessary to fire a volley of musketry into the crowd. A weaving mill in Derbyshire had been broken into by a mob who feared that its machinery would take away their jobs. The mill's looms had been smashed with hammers, and its wheel-shaft damaged by fire, causing the magistrates to call out the local militia. He turned back to the report from Spain. A battle had been fought at Sorauren. He had never heard of the place, and he wondered if it was in France or Spain, for the border was intricate in the Pyrenees, but then he reflected that *The Times* would surely have said if any British troops had crossed the frontier. He wanted to be there when it happened. He wanted to be there with his own regiment.

The clock struck twelve and the door behind him opened. 'Richard! By all the Gods! Richard!' Sharpe turned, startled by the good-natured interruption. A one-armed man, elegantly dressed in civilian clothes; a handsome man, smiling in unforced welcome, faced him. 'My dear Sharpe! I had business with the Adjutant General and the porter told me you were here!'

'Sir!' Sharpe smiled in genuine pleasure.

'My dear Richard! How very good to see you, and almost properly dressed!'

Sharpe shook the one hand. 'How are you, sir?'

'My dear fellow! I'm wondrously healthy. You look very good yourself, very good indeed.' The Honourable William Lawford was pumping Sharpe's hand up and down. 'Except for your face. Had a fight with a cat?'

Lawford was plumper than in the days when he had been the South Essex's Lieutenant Colonel, and much plumper than when he had been a Lieutenant in India and Sharpe had been his Sergeant. They had been imprisoned together by the Sultan Tippoo, and in those days Lieutenant Lawford had been thin as a ramrod. Now, out of the army, and evidently prospering as a civilian, he had spread in the waist and his handsome face was rounded with good living and success. 'What are you doing here, Richard?'

'I'm hoping to see the Duke.'

'My dear fellow! You'll wait in vain! He's gone to Windsor and I doubt we'll see him again this week. You'll take some lunch?'

Sharpe hesitated, but Lawford's certainty that the Duke would not be returning to the Horse Guards swayed him. 'Yes, sir.'

'Splendid.'

Lawford had a carriage; a rich, high, open vehicle drawn by four horses and driven by liveried servants. They crossed the parade ground at a fast clip and Lawford raised his cane to acknowledge a greeting from a horseman who came from the park. He smiled at Sharpe. 'I heard you were in London. You saw Prinny, yes?'

'Yes.'

'What a fool he is! Almost took my head off with the sword when he gave me the knighthood.' He laughed, but Sharpe sensed that the true message being given was that Lawford was now Sir William.

'You were knighted?'

'Yes.' Lawford smiled modestly at Sharpe's evident admiration. 'All nonsense, of course, but Jessica approves.'

Sharpe gestured at the coach they sat in. 'You must be prospering, sir!'

'That's kind of you, Sharpe!' Sir William smiled. 'I've a few acres these days. I'm in the Commons, of course.' He laughed as though it was a minor thing. 'I sit as a magistrate and send a few villains to Australia as well. It keeps me busy, what? Ah! Here we are!'

They had passed St James's Palace, stopped on the hill beyond, and servants hastened to open the carriage door. Lawford gestured Sharpe forward, then up some steps into a great hallway where Sir William was greeted by obsequious servants. It was evidently a gentlemen's club. Sharpe was relieved of his sword and ushered into the dining room.

Lawford took Sharpe's elbow. 'They do a cold spiced beef, Richard, which I really must recommend. The salmagundi is truly the best in London. Turtle soup, perhaps? Ah, this table, splendid.'

The meal was excellent. It seemed odd to think that their last meeting had been in the convent at Ciudad Rodrigo where, the city still stinking of fire and cannon-smoke, Lawford had lain in bed with his left arm newly amputated. Lawford laughed at the memory. 'Seems I was damned lucky to miss Badajoz, yes?'

'It was bad.'

'You survived, Richard!' Lawford raised his glass of claret and signalled with his head for the waiter to bring another bottle.

Cigars were given to them and Sharpe admiringly watched the skill with which Lawford used his one hand to clip and light the cigar. He refused to let the waiter do it, preferring, he said, always to cut his own. He blew out a plume of smoke. 'So why on earth were you trying to see York?'

Sharpe told him. He wanted to tell someone, and who better than this Member of Parliament, magistrate, and old soldier with whom he had fought on two continents.

Lawford listened, sometimes asking a question, more often prompting Sharpe to continue. His shrewd eyes watched the Rifleman and, if the story of Foulness astonished him, he took care to hide it. Indeed, the only real surprise he showed was when Sharpe described the attempt in the rookery to murder him.

When the tale was told Lawford put his cigar down and sipped at some brandy. He swirled the liquid in his glass and stared at Sharpe. 'So what's your private interest, Richard?'

'Private?' Sharpe was puzzled.

Lawford retrieved his cigar and sketched a gesture in the air, leaving a trail of smoke. 'What do you personally want out of it?'

Sharpe paused. This was not the moment to talk of Jane Gibbons, or his wish to save her from an odious marriage. 'I just want men to take to Spain. I want a Battalion to fight into France.'

'Ah!' Lawford seemed surprised that Sharpe should want nothing more. 'I see, I see. Who else have you told?'

'No one.'

'Except your Sergeant, of course. He's well, is he?'

'Yes, sir.'

'Do tell him I asked. Splendid fellow, for an Irishman.' Lawford frowned. 'You say he killed a militia man?'

'We killed one.'

Lawford smiled at the 'we'. 'A trifle clumsy, perhaps? Better not to have done it.'

'They were trying to kill us!'

'Bound to be questions asked, Richard, bound to be! Fellows will be up on their hind legs embarrassing the government. It's really too bad.'

'Say they were chasing smugglers!' Sharpe could not understand this concern for a dead militia man that did not seem extended to Sir Henry's peculations.

'Brilliant! Smugglers! Very good, Richard. We'll do that.' He leaned forward and laid the stub of his cigar on a silver plate.

'You do have some proof of these auctions, Richard, of course? Account books, records, tedious paperwork?' He smiled.

'Accounts?'

'Proof, Richard, proof.'

'I saw it!'

Sir William shook his head slowly, then sipped his brandy. 'My dear Sharpe! All you saw were some soldiers on Simmerson's lawn! The rest is surmise!' Sharpe had said nothing about Jane Gibbons or what she had told him, though now, facing Lawford's sceptical face, he doubted whether her testimony would add any weight to his argument.

'I saw . . .'

'I know what you say,' Lawford smiled to take the sharpness from his words, 'but we shall want proof.'

Sharpe leaned back. He felt uncomfortable in this lavish room among these fat men whose chins bulged and wobbled over their silk stocks. 'I heard Lord Fenner say there was no Second Battalion, except as a paper convenience, and I've proved him wrong.'

'There is that,' Lawford smiled. 'A greedy man, Fenner. Rich as Croesus, but always eager for more. Not a fellow I'd choose as an enemy, at least not without proof, eh?'

'The proof is at Foulness. A day's march away!'

'I'm sure it is.' Lawford held up his one hand in a placatory gesture. His other sleeve was pinned across his coat. 'The nub is York.'

'York?'

'The Duke. Foolish Freddie.' Lawford smiled again. 'Doesn't want another scandal, that's for sure! He had to resign for two years as it was. My dear fellow, thank you.' Sharpe had poured more brandy as Lawford cut another cigar. 'I think you'd better leave it to me, Richard.' Sharpe said nothing, and Lawford leaned forward persuasively. 'Let me patrol around it, eh? Will you let me do that, Richard? Say to the end of next week?' He laughed. 'That'll give you a chance to watch Prinny's battle of Vitoria, yes? You'll enjoy that!'

Sharpe was not happy with the suggestion, but he accepted that Sir William moved in circles that understood these matters, while he was a friendless soldier in a capital city where no one cared about him. 'Why don't I just see the Duke of York?'

'Richard!' Lawford said in a pained voice. 'You'll only upset him, and you know how liverish that damned family is! My dear Sharpe! If I was facing a French army I'd be delighted to have your help, can't you see you need mine now? You want your men, yes?'

'Yes.'

'Then I shall do my damnedest! I can't promise anything, of course, but I think I can extricate you. Where are you lodging, Richard?'

'Rose Tavern. It's in Drury Lane.'

'I do know where the Rose is, Richard,' Lawford said testily, then noted the name in a silver bound notebook. 'Give me two days, then meet me here for luncheon. You can do that? And don't worry about disobeying those orders to go back to Spain, I'll make sure there's no undue fuss there.'

Sharpe frowned. 'Can I ask what you propose to do, sir?'

'Do?' Lawford snapped the notebook shut. 'The proper thing, the clever thing. A few quiet words, Richard, here and there. Thank God Parliament's recessed so we can keep the whole damned mess secret. And you, Richard,' he stabbed at Sharpe with his fresh cigar, 'are going to do nothing. You will keep quiet. No stirring up the enemy from the skirmish line? This is London, not Spain!' He laughed. 'Perhaps we can tempt you to dine one evening? Lady Lawford would never forgive me if I didn't snare you for one night.'

'That's kind of you, sir.'

'Nonsense!' Lawford smiled. 'Just leave it all to me, Richard!' He picked up a strawberry left over from luncheon and popped it into his mouth. 'Just leave it to me.'

'Yes, sir.'

Lord Fenner met his guest in the library. His Lordship was not pleased.

Lord Fenner was in the habit of asking the Lady Camoynes to visit him in the early evening, thus leaving his nights free for the pursuit of other pleasures. This evening, as Lord Fenner closed the library door, the Lady Camoynes waited upstairs and Lord Fenner, instead of watching her undress, was forced to be polite to this unexpected and unwelcome guest. 'I usually take a glass of brandy at this hour. You'll join me?'

Sir William Lawford smiled his assent. He appraised the pictures that hung between the shelves, noting a fine small drawing of ships at sea and a very good Reynolds. 'Your mother?'

'Yes,' Lord Fenner had barked his order for the brandy. 'You said this business was urgent, Sir William?'

'I would hardly disturb your Lordship otherwise.' Lawford ignored his host's barely disguised rudeness, admiring instead a Roman bust of a woman with tightly rolled hair. Everything about this room, from its books to its fine hand-painted Chinese wallpaper, testified to the exquisite taste and wealth of Lord Fenner. Lawford accepted his brandy, waited until the steward had left, then sat in the chair Fenner offered. 'Your Lordship's most excellent health.'

'And yours.' Fenner sat down. He was dressed in a black suit, with a white silk waistcoat and stock. He tried to guess, from Lawford's demeanour, just what kind of business was so urgent as to preclude an appointment, but the younger man's face was unreadable. Fenner was remembering what he knew of Lawford; an ex-soldier who now sat in the government's interest on the green-leather benches of the House of Commons. Fenner crossed his legs and brushed at a boot-tassel. 'You'll forgive me, Sir William, if I tell you that I have other engagements this evening?'

'Quite so,' Lawford smiled. 'I think you'll hear me out, though. We both, after all, share an interest in making certain that no scandal disturbs our administration? This is very good brandy! My smugglers bring in a most inferior article.'

'You spoke of scandal.'

Lawford stared at the thin, pale face with its aquiline nose. 'Girdwood, Foulness, auctions. You permit me to smoke?'

Lord Fenner was too astonished to offer or refuse permission. He said nothing until Lawford had cut and lit a cigar with his one hand, then he made his nasal voice deliberately calm. 'You confuse me, Sir William.'

'Confuse you?'

'You play at riddles like a child.'

Lawford shrugged apologetically. He was nervous. This handsome lord, a government minister, conveyed such an air of elegant gravity that it seemed unthinkable that he should be bound up in so squalid an affair as Foulness. Lawford smiled. 'I do not, for one moment, sir, imagine that you know of what I speak. Let us, though, assume that you have some influence over those who might? Sir Henry Simmerson, perhaps?'

Lord Fenner showed none of the relief that he felt. Lawford was showing his cards, and though the first cards had horrified Fenner, this last demonstrated that Sir William did not seek his disgrace. Fenner's voice was still cold and toneless. 'We can assume that, Sir William.'

Lawford, who had half-expected to be forcibly ejected from the house, even challenged to a duel, knew now that Sharpe's

209

accusations were right. Lord Fenner had admitted nothing, but the very fact that he would talk proclaimed that there was much to admit. Sir William rested his cigar to take up the brandy. 'Should news of Sir Henry's peculations at Foulness become public, my Lord, I need hardly tell you the result.' Nor did he; another scandal to rock the government, cries of treason, of corruption, of demands for inquiries and God knows what else.'

Fenner sat very still. 'How could it become public?'

'Because Major Richard Sharpe is in full knowledge of the facts.' Sir William smiled. 'He attempted to see the Duke of York today. York's aide sent for me, knowing that I had been Sharpe's commanding officer, and I have, so far, kept him silent. You owe me thanks for that.'

Fenner somehow managed to hide his horror. Sharpe was alive? His Lordship had thought it strange that his hired assassins had not come to collect their reward, but nor had Sharpe ever appeared again and Fenner had persuaded himself that the troublesome Rifleman was safely dead.

The door to the drawing room creaked ajar and Fenner supposed that Anne Camoynes was listening there. God damn her! He dared not close the door lest the movement be interpreted as nervousness and, to cover his astonishment and consternation, he lit a cigar for himself and forced insouciance into his voice. 'You say Sharpe spoke to you?'

'At great length. A very remarkable man, my Lord. I knew him as a sergeant. He has a talent for battle, but not, I think, for politics.' Lawford smiled as though such a lack in a man was to be pitied. 'He is an intemperate fellow, often foolhardy, and not easily dissuaded. He pointed out to me, with commendable passion, the need for veteran Battalions to be kept in Spain. His own Battalion, as your Lordship knows, is in danger of dismemberment and he feels, not without cause, that it has yet a great contribution to make in the invasion of France. If he feels that it is being deliberately denied replacements, then he could make an unwelcome noise. Your Lordship comprehends me?'

Fenner nodded. How, in God's name, had Sharpe discovered Foulness? Fenner would dearly love to know, yet to ask was to reveal too great a concern.

'Fortunately,' Lawford went on, 'he has no absolute proof, so his opportunity for embarrassing our government is slight. He has agreed to do nothing until the day after tomorrow, my Lord, and to leave the resolution of this affair entirely in my hands.'

Fenner bowed to Lawford, a gesture that did express relief, for now he knew what he must deal with. Not with some rogue Rifleman whose passion and enmity scared His Lordship, but with another politician, a man who understood that compromise was the very finest of the arts. 'You have suggestions, Sir William?'

'Mere thoughts,' Sir William smiled. 'I really do not know if there is anything amiss at Foulness. A strange name, yes?' Lord Fenner smiled, for the words told him that Sir William had not come to preach morality, but to make his bargain. Lawford drew on his cigar. 'My concern is with Major Sharpe. I owe him a great deal, sir, including my life. You will sympathise with my wish to extricate him from this entanglement. I would not want him punished, nor in any way see his career harmed, indeed, I would like to see it advanced. If he is guilty of anything, my Lord, it is merely an excessive devotion to his duty.'

Lord Fenner nodded. 'You say he is in London?'

'I did not. I said he has agreed to do nothing until I speak to him in two days.'

'What does he want?'

'His Battalion.'

Lord Fenner knew that now he had to play a card of his own. 'But if there is no Battalion, Sir William, he cannot have it.' Fenner's gaze was challenging.

Lawford knew that Lord Fenner, by his last statement, was saying that the physical evidence at Foulness, the men, the camp itself, all signs of the hidden Battalion, would be removed. The men would be sent to different depots throughout Britain, dispersed in sections, while the tents and buildings would be destroyed. There could be no disgrace for Lord Fenner, for there would be no evidence of any kind. Lawford smiled. 'I thought, my Lord, that he might be given command of a Rifle Battalion in the American war? We need good men over there.'

'America?' Lord Fenner thought it would do very well; a minor, scrappy war being fought three thousand miles away. No one cared what happened in America. 'We could doubtless arrange such a thing, so long as he keeps silent about this preposterous business.'

'If there's no evidence, my Lord, what does it matter?'

Fenner said nothing. There was only one proof that could destroy him, and that was the secret records of the Battalion auctions, and they, he knew, were safe. Even if Major Sharpe should produce the men themselves, what could they prove? They were listed as a Holding Battalion, so the men were accounted for. The officers might bleat about auctions, yet they had taken the money and so risked punishment, while not one officer, apart from Girdwood, knew of His Lordship's involvement.

Sir William tossed his cigar into the empty hearth. 'I have your permission to return and speak with you tomorrow, my Lord? I would not ask you for a precipitate decision.'

Fenner stood. 'America?'

'It would be most suitable. A Battalion command, of course.

Nothing less.' Lawford was ensuring that Sharpe did not suffer. The scandal would be avoided, the government safe, and Sir William's own reward could wait.

'Of course.' Fenner held a hand out to guide his guest towards the door. 'I really am most obliged to you, Sir William. Men of sense and discretion are rare commodities these days. We must make sure your talents do not go unrewarded.'

'Thank you, my Lord.' Which meant that Lawford could now look for a government post, something unburdensome but with a welcome salary.

Lord Fenner did not summon his steward, but opened his front door himself. 'I shall look forward to your return tomorrow. You have a coat, a hat?'

Sir William stood on the step in the gentle London dusk, and thought that it was a good evening's work. There would be no scandal, no ribald jeers in Parliament. Instead the criminal evidence would be quietly hidden and Richard Sharpe, whom Lawford liked, would get a just reward. He would be promoted, he would have a Rifle Battalion of his own, and no one, except the enemies against whom that Battalion was matched, would suffer. No one. Lawford smiled as his groom opened the carriage door.

Lord Fenner, from his front windows, watched Sir William's coach go towards St James's. Lord Fenner was not happy. He had been found out, yet he was sensible of the fact that Sir William had been most delicate. Sir William wanted a reward; why else had he come? His price was Sharpe's future. Lord Fenner would rather have seen Sharpe flayed alive, but the man's promotion was a very cheap price to pay.

He turned to the drawing room, opening the door that had been left ajar, to find the Lady Camoynes leafing through a book. 'How long have you been here?'

'A while, Simon.'

'You heard?'

'That is why I came to this room.' She smiled at him, her green eyes bright in the lamplight. 'You might care to know, Simon, that Lawford has a most expensive and ambitious wife. You are fortunate.'

'Fortunate?'

'That you will be able to bribe him into silence. A Battalion for the Major and a salary for Sir William.'

'You disapprove.' He said it to mock her, to diminish her. She was his creature, in his debt, in thrall to his whim for the future of her son and his inheritance.

'If it was I, Simon,' Lady Camoynes closed the book, 'I would use the knowledge to destroy you.'

He laughed. 'But it is not you, and your place in my house, Anne, is upstairs.'

She dropped the book and, without another word, turned and left the room. Lord Fenner followed her up the stairs, his appetite, as ever, sharpened by the apprehension of this demonstration of his power. The evening was yet young, and he would do mischief.

CHAPTER THIRTEEN

Most Londoners claimed that the Vauxhall Gardens were past their prime, that the delights of London's oldest pleasure garden were faded, mere shadows of outrageous past joys, yet Sharpe had always liked Vauxhall. As a child he had come here from the rookery, sent to pick pockets in its shadowed walks and about its extraordinary pavilions, grottoes, lodges, temples, statues, and porticos. It was lit by a myriad of lamps, mostly shaped as stars or sickle moons, lamps that were strung among the trees at different heights so that, from any part of the garden, it seemed as if a visitor walked like a giant amongst a galaxy.

He had been summoned here, brought by a scented note written in a woman's hand that reminded him of startling green eyes. He had been at the Rose Tavern, reunited with d'Alembord, Price and Harper when the note had come. There was one other piece of mail for him, waiting since the day he had fled London, a great embossed piece of gilded card that ordered Major Richard Sharpe to attend upon His Royal Highness, the Prince Regent, at ten in the forenoon of Saturday, 21st August, at the Reviewing Stand by The Ring in Hyde Park. Sharpe, sourly thinking of the joys of watching garrison troops re-enact a battle at which none had been present, had pushed the card into his pouch. Then had come the scented letter, the mysterious summons to these gaudy, heady, music-filled gardens.

Vauxhall was crowded this night. All kinds of persons came here, from the highest to the lowest, to this place where the titled and rich mixed with anyone who could pay the few pence admission. Many of the women, and a few of the men, wore cheap black masks. Some women carried their masks on short sticks, holding them before a face that would be recognised. Others were masked in the hope that onlookers would think the hidden face famous. It was a place for fantasies, where the dim lights disguised tawdry clothes, and the plaster grotesques fleshed out hopeful dreams.

The letter had named no place in the garden, nor any time for a rendezvous, and Sharpe walked slowly through the great spread of pleasures. He looked at each masked face, but if the woman who had sent him the letter was here, he saw no sign of her. Two soldiers saluted him, but other soldiers in the crowd, seeing an officer approach, pretended not to notice him so that they would not have to diminish themselves in the eyes of their girls by giving a salute. He passed the central pavilion, four storeys high, in which an orchestra played about the base of the great organ. Couples danced beneath the lamps. A woman, on an elevated stage, sang a sentimental song. Beneath the pavilion's canopies one of Vauxhall's restaurants did brisk business.

He went down one of the long, gravelled walks between the intricate hedges which, within their depths, held small, private chambers where couples could retire. Children learned the arts of stalking among these hedges. He saw them now, creeping into angles of the neatly cut box to watch the lovemaking.

He passed a lodge built beside a fountain. The pool of the

216

fountain was thick with rubbish, but at night, under the coloured lamps, the dirty water was glazed with magical gold. A statue of a naked goddess smiled at him from beside the lodge door, while from one of the private rooms within came the sound of a violin. One of those rooms was unshuttered and, through the open windows, Sharpe saw three young women sipping wine and looking invitingly and expensively towards the strollers beyond the fountain.

The pigeons of Vauxhall kept revellers' hours. They strutted on the walks, knowing there were more pickings when the lamps were lit than during the empty hours of daylight. Children chased them fruitlessly. Sharpe turned back towards the beckoning sound of the orchestra in the central pavilion, and, in the warm night, he wondered if it was cold in the high passes of the Pyrenees. Even in summer there could be bitter nights in those hills where the French, so surprisingly, had launched a counter-attack on Wellington. The newspaper had hinted that the attack had been repulsed, but Sharpe wished he was there to know for certain. He wondered what the men left in Pasajes would think if they could see him now, strolling in London's careless pleasures while they listened to the distant guns that besieged San Sebastian.

He shook off the whores who fell into step with him, refused the hawkers who tried to sell him confections or toffeed apples, and stalked like a dark figure through the gaudy crowds. His scarred face, that still bore the marks of Girdwood's cane, was grim in this place of music and discreet sin. He felt as out of place here now as he had in Carlton House. He looked at laughing faces, drunken faces, sad faces, and tried to work out what lives those faces hid. Were they clerks and seamstresses snatching a few hours' pleasure from a long, drab life? What worries did they have? Did they care that the French had come south again, that the British had repulsed them, that men died in the Spanish rocks? He thought not. London, like England, welcomed victories but wanted nothing more to do with the war. Even Isabella, Harper's wife, had noticed it. No one was interested. No one cared about the fate of the soldiers. Isabella wanted to go back with her husband, pleading with him not to leave her in this fat, rich city where no one cared and no one understood and where she would be ignorant of her husband's life or death.

Sharpe bought himself some ale and took it to the edge of a pool. He sat and watched the real gentlemen, laughing confidently as they strode, long canes in their gloved hands, among the lesser folk. He was not welcome among their kind. He knew that. He was welcome in Spain, for there he won battles and was judged by the standards of bullet and blade, but here, in London, he was made to feel clumsy beside Sir William Lawford's suaveness. Even in Carlton House, where he had been so flattered by the Prince, he had been nothing more than a freak on show like the Siamese Twins or Bearded Lady of the hiring fair. He was useful because he was ruthless. He saw it sometimes in the faces of men in Spain, men who were appalled by what he did, yet glad that he did it.

'Got a penny, Colonel?'

A small boy, no more than six, with a grubby face and torn trousers, stared belligerently at Sharpe. The child, as Sharpe used to do, had climbed the wall, risking the broken glass embedded in its top. Would the boy believe him, he wondered, if he told him that the 'Colonel' had once been one of the ragged urchins who came here to steal? 'What do you want it for?'

'Something to eat.'

'Just one. If you ask me for another I'll clout your head off. And if you send your friends to ask me I'll come and find you and bite your eyes out. Understand?'

The boy grinned. 'Tuppence?'

Sharpe gave him a penny. 'Now bugger off.'

'Want a girl, Colonel?'

'I said bugger off!' The boy fled, going to buy gin as Sharpe had known he would.

He thought of Jane Gibbons, and the memory of her made him feel guilty that he had come so expectantly to these gardens to meet another woman. He wondered, for the hundredth time, why he was so sure he must marry her. He did not know her, indeed, he had met her now just three times. He knew nothing of her, except that she was beautiful and she had helped him. He recalled her face, mischievous, so full of life, so lovely as she had spoken to him on the boathouse steps, yet what, he asked himself as the parade of fashion and display went past him, could he offer her? Ruthlessness? The talent to demand men's death to defeat the French?

What use was he? He could send a skirmish chain forward, he could impose their fire on the enemy, and he could kill. Year after year, nineteen years in all, he had killed. He knew when to kill, when not to kill, and he thought, as he looked at the vacuous faces and listened to the empty laughter, that these were the people he fought for. And again, as he watched a young man drunkenly dance some ludicrous steps in front of a laughing girl, he knew that, should he have been born in France instead of England, he would have worn the red epaulettes of the French *voltigeurs* with the same pride as he wore his green jacket and he would have killed the British officers of the skirmish line with the same skill with which he now made Napoleon's light troops leaderless.

He finished the ale. The orchestra was playing a waltz. What life could he have with Jane Gibbons? Or with any woman? What would he do with himself if there was no war? He had become so hardened by it, so craving of its excitement, so sure of himself within its achievements, what would he do with twenty-four hours a day? Even with the money of the diamonds, what would he do? Plough? Grub up new land? Breed cows? Or would he, and he dimly saw the possibility though he dreaded it, stay in the army to insist that it must never change from the machine that had defeated Napoleon? He would have a servant to clean his uniform, a horse to parade on, and a fund of memories with which to bore and awe young officers. The soldiers of Britain's army, he reflected, were not there out of choice, but of necessity. It was an army of failures, bonded by victory, and, unlike their conscripted French counterparts, most had no life to go back to, no home to return to when the war was done. The army was home, the Regiment was family, and Lord Fenner threatened both.

'You are a fool.' The voice came from behind him, from beyond the angle of the pool's parapet. He stood and turned. She watched him. She was masked with a cheap black mask, but there was no hiding her piled red hair that was held with pearl clips. She wore, on this warm August night, a dress of lilac silk that clung to her body in a fashionable sheath. A shawl of dark lace was over her bare shoulders. He remembered, from the night when he had met her at Carlton House, that she was beautiful, and oddly the cheap black mask only enhanced that beauty. He half bowed, clumsy and unsure of himself.

'Ma'am.'

'You've been looking very grim. Had you realised your own foolishness?' She put her parasol into her other hand and offered her elbow. 'Walk with me.'

They went down one of the gravel walks that was edged with

the intricate box hedges, and Sharpe saw how the men eyed her body and looked enviously at him. Two of the watchmen who guarded Vauxhall were dragging a feebly protesting drunk towards the gate and one of them, perhaps an old soldier, grinned at Sharpe and sketched a salute.

She walked slowly, her head high, her voice amused. 'They'll think I'm your whore, Major.' He did not know what to say, and she laughed mockingly at him. 'Wives don't dress like this.'

'They don't?'

'This is how you attract a husband, Major, but once he has married you he begs you not to dress like it again.' With arrogant aplomb she swept a child from her path with her parasol. 'Just as a man falling in love with an actress begs her to leave the stage, even though her profession was exactly what attracted him to her in the first place. You have been,' she went on in the same bored voice, 'excessively foolish.'

'Foolish?'

'You go to the Horse Guards, even though you had been ordered back to Spain, and you behave with childish mystery. The Horse Guards, not being foolish, sent for Sir William Lawford, knowing he had been your Colonel, and you, in your innocence, tell him everything. Do you think we might sit here? They serve a smuggled champagne which is bearable, and fortunately too expensive for the rabble to afford.'

They had come to a place where, beneath lamps hung in the branches of great oaks, tables of white-painted iron were set before a small restaurant. An aproned waiter took her order and obligingly moved the nearest tables away so they would not be overheard.

She had her back to the restaurant and to the people who walked past its small garden. She took off her mask, and her green eyes stared at him with apparent scorn. 'Take your shako off, Major. You look like a groom waiting on me.'

He put it on the table to which, in a moment, the waiter brought the champagne, some bread, and one of the strange jellied-meat loaves like the one Jane Gibbons had given him just the night before. Now it seemed like a month before. 'What is it?'

She smiled at his ignorance. 'A galantine. Aren't you curious how I should know your business so well?'

'Yes, Ma'am.' He poured the champagne. He wished suddenly that he had a cigar.

She sighed, perhaps because he had not asked her directly how she knew so much, and cut into the galantine. 'You are also a lucky fool. Sir William is an ambitious man. He chose not to speak with the Horse Guards, but with Lord Fenner. Do try the galantine, Major. It might not be ration beef,' she said the last two words with a sneer, 'but it won't slay you.'

'Lord Fenner?' Sharpe could not believe that a man he thought a friend had gone to his enemy. 'He went to Lord Fenner?'

'Who will make a small bargain with Sir William.' She laughed at Sharpe's expression. 'Fenner, Major Sharpe, has patronage. He can give Sir William a small *pourboire*. Don't you know how these things work?'

'A *pourboire*?' He stumbled over the unfamiliar word.

'A small reward, alley-cat.' She sipped her champagne and her green eyes searched his expression. 'You look like an alley-cat, a very handsome one.'

Sharpe was groping for meaning in her words, for sense. He could only translate what she had said so far as desperate failure.

She nibbled at the bread. 'Sir William wants to avoid a scandal. He won't get you your Battalion. That's what you want, isn't it?' He nodded, and her green eyes seemed to mock him. 'He doesn't want you hurt, but he'll protect the government first.' She smiled at Sharpe. 'You do understand me, Major? Sir William wishes you no harm.'

222

But Sharpe was still trying to make sense of Lawford going straight to Lord Fenner. 'Why did he go to him?'

She smiled at the alarm in his voice. 'To feather his nest, of course.' She said the vulgarism brutally. 'Lawford wants higher office and he has a most expensive wife. Or perhaps he wants a peerage? Above all he wants the scandal hidden so that he stays in office. The evidence will be destroyed, Major, and no one will ever know, except for you.' She pointed a knife at him. 'You're the embarrassment. They tried to kill you once, but they can't do that again. I would guess, Major, that they'll send you to a remote Canadian garrison? Or perhaps you'll be given the command of a penal settlement in Australia. I imagine you'd like Australia.' She had decided not to mention that Sharpe was to be given his own Rifle Battalion. He might, she thought, accept such an offer and then she would lose a man who could help her.

Sharpe frowned. 'But Lawford promised . . .'

'Lawford promised nothing!' She said it sharply. 'He's a politician, Major. He'd like to give you what you want, but not at his own expense.'

'How do you know all this?' Sharpe was astonished by her. He presumed she was like the Marquesa; a subtle, pretty woman fascinated by the ways of power.

Lady Camoynes leaned back in her uncomfortable iron chair. Behind her, in the restaurant, a string quartet played. She stared at the Rifleman, and she resented the fact that he was so handsome and so base-born. 'I just know.'

'How?'

She would not reply. She wanted to tell him, because she liked him, but the truth was too hurtful. The truth had given her hatred, a hatred that had brought her here.

She would have liked to tell this Rifleman about the monstrous debt her husband's death had left owing to Lord

Fenner, a debt she paid in Fenner's bed, a debt of humiliation. She had listened this night at the library door, listened shamelessly, for she was a woman who knew that all knowledge is power. She would hurt Lord Fenner if she could, and if to hurt him she must keep from Sharpe the knowledge that he was to be offered promotion and a Battalion of Green Jackets, then she would do it. She would destroy Fenner, and with him the debt, so that her small son, who had inherited the Earldom of Camoynes would not inherit the great debt too.

She would have liked to tell Sharpe all this, but her habits of secrecy were too strong and her fear of his pity too great, so instead she stared defiantly at him. 'I know it all, Major. I know about Foulness, about Sir Henry, about Girdfilth or whatever he's called. I met him once, grovelling in Fenner's house. He's going to marry Simmerson's niece, which seems very suitable. She can't be much of a catch, though I suppose she'll inherit his money.' She raised her eyebrows. 'Have I said something?'

'No, Ma'am.' Sharpe had blushed at the mention of Jane. He stared at the table top. 'No.'

She still looked curiously at him, then shrugged. 'Let us just say, Major, that I am here because I wish to destroy Lord Fenner. I want him clawed into little fragments and you, alley-cat, can do it for me.'

'How?' He was thinking of Jane Gibbons and her soft, lively beauty bedded with Girdwood.

She gestured at the champagne and he poured more into her glass. He had hardly touched his own. She smiled. 'You want your men?'

'Yes.'

'Nothing else?'

'I want the auctions stopped. I want Girdwood punished.'

'Then I'll do it for you. With pleasure. But you have to bring me one thing, Major, and soon.' He looked at her, saying nothing, and her green eyes stared into his. 'There must be proof, Major. Accounts, letters, anything on paper. Bring them to me.'

He was about to say that he did not know where to find them, but the words sounded feeble in his head so he checked them. Lawford had also wanted proof, yet now Lord Fenner was alerted and doubtless would be taking precautions against the discovery of any such proof.

She leaned closer to him. To the people who walked past the small embowered restaurant garden it seemed as if they were a pair of handsome lovers; an officer and his lady. 'I will promise you, Major, that I will give you what you want.'

'I don't even know who you are.'

'I'm called Lady Camoynes. The Dowager Countess Camoynes.' She seemed to offer the name as a token of her trustworthiness. 'Bring me that proof, and you can ask for anything you want of the Horse Guards. They'll give you an army to keep you quiet. You want a Rifle Battalion of your own? They'll give it to you.'

He smiled at the thought. 'Where do I find you?'

'You don't. Take the proof to the Rose. I'll send a servant every day to see if you have it.'

He would have to go back to Foulness, and swiftly. If proof existed, it was there. He shrugged. 'You know about it, I do, isn't our word enough?'

She closed her eyes as if in exasperation. 'I am a woman, and you're no one, alley-cat, no one.' She opened her eyes. 'They are politicians and men of standing.' She said it mockingly. 'Whom will they believe?'

'Won't they already have destroyed the proof?'

'Not yet. Lord Fenner will do nothing until he's met Sir William again. You have one day, when they think you're doing

225

nothing. After tomorrow night?' She shrugged. 'They'll destroy the proof, Major, and in three days' time there'll be no men at Foulness. They'll march them away, they'll scatter them in a hundred depots and garrisons! It will never have happened, and if you claim that it did they'll call you a fool and strip your commission away.'

She leaned back and sipped her champagne. Sharpe said nothing. He had thought it would all be so simple, that he would reveal what he had discovered and that an outraged army would thank him, give him what he wanted, and then, before going back in triumph to Spain, he would visit the big brick house on the marshes and demand to see Jane Gibbons. Instead, everything he had discovered would be hidden and denied, and he would be treated as an embarrassment and a fool.

She finished her champagne, stood up and the waiter scuttled through the tables as she laced the mask back onto her face. Sharpe paid the man and followed Lady Camoynes back into the Gardens.

She walked towards the central pavilion, stalking, imperious and beautiful, in the centre of one of the walkways. 'You will have to do what is necessary swiftly, Major.'

'Indeed, my Lady.'

'You'll leave tonight?'

'In the morning.' He was planning already, knowing that he must remove more than just paperwork from Foulness.

'Good.' She steered him by the arm towards a dark gap in the box hedges. 'These are not pleasure gardens for nothing, alley-cat, and tonight, for reasons that are none of your business, I need a real man. Find us somewhere private.'

He smiled, and led her into the tangle of box where, long ago, he had learned his earliest lessons of fieldcraft. Tonight he would lie with her beneath the leaves, and in the morning, as a full Major of His Britannic Majesty's army, he would return to Foulness. He had thought, by escaping over the marshes, that his task had been completed, but this woman, who clawed at him and loved him as though this was her last night on earth, had told him that the fight had just begun.

CHAPTER FOURTEEN

'Property of a widow, sir.' The owner of the livery stables
wiped his palms on his leather apron, spat tobacco juice at a
cat that sunned itself on his cobbles, then ran a hand along
the springs of the carriage. 'I grant you it ain't clean, Major,
but in very nice trim! New axles! New splinter-bar I put on
myself. Take you anywhere!' He slapped one of the iron-
rimmed wheels. 'Tell you the truth, Major, I was thinking of
using it for myself.'

'I need it for a week.'

'Horses too?'

'And groom and driver.'

The owner, a portly, bald man with knowing eyes, looked
again at Sharpe's new uniform, as if gauging what it cost, then
shook his head as though what he was about to say pained him
greatly. 'Of course I can give you a special price, Major, always
like to help the military, I do, but it ain't cheap! I mean hiring
a four-horse carriage, Major? It ain't a sedan chair!'

'How much?'

'And horses! You'll have to change, of course, or are you
staying in town?'

'We'll be changing horses.'

'There's the return fee on them, deposit on the vehicle, on
the horses, then there's their feed, wages of the men if I can

find a couple for you, their feed, hire of the carriage, deposit on the harness. Adds up, Major.'

'How much?'

'Drivers need to sleep somewhere, Major.' He was eyeing Sharpe's weapons, wondering how much he dared ask. 'You ain't going abroad, Major? Just my little joke, sir.' He sniffed. 'Still, seeing as you're the army and as how our lads are beating Boneypart, Major, I think I can do it for thirty guineas, plus the deposit and return fees, of course. All payable today, Major. Cash.'

'Fifteen.'

The stable owner stared at Sharpe in amazement, then gave a short laugh to demonstrate that the soldier must have misheard. 'This is a quality vehicle, Major! It's not your trades-man's cart! There's nobility who'd like this one, Major!'

They settled on twenty-five guineas, which still gave Sharpe the disquieting sense that he had been cheated, and he was forced to leave a bond for a further two hundred guineas against the loss of the carriage, then he was forced to wait while the owner found a coachman and a groom who were willing to be hired for the week. Travelling by carriage was far faster than by saddle horse, which was one reason Sharpe had chosen to hire a vehicle, the other being that he could use it to remove the mounds of paperwork he expected to find at Foulness, but as he waited for the problems to be solved there were moments when he thought he would have preferred to walk. D'Alembord, Price, and Harper, on the other hand, were in high spirits because of what the day promised.

Sergeant Harper, delighted to be back in uniform, was equally delighted with the carriage. He had never travelled in one before, and he stared fixedly through the window for the sheer pleasure of watching a landscape beyond glass. 'This is grand, sir! This is just grand!'

'Cost me a bloody ear-ring.'

'You'll just have to marry a one-eared woman, eh?'

Lieutenant Price groaned. 'I forgot your Irish wit, Sergeant.'

Sharpe had told all three that they need not come with him, and all three, as he had hoped, had refused to abandon him. D'Alembord, sitting opposite Sharpe, looked out at the dull marshes over which the road led, level and monotonous, towards West Ham. 'You think Lord Fenner's already sent a message to this Girdwood?'

'Maybe.' But if the Lady Camoynes was right, then Sharpe had this one day at least. She had been licking his face, spreading the blood over his skin from the wounds that she had re-opened with her teeth. 'They think you're asleep, alley-cat. So don't wait. Don't talk to Lawford. Just go.' Sharpe had obeyed her, driven into precipitate action by her assurance that Sir William Lawford, by going to Fenner, would betray the men at Pasajes.

They changed horses at Stifford, and again at Hadleigh, and the driver and groom, both promised a bounty by Sharpe if they completed the journey before sundown, worked fast. At Hadleigh, their last stop, where the old castle stood above the Thames Estuary, Sharpe bought saddle horses. He had been that morning to St Alban's Street to find, to his pleasure, that the first money from the sale of the diamonds had arrived, then, to make his plans possible, he had withdrawn a great draft of the cash. This week, he knew, the money he had stolen from the French would be put to work for the British.

They were close now. Sharpe, as the ostler backed the fresh horses into the harness, called Harper and the two officers to his side. 'Remember why we're here. We need their record books, and we have to take the men away from Foulness so Fenner can't hide them again. That's all. We're not going to punish anyone.' They nodded. It was the twentieth time he had told them, but he was nervous. He planned to find the proof which he was sure existed, proof that he could send to the green-eyed lady who wanted her vengeance on Fenner, then he would march the men to Chelmsford and there formally enlist them into the First Battalion and protect them while the proof worked its magic in London. 'Remember. We're not punishing anyone.'

'I'm still looking forward to it.' Harper laughed. 'By God, I am!'

Sharpe smiled. 'There is a vengeful streak in you, Sergeant Harper.'

'By God, sir, and you're right.' Harper grinned, and they went on to Foulness.

At six o'clock, as always, Lieutenant Colonel Bartholomew Girdwood sat in his office and wrote, in his small, neat hand, the progress reports of his Companies. 'Number four's ready for musket training?'

'Yes, sir.' Captain Smith sat stiffly in front of the desk.

'Good, good!' Girdwood made a mark on his chart. From the parade ground came the bellow of orders. He tapped his newly tarred moustache with the shaft of his pen, making a sharp, rapping noise. 'How many men did Havercamp bring today?'

'Ten, sir.'

Girdwood grunted. 'Getting near harvest. Always a bad time. Is he leaving tomorrow?'

'Yes, sir.'

'Issue him with funds.' He frowned. 'Is that a coach?'

'Sounds like it, sir.'

Lieutenant Colonel Girdwood presumed Sir Henry had come, as he often did of an early evening, to inspect the camp. He would find nothing amiss, except, of course, the burned-out stables. The memory of the fire, and the thought of the two deserters, hurt him. One of them, the Irishman, had dared to fire at him! 'I suppose it would be expecting too much to have any news from the militia?'

'Nothing as yet, sir.'

'My God! Real soldiers would have found those bastards days ago. They've gone, Smith!' Girdwood shook his head sadly. 'We won't see them again!'

Hooves sounded outside. The noise, coupled with the jangling of the coach's trace chains, reminded Girdwood that Sir Henry was planning to stay in London until after the Prince Regent's victory parade, and he glanced stiffly towards the door. 'See who it is, Smith.' No one, in Girdwood's view, had any business coming here, no one. The vicar of Great Wakering had arrived once, having talked his way past the bridge guard, to offer spiritual solace to the camp, but Girdwood had ordered the man away and told him never to come back. He wondered if this was the vicar returning and he shouted through the open door after the Captain. 'And see the filth off, Smith! Smartly!'

'Sir!' The shout was a despairing one, cut off almost as soon as it was begun, then the door was snatched open and Girdwood, gripping the table's edge, saw a tall man silhouetted in the doorway. Instantly a pang of guilt stabbed through him, for the man wore uniform and a sword, and the moment that Girdwood had feared despite all Sir Henry's reassurances seemed to have come. An officer had come to arrest him!

'See what filth off?' the man asked.

Girdwood stood. He could see, now that the man had walked into the room and shut the door, that the unwelcome visitor was a Rifle Major. Girdwood outranked him, and despite the fear he still felt, he made his voice harsh. 'You will leave this office, Major! Now! You did not have my permission to enter.'

The Major took off the shako that had shadowed his face

and dropped it casually onto a chair. He put his hands on Girdwood's table, leaned forward, and smiled into the Lieutenant Colonel's face. 'Remember me, Bartholomew?'

Girdwood stared, not sure if the face was familiar or not. The two fresh scars on the Rifleman's face were dark with dried blood, and the sight of them, and something about the eyes that stared so implacably at him, brought to Girdwood's mind a memory of the two deserters. 'No.' He had not meant to speak aloud. He shook his head, shrank back in his chair. 'No!'

'Yes.' Sharpe picked up Girdwood's cane and the Lieutenant Colonel was helpless to protest. 'You know me, Girdwood, as Private Vaughn. Or perhaps you just remember me as filth?'

'No.'

Sharpe tapped the cane into his palm. 'Do you make it a habit, Girdwood, to strike recruits? Or hunt men through the marshes?'

'Who are you?'

Sharpe had been speaking softly, but now, with a savage, sudden blow, he cracked the cane onto the table to spill ink over Girdwood's careful charts, and his voice was loud. 'I am the man, Girdwood, who's in charge of this Battalion. You are relieved.'

Girdwood stared. He could not imagine how a deserter, one of the filth of this camp, had suddenly come into this office as a full Major. He found it hard to make his voice coherent, but he managed. 'You have orders?'

'I have orders,' Sharpe lied. 'Of course I have bloody orders! You think I'd come to this place just for the pleasure of your filthy company?'

Girdwood knew he should be showing more bravado, but he was powerless to move and his voice, that was normally so harshly confident, was barely more than a whisper. 'Who are you?'

'My name, Girdwood, is Major Richard Sharpe, First Battalion the South Essex, and until three days ago, sometimes known as Private Vaughn.' Sharpe saw the terror in Girdwood's eyes, and felt no pity. 'The man you hunted through the marshland, Colonel, was Regimental Sergeant Major Harper. An Irishman. You may remember that he once captured a French Eagle.' Sharpe pointed with his cane at the gleaming badge on Girdwood's shako. 'That one.'

'No.' Girdwood was shaking his head. 'No. No.'

'Yes.' Sharpe tapped the cane into his hand again, then, with sudden, terrible speed, he lashed it into Girdwood's face, not to cut him as Sharpe was cut, but to ruin the careful sculpture of the shaped moustache. The blow shattered the shining pitch and a lump of tar hung pathetically down at the Lieutenant Colonel's lip. Sharpe stared at him. 'You spineless bastard. Dally!'

D'Alembord pushed the door open and stamped in with a wondrous display of military precision. 'Sir?'

'This is Lieutenant Colonel Girdwood. He is under arrest. You will conduct him to his quarters, search them for any papers belonging to this Battalion, and, if he gives you his word of honour, you will leave him unguarded.'

'Yes, sir.' D'Alembord looked at the small man with his ruined, broken moustache, and smiled. Then he remembered that he was supposed to be solemn. 'Of course, sir.'

Sharpe snapped the silver-headed cane in two and tossed the fragments onto Girdwood's lap. 'Get up, sir, and bugger off.'

Outside, as he followed d'Alembord and his prisoner, he saw a group of men gawping at him. He ignored them. 'Lieutenant Price?'

'Sir?'

'Start going through the papers in this office.' He tossed Price his rifle. 'And Harry?'

'Sir?'

'If anyone tries to stop you, shoot them.'

'Yes, sir.'

Sharpe untied his horse and mounted. He was beginning to enjoy himself.

Sergeant Lynch was not enjoying himself. He had been bawling at his squad, making them form a column of four on the centre files, swearing at the filth because they were getting it wrong, when he was suddenly aware that the men, instead of looking at him, were staring past him and that their faces, above the constricting leather stocks, were showing looks of astonishment and even delight. 'Look at me, filth!' They ignored him, and suddenly a voice bellowed behind him, a voice even louder than his own.

'Look at me, filth!'

Sergeant Lynch turned.

Private O'Keefe stood there, except that he was not a private any longer, but a Sergeant, a huge Sergeant who had a rifle slung on one shoulder, a huge mouthed seven-barrelled gun on the other, and a sword-bayonet at his belt. Harper, grinning, stamped to attention a single pace away from Sergeant Lynch. 'Remember me, filth?'

Lynch stared up at Harper, not knowing what to say or do, and the huge Irishman smiled back. 'Say, "God save Ireland", Sergeant Lynch.'

Lynch said nothing. The back of his neck, so acute was the angle at which he had to hold his head, was hurting because of the leather stock.

Harper raised his voice. 'My name, filth, is Sergeant Major Patrick Augustine Harper, of Donegal and proud of it, and of the First Battalion of the South Essex and proud of that too. You, Sergeant Lynch, will repeat after me; God save Ireland!'

'God save Ireland,' Sergeant Lynch said.

'I can't hear you!'

'God save Ireland!'

'It's grand to hear you say it, John! Just grand!' Harper looked past Lynch and saw the squad grinning at him, slouching in their ranks. 'No one stood you at ease! Shun!' They snapped to attention. Charlie Weller was staring at Harper as if the huge Irishman had just landed on a broomstick. Harper winked at him, then looked again at the Sergeant. 'What were you saying to me, Johnny Lynch?'

'God save Ireland.'

'Louder, now!'

'God save Ireland!'

'Amen. And may the Holy Father pray for your soul, John Lynch, because, by Christ, it's in danger from me.' Harper turned away from him, took a great breath, and shouted across the parade ground. 'Talion! 'Talion will form line on number one Company. To my orders! Wait for it!' Officers stared. Sergeant Major Brightwell began striding over the vast area, but Harper's voice seemed to double in intensity. 'No one told you to move, you great lump! Stand still!'

It was grand to be alive, Harper thought, just grand! Even to be a soldier in this army had its moments of pure joy. He grinned, filled his lungs again, and ordered the Battalion to form up on parade.

'Private Weller!' Sharpe had ridden to the front of the parade. Harper stood beside him. 'Weller! Here! March, lad! Don't run!'

Weller, grinning like an imp, marched to Sharpe, stamped to attention, and stared up at the Rifleman as if he did not believe what he saw. Sharpe smiled at him. 'My name, Charlie, is Major Richard Sharpe. You call me "sir".'

'Yes, sir.'

'And the Sergeant Major has instructions for you. Listen to him.'

'Yes, sir.'

Sharpe left them, riding his horse slowly forward and staring at the Battalion which, dressed in its blue and grey, was stretched over the parade ground. He came from the east so that the setting sun was on his face and, dazzled by it, he could hardly see their faces. He looked down at Brightwell, and the man stared up at Sharpe with horror in his eyes. 'Sergeant Major?'

'Sir?'

'Punishment order. Now!'

Brightwell ordered the Companies to form three sides of a hollow square. His voice was uncertain as he did it, an uncertainty that was reflected on the faces of the sergeants and officers. They had all heard the words 'punishment order'.

Sharpe turned and saw Charlie Weller running off the parade ground. 'Sergeant Major Harper?'

'Sir?'

'Stand the men at ease.'

The men watched him. Sharpe estimated there were more than five hundred men here, enough to be considered a full Battalion in Spain, and he hoped that sufficient of them were trained to take their places in the line. He had ordered them into punishment order, not because he planned any action against the sergeants or officers, but because it was the most convenient formation for every man to hear his voice. 'Take your stocks off!'

They obeyed. Some grinned, others looked worried. Some, a few, recognised him as Private Vaughn, and others listened to the sudden rush of whispers that went through the Battalion like a wind through standing corn.

'Quiet!' Harper's voice brought an instant silence.

Sharpe rode forward. 'My name is Major Richard Sharpe. I come from the First Battalion of this Regiment in Spain. I am going to take some of you back to Spain.' He let that sink in as he turned and watched the faces of the men on the flanks, the only ones who were not silhouettes in front of the setting sun. 'Tomorrow we begin our journey! We will be going to Chelmsford. In a few weeks, perhaps less, some of you will go to our First Battalion with myself and with Regimental Sergeant Major Harper. You may have heard of him. He once captured an Eagle from the French!'

The sergeants, he could see, were staring in shock at Harper. The officers looked white.

'You are therefore dismissed from duty this night! Reveille will be at three in the morning, we march at five! You will pack your kit this night. Your stocks you will throw away. You will not be charged for their loss.' That caused a small, uncertain cheer that grew when they realised that neither Harper nor Sharpe was inclined to stop it.

Sharpe waited. 'Officers will report to the Lieutenant Colonel's office in five minutes! Sergeants to their Mess at the same time. Sergeant Major Harper! Dismiss the parade!'

Harper stepped forward, but before he could shout the dismissal order, a voice interrupted him. A strong voice, coming from the left of the Battalion, as Sergeant Horatio Havercamp filled his lungs. 'Three cheers for Major Sharpe, lads! Hip, hip, hip!'

They cheered. Havercamp, with the same instinctive skill with which he dazzled crowds at country fairs, had read the Battalion's mood and now, as the last cheer died, and as Sharpe rode across to the big, red-moustached man, Havercamp grinned up at the officer. 'Welcome back, sir!' Sharpe considered the Sergeant. A rogue, no doubt, but a clever one. Havercamp smiled. 'I told you I'd have to call you "sir", sir.'

Sharpe crossed the index and middle fingers of his right hand. He kept his voice low. 'Like that, aren't we, Horatio? Many's the time we've shared a jar of ale, many's the time I've told you not to call me "sir"?'

Havercamp laughed, not in the least abashed at being reminded of his Sleaford claims. 'I was telling just as much truth that day as you, sir.'

'Then we shall have to have a truthful talk in the morning, Sergeant Havercamp.'

'Yes, sir.' Havercamp paused, then raised his voice so that the Battalion could hear him. 'And I told you so, sir.'

'Told me what?'

'Any of you could become an officer! Really quick!'

The men laughed, and Sharpe, hearing it, was glad. Men who laughed were men who could fight, and he began to believe that if he could just find the proof that a green-eyed lady needed, then the South Essex was anything but doomed. He had bluffed Girdwood, he had taken over the Battalion, and now all that stood between Sharpe and success were the hidden records. 'Regimental Sergeant Major!'

'Sir?'

'Dismiss!'

Sharpe pulled the reins of his horse and wheeled towards the offices. He was not a gambler, but he was taking a risk as great as any he had ever taken before the guns in Spain. He put his heels back and rode to save his regiment.

CHAPTER FIFTEEN

The sergeants stood to attention as Sharpe came in. None, except for Horatio Havercamp, caught his eye. Some flinched when Harper slammed the door. The huge Irishman's boots were loud on the wooden floor as he went to stand behind and to one side of Sharpe.

Sharpe, as the silence stretched almost unbearably, counted thirty-one men in the room. He had decided to start here, letting the officers sweat in Lieutenant Colonel Girdwood's old office. These men, the sergeants, were the men who really ran this camp. They were the trainers, the disciplinarians, the workers who took boys and made them into soldiers. Nine officers were more than sufficient for Foulness, but Sharpe knew that Girdwood would have needed as many sergeants as he could find.

He spoke softly, 'You may sit.'

Awkwardly, as if every noise they made might attract unwelcome attention, they perched on chairs or tables. Some remained standing.

Sharpe waited. He looked at each of them, again letting the silence put fear in them, and when he did speak, his voice was savage. 'Every one of you is going to die.' That froze them. Whatever they had been expecting, it was not that. They seemed hardly able to breathe as they stared at him. 'You're going to die because you're useless buggers. A dozen of you against one man!' He gestured at Harper. 'And you lost! You think the French are weaklings? You couldn't even catch the two of us! We ran circles round you! You feeble bastards! Brightwell!'

'Sir?' The Sergeant Major was sitting stiffly in an old armchair which trailed tufts of horsehair.

'I believe you owe Regimental Sergeant Major Harper one crucifix. Do you have it?'

Brightwell said nothing. His face, red and broken-veined anyway, was scarlet now.

Sharpe stared at him. 'I asked you a question!'

'No, sir.'

'No what?'

'Don't have it, sir.'

'Then you will pay him for it.' Sharpe looked for Lynch, and found him at the back of the room. 'Lynch!'

Lynch stood. 'Sir.'

Sharpe paced towards him, stopping halfway down the long, bare hut. 'I watched you commit murder, Lynch.'

Lynch was white. 'Colonel's orders, sir.'

'Go and lick out a latrine, now!'

'Sir?' Lynch looked horrified.

'Move!'

'But sir!'

Sharpe waited till the Sergeant reluctantly moved, then told him to stay where he was. 'You see, Lynch. There are some orders you choose to obey and some you do not. Sit down, you bastard. Your punishment for that murder is delayed.'

Sharpe's feet echoed on the bare boards as he walked back to the front of the room. One of the sergeants was nervously fingering dominoes left on a table, and his fidgeting pushed a tile over the edge. The clatter of its fall seemed unbearably loud, making some of the sergeants jump as if it had been the sound of Sharpe cocking a rifle.

Sharpe turned. 'I have taken over command of this Battalion as of this evening. The senior captain is now Mr d'Alembord. The head of this Mess is Regimental Sergeant Major Harper. As you are aware, the Sergeant Major and I had to use unusual methods to find you. Whatever happened to myself and the RSM in this place is now forgotten. It is over. There will be no recriminations for anything that happened to us, no punishments, nothing.'

They stared at him, surprised by the leniency. 'So listen to me. I know what has been happening here. The army knows. Every one of you, every single one of you has earned a prison sentence or worse.' He was making it up as he went along, but their submission told him that he was on target. 'But the army, in its wisdom, is not going to pursue charges, not if you bastards now do as you are told and do it well!' Not one of them moved. The last rays of the sun slashed through the drifting dust in the air.

'There will be no more selling of recruits. We're marching to Chelmsford tomorrow. We're going, eventually, to Spain. I'm leaving you miserable bastards in your present ranks, and I expect you to earn that trust! You are accountable to the Regimental Sergeant Major and if any of you do not like that, then I suggest you take it up with Sergeant Major Harper personally. I can tell you from personal experience that he has no objections to settling quarrels in private.'

Harper kept his rigid pose, but slowly, very slowly, a smile appeared on his face. No one smiled back.

Sharpe was nearly through with them. 'I assume that all of you remember how real sergeants behave? That is how you will behave. There will be no punishments except those sanctioned by your Company officer, or the officer of the day, or by myself, and all such punishments will be recorded in the Battalion book. And if I discover any one of you trying to get round that order, I will punish that man myself, in private, and alone, and without entering it into the book. Two last things.' He did not raise his voice, and only Harper knew how desperately Sharpe meant these final words. 'If any man out of any of your Companies deserts on tomorrow's march, I will punish you for that desertion. There will be march orders in three hours; be ready for them. And one last thing.' There was a small stir as they looked up at him. So far, beyond insults that they deserved, he had not been harsh.

His face was full of disdain. 'If any of you are frightened of going to Spain and wish to stay with a properly constituted Second Battalion, give your name to the RSM. On your feet!' He waited till they were standing. 'Good evening.'

He left, stopping only to mutter a question to Harper. 'Any sign of Charlie?'

'Nothing, sir.'

'Don't wait if he has news. Just find me.'

'Yes, sir.'

Sharpe crossed to the office and there he gave much the same to the officers, though he also offered them a chance to resign their commissions this very night if they so wished. 'Just don't be here in the morning, you understand?'

There was silence. There were the two Captains; Smith the senior man, and Finch the junior, with six Lieutenants. They all looked old for their rank, and Sharpe supposed that Girdwood had hand-picked each of them. Doubtless they were filled with resentment against an army that had let younger men be promoted over them, that had even allowed a man from the ranks, Richard Sharpe, to be a Major. He was equally sure, though he did not yet have any proof, that their rancour had been assuaged by generous payments from the profits of Foulness.

'I know what this place is.' Not one of them, just like the sergeants, would catch his eye. 'You're bloody crimpers! Hardly a gentleman's trade, is it? And thieves.'

Captain Finch, his head still bandaged from the thump Harper had given him with his pistol butt, looked angrily at Sharpe, but the Rifleman stared him down. 'I had to find this place by bloody joining up! And what do I find? Thieves masquerading as gentlemen. Common bloody criminals. You! Captain Smith?'

'Sir?' Captain Hamish Smith, five years older than Sharpe and with prematurely grey hair and sunken cheeks, looked timidly at the Rifleman.

'Where's the Battalion chest?'

'In that cupboard, sir.'

'Open it.'

'Locked, sir. Colonel has the key.'

Sharpe took his rifle. They watched in silence as, with the practised, quick efficiency of a trained Rifleman, he loaded the gun. When the rifle was primed, he opened the cupboard, dragging the great, padlocked chest onto the floor, and held the muzzle against the steel padlock.

They flinched as the bullet ripped the hasp away from the chest with a burst of splinters and a shrieking of torn metal. 'You! Tell me your name again.' Sharpe pointed to a tall, long-faced Lieutenant who had been guarding the bridge when Sharpe arrived and who still looked shocked from the savage words that had answered his challenge there.

'Mattingley, sir.'

'Count the contents.'

Sharpe had kicked the lid open. He could see bags of coin and a pile of banknotes, but he could see no ledgers or papers.

Lieutenant Price, in his search of this office, had likewise found no incriminating documents. The only proof Sharpe had, at this moment, of Sir Henry Simmerson and Lieutenant Colonel Girdwood's illegalities was the Battalion itself. The proof he so desperately needed was not here, and he prayed that d'Alembord would find it in Girdwood's quarters.

He gave the orders for the next day as Mattingley counted the money. When the orders were given, he stared at each man in turn. 'I will say one last thing. I do not know, nor do I much care, whether the army will punish your thievery and crimping. I do know this. The attitude of the Horse Guards will be much affected by the behaviour of this Mess over the next few days.' The truth was that he could not control the Battalion without these men or the sergeants, and, though he despised them and would have gladly seen each one broken and dismissed, he needed them. 'My object, gentlemen, is simple. I wish our Regiment to be part of the invasion of France. It is to that purpose that I am here, and if you help me in that purpose then I will do what I can to ensure your own personal survival.' He looked at Mattingley. 'How much?'

'Two hundred and four guineas in coin, sir. Forty-eight pounds in note.'

'This room will be locked and guarded tonight. If I find anything missing, any papers, any money, then I will know who to question. Captain Smith? I'll trouble you to stay here. The rest of you gentlemen are dismissed.'

He watched them file from the door. D'Alembord waited outside and Sharpe gestured for him to enter. 'Anything?'

'Nothing, sir.' D'Alembord had searched Girdwood's quarters, even those of his servant. 'Except some poetry.' He grinned, and it was a relief to Sharpe, after the last half hour, to hear an honest voice with humour in it.

'Poetry?'

'He's written reams of it, sir, very much of the drums of battle variety. The word rattle comes in frequently as a convenient rhyme,' d'Alembord smiled. 'But no papers. He's also given his word that he won't leave his quarters tonight.'

'But no papers, Dally?'

D'Alembord smiled sympathetically at Sharpe's disappointment. 'I fear not, sir.'

So Sharpe was still without written proof. He swore softly, told d'Alembord to sit, then, with Smith's help, went through Girdwood's charts and training records to determine which men were ready for battle, and which not. That news, at least, was satisfying. Two hundred and forty-three men, including the two guard Companies, were either fully, or close to being fully trained. D'Alembord smiled. 'It's enough, sir.'

'More than.' Sharpe rubbed his eyes. He had stayed too late in Vauxhall Gardens, and had had small sleep. 'I want those guard Companies broken up in the morning, Dally.'

'Yes, sir.'

'Form the trained men into four Companies. The rest stay in their squads. You take one Company, Harry another.' He paused. He needed two more Company commanders. 'What are those lads at Chelmsford like, Dally?'

'Carline might do.' D'Alembord said it grudgingly. 'Merrill and Pierce are bloody milksops.'

'We'll give Carline one Company, the other will have to wait.'

'Yes, sir.'

Sharpe saw the pathetic eagerness on Captain Smith's face to be given the fourth Company. He ignored it for the moment, drawing to him, instead, the great piles of attestation forms that Price had discovered in this office. There was one for each man and, just as when Sharpe had made his mark on one of these forms in Sleaford, none of them had the name of the

Regiment filled in. 'Dally. Find some clerks. Put the First Battalion, South Essex, on every god-damned form. And lose O'Keefe and Vaughn from the pile, will you?'

D'Alembord looked at the huge pile, and nodded. He knew how important the task was. Once at Chelmsford the Battalion was still not safe from Lord Fenner, but if these forms, above a magistrate's signature, stated that the men were part of the First Battalion, then they would constitute some kind of proof that the men existed and might confuse whichever officer tried to march away the Second Battalion. Sharpe would guard these forms well, staying with them until his proof had reached Lady Camoynes in London. If the proof ever came.

D'Alembord left with the attestations and Sharpe stood up. He paced up and down the floor, watching the grey-haired captain who sat miserable and ashamed in one of Girdwood's stiff chairs. He was also, Sharpe could see, eager to please his new master.

'How much money, Smith, did Girdwood fetch for each man?'

Hamish Smith blushed. He spoke reluctantly. 'Fifty pounds.'

'That's what I thought.' Sharpe did not betray the sudden relief he felt because that answer was the first direct proof he had that the Battalion had been crimping. He had Jane Gibbons' word, and that of Lady Camoynes, but Smith was the first man of the Battalion to confirm it.

'Of course it varied.' Smith was rubbing his hands together, twining his fingers, fidgeting unhappily. 'Some auctions were more profitable.'

'Who bought them?'

'Foreign postings,' Smith shrugged. 'West Indies mostly, some in Africa.'

That made sense. The regiments posted to the West Indies lost far more men than the regiments in Spain, most of them to the dreaded yellow fever. Recruits were hard, almost impossible to find, and by selling men to such regiments Lieutenant Colonel Girdwood had made sure that the evidence of his peculation was carried far away to an early grave.

Smith looked sheepishly up at Sharpe. 'I'm sorry, sir.'

'You're sorry! Christ Almighty! What about the men you've sent abroad!' There was no answer. 'Why did you do it?'

Smith paused, then the words tumbled out. He had been a Lieutenant, passed over for promotion, in debt, unable to buy a Captaincy, and, seemingly like a gift from heaven, Girdwood had offered this chance. Smith, like Finch, had bought his Captaincy and paid off the debt with the crimping profits. He looked up at Sharpe. 'I've been a soldier for twenty-four years, sir!'

Sharpe knew that desperation. He had felt it himself. He had struggled to be made a Captain, and only fortuitous interference by the Prince of Wales had afterwards made him a Major. For a man without money, promotion was hard, and if that same man, like Smith, was not serving in a fighting Battalion where dead men's shoes created vacancies, it was virtually impossible. Bartholomew Girdwood had offered another way, offered all these men a rise in rank so that their pensions would be higher and their futures more secure.

Smith dropped his eyes. 'What does happen to us, sir?'

'Nothing. Not if you do as I tell you.' Sharpe wondered what Smith would think if he knew that Sharpe had no orders to be here, that every order from now on was unsanctioned by the army, that Sharpe was, quite literally, stealing this Battalion. 'So where are the records, Smith?'

'Don't know, sir. The Colonel kept them.'

'He's getting married, I hear?'

'Yes, sir.' Captain Smith smiled shyly. 'He doesn't like her dog.'

'Perhaps he won't have to live with it now. After this.'

Smith nodded slowly. 'No, sir. I suppose not.'

Sharpe wondered if Jane Gibbons had given, even reluctantly and under duress, her approval to the marriage. Perhaps, unless Girdwood was disgraced, she thought the marriage inescapable, and again Sharpe wondered where the proof for that disgrace would be found. 'He writes poetry, does he?'

'About war, sir. When he's drunk he reads it aloud.'

'Christ,' Sharpe laughed. 'So what did you do with the bounty money?'

Smith, who had been relaxing as Sharpe's mood turned affable, suddenly frowned. 'That was ours, sir, and the sergeants'.'

'And I suppose no man ever got paid here?'

'Only the guard Companies, sir.'

Sharpe looked at the charts on the desk. 'So, not counting the guard Companies, you've got four hundred and eighty-three men?'

'Yes, sir.'

'Then they'd better get some pay tomorrow, hadn't they?' He kicked the Battalion chest. 'Five shillings each. Not much, is it?' And that, he thought, would take nearly half of the money in the chest.

'They'll run, sir,' Smith said.

'No, they won't.' Sharpe said it firmly, though he hardly believed it. These men had been ill-treated, and, given money and the open road, there would be a strong temptation for them to flee at the first opportunity. 'You lead men, Smith, you don't drive them. And if you find yourself on a battlefield with those men, you'll need them. They aren't filth, Smith, they're soldiers, and they make the best god-damned infantry in the world.'

'Yes, sir.' Smith said it humbly and made Sharpe feel pompous.

'I want a list of the sergeants by morning. Who's good, who's bad, who's useless.'

'Yes, sir.'

'We just get them safely to Chelmsford where they belong, that's all.' It was not all. Sharpe wondered how he was to protect these men if he did not receive written proof that he could send to London. In two or three days, he knew, he might have all hell itself descend on the Chelmsford barracks. He needed the records of the auctions.

The door opened suddenly, without any knock, and Patrick Harper burst into the room with an excited look on his face. He saw Captain Smith and, thinking that Sharpe would not want this news spread about the camp, dropped into Spanish. 'The lad's come back, *señor*. He's travelling.' He grinned.

Sharpe picked up his shako and rifle. It was oddly pleasant to hear Spanish again, and he replied in the same language. 'On foot or horse?'

'Horse.'

Which all meant that Charlie Weller, placed as a hidden sentry to watch Lieutenant Colonel Girdwood's quarters, had reported that the Colonel had broken his word and fled. Sharpe had expected it.

Sharpe switched back to English. 'I want a guard on this room, Sergeant Major. No one is to enter without my permission. No one.'

'I understand, sir.'

The officers waited outside, as though they had feared that Captain Smith, left alone with Sharpe, might be eaten alive. Sharpe, as he reloaded his rifle and waited for his horse to be brought, advised them to get some sleep. 'Unless you're leaving us, gentlemen?'

No one replied. They watched as he mounted, as he wheeled the horse, and as he rode into the night. Captain Smith, who had left his shako in the office, thought to order the door open, but one look at the huge, respectful Irish RSM, who carried eight loaded bullets in his two guns, persuaded Smith that this night, and perhaps in all the army nights to come, it would be better to obey orders. He walked away.

While Sharpe, sword at his side and rifle on his shoulder, galloped after his enemy who would lead him, he suspected, towards the house with the eagle weathervane, where a girl of mischievous beauty lived, and a house which, as Sharpe had guessed ever since the search of the office had proved barren, would hold the papers he needed to destroy his enemies.

CHAPTER SIXTEEN

It was a night like the one on which he and Harper had escaped. There was the same sheen of moonlight on the marshes that turned the grasses and reeds into a shimmering, metallic silver. On the flat stretches of water that flooded the mudbanks at the creek mouths, Sharpe could see the black shapes of waterfowl. From far off, where the rising tide raced over the long mudbanks of the shore, there came, like a distant battle dimly heard, the sound of seething water. Once, as he put his horse to an earthern bank that dyked farmland from the marsh, he saw the white, fretting line of waves far to the east, and, beyond it, a dark shape in the night that was a moored ship waiting for the ebb. A tiny spark of light showed at its stern.

Sharpe rode cautiously. He could see the small figure of Lieutenant Colonel Girdwood ahead of him, and Sharpe slowed to make sure that the Colonel did not realise he was being followed. At the place where the track went north Girdwood turned, confirming Sharpe's suspicion that he was going to Sir Henry's house. Sharpe waited until the horseman had melded into the far shadows of the night, then followed.

He splashed through the Roach ford. He seemed alone now in a wet land, but behind him he could see the flicker of lights where the Foulness Camp lay, while, ahead of him, Sir Henry's house was a dark shape spotted with brilliant candlelight. Sharpe paused again beyond the Roach, standing his horse beside a tall bed of reeds and he heard, distinct over the flat, still land, the sound of big iron gates being pulled open. When he heard them close, and knew that Girdwood was safe inside the sheltering garden wall, he put his heels back and went on.

Sharpe rode to the right of the house, following the route he and Harper had taken three nights before. Hidden from the house by its front garden wall he dismounted, led the horse down into the creek bed, hobbled it, then went on foot down the sucking, muddy creek. The rising tide had half-filled the channel, forcing Sharpe to one side. He could smell the rotting vegetation that his squad had grubbed up under Sergeant Lynch's command.

The boathouse was locked again, but it was a simple matter to use the bars of the gate as a ladder. Sharpe, his rifle on his shoulder, pulled himself up to the arch's summit, peered over the top to see the east lawn deserted, then rolled onto the grass. He stayed there, a shadow at the lawn's edge, listening for guard dogs. He could hear none. The tall windows which opened onto the banked terrace above the lawn were lit, their candle-light rivalled by the moon which showed every detail of the house in black and silver.

He wondered if Sir Henry had returned. There would be consternation in London if Lord Fenner, finding Sharpe gone from the Rose Tavern, believed him to have come here, and who better than Sir Henry to come to Foulness to hide all evidence of wrongdoing?

He walked forward, his shadow cast before him, but no one saw him, no one called an alarm, and he crouched in safety at the top of the bank and stared into the rooms.

On his left was an empty dining room, its table showing the litter of dinner. On the wall over the mantelpiece was a huge picture like the one in the entrance hall of the Horse Guards; British infantry lined beneath the battle's smoke.

In the second room, less brightly lit, he saw Girdwood. It was a library, its shelves scantily provided with books, but its walls lavish with weapons. A rosette of swords surmounted the doorway opposite Sharpe, while muskets were racked above the fireplace. Lieutenant Colonel Girdwood, his back to Sharpe, was opening the drawers of a bureau. From it he took a brace of pistols, fine-looking weapons with silver handles, then two red leather-bound books with page edges marbled in bright colours.

Sharpe had planned to follow Girdwood from the house, reasoning that he could more easily take the auction records on the lonely marsh road than in a house where Sir Henry's servants could and should resist him. Sharpe was ready to run back across the lawn, jump into the creek bed and find his horse, but, as Lieutenant Colonel Girdwood pushed the books and pistols into a saddlebag and buckled it, so a servant came to the library door and spoke with him. The servant seemed to gesticulate, inviting Girdwood to another room, and Sharpe, rather than running for his horse, waited.

Girdwood buckled the last strap, dropped the bag on the library table, and followed the servant into the hallway. They turned to their right, and Sharpe, still on the slope of the bank beneath the terrace, sidled that way.

He saw a sitting room. A grey-haired woman sat with her back to the window while, beside the empty fireplace, a book on her lap, sat Jane Gibbons. Lieutenant Colonel Girdwood, introduced into the room, bowed to his fiancée. The servant who had fetched Girdwood crossed to the girl's side and picked up the small white dog to keep it from annoying the Colonel.

Sharpe watched for a few seconds, then went back to the library window. The room was empty, the saddlebag left on the table, and within that leather bag, he knew, were the books that would finish Lord Fenner, Sir Henry, and Girdwood. Sharpe stared at the bag, knowing he could take the books now, and then, remembering that hesitation was fatal, he unslung his rifle and opened the small brass lid that covered a compartment carved in the butt.

Inside the compartment were the tools that were used to clean the rifle's lock and to draw a bullet after a misfire. There was a stiff brush, a small screwdriver to take off the plate, a one-inch iron nail that held the tension of the mainspring when the cock was dismounted, a small, flat, round oil can, a wormscrew that fitted on the ramrod to draw a bullet, and a metal bar to give leverage on the ramrod when screwing down onto the misfired round. He took the wormscrew, torque bar, and screwdriver, closed the butt trap, and moved over the gravel terrace to the library door.

His sword clanged as he stooped, but there was no pause of alarm in the indistinct noise of voices from the next window on the terrace. He ran the slim screwdriver blade between the leaves of the window, pushed gently to confirm that it was latched, then saw where the shadow, thrown by the candles within the library, betrayed the presence of a lock-tongue.

There was no keyhole on the outside of the door, but the wormscrew, provided by His Majesty, was a perfect cracksman's tool. He slotted the torque bar onto one end, so that it looked like a grim corkscrew, and worked the screw tip to where he knew the tip of the lock-tongue would be. He turned it.

The screw point grated, screeched, and he pushed it further into the gap of the doors, breaking the old wood, turned again, and the wood creaked alarmingly as the strain came onto the metal, then, with a click that he thought must raise the dead, the lock-tongue shot back.

He froze. He could hear nothing except the low voices and the far-off mutter of the sea. He pushed the latch down, pressed gently on the door to see whether there were bolts both top and bottom and, to his surprise, the door swung back. The servants had not bolted it, perhaps waiting to do so when they closed and barred the heavy shutters.

He left the garden door open one inch, then silently crossed the bare, polished wooden boards and, praying that the hinges would not creak, closed the library door. He bolted it. Now, should anyone come to the library, he could leave with the books and be on his horse long before they could break down the door or think to use the garden entrance.

He smiled as he unbuckled the saddlebag and took out the two heavy books. He opened one. On the flyleaf, in neat handwriting, was written 'The Property of Bartholomew Girdwood, Major'. The 'Major' had been crossed out and, next to it, was written 'Lieutenant Colonel'. Then Sharpe's smile went, for the heavy volume was not an account book at all. It had no pages of ruled columns, no closely written figures that would add up to Sir Henry Simmerson's disgrace. It was an ordinary book, entitled *A Description of the Sieges of The Duke of Marlborough*. Sharpe riffled its pages, seeing only text and diagrams. The second book, equally bare of figures, was called *Thoughts on the Late Campaign in Northern Italy with Special Reference to Cavalry Manoeuvres*. There were no other books in the saddlebag, just sheafs of paper that proved to be verse, all written in the same meticulous hand. Sharpe stood, frozen. He had pinned all his hopes on finding the auction records in this house, and instead he had found two books of military history. He pushed them, with the poetry, back into the saddlebag and buckled it.

He turned to re-open the door, planning to leave the room as he had found it so that no one would know an intruder had been in the library. He unbolted the door, turned the lever, and pulled it ajar. Then he froze again.

When he had closed the door, caring only about the noise of its hinges and the grating of its bolt, he had been aware that the entrance hall to the house was as packed with weapons as the library in which he stood. Rosettes of bayonets and fans of lances vied with hung pistols and crossed swords. The weapons could have furnished a small fortress, yet it was not the carefully arranged armaments that caught his attention, but rather what, when he had glimpsed them before, he had taken to be the draped folds of curtains.

But he was not seeing curtains. He was seeing two great flags. Each was thirty-six square feet of coloured silk, fringed with yellow tassels. The staffs were proudly topped with carved crowns of England. He was seeing the Colours of the Second Battalion of the South Essex which, against all honour and decency, had been brought to this house and hung in its hallway like trophies of battle.

Sir Henry Simmerson had thought himself a great soldier, yet, when he faced the French in battle for the first time, he had lost a Colour. The second time, he had run away. Now Sharpe was seeing the man's home, seeing the fantasy of a career. The house was filled with weapons, with pictures of soldiers, with models of guns, and now this!

Sharpe felt a terrible anger at the sight. The flags were the pride of a Battalion, the symbols of its purpose. These great squares of silk were as out of place in this house as the French Eagle was in the Court of St James's, yet at least the French Eagle had been to war, had been won in a fight, while these flags, these pristine, new flags, had never flapped in a musket-fogged wind or drawn men towards their signal as the enemy fire thundered and whipped at the line. They had been purloined to feed Sir Henry's fantasies, just as the Battalion had been purloined to fill his pockets.

The door to the sitting room clicked open and Sharpe, standing in the doorway to the library, knew he could not reach the window undiscovered. There was one place only to hide and he stepped, praying his sword would not knock on wood, behind the angle of the open library door.

Lieutenant Colonel Girdwood's voice sounded just inches from his ear. 'You will forgive my haste, Miss Jane?'

'It seems extravagant, sir.'

Girdwood's footsteps sounded on the floorboards. Sharpe heard the saddlebag scrape on the table, then Girdwood chuckled. 'When the army summons a soldier, dear Miss Jane, all we may do is obey with alacrity. It was ever thus.' His footsteps paused the other side of the door. 'One day, perhaps, when my service is over, I might look forward to a leisure spent ever at your side.' His heels clicked together, his spurs ringing. 'Mrs Grey? May I wish you a good night?'

'Thank you, sir. You have your books safe?'

'Most safe.'

'And I pray you give Sir Henry our most dutiful regards.'

'It will be my pleasure.' There were more footsteps in the hall, the sound of the front door opening, and Sharpe stood, silent and still, debating whether to leave now. Perhaps, on the moonlit road, he could force from Girdwood the whereabouts of the accounts.

Yet before he could move, the sound of hooves on

258

gravel was abruptly cut off by the closing of the front door, and voices murmured outside the library. They were close, and coming closer. 'I shall take your aunt her medicine, Jane.'

'Thank you, Mrs Grey.' Jane's voice was demure.

'And you will go to bed?' It was as much an order as a question.

'I shall fetch my book first, Mrs Grey.'

'Then goodnight.' Sharpe heard footsteps on the hall floor. He was staring at the window. If a servant came to bolt the window-doors, then fold and bar the shutters on the night, surely he must see Sharpe behind the door? He held his breath as footsteps sounded in the room again.

'I'll lock the windows, Miss Gibbons?' The voice was just the other side of the door.

'I'll do it, King.'

'Thank you, miss.'

Sharpe was in shadow. The room smelt musty and damp. He heard steps in the room, a key in the lock, then the squeal of a drawer opening. He guessed Jane Gibbons was looking into the bureau from which the books and pistols had been taken. The drawer closed, was locked again, then Sharpe saw her. She walked to the window-doors, closed them and seemed to show no surprise that one leaf had been ajar onto the night. Then, as she stooped to push the lower bolt home, she became completely still.

Sharpe could see her golden hair was in ringlets. She wore a blue dress, white-collared, with a tight, old-fashioned waist that showed her slim hips.

She was staring at the floor.

There was mud there, brought in on Sharpe's boots from the creek bed, mud that led to his hiding place.

She straightened, turned, and raised her eyes slowly, following the trail of dry mud until she was staring into the shadow beside the door.

She jumped when she saw him, but did not cry out. Sharpe stepped sideways, out of the shadow, and they stared at each other, neither saying a word. He smiled.

For a moment he thought she was going to laugh, so mischievous and delighted was her face, then, decisively, she crossed to the door beside him. 'I have to talk with you!'

'Here?'

She shook her head. There was a pergola in the garden, built at the corner of the north wall, and she would join him there. 'You'll wait?'

'I'll wait.'

He waited in the dark shadow of the roses that grew unpruned about the lattice shelter. There was a seat in the pergola that ran around a table made of rough planks. The sea, far off to his right, seethed, faded, then seethed again. He had come here to find the missing Battalion's accounts, and instead he waited for a girl that he imagined he loved.

He had waited twenty minutes and was beginning to think that she would not come when he heard the creak of a door, and, seconds later, saw a dark-cloaked figure running over the grass. She slid into the shadow, sat, then looked nervously back at the upper windows of the brick house that were glowing with lamplight. 'I shouldn't be here.'

He stared at her, suddenly not knowing what to say, and she bit her lower lip and shrugged as if she, too, was suddenly uncertain.

'Thank you for the food and money,' Sharpe said.

She smiled and her teeth showed white in the moonlight that filtered through the roses. 'I stole it.' She spoke barely above a whisper. She shuddered suddenly, perhaps remembering the man who had died in the marsh that night. 'I shouldn't be here.'

He realised that, for all her vivacity, she was frightened. He put his hands slowly over the table and covered hers. 'I shouldn't be here either.'

'No.' She did not move her hands that were, even though it was a warm night, bitterly cold. 'No, you shouldn't.' She smiled a little uncertainly. 'Why were you in the house?'

'I wanted to find the records of the auctions. There must be records? Accounts?' His voice tailed off, for she was nodding assent.

'There are. In London.'

'London?' In his disappointment he spoke too loudly, and she looked, fear on her face, towards the house. He lowered his voice. 'I thought Girdwood was taking them out of the drawer.'

'He keeps some things there. Books, pistols.' She shrugged. 'He said he'd been ordered to London, and I suppose he wanted the pistols for the road. What's happening?'

He told her what he had done that day, how he had stripped Girdwood of his command. He did not tell her that he had no orders to take the camp under his authority. 'But I need those accounts.'

'They're only here for the auctions. I write them and my uncle takes them back.'

'You write them?'

'My uncle makes me enter the figures.' She left her hands in his and, in a low voice, told him of the money that had flowed through Foulness. Sir Henry Simmerson had made more than fifteen thousand pounds, Lord Fenner the same, and Lieutenant Colonel Girdwood about half. They had spent three thousand and eight hundred pounds for expenses. She smiled,

261

as if at her own precision. 'They're in two big books, red leather books.'

'Where?'

'In my uncle's town house.'

'Where in his house?' Sharpe was wondering if his ancient skills would have to be put to a sterner test.

'I don't know. I don't go to London often.'

'You don't go to London?'

She heard the astonishment in his voice, as if he had expected her to dazzle London's society and as if that expectation had given him the irrational envy people feel about the undiscovered life of someone they desire. She stared at him. 'You don't understand, Mr Sharpe.'

'I don't understand what?'

She did not answer for a long time. The waves beat at the mudbanks behind Sharpe, water sucked and gurgled in the creek bed, then she pulled her hands free, rubbed her face, and began talking. 'My mother was the younger daughter. She married badly, at least that's what my uncle thinks. You see, my father was in trade. He was a saddler. He was successful, but it's still trade, isn't it? So I'm not well-born enough to go into society, and I'm not rich enough for society to come here.' She gave the smile again, rueful and fast. 'Do you understand?'

'But your brother . . .'

She nodded quickly, understanding the question. Her brother had presented the appearance of aristocratic birth and breeding; it had made him into a loud, arrogant, insensitive and elegant lout. 'Christian always wanted to be fashionable. He worked hard at it, Mr Sharpe. He aped the accent, the clothes, everything. And he inherited the money and lost most of it.'

'Lost it?'

'Horses, clothes.' She shrugged. 'But I imagine he made a

good soldier.' She could not have been more wrong, though Sharpe said nothing. Jane pushed hair from her forehead. 'He wanted to go into the cavalry, but it was too expensive. We weren't rich. At least, not as rich as Christian would have liked.' She said her parents had died eleven years before, when she had been thirteen, and she and her brother had come to this house where her mother's sister was Sir Henry's wife. Lady Simmerson was ill. Jane shrugged. 'Or so she says.'

'What do you mean?'

The quick smile again, shy and dazzling, and she looked behind her as though worried that a servant might be watching from the moon-glossed windows of the house. 'She doesn't leave her room, hardly her bed. She says she's ill. Do you think a person can be so very unhappy that they think they're ill?'

'I don't know.'

She looked at the table top. She pushed a leaf between two of the rough planks and he saw how the white cuff of her dress was darned with small, neat stitches. 'I don't think she wanted to marry my uncle, but women don't have a choice, really.' She talked very softly, not just because she feared her voice carrying, but because she had never talked like this to anyone. She said she should have been married herself, two years before, but the man had lost his fortune and Sir Henry had called off the wedding.

'Who was he?' Sharpe asked with a stab of jealousy.

'A man from Maldon. It's not far away.' Now she had been told she was to marry Bartholomew Girdwood.

'Told?'

She gave her sudden, enchanting, mischievous smile, that always, Sharpe was noticing, left a residue of sadness on her face. 'I ran away when it was arranged. My uncle brought me back.'

Sharpe wondered if that was why she had been in the carriage on the day when he and Harper were being marched as recruits to Foulness. 'Ran away?'

'I have a cousin who married a vicar. Celia said I should come to them, but my uncle knows the man who owns the living, and you can imagine what happened.' Doubtless Sir Henry had threatened the vicar with the loss of his parish and livelihood. She smiled at Sharpe. 'I wasn't much good at running away.'

'Are you frightened of Sir Henry?'

She thought about it, her hands linked on the table top, then nodded. 'Yes. But most of the time he's in London. He's only here for a few days at a time.' She looked out over the moon-washed marshes to where, now at its height, the tide was pushing waves across the drowned mudflats in shimmering, silver sheets that broke in small, bright spurts of foam where they met the river's push. 'So here I am. I'm a companion to my aunt, I talk with the housekeeper, and sometimes, when my uncle's at home, I have to be a hostess for his dinners.' She smiled. 'That means soldier's talk.'

'Girdwood?'

'He's always here.' She said it with a rueful laugh. 'My uncle likes him. They talk for hours and hours about battles and tactics?' She made the last word into a question as though she was not accustomed to using it. 'But I suppose all soldiers do that?'

He shook his head. 'Most of the soldiers I know talk about what they're going to do when the war ends. They want to own a piece of land. I think they dream of never seeing a uniform again.'

'And you?'

He laughed. 'I don't know what I'll do.' He remembered his sad thoughts as he had sat on the pool's parapet in the Vauxhall Gardens, his drab presentiments of a soldier in peacetime.

She sighed. 'You need the books badly?'

'Yes. I have to have proof, you see.'

'Yes.' She nodded. 'I want to help you, but it's hard.'

'Hard?' He wanted to take her hands once more, but was uncertain whether the gesture would be welcomed. Her head was lowered, and the moonlight cast the shadows of her eyelashes in long, thin lines down her cheeks that abruptly vanished as she looked up at him.

'I can take the risk, you see. I can try to find them for you. I would like to do that, really. But I shall be punished.'

'Sir Henry?'

'He beats me.' She was not looking at him, but across the marshland to the small waves.

'He beats you?'

'Yes.' She said it as if it was the most normal thing in the world. 'He let Girdwood watch the last time, because he thought the Colonel should know how to treat a wife. He uses a cane. He doesn't do it often; not very often, anyway.' She gave a small laugh, as though indicating that she was not seeking his pity. Sharpe felt inadequate to say anything, and kept silent. She shook her head. 'There are marks on his study walls. He thrashes, you see, and the cane scratches the plaster. He gets very angry.' The last words were said limply, as though she could not truly describe the beatings. In the silence that followed her words Sharpe heard a clock chiming in the house. He counted ten beats and, when they were done, she looked up at him. 'What happens if you don't have the books?'

He did not know. Everything he had planned for these next few days depended on the accounts. He had been so sure that they would be here, that he could ambush Girdwood and take them, and then march the men to Chelmsford where the Battalion would wait. He had planned to send d'Alembord to the Rose Tavern, but without the books he had no proof. He had nothing. He looked into her huge eyes, shining with reflected moonlight, and he let his gaze linger on the shadows beneath her cheekbones and on her neck. He smiled. 'Do you remember that you gave your brother a locket with your picture inside?'

'Yes.' She sounded surprised.

'I wore it after his death.'

She smiled shyly, knowing the message he was giving her, yet not sure what to say in return. She looked down at the table. 'Do you still have it?'

'I was taken prisoner earlier this year. A Frenchman has it now.' Sharpe had worn it as a talisman, as all soldiers have talismans against death. 'I expect he wonders who you are.'

She smiled at the thought, then looked up at him. 'I want you to have the books.' She said it hurriedly. 'But I'm afraid.' She was scared because, once Sharpe had the books and his victory, she would be left to her uncle's revenge.

Sharpe touched her hands again. It seemed, at that moment, as brave an act as climbing the blood-slicked breach at Badajoz. 'Why do you want to help me?'

She gave the quick, mischievous smile. 'I never forgot you.' She said it very softly. 'I sometimes think that it's because my uncle hates you so much. If you were his enemy, you had to be my friend?' She inflected the last word as a question, then gave a low laugh. 'He envies you.'

'Envies?'

'He'd like to be a big, brave soldier!' she said scornfully. 'What did happen to him in Spain?'

'He ran away.'

She laughed. Her hands were still in his, unmoving. 'He always talks about it as if he was a hero. Did Christian take that Eagle?'

266

'He was close.'

'Meaning he didn't?'

'Not really.'

She shook her head, as if remembering all her uncle's lies. 'I've always wanted to see Spain. There was a girl from Prittlewell who married an artillery Major. She went to Spain with him. Marjory Beller? Do you know her?'

He shook his head. 'No. But there are a lot of officers' wives there.'

She was silent for a long time. She looked down at his hands that were still on her hands. 'I could go to London, but I'd need some money. I know some of the servants in his house because they visit us here. I could perhaps find the books.'

He said nothing. There were too many uncertainties in her words for Sharpe's peace of mind and, though his spirit soared that she wished to help him, he feared too for the punishment that she risked.

She bit her lip. 'But what if I can't find them?'

'I'll have to think of something else.' He said it lightly, yet without the proof he had nothing. He could perhaps order Captain Smith and the other officers to write their confessions, but then he remembered Lady Camoynes' words; what hope did such witnesses have against the evidence of peers and politicians and men of high standing? Sharpe, without the account books, needed allies of equal weight, and suddenly that thought, the thought of allies, gave him an outrageous, wonderful, impossible idea. The idea, that rose like a great sheet of flame in the darkness of his head, was so splendid that he smiled and gripped her hands hard. 'I don't need them, truly!'

'You don't?'

The idea was seething in him, making his words tumble out.

'It would be wonderful to have them. It would make things easy. But if not? I can manage.'

'But it would be helpful to have them?' She said it earnestly and he realised, suddenly, that this girl wanted to help him.

'Yes, of course.'

'Would you like me to try for you?'

He nodded, 'Yes.'

'How do I find you?'

'Next Saturday.' He took one hand from hers and pulled some guineas from his pouch that he put on the table. 'Do you know Hyde Park Gate? Where Piccadilly ends?' She nodded. He pushed the coins towards her. 'I'll be there at midday, and if you have the books then we'll beat them, but if not? We'll still win!'

She smiled at the enthusiasm in him, the sheer, sudden hope that had given him energy. She stirred the ten coins with her finger. 'I'll be there. I'll bring the accounts.'

'And no one will punish you.' He held her hands tight. 'I have money, more than enough.' For a moment he was tempted to tell her about Vitoria, about that battlefield of gold and jewels, of silks and pearls. 'You can go where you like. You can run away.'

She laughed. Her eyes were bright on his. 'I'm not very good at running away.'

He stared at her, overwhelmed by her face, by a beauty that was precious and rare, and he thought of all the things he had wanted to say to her, had dreamed over the years of saying, and suddenly knew that now they must be said, or, perhaps, never be said at all. Sharpe had often taken risks, he had often, on the spur of a sudden thought, and without thinking of consequences, done things on a battlefield that had made his name famous in Wellington's army. He had climbed a breach where hundreds lay dead, acting on the snatched opportunity because the thought led instantly to the deed and, though caution was wise in soldiering, hesitation was fatal. Yet now, when he spoke, listening with astonishment to his words, he thought he was taking a risk greater than any he had chanced in Spain. 'Then you must marry me.'

She stared at him in frozen silence. He had said it so quickly, so casually, with a friendly tone as though it was a thought that had just settled in his head. She pulled her hands away, despite the pressure of his fingers, and he regretted the words instantly.

'I'm sorry.'

'No, no.' She shook her head in embarrassment.

A door closed inside the house, a dull click that seemed to echo menacingly about the garden. She turned at once, staring at the windows as if, from their blank sheen, she could tell what happened in those weapon-hung rooms. 'I have to go! Mrs Grey sometimes comes to my room.'

'I am sorry, truly.'

'No.' She shook her head again and stood. The door sounded again, and this time she shuddered. 'I must go!'

'Jane!'

But she ran. She seemed very frail and slim in the moonlight. Sharpe watched her until she went into the shadows at the side of the house and was gone.

He stayed in the pergola, his head in his hands, and cursed his clumsiness. He had dreamed of this girl for four years and, given a chance to talk with her, he had stamped clumsily where only delicacy was needed. His proposal of marriage echoed in his ears to mock him, and he wished, with all the vain hope of a fool, that he could take the words back. He had lost her. She would not come to London. The guineas he had given her were still on the table, fool's gold in the moonlight.

He waited until the last lights were out in the house, and

only then did he move. He plucked a single rose from the pergola and, like a shadow in darkness, went down into the creek that was flooded with the high tide. He left the coins behind.

He rode empty-handed to Foulness. He did not have the evidence he needed, nor, he thought, was it likely that it would come. She had wanted to help, and he had frightened her. He would have to do the desperate thing now, the reckless thing; he would use the Battalion itself as a weapon against the crooks and fools. He might still win, but what he had lost tonight would make all the victories to come seem hollow. He was a fool.

CHAPTER SEVENTEEN

The morning was chaos, as Sharpe had known it would be chaos. The men were willing enough, but the Foulness officers and sergeants seemed incapable of solving the smallest difficulty. 'Sir?' Sharpe turned to see Lieutenant Mattingley frowning unhappily in the moonlight before dawn.

'What is it, Lieutenant?'

'The cauldrons, sir. We haven't got transport.' He waved feebly towards the huge iron pots, each of which was large enough to boil a beef carcass whole. 'We can't carry them, sir.'

'Lieutenant Mattingley,' Sharpe spoke with a patience he did not feel, 'imagine that within two miles of this place there were ten thousand Frenchmen who wanted nothing more than to blow your skull apart. Further imagine that you had orders to retreat. What would you do with the cauldrons if that was the case?'

Mattingley blinked, thought about it, then looked tentatively at Sharpe. 'Abandon them, sir?'

'Exactly.' Sharpe turned his horse away. 'Do that.'

He abandoned the tents too. There were no mules to carry them, any more than there was transport for half the equipment that had been fetched to Foulness. The hired carriage became the Battalion office, its interior crammed with papers that would all need to be sorted out in Chelmsford. The

Battalion chest, which now held the precious attestation forms as well as the money, was pushed between the carriage seats.

'Sir?' Captain Smith saluted Sharpe. Smith saw, by the pale moonlight, that the Major wore a rose in his top buttonhole, but Captain Smith was not the kind of man to ask why.

'Captain?'

'Lieutenant Ryker's gone, sir.' That was one officer who had decided to resign rather than stay with the Battalion. 'And, sir?'

'Well?'

'The Colonel's gone too, sir!' Smith sounded shocked.

'Good! Good!' Sharpe was forcing himself to sound cheerful. Most mornings, as Harper knew well, Sharpe was in a foul mood until the sun or a good march had warmed him, but today, with the uncertainty and chaos that surrounded him, he had to pretend that all was normal. 'You've found some drovers?'

'Yes, sir.'

'Get them moving!' Sharpe had ordered that men should be found who, before they joined the army, had been herdsmen. A dozen would be needed to drive the Battalion's ration cattle on the march. 'And, Captain Smith?'

'Sir?'

'Number four Company's yours!'

'Thank you, sir!'

He led them, a raggle-taggle Battalion, out of Foulness. As the dawn leeched the dark sky pale they approached a ford across the Crouch, and Harper, marching at the front of the column, was teaching the lead Company the words of 'The Drummer Boy'. 'Sing, you Protestant bastards! Sing!'

By the time they had crossed the Crouch, and the first stragglers were limping to catch up, the lead Company knew the first three verses. It was not a song that was heard much on Britain's roads, where the officers liked to pretend that the only marching songs were patriotic and stern, but the tune was catching, and the drummer boy's exploits extraordinary, and the men bellowed out the lines about the lad's pleasuring of the Colonel's wife with a gusto. Beyond the Crouch, as they approached a small village, Sharpe called a halt. Geese flew overhead. A miller cranked the sails of his mill to catch the wind, and Sharpe looked at the men who collapsed onto the side of the road and he decided that, given a chance, these men could fight as well as any in Spain.

They must be given that chance. He had no proof now, no evidence of the crimping, and Sharpe knew the evidence was lost. If he had been more gentle with Jane, if he had not blundered into a proposal of marriage on just the fourth time he had met her, then she might even now be planning to find the books. Yet he had frightened her away, before he could tell her where she might find lodgings or help, before any of the small, all-important details could be settled. His ten guineas were doubtless lost, scooped up by a servant, and Sharpe rode to a desperate risk.

'No proof then, sir?' D'Alembord rode alongside Sharpe.

'None, Dally.'

D'Alembord looked at the red rose in Sharpe's buttonhole, decided to say nothing, and gave a confident smile instead. 'We'll just have to get confessions out of these buggers.' He waved at the officers and sergeants ahead.

'Their word against Lord Fenner?' Sharpe shrugged. 'I think I've got a better idea.' He told d'Alembord his thought of the previous night, the outrageous, splendid, desperate idea, and d'Alembord, after hearing it, laughed. Then, realising that Sharpe was serious, he looked appalled. 'You can't do it!'

'I can,' Sharpe said mildly. 'You don't have to come.'

'Of course I'll come! The worst they can do is hang us, isn't it?'

Sharpe laughed, grateful for the support. He was finding this morning, this day, this march, a trial. Not just because of the foolhardy action he planned, but because he was bitterly regretting his stupid, impulsive proposal of marriage. He had shocked her. He felt a fool. He felt as if he had been given a chance to approach something precious and wonderful, and, with crass clumsiness, he had spoilt it. He tried to convince himself that he was fortunate she had not accepted him on the spot, but instead he felt only regret for his tactlessness.

Jane Gibbons haunted his thoughts to embarrass him, and his enemies haunted them to make him fearful. As soon as Girdwood reached London, the orders would be written for Sharpe's arrest. Doubtless Fenner would send to Foulness first, then to Chelmsford, and Sharpe watched the road behind his columns as though he expected to see the messengers galloping towards him. His lead over his enemies was slight, and each hour that passed as the unwieldy column trudged along the dusty road brought failure closer to him.

Sharpe knew he must not show his fears. He found Horatio Havercamp and called him to one side so that the Sergeant walked beside Sharpe's horse in an interval between Companies. 'Sir?'

'How much did you make, Horatio?'

'Make, sir?'

'Horatio Havercamp, I started in this army where you did. I know all the bloody tricks and a few even you haven't bloody learned. How much did you make?'

Havercamp grinned. 'We got the poor buggers' wages, sir.'

No wonder, Sharpe thought, the sergeants had been so keen to discover any small fault with a man's kit that would deserve a deduction from the pay. Those deductions made up the sergeants' extra income. 'So how much did you make?'

'Three pound a week? Varied a bit, of course.'

'Five pounds a week, maybe?'

'Say four, sir,' Havercamp grinned cheerfully. 'But it was all official like! Above board, sir. Orders.'

Sharpe looked at the sly face. 'You knew it bloody wasn't.'

'Didn't do any harm, sir, did it? The army needs men; they've always paid for crimping, so why not us?'

'But didn't you ever wonder what would happen when someone found out?'

The Sergeant still had his look of sly enjoyment. 'If you was going to arrest us, sir, you'd have done it. You haven't, which makes me think that you need us. Besides, have you ever seen a better recruiting sergeant than me, sir?' He grinned at Sharpe and took from his pocket the two golden guineas which, with his marvellous dexterity, he made come and go between his knuckles. 'It ain't every sergeant who can say he recruited Major Sharpe, is it?'

Sharpe smiled. 'Suppose that I think you'd be more useful to me in Spain?'

'I always heard you were a sensible man, sir. You find recruits here, sir, not there!'

'But there are no profits in it any more, Sergeant.'

'No, sir.' Sergeant Havercamp smiled happily. He knew the profits were still there, not perhaps of the same magnitude, but recruiters had to carry government cash, and if he organised just two fictional jumpers a week then that was two guineas to be split between himself and his corporals. Sergeant Havercamp knew he would do very nicely, even if, as was the usual practice, officers were sent with each party. Horatio knew how to fix an officer's purse as well as any man's. 'Anything else, sir?'

'One thing. Is there a Mother Havercamp? You know, the one the General chats to over the garden gate?'

Havercamp laughed. 'Haven't seen the old maggot in years, sir. Don't want to, neither.'

Sharpe laughed.

They came to Chelmsford in the middle of the afternoon, flooding the sleepy depot with men, and the problems that had plagued Sharpe before dawn were now magnified a hundred times. It was here that his real work had to begin.

He had been thinking of this moment ever since the idea had come to him across the table from Jane Gibbons. He had tried to anticipate the problems, but even so there were a thousand details he had not thought of, and, outside of d'Alembord, Price, and Harper, he had no capable men to cope with the chaos.

He did not have the proof he needed to shield these men from Lord Fenner, nor, he thought now, would that evidence come. If Jane Gibbons did help him, if she brought the accounts even at the very last moment, then he would be spared the desperate risk he planned, but without such proof he must do what his enemies had already done; he must hide the Battalion.

Not all of them, for not all were ready to do what he would ask of them. He split the four trained Companies away from the others, and to those four Companies he issued uniforms and muskets. The others, the untrained or half-trained recruits, he must leave here and hope that, within the next four days, no one would succeed in taking them away.

'Sir!' Charlie Weller broke the ranks of his squad and ran to Sharpe's side. 'Please, sir!'

'What is it, Charlie?' Sharpe was watching the barracks archway, fearing a messenger from London.

'I want to come with you, sir. Please?' Weller gestured at the four Companies in their bright new jackets. 'They're going to Spain, aren't they, sir!'

Sharpe smiled. 'You'll get there one day, Charlie.'

'Sir! Please! I can do it!'

'You're not even musket trained, Charlie! The French are good, you know. Really good.'

'I can do it, sir. Give me a chance!' There were tears in his eyes. He gestured towards Sharpe's rifle. 'I'll show you, sir!'

Sharpe pulled his rifle out of reach. 'So you can shoot a gun, but it's not like shooting rabbits. These bastards fire back.'

'Sir!'

Sharpe looked at Weller's desperation and he remembered how this boy had run after the recruiting party in the dawn. 'Tell Sergeant Harper you're in Lieutenant Price's Company.'

Jubilation exploded in the boy. 'Thank you, sir!'

'But don't get killed in your first battle, Charlie.'

He wished all the problems were that simple to solve. There were camp kettles to find, billhooks to issue, mules to steal from the militia stable, and all had to be done in a hurry because Sharpe knew he must be away from this place before any orders arrived from London. He split the sergeants between the two units, leaving Sergeant Havercamp to recruit from Chelmsford. He left Brightwell too, as Sergeant Major here beneath Captain Finch. Sharpe was not happy with the arrangement, but if he was successful in the next few days, then Finch and Brightwell would soon be relieved by better men. Sharpe kept Sergeant Lynch with his trained men. Sharpe wanted to have the renegade, vicious Irishman under his own eye.

The ration cattle had not arrived yet, and the coachman claimed that the carriage's splinter-bar was breaking, but relented when Sharpe promised him a gold coin if the wood stayed whole. Captain Carline, appalled by the sudden energy that was infusing the quiet barracks, went pale when Sharpe told him to prepare to march.

'We are coming back this evening, aren't we, sir?'

'Why?'

'I had dinner arranged . . .' His voice tailed away.

'Hurry, Captain!'

There were still more problems. Half the men's shoes had

broken down on the day's brief march, and there were not enough new shoes to be issued. Price went in search of men who had been cobblers before they joined the army. Most of the papers from Foulness were put into the offices, but Sharpe kept the attestation forms. These forms, all now saying that the men were in the First Battalion of the South Essex, would be embarrassing to Sharpe's enemies. They proved no wrong-doing, but the absence of the forms, in an army that thrived on paperwork, would make it almost impossible for Lord Fenner to scatter the men left in Chelmsford to other barracks. The attestation form was a man's passport in this army. Without it, he did not exist. Sharpe kept them in the carriage.

And at last, at seven o'clock, when the midges were dancing in the evening air over the gatehouse and the swallows darting above the Mess roof, the four Companies were ready. They paraded in full marching order, their equipment and weapons heavy on their shoulders. They believed that Sharpe, as an unwelcome exercise, was doing no more than marching them to the outskirts of the town and back. It was a belief that all but his three closest comrades shared.

''Talion! By the front!' Harper's voice was huge. 'Quick march!'

The four Companies, followed by the coach, went under the archway and turned west towards Chelmsford. Sharpe skirted the town, going north, and it was not until the tallest spire of Chelmsford had disappeared that he allowed himself a small measure of hope. He still kept them marching at a cracking pace, taking them down narrow, thick-grown lanes, losing them in a scented, soft country of orchards, hedges, and gentle hills. He marched them until the sun, huge and glorious, almost touched the western horizon. Then, where a meadow lay by a great covert of oak and beech, he stopped the exhausted column and called the officers to him. 'This, gentlemen, is where we sleep.'

Captain Carline, whose elegant breeches had been chafed thin by the ride, gaped at him. 'Sleep, sir? But we haven't got tents!'

'Good.'

They slept.

For two days he marched them westward. They slept rough, as they would in Spain, and Sharpe spared the men the parades and drills which had plagued them at Foulness. Not that he made it easy, but he tried, so far as it was possible in this plump, easy country, to give them a taste of what a campaign march was like.

At night they set picquets. To two of his Captains, Smith and Carline, a picquet was a smart group of men who stood to attention at the boundary of a camp and had no purpose other than to salute officers.

On the first night that Smith set the picquets, Regimental Sergeant Major Harper, hidden in a thicket of blackberries, put a bullet into a tree trunk beside the Captain. Smith jumped a foot in the air. 'Sir! Sir!'

Sharpe beckoned Smith to one side. 'If that was the French and not the RSM, you'd be dead. Hide the buggers.'

'Hide them?'

'If you were French, Captain, how would you approach this place?'

Smith frowned, then pointed to where the lane disappeared over the hill by a stand of elms. 'There, sir?'

'So guard it. And tell them I'll come looking for them.'

That night and the subsequent nights, about the officers' fire, Sharpe talked of battles. He did not do it boastfully, but because none of these men, except for d'Alembord and Price, knew what it was to face the French. He told them how to smell unseen cavalry, how to clean a musket on a battlefield, how to face a charging horse, how to make a billet out of nothing, and sometimes Sharpe would wander about the other camp-fires and tell the same stories to the men. Harper did it too, working his Irish magic so that, within two days, he could swear at them foully and they still grinned and tried to impress him with their endurance.

'They're good lads, sir,' Harper said.

They were, too, and they were beginning to want to go to Spain, but Sharpe sometimes feared in the night that their hopes would be dashed by his temerity. His idea, that might mean no proof would be needed, was a desperate gamble. He tried not to contemplate failure, and marched his hidden Battalion onwards.

The men were not spared all drills. Where they could, on common land or on the patches of heath that they discovered as they went further west, Sharpe would suddenly bellow at them to form square, or line, or a column of half Companies, and he had Lieutenant Mattingley at his side to time the manoeuvre. They got better each day, even began to enjoy the experience, and they were blessed with little rain, warm sun, and some back pay from the Battalion chest that was still kept in the hired coach. The money dwindled fast. It was used to pay millers for flour, farmers for beer, and innkeepers for ration ale.

On the third day Sharpe stopped the march. The men were harder than they had ever been, as dirty and ragged as any soldiers in Spain, and happier than he had dared hope. He made it a day of exercises, two Companies against two, games in which men tried to surprise picquets or conceal themselves in woodland; stalking games that would not be of great use to any of them unless they joined the Light Company, but which were a rest from the hard slog of marching. That evening, to the concern of the sergeants and officers, he let them go to the tavern in a nearby village, promising to flog any man who made trouble or who could not walk back to the bivouac.

'You won't see the filth again.' Sergeant Lynch, put into d'Alembord's Company, was surly still, ever ready to preach doom. Slowly, as the punishment he had expected did not materialise, he was regaining his old bumptious confidence. Charlie Weller still stared at him in hatred, remembering the death of Buttons.

Sharpe did not smile. He sensed the mutual hatred between himself and the Irish Sergeant. 'I am not a gambling man, Sergeant Lynch, but I will wager you one pound a man, which you can well afford, that every man will come back.'

Lynch would not take the bet and every man came back.

Twice Sharpe met senior officers, both riding close to their country estates, and both delighted to meet him. They nodded genially at the marching men. Sharpe said they were on exercise and neither officer thought there was anything odd in it, which meant that there was no hue and cry being made for a half Battalion missing in England.

Sharpe was certain that Lord Fenner would institute a search, but he guessed the search would concentrate on Chelmsford and then, perhaps, on one of the depots, like Chatham, from whence the replacements sailed to Spain. If he was found in the next two days, before he could lay on the display that he planned, then he knew he was doomed.

On the Friday morning, as the half Battalion turned south-wards, Sharpe called Lieutenant Mattingley to him. Mattingley, like Smith, wanted to impress Sharpe, wanted forgiveness, and he showed a doglike relief when he saw that Sharpe was smiling. 'Sir?'

'It is Friday, Mattingley.'

'Indeed, sir.'

'I want chicken for dinner.'

'Chicken, sir? There's beef left.'

'Chicken!' Sharpe waved to a woman who watched the men pass and who returned ribald comments as good as she got from the marching ranks. 'White chickens, Mattingley, to the number of sixty.'

'Sixty white chickens, sir?'

'White chickens taste better. Buy them. Steal them if we haven't enough money, but find me sixty white chickens for dinner.'

Mattingley wondered if Sharpe was proving to be just another eccentric officer. 'Yes, sir.'

'And Mattingley?'

'Sir?'

'I want a feather mattress. Keep the feathers.'

Mattingley was now convinced that Sharpe, who still wore a fading rose beneath his collar, was touched in the head. Too much fighting, perhaps. 'A feather mattress. Of course, sir.'

That night, before a dinner of stewed chicken, Sharpe rehearsed his half Battalion in a manoeuvre which had never, so far as he knew, been performed by any Battalion in the history of war or peace, a manoeuvre that made the men laugh, but which, until they performed it to his satisfaction, he insisted on practising. Some, like Sergeant Lynch, thought he was crazy, others just thought that the whole army was mad, while Harper, who bellowed the strange orders, knew that Sharpe's high spirits meant that they were about to go into action.

And indeed, in the next dawn, which showed the southern sky hazed by a great smoke, Sharpe dressed himself in his old uniform of battle, his scarred, faded, tattered uniform that bore no marks of rank. He made Charlie Weller, who was skilled with a needle, sew the laurel wreath back onto his old sleeve. 'I wore that jacket when we captured the Eagle, Charlie.'

'You did, sir?' Weller watched wide-eyed as Sharpe pulled the green jacket on, and as he strapped the great sword about his waist. 'Something special today, sir?'

'Yes, Charlie. It's Saturday the twenty-first of August.' Sharpe drew the sword and turned it so that the rising sun ran its pale light up the blade. 'A very special day.'

Weller grinned. 'Special, sir?'

'Special, Charlie, because you're going to London to meet a Prince.' Sharpe smiled, slammed the sword into its scabbard, then mounted his horse. He was going to a battle.

CHAPTER EIGHTEEN

The crowds gathered early in Hyde Park. The public enclosure was entered from the old Tyburn Lane, now renamed Park Lane to rid it of the odium of public execution. Once through the Grosvenor Gate there was a generous stretch of grass, defined by rope barriers, in front of the Reservoir where Londoners could walk, watch the proceedings, and buy ale, pies and fruit. The best views of the review and pageant would be had either from the top of the Reservoir bank, or else from one of the many tiers of seats that builders were permitted to erect and then hire out to the public. Behind the roped area, between the public enclosure and the Tyburn Lane, there were sacking screens for lavatories, whose owners sat collecting farthings from the more fastidious of the spectators.

There were pickpockets, whores, and more recruiting sergeants than there could possibly be recruits. Every beggar in London who could claim, rightly or wrongly, to be an ex-soldier made his way to Hyde Park in the belief that the day's crowd would be sympathetic to those wounded in Britain's wars.

Opposite the public enclosure, across the three-hundred-yard review ground that was criss-crossed by the park's public walks, was the Ring. The Theatre was at its centre, and round its perimeter the young bloods of London were accustomed to show off their horses and raise their hats to the ladies who took the air in open carriages. Not this day. Hiding the Ring from the public view was a great covered stand, hung with red, white and blue bunting, surmounted by five flagpoles. Four of the poles, those flanking the bare central staff, were already hung with flags; two union flags and, on the outer poles, the flags of Britain's closest allies, Portugal and Spain. The centre staff waited for the Prince Regent's standard. On the pavilion roof, above its banked, cushioned seats, was the Royal crest, flanked to its left by the escutcheon of the Duke of York and, to its right, by the three curling feathers that were the badge of the Duke's elder brother, the Prince of Wales.

On either side of the great reviewing pavilion were two more public areas, roped like the one before the Reservoir, but these were forbidden to the common people. The ropes of the two enclosures were of scarlet weave, tasselled with gold, and into the enclosures came the carriages of the rich. The leather coach hoods were folded down on this day of bright sunlight. In front of the carriages an open space was left where the wealthy could promenade, or ride their well-schooled horses to impress the ladies. There were sacking screens here too, but hidden behind the Ring's trees and tastefully draped with red bunting that quadrupled the price for their use. By ten o'clock the carriages were lined wheel to wheel, their horses unharnessed, and the women eyed their rivals from beneath pretty parasols as the men barked at servants to bring champagne or wine.

The celebrations were not due to begin until eleven, but already the huge open space between the two lines of spectators was busy with soldiers. A troop of Royal Horse Artillery raced spectacularly about the great rectangle, the wheels of their guns throwing up turf as the gun carriages slewed behind the galloping teams. A Guards band played.

In front of the carriage enclosures, where the women paraded in their summer finery, mounted officers showed off their horsemanship. This day such officers were lords of the park and, even though most had not been further from London than Bath, each man this day pretended to have survived the carnage at Vitoria. Their uniforms were thick with looping ropes of gold cloth, bright with chain epaulettes, and gorgeous with lace and silver. They saluted the ladies by touching casual fingers to their helmets, sometimes leaning down to take a glass of champagne, which, like a stirrup cup, was offered by friends. Assignations were made and more than one duel provoked.

The Royal stand filled gradually with senior officers and their wives, ambassadors and men of power from the clubs of St James's and Westminster. Servants brought tea, coffee, and wine. The huge, padded seats in the centre of the stand were still empty. The young officers, walking their beautifully groomed horses past the Royal stand, would salute its tiers and, like German clockwork toys magically in unison, three score of Generals and Admirals returned the honour.

Lord Fenner, as a Minister of State, had a seat in the Royal stand, but, twenty minutes before the Royal party was scheduled to arrive, he walked through the northern carriage enclosure, coldly greeting acquaintances, smiling sometimes at a woman whose favours he desired or had enjoyed, and once slicing with his cane at a servant who clumsily walked in front of him with a tray of glasses.

He saw the carriage he sought, and saw too how Sir Henry Simmerson, noting his approach, ordered a servant to open the door and fold down the carriage steps. Simmerson, the servant dismissed, beckoned Fenner inside. 'My Lord?'

'Simmerson.' Lord Fenner sat on the leather bench and disdainfully put his heels on the front cushion. He stared with distaste at the public enclosure opposite, then looked down at his immaculately polished boots in which, distorted by the curve of his toecaps, he could see twin reflections of his thin, distinguished face. 'Well?'

Sir Henry, sweating in his uniform, smiled beneath the tasselled point of his bicorne hat. 'My Lord.' He lifted a leather bag onto the seat between them and opened its flap. Inside were two, big, red leather-bound books. 'I assured you they were safe.'

'So I see.' Fenner's voice, even though he tried to keep it calm and aloof, betrayed his relief. 'The correspondence is there?'

'Everything is safe.' Sir Henry, whose bile and phlegm on hearing that Richard Sharpe still lived had not been relieved by three blood-lettings performed by his doctor, pushed the books towards Lord Fenner. 'I can assure you, sir, they're entirely safe in my house.'

Lord Fenner closed the flap as if the very sight of the incriminating accounts would harm him. 'Do I have to remind you, Simmerson, that I have more to lose than you?' Simmerson, insulted, said nothing. Fenner growled. 'Where is Girdwood?'

'He's joining me here, my Lord.'

Fenner shrugged, as if he did not care. 'And Sharpe?' Lord Fenner asked the question without hope of an answer. He stared from beneath the brim of his silk hat at a Household officer, plumes lifting elegantly to the rhythm of his trotting horse. 'Where, in God's name, is Sharpe?'

His Lordship had discovered half of the missing Battalion, without their attestations, marooned in the Chelmsford barracks. Yet of the other half, and of Major Sharpe himself, there was no sign. Lord Fenner, on hearing that Sir William Lawford had not kept Sharpe silent and inactive, had lost his temper; swearing at Lawford that he was a traitorous fool, and then, scenting the danger to himself, had begun to hunt for his enemy. Orders had been given for Sharpe's arrest, orders that had not been bruited abroad too loudly, for Fenner did not want to provoke questions from the Prince of Wales. 'What is he doing?'

Sir Henry, whose hatred for Sharpe had not diminished over the years, frowned. 'Chatham or Portsmouth?'

'We've looked there. Besides, he can't sail without orders! He must know that, unless he's mad!'

'He is mad.' Sir Henry ran a finger beneath his stock, then wiped the sweat onto the bench beside him. 'He's also insolent. I recommended his dismissal in '09, but my voice was not heeded.'

Lord Fenner listened to the complaint, as he had a dozen times before, and ignored it. He now felt that his first burst of temper on discovering that Sharpe still tried to fight him had been unnecessary. He had weighed the risks, and thereby drawn consolation. He had concern for the missing men, but not undue concern. He had always known that the scheme might have to end, and he had insured against it. The official records in the War Office and Horse Guards would show that the Second Battalion of the South Essex was a genuine Holding Battalion, and the only incriminating documents were the two record books which, as he had insisted, were now in his possession.

Which only left the missing men as an embarrassment, yet what damage could they cause? They knew nothing. The officers might, at risk of punishment, admit to taking money, but not one of them could prove that Lord Fenner was involved, for his Lordship had taken great care to stay deep in the shadows, letting others show themselves and earn the money he craved so badly. No one, apart from Simmerson and Girdwood, knew the extent of his involvement. Only Sharpe, outside of Foulness, was a danger to his Lordship, and without these account books Sharpe was helpless.

And Major Sharpe would be silenced. If the Prince of Wales insisted that he be retained in the army, then Lord Fenner would accept Sir William Lawford's proposal and send Sharpe to the war in America as a Rifle officer. Fenner smiled at the thought. 'We'll let the Americans kill him, eh?'

Simmerson shrugged. 'The Fever Islands would be a preferable solution, my Lord. Or the Australias.'

There was even a chance, Lord Fenner thought optimistically, that Sharpe could be quietly arrested, disposed of without public knowledge, and the men sent back to Foulness. The crimping had been more profitable than he had ever dared hope and it would be hard to give up that income. Sir William Lawford, of course, would have to be bribed into silence, but Lord Fenner was confident that Sir William would eagerly snap at office. Lord Fenner, though incommoded by Major Richard Sharpe, felt confident. He picked up the leather bag and pushed the carriage door open. 'I trust you will enjoy the day, Sir Henry.'

'I wish the same of you, sir.'

Fenner did not go directly back to the Royal stand. Instead he went to the Ring where his carriage was parked. He gave the bag to his manservant. 'Take it to the house.'

'Yes, my Lord.'

'Tell the steward to burn it.' He turned away. The evidence was destroyed, he was safe, and he would endure this tomfoolery in the park before returning to his town house to which, as his Lordship felt the need to prove his mastery of his world, he had summoned the Lady Camoynes to an early supper. And once she was used, he thought, there was the Prince's reception to attend. Lord Fenner, secure from scandal, had much to look forward to, but most of all he relished, with a piquant pleasure, the prospect of punishing Major Richard Sharpe for his damned insolence. He smiled, then took his seat once more in the Royal stand. The Review was about to begin.

The assembly area for the troops being reviewed, and who would, afterwards, perform their careful restaging of the battle of Vitoria, was to the north of the park. They would march past the Royal reviewing stand once, form up to the south by the King's private road, then march back with all bands playing behind the trophies that had been captured in Spain. The Eagles, eight of them, were to be carried in replicas of Roman chariots. They would follow the captured guns, going close to the Prince, circle to the north, then ride past the common folk in their enclosure. Some troops, men of the Middlesex militia, would stay to the south during the parade of trophies. Their task, eventually, was to play the role of the defeated French army.

At nine o'clock, long before Lord Fenner arrived, a young man in good country clothes had ridden into the assembly area. He looked, for all the world, like a squire's son, down for the season in London, and he cheerfully asked if anyone could direct him to Captain William Frederickson. No one could, for the Captain was in the Pyrenees, but the young man, so impressed by the officers' uniforms, seemed a welcome, if naive, admirer. He brought, too, a fine flask of brandy, and he chatted amiably with the junior officers, wished them joy of the day, and left when he had discovered the answers to all the questions Sharpe had posed to him.

'Well?' Sharpe greeted Price.

Lieutenant Price, changing out of a broadcloth coat into his red jacket, described the timetable of the day, the assembly areas, and gave the names of the parade's marshals.

Sharpe's moment was close now, and the fear was rising in

him like vomit. He clung to the desperate, foolish hope that Jane Gibbons might yet have rescued the ledgers, might yet be waiting in the park, but he knew such a hope was desperate. He must do what he had planned, and he must do it as if he knew he would win, for the soldier wins who believes in victory. Yet, victory or not, he would protect one man from defeat.

He went to Sergeant Major Harper. 'This is for you.'

Harper took the paper Sharpe gave him. 'What is it, sir?'

'A discharge. It says you were wounded at Vitoria.' Harper frowned. 'What would I want a discharge for?'

'Because, Patrick, either we're on our way to Spain tomorrow, or I'm in jail.'

'They won't jail you.'

'They will if they can. If it goes wrong, Patrick, get the hell out of it.'

'Run all over bloody Hyde Park with the Household Cavalry chasing me?' Harper laughed. 'Here.' He handed the discharge back.

'Keep it, and good luck.'

Sharpe reviewed his troops, his tattered, march-soiled troops, and, as the sun rose higher in a cloudless sky, he marched them south, through the leafy lanes from Hampstead towards London, and towards failure or the invasion of France.

The bands thumped and jangled, crashing out the good tunes of the army, and the troops marched in columns of half Companies past the Prince who, delighted by it all, raised a plump, gloved hand to answer their salutes. The swords of mounted officers flashed up as they rode past him, the Household Cavalry went by in a splendid jingle of curb chains with plumes tossing above their burnished helmets.

In front of the Royal stand, in three ranks, stood two

Companies of Foot Guards; the Royal bodyguard. Eight mounted officers flanked the line, carefully placed where their height would not obstruct the Royal view.

The Horse Artillery went past at such a pace that the earth seemed to thunder with their passing. Behind them, at a far more sedate trot, came a troop of Rocket Cavalry, the sticks of their curious weapons jutting up like sheafs of lances. The sight of them reminded the Prince that it had been Major Sharpe who had first proved their use against the French army, a use that the Prince had forecast and supported, and he twisted heavily in his chair to look for Lord John Rossendale. 'Sharpe here?'

'No, sir.'

'Deuced odd!' The Prince looked at his brother, the Commander in Chief of the Army. 'Got any of those fireworks in Spain, Freddie?'

The Duke of York did, but only at his brother's insistence. Like the rest of the army, he believed rockets to be a dangerous, mad invention. 'A few,' he grunted.

'Wish we could fire one now.'

'You can't. London's too valuable.'

The Prince laughed. He was having a fine time, dressed in his uniform and imagining that he was about to lead these splendid men into battle. He sometimes dreamed that Napoleon invaded England and no General was conveniently at hand, and so, mounted on his horse, the Prince himself led the Household troops to meet the Tyrant. He won, of course, and brought Napoleon caged to London. It was a fine dream. The cheers would ring in his head. 'Who's this?' He waved towards a Battalion of infantry that came behind the Rocket Troop.

Lord John Rossendale bent forward. '87th, sir, First Battalion. One of yours.'

'Mine?'

'Prince of Wales' Own Irish, sir.'

'Splendid!' He waved at them. 'Well done! Well done!' He turned back to Rossendale. 'How many Regiments do I have?'

'One of Dragoon guards, sir, two of Light Dragoons, and three Regiments of the line.'

The Prince heaved himself closer to his aide and dropped his voice so that he could only be heard five tiers away. 'And how many has he got?' He stuck a thumb towards his brother.

'Just one Irish Regiment, sir. The 101st.'

The Prince laughed and turned to his brother, the Duke of York. 'Hear that, Freddie?'

'I've got the whole damned army. And you're supposed to salute it.'

The Prince was enjoying himself. It was a splendid summer day and the crowd was remarkably friendly. For a change not a single jeer had greeted him, and the troops looked marvellous. He called for a glass of champagne, and waited for the parade of trophies.

Sharpe left the Edgware Road at the Polygon and marched his half Battalion west towards the Queen's Gate of Hyde Park.

There were few people in the streets, most having been drawn to the entertainment in the park, but a few urchins, shouldering sticks, fell in step with his men.

It was odd, Sharpe thought, how this felt like a wartime action. He had no permission to bring these troops to London, so he was, in effect, on enemy territory. His target lay to the south, but he was hooking round west to sneak up on it and, just as if this was a real surprise attack on an enemy's flank, he must stay hidden till the very last minutes.

He was leading his men through the smart, new houses of

Polygon Street, their facades brilliant white in the sunlight. Maids stared at the men from the black railings that guarded the cellar steps, and sometimes faces would peer from the curtained windows above. Sharpe, mounted on his horse, could see into the parlour windows and, thinking of his action as a secret approach march, he feared that he might lead his men past the house of a senior army officer who, like a French *tirailleur*, would ambush them.

They marched without singing. To many of these men, like Charlie Weller, this was their first sight of London. It astonished them. So many rich, high, ornate houses, so many people, so many kitchen chimneys, so much horse-dung, so many carriages, so much to look at and be amazed by. Houses as tall as church spires, rows of them, and never the comforting sight of hills and trees at the end of a street to remind a boy that the country was always a short walk away. Hyde Park, which was sometimes visible through streets to their left, was not countryside. It was a great expanse of rolling lawn, dotted with trees, just like the squire's park which was forbidden territory to any but the most impudent poachers.

They could hear the bands behind them and, sometimes, a cheer that would grow, swell, and fade on the breeze. A signal gun sounded, a blank charge of powder blasting into the hot, early afternoon air, and to Sharpe the sound was utterly familiar, while, to his men, it was an awesome reminder of what might face them in Spain and France.

They turned into the Queen's Gate. There was no one to challenge them. The urchins still accompanied the troops, shouting out the steps in imitation of the sergeants. One got too close to Sergeant Lynch and reeled off the road with a well-aimed clip to his ear. At the Serpentine, Sharpe called a halt and ordered the officers to gather round him.

All the officers were mounted. He trotted with them over

the grass, away from the four Companies. He was not sure of what he should say, but, now they were so close to the target, he expected trouble and these men had to know how to deal with it.

'We're here at the Prince Regent's invitation.' That shook them. It was not true, for the invitation hardly requested Sharpe to bring a stolen half Battalion with him, but the lie might give them confidence. 'However, there's been the usual army buggery so the parade marshals don't know about us. Understand?' They did not, but Sharpe's voice discouraged an exploration of the misunderstanding.

Captain Smith looked desperately worried, while Captain Carline, who had grumbled all week about the lack of comforts on the march, plucked at his uniform in an attempt to make it look fit for Royalty.

Sharpe felt a sudden terror of what he was about to do. 'If any officer, I don't care how senior, demands to know why you're here, refer them to me. That's all you do! Send them to me. My orders are the only ones you obey. Mine only!'

'What are our orders, sir?' Captain Smith asked nervously.

'There is to be a re-enactment of the battle of Vitoria. Our orders are to take part in that. We're to be the French. We stay in close order, you listen for my commands, and you ignore all others! As French troops today we don't obey British officers.' He grinned, and some men grinned with him. D'Alembord and Price, who knew the truth of it, looked solemn.

'We ignore senior officers, sir?' Captain Smith frowned. 'Can we do that, sir?'

Sharpe had been offering carrots all week, now, he thought, it was time for a bitterer diet. 'You do what I say, Captain, just what I say. Every god-damned officer from Foulness has deserved worse than you're going to get. Your only chance of survival, of honour, lies in my hands. So don't upset me, or I will recommend your dismissals, trials, and imprisonment.' That, after Sharpe's friendliness of the past days, brought silence.

None of them, except d'Alembord and Price, knew what he did. Yet the habit of obedience was strong in them so that, until an officer more senior than Sharpe gave them conflicting orders, they would obey him. That was what had brought Sharpe this far with their dubious help, but now he was taking them into a place that teemed with senior officers, with more Generals than Wellington had Battalions, and, for these crucial hours, he had to bind their obedience with something other than mere habit. He used the threat, and he trusted the threat would keep them docile.

He twisted to stare at the Review. He could see the Ring and, flanking it, the two lines of carriages. No one looked his way. He was far from the Hyde Park Gate, but he could see no golden-haired girl in that direction, only a few grooms who exercised horses behind the carriage parks and who thought nothing strange this day about soldiers waiting by the Serpentine. Sharpe stared a long time, looking for Jane Gibbons, but he did not see her. He turned back. 'The main thing, gentlemen, is to enjoy this.'

'Enjoy it, sir?' Smith asked.

'Of course, Captain. We're going to win a battle.' Sharpe laughed, though he felt despair too. 'To your Companies, gentlemen!' She had not come. She had not come, and his best hope was gone. Now he must fight.

Sharpe took his place at the head of his men. He was glad to hear the bands playing for it filled him with the right warlike spirit. The music; heart-stirring martial tunes, came faint over the park's grassland, and the big drums punched the warm air like cannon-fire. Regimental Sergeant Major Harper, marching

Sharpe's force towards the Review, unconsciously called the steps to match the music's rhythm. The men marched in silence, muskets shouldered, and, though they marched in the heart of England itself, they were marching to war.

CHAPTER NINETEEN

Jane Gibbons' journey to London had not been hard, a carter from Great Wakering had carried her to Rochford, and from there she had paid to travel in a stage that dropped her at Charing Cross, but London filled her with dread. She had visited it before, but never on her own, and she knew no one. She had money, eight of the guineas were left of those that, in a dew-wet dawn, she had rescued from the table in the pergola.

She carried two bags, a reticule, a parasol, and Rascal was on a leash. She was glad of the small white dog. The smells of the city were strange, the people frightening, and the noise overwhelming. She had never seen so many cripples. On her previous visits, insulated from the misery by the glass windows of her uncle's coach, she had not realised how much horror stirred and shuffled on London's pavements. She stooped to pat the dog. 'It's all right, Rascal, it's all right.' She wondered how she was to find him food, let alone shelter for herself.

'Missy!'

She looked up to see a well-dressed man tipping his hat to her. 'Sir?'

'You look lost, Missy. From out of town?'

'Yes, sir.'

'And in need of lodgings, I warrant?' He smiled, and because three of his teeth were missing and the others so blackened that it was hard to see them, she shuddered. He stooped for her large bag. 'You'll allow me to carry it?'

'Leave it!'

'Now, Miss, I can tell . . .'

'No!' Her voice attracted curious glances. She turned away from the man, struggling with her ungainly luggage and wondering whether it had been truly necessary to pack so many dresses, as well as the silver-backed hair-brushes and the picture of the boats she liked so much. She had her jewellery, those small few pieces of her mother's that Sir Henry had not taken, and she had her parents' portraits. She had the first two cantos of *Childe Harold*, her paints, and a vast iron flintlock pistol taken from her uncle's library wall which she was not sure would work, and for which she had no ammunition, but which she thought might frighten away any assailants. She lugged it all west, past the Royal Mews where, it was said, a great space would be made to commemorate Nelson and Trafalgar. She turned into Whitehall.

Twice again men offered her lodgings. Clean lodgings, they said, respectable, run by a gentlewoman, but Jane Gibbons was not so foolish as to accept. Other men smiled at her, struck by her innocence and beauty, and it was those errant looks, as much as the bolder approach of the pimps, that drove her to seek refuge.

She chose sensibly. She picked her helpers as carefully as Richard Sharpe chose his battlegrounds, and the chosen pair was a gaitered cleric, red-faced and amiable, and his middle-aged wife who, like her husband, gaped at the London sights.

Jane explained that she had been sent to London by her mother, there to meet her father, but he had not been on the Portsmouth stage and she feared he might not now come until the next day. She had money, she explained, and wished no

299

charity, but merely to be directed to a clean, safe place where she might sleep.

The Reverend and Mrs Octavius Godolphin were staying in Tothill Street, at Mrs Paul's Lodgings, a most respectable house that ministered to the visiting clergy, and the Reverend and Mrs Godolphin, whose children were grown and gone from home, were delighted to offer their sheltering wings to Miss Gibbons. A cab was summoned, Mrs Paul was introduced, and nothing would suffice but that Miss Gibbons should accompany them to evensong and then share a shoulder of lamb for which they would not dream of taking payment. She went safe to bed, secured from an evil world by the multiplicity of bolts and bars on Mrs Paul's front door, and the Reverend Godolphin reminded her to say her prayers for her father's safe journey on the morrow. It all seemed, to Jane, like a great adventure.

The next morning, Saturday morning, when prayers had been said around Mrs Paul's great table, Jane persuaded the Reverend and Mrs Godolphin that she had no need of their company to wait at Charing Cross. The persuasion was hard, but she achieved it and, leaving her luggage and Rascal under the watchful eye of Mrs Paul, she took a cab to her uncle's house.

She watched the house from the street corner, half hidden by plane trees, and after a half-hour she saw her uncle leave in his open carriage. Her heart was thumping as she walked down Devonshire Terrace and as she pulled the shiny knob that rang a bell deep in the house. She saw soldiers marching at the end of the street, going towards the Queen's Gate of the park, then the door behind her opened. 'Miss Jane!'

'Good morning.' She smiled at Cross, her uncle's London butler. 'My uncle sent me to fetch some books for him.'

'This is a surprise!' Cross, a timid man, smiled as he beckoned her inside. 'He did not mention that you were in London.'

'We're with Mrs Grey's sister. Isn't the weather lovely?'

'It won't last, Miss Jane. Some books, you said?'

'Big red account books. I expect they're in the study, Cross.'

'Leather books?'

'Yes. The ones he brings to Paglesham every month.'

'But I distinctly remember the master took them with him. Just now!'

She stared at him, feeling all her hopes crumble. She had so wanted to do this thing for Major Sharpe, a man who had given her hope and pleasure if only because of her uncle's enmity towards him. 'He took them?' Her voice was faint.

'Indeed, Miss Jane!'

'Cross!' A voice barked. 'My boots, Cross! Where the devil are my boots?' Lieutenant Colonel Bartholomew Girdwood opened the parlour door and stared into the hall. His eyes widened. 'Jane?'

But she had gone. She snatched open the heavy door, threw herself down the steps, and ran as if every pimp in London chased her.

'Jane!' Girdwood shouted from the top step, but she had gone. Far away, from the park, he heard the music which reminded him that he was late for the Review. Damned strange, he thought, but he had never truly understood women. Women, dogs and the Irish. All unnecessary things that got in the way. 'God-damn it, where are my boots? Is the cab coming?'

'It's been sent for, Colonel, it's been sent for.' Cross brought the boots and helped the Colonel dress for the great celebration of the battle of Vitoria which, this fine day, would grace the Royal park.

The massed bands played the inevitable 'Rule Britannia' as the French trophies were paraded about Hyde Park. Enemy guns, a mere fraction of the artillery that Wellington had captured, led the procession that was bright with the flags and guidons that were the lesser standards of the French. The flags were serried in colourful abundance, but it was the eight Eagles, brightly polished and held erect in gaudy chariots, that fetched the warmest applause.

Each French Regiment was given an Eagle standard. Not all of those on display had been taken in battle. Two, Sharpe knew, had been found in a captured French fortress, neither of them incised with their regimental numbers, obviously stored against the day when they might be needed for fresh units. One had been thrown from a high bridge by a trapped French unit, and it had taken days of diving by Spanish peasants to bring the trophy up from the river bed. They had presented it to Wellington and now, as if it had been taken in battle, it was solemnly paraded past the Prince of Wales.

The others had been fought for. There was the Eagle of Barossa, captured by the Irish 87th, which, like the Talavera Eagle, had been taken by a sergeant and an officer together. Harper stared at the distant procession. 'Which one's ours, sir?'

'The first one.'

Captain Hamish Smith, seeing for the first time the distant gleam of a French Eagle, looked in some awe at the two Riflemen. They had actually done that most splendid thing, brought an enemy Colour from a battlefield, and no soldier, however grubby his career, could fail to be moved.

'We've captured more than eight,' Harper said cheerfully.

'More, RSM?' Smith asked.

'There was two taken at Sally-manker, sir, but the lads broke one of them up, so they did. Thought it was gold! I heard of another one sold to an officer. Be murder if anyone found out!'

Sharpe laughed. He had heard the rumours, but had never known if they were true.

He had marched the half Battalion across the Serpentine bridge, then turned eastwards along the King's private road. He had stared towards the Hyde Park Gate, but Jane Gibbons was not there. He told himself that he had not expected to see her, which was true, but he was disappointed just the same. Now the men were at the southern assembly field, deserted by all the troops except some disconsolate militia who today had to pretend to be the French. They wore grubby blue fatigue jackets and carried red, white and blue tricolours; miserable thin flags run up for the day and which were doubtless destined to be captured before the afternoon was done.

The rest of the parade troops were at the northern assembly area, drawing themselves up for the magnificent advance, with artillery flanking, which was supposed to represent the final stage of Vitoria when Wellington's army, stretched across a river plain, had swept the French in chaos from Spain.

The trophies were at the northern end of the review ground. They had gone past the Prince, the Duke, the carriage parks, and now they were carried by the Battalions of the Review before turning back to be displayed to the packed public enclosure.

'Sir?' Harper's voice was a warning.

An infantry captain, harassed and hot, was trotting his horse towards them. He carried a sheaf of papers. Sharpe kicked his heels to meet the man halfway. 'Fine day!'

The captain could not distinguish Sharpe's rank. He frowned at the South Essex's yellow facings and looked with shock at the faded, tattered uniform Sharpe wore.

'You're . . . ?'

'Major Richard Sharpe. You?'

'Sir? Mellors, sir.' The captain threw a hasty salute. 'Sharpe, sir?' He sounded uncertain.

'Yes. All going well, Mellors?'

'Absolutely, sir. You're . . .' The captain hesitated.

'What's the news from Spain?'

'Spain, sir?' Captain Mellors was understandably confused. 'Wellington threw them back, sir. Over the Pyrenees.'

'Splendid! We in France yet?'

'Not that I've heard.'

Thank God for that, Sharpe thought. He wanted to be back in Pasajes before the British marched north. 'Carry on, Captain! Well done!'

Mellors blinked. 'You're sure you're supposed to be here, sir?' He was staring at the South Essex. Without their stocks, and with their uniforms stained by the week's marching, they looked an unlikely unit to be brought to this Royal Review.

'Absolutely!' Sharpe smiled. 'Colonel Blount's orders. Someone has to clear up after this lot.'

'Of course, sir.' The explanation made Captain Mellors much happier. Blount, as Harry Price had discovered, was in charge of the day's arrangements, and it made sense to the Captain that some troops had to have the fatigue of clearing the equipment from the park. 'You'll excuse me, sir, but you are the . . . ?'

'Yes.' Sharpe interrupted him, and nodded towards the gaudy chariot that led the parade of captured standards down the line of cheering public. 'That's mine.'

Mellors beamed. 'Might I shake your hand, sir?'

Sharpe shook hands. 'You don't mind if my men watch from here, do you?'

'Of course not, sir.' Mellors was only too eager to please a man who had actually captured one of the trophies.

'Warn your fellows that we're here.'

'Of course, sir.' Mellors saluted again. 'It's an honour to have met you, sir.' But Sharpe was not listening. He was staring

304

eastwards and his face was suddenly lit with a pleasure so great that Mellors twisted in his saddle. 'My word, sir!'

She was dishevelled, hot, worn out by running, but she could still elicit admiration. She was beautiful. Sharpe kicked his heels back. 'Jane!'

'Suffering Christ have mercy on us.' Regimental Sergeant Major Harper saw his officer swing from the saddle to clasp the girl into his arms. 'Bloody hell!'

'Sergeant Major?' Captain Smith was nervous.

Harper sniffed. 'Not my place to criticise officers, sir,' which he usually said when he did, 'but you'll notice there's a woman here, sir, and women and Mr Sharpe are not the gentlest mixture in the world. Trouble, sir! Trouble!'

'It's Sir Henry's girl!'

'That's what I said. Trouble.' Harper swivelled to face the half Battalion. 'Take your bloody heathen eyes off her! You've seen women before! Eyes front!'

She was panting, exhausted by her journey through London, and she was in his arms. She struggled to speak through her laboured breath. 'He's got them.'

'You came.'

'He's got them!'

'He's got what?'

'The books!'

'It doesn't matter.' Nothing mattered at this moment except that she was here, where the cut grass was fragrant, where he almost trembled as he stared at her. 'You came!' He had not known such happiness could exist, something insane and blossoming, something to fill a world.

'I had to. He was there, you see. He's put tar on it again. It's so horrid.' She laughed, as filled with stupid, bubbling happiness as he was. 'My uncle's got the books.'

'It doesn't matter.'

She looked at his jacket, torn and patched, still marked with his dried blood and the blood of enemies. 'That's terrible!'

'It's the jacket I fight in.'

She fingered a rent. 'I can see why you want a wife.'

He held her still, his arms on her shoulders, and for a few seconds he thought he could not speak.

'You mean?' She said nothing, and he could hear nothing but her breath, feel nothing but her body, see nothing but her eyes.

'Jane?'

'I can't go back. Ever.'

'I don't want you to.'

'I mean we shouldn't.'

'No.'

'I don't know you.'

'No.'

'But I will marry you.' She looked so solemnly at him, he blinked, and for this glorious moment there was no war, and no crimping, and no bands playing, just her eyes and a happiness that was greater than he thought he could manage. He swallowed. 'I would be most honoured.'

'And I, Mr Sharpe.'

There was an awkward silence. He smiled. 'I thought I had offended you.'

'It was sudden, I was frightened.' She bit her lower lip. 'But I did hope you'd ask.'

He laughed, awkward still, then turned. 'Sergeant Major!'

'Sir!' Harper did not walk to Sharpe, he marched. He did it as though the eyes of the guards were on him, as though he came to take the surrender of the Emperor of the French himself. He stamped to attention and his hand snapped into a crisp salute. 'Sir!'

'You remember Miss Gibbons, Sergeant Major.'

'I do, sir.' He winked at her, an outrageous gesture.

'We are to be married.'

'Very good, sir.'

'And when we advance, Sergeant Major, I want a good man left with her. Private Weller, perhaps?'

'Very good, sir.'

'Advance?' Jane looked up at him.

Sharpe took a deep breath as he plunged back into this desperation. 'We have no proof of the auctions. I need these men, otherwise a Regiment dies. I have to do something,' he paused, looking for the right word, 'dramatic.'

'He means foolish, Miss,' Harper said helpfully.

'I see,' she smiled.

Sharpe detected an unhealthy alliance developing already between these two, a repartee at his expense, but he ploughed on. 'I need to prove these men exist, that they are not a paper Battalion, and I need a powerful ally against my enemies. You understand?'

'Entirely. What will you do?'

'I intend,' he said grandly, 'to place the men under the protection of the Prince Regent.'

'He's here?'

Sharpe took out his telescope, extended its tubes, and propped it on the saddle of his horse so that she could see the Prince where he inspected the soldiers who would re-enact the battle.

'He's very fat.' She took her eye away and looked at the telescope itself, a gorgeous instrument encased in a barrel of ivory and gold. She read the French inscription aloud. '"To Joseph, King of Spain and the Indies, from his brother, Napoleon, Emperor of France." Richard!' It was the first time she had used his name. 'Where did you get it?'

It had been a gift from the Marquesa, but Sharpe thought that was better unsaid. 'At Vitoria.'

'It really belonged to King Joseph?'

'It did. Would you like it?'

'Only when I've bought you another. Do you think Napoleon held this?'

'I'm sure.'

A gun fired at the far end of the field, startling pigeons into the sky. The Prince and his entourage were back in the pavilion. A trumpet blared, drumsticks fell onto taut skins, and the militia started forward. Mounted officers with speaking trumpets announced to the separate crowds that they watched the advance of the French army, to which event the spectators in their carriages gave polite applause and the public enclosure lusty jeers. The militia had to split in their advance, to pass either side of the trophies which now were parked in a solid phalanx to the south of the review ground. Seeing them there made Sharpe remember the Colours that Sir Henry had purloined to display in his house. He turned and looked at his men. It would do them good to march beneath a standard.

'Patrick?'

'Sir?'

'If you need me, I'm over there!' He pointed to the trophies. 'Would you look after Miss Gibbons?' He smiled at her, left the telescope in her hands, then pulled himself into his saddle.

Harper looked down on Jane. 'I'm very happy for you, Miss.'

She smiled so beautifully that he truly was. 'What's he doing, Sergeant?'

'There are some times, Miss, when I don't ask, I just pray.'

She laughed, and Harper began to think she might even be a good thing for his officer who now reined in beside the trophies in their chariots.

The 'chariots' were mere two-wheeled carts that had been tricked out with painted cardboard. They were parked in front of the gleaming French guns, each with its wreathed 'N' on the barrel that made Sharpe think of Spain and the number of times he had faced such guns. Some of these captured guns had tried to kill him, perhaps at Badajoz or Salamanca, yet now they stood, polished and docile, in a London park. He shouted to the men with the standards, 'Who's in charge?'

A major frowned at him. 'Who the devil are you?'

'Sharpe. Major Richard Sharpe, and I'll trouble you to be civil. I'm here for that!' He pointed at his Eagle, a green laurel wreath draped about its plinth, its one wing still bent where he had killed a man with it.

'You can't . . .' the major started.

Sharpe produced the embossed, engraved invitation card, unfolded it, and waved it at the major. 'Orders of His Royal Highness!'

'Who did you say you were?'

Sharpe smiled. It was pleasant, sometimes, to use the prestige that the Eagle had given to him. 'I'm the man who captured it.'

'Sharpe?'

'Yes.' The happiness of Jane's arrival still worked in him. He could not fail now! She was going to marry him, and that was a token of success, of a victory greater than this Eagle.

The major was torn between his orders, which were not to let a single captured trophy out of his sight, and this privilege of meeting the man who had provided the first of these Eagles. Sharpe's uniform disturbed him, but the engraved card seemed impressive. Sharpe smiled again. 'It's all nonsense, of course, but Prinny wants to see us with it.'

Understanding dawned on the major. 'Those are your men?'

'Yes.'

'And you're showing him what they looked like in Spain, eh?'

'Exactly.'

'Splendid.' The major smiled. 'You'll bring it back?'

'I did before, Major.'

The major laughed, gave the order, and the Eagle was handed to Sharpe who, hoisting it up, and almost wishing that it had its magnificent flag attached to the staff, galloped with it to his men. It would go into battle one last time. He smiled at Jane. 'There.' He lowered it so she could touch it. 'Napoleon handled that as well.'

'This is the one you captured?'

'With Patrick.' He tossed the standard to the Irishman. 'Harps! Here!'

The officers from Foulness crowded about it, then Harper paraded it down the ragged ranks, letting men touch it, letting them take from it some of the magic of a far-off battle. Only Sergeant Lynch showed an ostentatious disinterest in the trophy, turning his back and walking some yards away from Harper's triumphant progress.

Sharpe watched what happened to his north. The militia had formed a line across the great rectangular arena, and now he heard the bands strike up from the far side of the park, and he knew that the moment was close. Timing now, as in every battle, was everything. 'Jane? You'll have to stay here.'

'You're nervous.'

He smiled. 'Yes. But I'll be back.'

'And afterwards?'

'We go to Spain.' He twisted in the saddle. 'RSM?'

'Sir?'

'Private Weller to his duty, the Eagle to me, and form columns of half Companies!'

'Sir!'

Now he must forget Jane Gibbons. Now, like any married officer in Spain, he must leave her behind and fight his battle. He took the staff of the trophy and propped it on his right boot so that the glittering Eagle was above his head. 'Fix swords!'

In his nervousness he gave the old command of the Rifles. He saw the puzzled faces. 'Fix bayonets!' If it was to be done, then let it be done in style.

They made a tight formation, eight half Companies paraded one behind the other, with Sharpe at their head. D'Alembord led the first Company, Price the last, so that Sharpe's loyal officers, the ones most likely to take the wrath of the marshals, were on the outer edges of his formation. He looked once at Jane, then raised his voice again. 'The South Essex will advance!'

There was a cheer from the crowd which meant that the British forces were marching from the northern assembly area. The guns fired a powder charge for the last time, their smoke drifting realistically over the grass, and the militia, their muskets unloaded, pretended to aim and fire at the gorgeous array of men, brilliantly uniformed, polished, and drilled, who advanced with bayonets and muskets beneath their great, splendid flags.

Sharpe gathered the reins of his horse. 'By the right! Quick march!'

The half Battalion of the South Essex marched.

There were two thousand soldiers in this place, all of them prinked and gleaming, and into their midst, without orders, Sharpe was marching fewer than three hundred scruffy, dirty men beneath a standard of the enemy.

No one noticed them, except for the major in charge of the trophies who raised a hand in friendly salute.

They marched. Harper called out the step, his voice loud and confident. One of the militia sergeants turned, looked at them, and wondered why the column of men which, though he did not know it, looked like a French attack formation, approached so menacingly from his rear.

Sharpe was leading them to the centre line of the review

ground. The militia were falling back, leaving a few men pretending to be dead on the ground. A militia officer noticed Sharpe.

They were well in view of all the stands now, of all the spectators, but all eyes were on the splendid advance of the British troops, Colours flying, whose bands filled the park with the music of triumph. Only the militia, seeing the column coming to their rear, were glancing nervously behind like troops fearing encirclement on a battlefield.

The marshals suddenly saw them. Sharpe saw two coming, saw the turf flung up behind the galloping hooves, and he called back to Harper to speed the march, to close the half Companies, and this was the challenge, this was the moment he had planned. Now, just as in battle, he had to close his ears to everything that might distract him, ignore everything that was not concerned with his victory. He did this for the men in Pasajes, for the men who lay in graves across Spain, for the girl who watched him.

'You! Who are you?' It was a cavalry captain, standing in his stirrups and bellowing the angry challenge.

Sharpe ignored the man. 'Clear ranks! Clear ranks!' He shouted the order at the militia ahead of him, using a voice which had been forged on parade grounds and practised on battlefields.

'Halt!' A colonel was beside him now. 'Halt your men! I order it!'

'Prince's orders! Out the way!' Sharpe snarled it. He hefted the Eagle higher, and the colonel, thinking that the metal trophy was about to strike at him, sheered his horse to one side.

'Who the devil are you?'

'King Joseph of Spain. Now bugger off!' Sharpe's voice was vicious, his face a savage mask. The curse astonished the colonel, then Sharpe forced his horse into the widening gap that the splitting militia men were making for him. 'Close up, Sergeant! Close up!'

The field was shouts and music, blank muskets peppering the air with smoke, and Sharpe shouted the order again, the commonest order of all on a battlefield when files have been flung down by cannon-fire and men shuffle towards the centre of the line and load their guns. 'Close up! Close up!

The colonel was spurring after him, but Sharpe was not looking at the man. He was watching the approaching infantry instead, judging how long it would take them to cover the one hundred yards that separated them from the front of his column. 'Left wheel! Smartly now!' The colonel tried to grab Sharpe's rein, but the Eagle swung at the colonel's horse, striking it over the face so that the beast swerved, reared, and Sharpe was clear. 'Close ranks! Close ranks!'

He had driven a path of destruction through the carefully reconstructed battle. Instead of the minutely rehearsed defeat, the 'enemy' now seemed to be fighting back, bursting through the centre of the line to advance against the astonished victors.

'Stop!' the colonel shouted. More marshals were spurring towards the small, ragged column that suddenly, to Sharpe's bellowed orders, wheeled left to march directly towards the Royal pavilion. 'March! Heads up! March!' Sharpe put the Eagle, with the horse's reins, into his left hand and, with a surge of excitement because he could see his target now, the object of these days of marching and hiding, he drew his great sword. His horse, unused to such commotion, stepped in small, nervous steps, and Sharpe pressed his knees against its flanks to keep it going steadily towards the Prince Regent.

The Royal bodyguard stared in shock at the men who approached them. The right flank of the British advance, loud with cavalry calls, checked because their way was blocked, while the left flank, unobstructed, kept marching forward to throw the whole practised symmetry of the advance into skewed disorder. Four officers now screamed at Sharpe, one shouted at the South Essex to halt, but Harper's voice was louder than any of the marshals and, despite the nervous glances of their officers, the men marched on. Sharpe was ahead of them. He could see the Prince now, and a man beside him who could only be the Duke of York, and he half turned and shouted the next order at Harper. 'Deploy!'

They formed line, facing and outflanking the bodyguard, and Sharpe could see the consternation in the Royal stand as men realised that this careful day had been driven into chaos by the dirty, unkempt troops who, with fixed bayonets, now faced the Regent of England, his brother, and the cream of society. The Prince, standing now, was twenty yards from Sharpe, staring at the mounted officer who held the French Eagle high in the air.

'Guards!' An officer on the flank of the bodyguard who feared that a volley of musketry was about to soak the Royal stand in blood, shouted at his men to load their weapons.

Sharpe ignored the threat. He rested the sword on his saddle, took off his shako, and stared at the Prince who, recognition dawning, smiled with sudden delight. Sharpe looked down to Harper. 'RSM? Now!'

This was the manoeuvre they had practised, the manoeuvre never before seen on a battlefield or parade ground, and Sharpe's men did it before the astonished eyes of the Foot Guards whose ramrods were still thrusting down the unnecessary bullets. The Royal stand, Lord Fenner, the whole bright array of the disordered parade watched as the strange, scruffy troops grounded muskets and, to the orders of a massive sergeant, removed their shakos.

Sixty white chickens had given the men a splendid meal and a fine flock of feathers. Each man had been issued with three white feathers, which now, like Sharpe, they pushed behind the badges of their shakos so that, after a few seconds, when the shakos were back on the men's heads, each wore the badge of the Prince of Wales white against their black headgear.

The Prince was charmed by the feathers. The Duke of York stared in fury. Sergeant Harper shouted the command for the general salute.

Sharpe had no proof that this Battalion had been stolen, that its masters were criminals, so now he was trying to put these men under the protection of the Prince Regent, of the fat man who nodded with pleasure as Sharpe lowered the Eagle in submissive homage. Sharpe, who could prove nothing against Lord Fenner, would harness the immense patronage and influence of the Regent of Britain and, even though the Prince Regent had no formal power over the army or the War Office, Sharpe could not see how his enemies could prevail over the Prince's wishes. Sharpe was presenting these men to the Prince in the hope that the Prince would become their ally and protector, and the Prince was delighted. 'What Battalion is it, Rossendale?'

Lord John Rossendale saw the yellow facings. He trained the Prince's spyglass on one of the shakos so that he could see the badge of the chained eagle. 'South Essex, sir.' He said it with some astonishment, remembering that Lord Fenner had denied the Battalion's corporeal existence.

'Mine now, eh? Mine! Splendid!' Sharpe, his sword held vertically in the salute, could not hear the Prince. Jane Gibbons, sharing the telescope with Charlie Weller, clapped as she saw the feathers on the shakos.

''Talion!' Sergeant Harper's voice rode over the protests of the massing marshals. 'Three cheers for His Royal Highness! Hip, hip, hip!'

They cheered. Some of the feathers drooped or fell, but it did not matter, the Prince was charmed. 'Major Sharpe!'

Sharpe knew his victory was not complete. He must talk to the Prince. He saw the beckoning fat hand and tried to push his horse forward to lay the Eagle before his Prince, but other orders were being shouted, and mounted men were pressing about his horse. A colonel of the Blues snatched the Eagle from him and a major wrestled for his sword. Another hand seized his bridle and pulled him away from the Royal pavilion.

'Major Sharpe!' The Prince called again, but the Rifleman was surrounded by marshals and officers, angry mounted men who jostled him away.

'Your Royal Highness?' Lord Fenner had hurried along the tier of seats. 'Your Royal Highness?'

'Fenner!'

'I trust your Royal Highness liked our small display.' Lord Fenner, seeing the Prince's happiness, was thinking fast.

'Monstrous good, Fenner! I like it! The men who took the Eagle, eh? Dressed as they were that day. I do like it, indeed, yes. Thank you, Fenner! I like it very much! Rossendale!'

'Sir?'

The Prince was trying to see Sharpe in the confusion, but there were too many mounted men. 'Tell Major Sharpe I expect him at our reception this night.'

'Of course, sir.'

The Duke of York, appalled at the shambles that had been made of his display, ignored his elder brother's delight. 'He's under arrest! Maxwell!'

A full General of the Guards came close.

'Take him to the Horse Guards now! I'll have his damned

head for this, by God I will!' He turned to Fenner. 'What the devil's going on, Fenner?'

'I think I can explain, your Royal Highness.' Lord Fenner smiled pacifically. He watched General Maxwell ordering an escort for Sharpe, and Lord Fenner, seeing the arrest, knew that Sharpe had gambled and lost.

'What is happening, Freddy?' the Prince asked plaintively.

'Not a god-damn thing.' The Duke of York signalled the marshals to extricate the parade from its sudden chaos and carry on with the battle. He turned and waved his fat hands at the spectators in the Royal stand who, alarmed for their safety, stood in confused worry. 'Nothing to worry you, nothing to worry you at all! Sit!' He plumped himself down, face outraged, as an example to the spectators.

Sharpe had marched a flank march, surprised the enemy, and lost. His escort closed about him and hurried from the field. He had not reached the Prince, he had failed.

While across the park, puzzled and hot, the Reverend and Mrs Octavius Godolphin agreed what a pickle the regular army had made of the afternoon! Not nearly so smart as the local Fencibles on parade! And to come all this way just to see muddle and shambolic chaos? Thank God for the Navy, the Reverend Godolphin fervently thought, then took his wife to Mrs Paul's for tea.

CHAPTER TWENTY

The room was upstairs in the Horse Guards. It was a large room, comfortably furnished, its papered walls hung with maps of fortresses and its chairs upholstered in fine leather. Expensive white candles burned pure, still flames above tables and desks.

Lord Fenner, papers spread before him, sat in the place of honour. At his side stood General Sir Barstan Maxwell, his round face still scarlet with fury at this upstart Rifleman who had destroyed the carefully rehearsed celebrations. At a side table, well lit by the tall candles, a clerk scratched down the records of the proceedings. Behind them all, in a deep, comfortable window, sat Sir Henry Simmerson whose joy at this humiliation of Richard Sharpe was complete. Downstairs, in the courtyard of the Horse Guards, Girdwood guarded Sir Henry's niece who had been found stranded in the park with a common soldier. This night, Sir Henry had promised her, she would be flogged till her bones were chalk.

Major Richard Sharpe stood in the room's centre. His sword, rifle and telescope lay on the wide table before Lord Fenner.

He had gained, though it was very cold comfort to him, a partial victory. He had saved the Battalion. He had produced it before the Commander in Chief, indelibly impressed its existence upon the Prince Regent, and there could be no denials now that it was merely a holding Battalion, a paper convenience for the administration. Within the last hour, together with a formal invitation for Major Sharpe to attend Carlton House this evening, there had come a paper, magnificently sealed, which said it was His Royal Highness the Prince Regent's pleasure that, henceforth, the South Essex Regiment should be known as the Prince of Wales' Own Volunteers. An accompanying letter thanked Lord Fenner for the moment of pleasure that the donning of the feathers had given to His Royal Highness, and reminded Lord Fenner of the reception that would be held that night at Carlton House. Fenner intended to be present, but, before leaving the Horse Guards, he would destroy this impudent man who had defied him. 'You had orders to return to Spain, Major Sharpe.' His nasal, precise voice was quiet. 'You disobeyed.'

'You know why.'

Fenner's long white fingers tapped the papers on his desk. 'Your insolence is noted.' The clerk's pen scratched ominously as Fenner looked at his own notes. 'You failed to obey an order, Major, that directed you to our army in Spain. That is tantamount to desertion.'

'And you're a bloody crimp, and that's robbery.'

'Silence!' General Sir Barstan Maxwell thumped the table with his fist, shaking the tall candles so that their flames shivered. 'You are an officer! Try to behave like a gentleman!'

Sharpe looked at the General, a Guardsman. 'These gentlemen, sir, have been disguising a Battalion as a holding unit, crimping the men to their own profit, and stealing their wages.'

Lord Fenner gave an easy, soft laugh. He leaned back in his chair and waved at the clerk who, frightened by the sudden thump on the table, had stopped writing. 'Write it down, man, write it all down! Write that Major Sharpe is formally accusing His Majesty's Secretary of State at War of "crimping" – is that the right word, Major?'

'Thievery will do.'

'Write that as well! You can, of course, substantiate these accusations, Major?' Fenner smiled. Sir Henry snorted, and General Sir Barstan Maxwell glared at Sharpe.

Sharpe could not. He had thought that by putting himself under the Prince of Wales' protection he would be safe from any proceedings such as these, but he had misjudged the situation. He had misjudged it terribly, and he knew that in this lavish, expensive room his career had come to an ignoble end. Not just his career, but that great bubble of happiness that he had experienced with Jane. There could be no marriage now. Sir Henry had crowed that she was in his carriage, that she would return home, that she was not for him. Sharpe, who had worked to disgrace these men so that Girdwood could not marry Jane Gibbons, was to be broken instead.

Another clerk knocked at the door, entered the room and, without looking at Sharpe, just as a jury would not look at a condemned man, carried a leather folder of papers to the desk. He selected one sheet and gave it to Fenner who read it, signed it swiftly, then looked up at Sharpe. 'That letter, Major Sharpe, informs His Royal Highness that you cannot, by my orders, attend on him this night. Nor indeed on any other night. Give me the postings!' He took another piece of paper from the clerk, ran his finger down the list, and stabbed with his nail. 'That one.'

'Very good, my Lord.'

'Write it now!'

'Of course, my Lord.' The clerk withdrew.

A clock chimed eight in the corridor outside. Lord Fenner smiled. 'The Prince of Wales' Own Volunteers,' he said the new name with a sneer, 'will proceed forthwith to Spain, Major, but not with your presence. They will be commanded by Lieutenant Colonel Bartholomew Girdwood. I am sure that under his command they will acquit themselves nobly.'

'Indeed so,' Sir Henry interjected. It had been his idea that Girdwood should be given command of the First Battalion and that he should take to Spain, along with the trained men from Foulness, the officers from the disbanded camp. He and Lord Fenner, reluctantly but sensibly, had agreed that, because the Battalion had surfaced so dramatically, it would be prudent to abandon the business of selling recruits. They would not, they convinced themselves, lose much money thereby. The war could not last long. The northern allies had agreed to fight again, France was beleaguered, and Fenner was certain that peace was within sight. He and Simmerson had made themselves a tidy fortune, and now, thanks to Sharpe's arrest, they could avoid all scandal.

Sharpe said nothing. There was nothing to say.

'You, Major Sharpe,' Fenner stared at him with triumph and distaste, 'have a new posting. You will leave in two days' time, and until then, Major, you are under arrest. You will be captain of a convict guard in Australia.'

Sir Henry Simmerson could not suppress a bark of sudden laughter. 'There are no tailors in Australia; you should feel most welcome!'

Fenner smiled at the jest and looked at Sir Barstan Maxwell. 'The Duke will agree?'

'He will think it far too lenient, my Lord.' Maxwell sniffed. 'But if you propose it, he will agree.'

'I am being lenient,' Lord Fenner said magnanimously, 'because it is undeniable that Major Sharpe has served his country well. We must all hope, General, that a sea voyage will restore his wits.'

'The Duke will be so informed.' General Sir Barstan Maxwell, who would have preferred to see Sharpe hanged, drawn and quartered, sounded grudging. Nevertheless, a posting to Australia was tantamount to a prison sentence. Sharpe would never return, he would be forgotten.

'Good.' Fenner closed the silver lid of an inkpot with a snap. 'Your orders are being written now, Major. You will wait in the guardroom for them. Ah! It seems they're here already!' There had been a discreet knock on the door. 'Come!'

It was indeed the clerk who had been instructed to draw up Sharpe's orders, but, instead of bringing them to the desk, he hovered uncertainly at the door. 'My Lord?'

'You have the orders?'

'They're being written, my Lord. It's your wife, I fear. I did say your Lordship was not to be disturbed, but she is most insistent.'

'Very insistent.' The voice, precise and confident, came from the door. Fenner, who was unmarried, stared in consternation, not at the clerk, but at the woman, tall and green-eyed, smiling sweetly, who walked into the room and imperiously waved the clerk away. The Dowager Countess Camoynes, an evening cloak draped over one arm, waited until the door was shut, glanced at Sharpe, then spoke. 'I called myself your wife, Simon, to persuade that boring little man to let me in here. Sir Henry? Please don't stand up.' She smiled at Simmerson who had made no move to stand, then looked quizzically from Sir Barstan Maxwell to Lord Fenner. 'Do please present me.'

'Anne?' Fenner's voice was an indignant growl.

'You do remember me! How very charming of you. Just as I remember Major Sharpe. I trust I find you well, Major?'

Sharpe stared at her. He said nothing. He was trying to work out how he had miscalculated so badly, failed so terribly. He was blaming himself for halting the half Battalion so far from the Royal stand. He should have smashed his way through the ranks of guards to the balustrade behind which the Prince had sat. He could have wept for Jane. They had been like children, thinking love a game that bravery could win, but the bastards had won.

Lord Fenner frowned. 'My dear Anne, I am engaged on the business of state.'

'Introduce me, Simon!'

Fenner reluctantly stood. He cleared his throat. 'General Sir Barstan Maxwell, I have the honour of naming the Dowager Countess Camoynes.' He made the introduction peremptorily. 'I presume you can wait, Anne?' He said it with a bad grace, his confidence returning after the shock of her entry.

'Of course I can wait, Simon. I merely wanted to be sure you had not forgotten that I was having supper with you tonight?'

'I had not forgotten.' Fenner sat down and pulled his chair close to the table. 'But I am delayed and will be obliged if you would wait outside, my Lady.'

'As you ask so graciously, my Lord, I will. I am honoured to have made your acquaintance, Sir Barstan.' She smiled at the Guards officer, then at Sir Henry, and finally gave Sharpe a cold, unfriendly look. 'Your uniform is a disgrace, Major.'

Sir Henry Simmerson, who had said the same thing at the commencement of the evening's business, gave a snort of delighted agreement. Lady Camoynes smiled at him, then looked back to Sharpe. 'You are also most remiss, Major.'

'Anne!' Lord Fenner said testily.

'A moment, Simon.' She chided him sweetly, then looked imperiously at Sharpe. 'Most remiss indeed, Major.'

'Remiss, Ma'am?'

She brought her left hand from beneath her cloak. 'You promised me this, but what is a soldier's promise? A mere bauble, yes?' She smiled. She held a red leather-bound book in her gloved hand. 'I had to find them for myself! Your steward, Simon? He wanted to know what he was to burn, so he was still reading them when I arrived for our little supper. Servants are so curious about us, aren't they?' She smiled at Lord Fenner.

'I have the other one. It's quite safe, of course, rescued from the flames. It has some letters inside signed by you. How careless of you not to destroy them. Do hold this book for me, Major.' She turned a chair to face the large table. 'I think perhaps I'll stay now, Simon. I am so fascinated by your business of state.'

General Sir Barstan Maxwell thought the world had gone mad. The Rifleman was smiling, leafing through a ledger book at which Lord Fenner and Sir Henry, white-faced and aghast, stared with disbelief. The Dowager Lady Camoynes sat, and on her elegant and disdainful face there came an expression of alert and intelligent anticipation.

The clerk was suddenly no longer needed. His records of the evening's transactions were taken by Lord Fenner and ripped into two. 'My Lord!' General Maxwell protested.

'Sir Barstan, this is not your business. Go, man!' This last to the clerk who, flurried by the evening's strange turn, dropped his pen and fled to the door.

General Sir Barstan Maxwell stared at the torn record. 'My Lord, I insist this is done properly! I must insist!'

'It is being done properly. Sir Barstan.' Lady Camoynes was suddenly dominating the room. 'Most properly indeed. If it is done any other way, my dear General, there is likely to be a most horrid scandal. Is that not true, Simon?'

The General looked at Lord Fenner, who, under Lady Camoynes' gaze, nodded weakly in confirmation.

She laughed. 'A splendid scandal, General. I do think your master of York will want us to keep it a secret, don't you? Freddie's had quite enough trouble already.' There was no one to dispute her words as she looked at Sharpe. 'Perhaps, Major Sharpe, you have some few requests to make of Lord Fenner?'

'Requests?'

She made a disappointed face at him. 'I assume you want a favour of Simon?' She gestured at Lord Fenner. 'I do believe this would be an opportune moment to ask. My own small requests,' she smiled at Lord Fenner, 'will wait.' She ruled the room. Sir Henry, who had delivered the books to be burned, felt his heart beating with a dangerous rapidity.

Lady Camoynes sighed. 'Do hurry, Major.'

Sharpe, torn from the pit of defeat to this sudden, dizzy success, obeyed. He would go to Spain with the trained men of the Prince of Wales' Own Volunteers. Lord Fenner agreed. His costs over these last weeks would be paid to his account at Messrs Hopkinsons and Son of St Alban's Street. Lord Fenner frowned. 'How much?'

'Two hundred guineas,' Lady Camoynes said. 'In gold. Is that enough, Major?'

'Indeed, my Lady.' It was a huge profit.

'Then do proceed, Major Sharpe.'

The back pay of the Battalion would be restored. The Second Battalion would be properly established at Chelmsford and given new officers. It was all agreed. The Colours would be taken from Sir Henry's house to the barracks. Sir Henry, unable to speak, nodded. Sir Barstan, outraged that the Colours were in Sir Henry's house in the first place, snorted angrily. Sharpe smiled. 'And there will be no changes, none at all, in the officers you have selected to go to Spain.'

Fenner stared as if he had misheard Sharpe. 'You mean . . .'

Sharpe's voice was loud. 'I mean that I wish to serve under Lieutenant Colonel Girdwood's command.' Sir Henry was frowning.

Fenner, defeated, was still puzzled. 'If Colonel Girdwood still wishes to command, Major, you will serve under him?'

'That is my wish.'

Lady Camoynes smiled. 'You've finished, Major?'

'Indeed, Ma'am.' His other request was none of Lord Fenner's business, no one's business but that of Sharpe and of the girl who waited downstairs.

Lady Camoynes reached out a gloved hand. 'I would be most grateful for the book, Major. Simon and I will meet tomorrow, won't we, my Lord?' Fenner nodded, scenting the humiliation that was to come. Sir Henry Simmerson still gaped at the book she now took from Sharpe. Lady Camoynes opened its pages, showing a spread of ledger columns. 'You like the book, Sir Henry? I have two for sale.' She stood. 'Major? Shall we leave?'

'Of course, my Lady.'

'Major Sharpe!' It was General Sir Barstan Maxwell, making one last effort to serve his master with honesty. 'You were telling the truth?'

Lady Camoynes held up a hand to stop Sharpe's reply. She smiled at the General. 'The truth, dear Sir Barstan, is whatever Lord Fenner and I decide it shall be. And it will prove, dear Simon, a most expensive commodity. Goodnight, gentlemen. Come, Major.'

He took his weapons and telescope from the table, gave his rescuer his arm, and left in triumph.

Sharpe pulled open the door of Sir Henry's coach. 'Sir?'

Girdwood, seeing Sharpe, gaped. He made a small noise of terror, a shrew-like noise. He saw the sword at Sharpe's side and the rifle on the tall man's shoulder, and his voice was tentative as though he saw a ghost of a man meant to be consigned to the Australian wilderness. 'You want me, Major Sharpe?'

'In my own time, sir.' Sharpe smiled. There were men whose flesh had long been flensed from their bones whose last sight on earth had been that smile. 'But for the moment I have come for Miss Gibbons.' He held out his hand. 'Jane?'

Girdwood lifted a weak hand as if to stop her, but there was a scrape, a flash of dusky light on long steel, and Sharpe's sword was gleaming in the courtyard. 'Sir?'

Girdwood stayed very still. Sharpe sheathed the sword and handed the girl down to the cobbles. 'Jane. I have the honour to present the Dowager Countess Camoynes.' He bowed to the Countess. 'Jane Gibbons, Ma'am. We are to be married.'

The Countess looked the girl up and down with a critical eye. 'Have you agreed to marry him, Miss Gibbons?'

'Yes, my Lady.'

'He's more fortunate than he deserves. He's an alley-cat, aren't you, Major?'

'If your Ladyship says so.'

She looked at him with a humorous, challenging expression. 'She does. Where do you go to this night, alley-cat? I have a carriage and I'm feeling generous.'

'Carlton House,' Sharpe smiled. 'We are invited.'

'Dressed like that? I suppose you can say it's a costume ball. Very well! We shall all go to Prinny's! Jane and I can turn up on the arm of a hero. Dear Miss Gibbons,' and the Countess offered Jane her hand, 'do me the honour of waiting in my carriage.'

When the Countess had Sharpe alone she stared up at him. 'You didn't tell me about her?'

'There seemed no need.'

She smiled. 'True. One hardly discusses one's intended while under Vauxhall's bushes.' She laughed. 'You wouldn't do that, Major, would you? I would, but not you. You're too kind. Did anyone ever tell you that you were kind?'

'No, Ma'am.'

'Don't call me "Ma'am". You make me sound ancient.' Her

fingers were touching the silver whistle on his crossbelt, and her startling green eyes were filled with amusement. 'If you weren't such an alley-cat, I might have taken you for myself.'

'I would have been most fortunate.'

'Thank you. Are you in love?'

Sharpe was embarrassed. 'Yes. Yes, I am.'

'Whatever love is. It will probably end in disaster, of course.'

Sharpe frowned. 'You think so?'

She laughed. 'Not if you look after her, and I think you're quite good at that.' She smiled. 'She's very pretty, if you like that innocent colouring. You have good taste in women, Major. I wanted to thank you.'

'Thank me?' Sharpe was feeling confused.

'You didn't get the proof for me, did you? But you were still on the battlefield, Major, and you were an ally of memorable strength.' She turned towards her coach. 'Now come along. It's not done to keep a Prince waiting, not even that fat fool.' She laughed, for she had won, and she would have her revenge, and because her son was safe.

Victory was suddenly very sweet. The Prince thought Sharpe's uniform 'monstrous good'. He was kindness itself to both of them.

'Who is she?' Sir William Lawford watched Jane Gibbons, who had been drawn away by Lord John Rossendale.

'I'm marrying her. She's called Jane Gibbons.'

'Gibbons? Gibbons?' Lawford frowned. 'Never heard of them.'

'Her father was a saddler.'

'Ah!' Lawford smiled. 'I wouldn't have heard of her then, would I? Still, she'll be a good match for you. Pretty, eh?'

'I think so.'

328

Lawford stared at Sharpe in silence for a few seconds. 'So you're feeling pleased with yourself, eh? You did it all on your own, didn't need my help?'

'I hope you were not offended, sir.'

'Offended! Lord, no. You were a fool, Richard. Do you know what a damn fool thing you did today? Do you know? You're lucky to have a head on your shoulders, let alone your damned Majority.'

'I'm sure, sir.'

Lawford, with his wonderful dexterity, struck a light with his tinder-box and lit a cigar. 'Do you know what I had arranged for you, Richard?'

'Arranged for me, sir?'

'A Rifle Battalion of your own. Yours. Rifles. Lieutenant Colonel Sharpe.' He smiled to show how foolish Sharpe had been in distrusting his help. 'Admittedly in the American war, but we can't have everything.'

A Rifle Battalion of his own? Sharpe felt the dreadful lure of the bribe, the savage lust for such a wonderful instrument of war to be given to him, and then he remembered the disconsolate men on the wharves of Pasajes, the men in faded, patched red coats who trusted him to bring them back their pride from England. 'I couldn't have accepted, sir.'

'Easy to say when you don't have the choice,' Lawford laughed. 'So you thought you didn't need me, eh?'

'But I do, sir.' Sharpe wondered how Lawford could have so misjudged him. Did Sir William really believe that Sharpe would abandon men for a promotion? The thought hurt, but he would not show it. He smiled instead. 'I want a service from you, and perhaps I can offer you one in return.'

Lawford, with a politician's distrust, frowned at the thought of a bargain not of his own invention. 'What can you offer me, Richard?'

329

Sharpe was awkward for this was not his territory. 'It occurs to me, sir, if you'll forgive me, but if you talk with Lady Camoynes, you might find that she has sudden influence in the Horse Guards and War Office. I should do it swiftly, sir, say tonight? I suspect there will be promotions, sir, within the government.' Lawford, who hardly expected to receive that kind of advice from a man who had once been his Sergeant, stared with some pique at Sharpe.

'You know the Lady Camoynes?'

'Not well,' Sharpe said hastily. 'She was kind enough to speak to me once or twice.'

Lawford grunted. 'I hope you were polite, Richard.'

'Indeed, sir,' Sharpe smiled. 'I was very humble.'

'Good.' Lawford looked at the dreadful, battle-stained green jacket. 'Because you do sometimes seem to have difficulty in knowing your proper place.'

'Yes, sir.'

'And what favour can I do for you?'

'I think, sir, that Lieutenant Colonel Girdwood will be trying to resign his commission and I would be grateful, sir, if it could be put to him that unless he accepts command of the First Battalion in Spain then criminal charges might be brought? Would that be possible?'

Lawford blew a long stream of cigar smoke as he watched Sharpe. 'And why, in the name of God, do you want to serve under Girdwood?'

'I don't intent to serve under him, sir.'

Sir William smiled very slowly, understanding. 'I think I know the right ear, yes. May I say I'm glad that I am not your enemy, Richard?'

'I'm glad of that too, sir.'

He took Jane Gibbons away from the court. He was going back to Spain, and there were a hundred things he wanted to do before the Battalion left. They walked down the massive staircase towards the octagon room, and Jane suddenly gasped and gripped his arm. 'Major!'

'You can call me Richard now.'

She was not listening. She stared fearfully towards the bottom of the staircase.

The defeated, knowing that the next day they would buy themselves out of scandal, and eager to stop the smallest rumours from sullying their reputation, had decided to brazen this night out. They had come to Carlton House. Lord Fenner saw Sharpe and stepped back so that he would not be forced to recognise his enemy.

But Sir Henry Simmerson, who had just handed his cloak to a servant, did not have the same sense. He stared in outraged anger. His niece, dressed in her simple blue country dress, was coming down the Prince Regent's stairs on the arm of the man Sir Henry hated most in all the world. 'Jane! I ordered you home! I'll have the skin off you!'

'Sir Henry!' It was Sharpe who replied. His voice, echoing in the marbled splendour of the hall, seemed unnaturally loud. He put his right hand over Jane's to calm her fears.

Sir Henry stared at them, and Sharpe, in the same loud voice, spoke two brief words that, though much used in Britain's army, were rarely heard in Carlton House. Then, with his bride on his arm and his sword at his side, he went into the night. He was going to Spain.

EPILOGUE

France

NOVEMBER 1813

EPILOGUE

Dawn showed a landscape whitened by frost and slashed by dark valleys. Smoke, like wisps of morning mist, drifted from the steep hillsides where troops brewed tea or cleared their muskets of an overnight charge. Men, stamping their boots and slapping their mittened hands against the cold, stared northwards at the heaped hills that were rocky, precipitous, and held by the enemy.

Sergeant Major Harper laughed. 'You look disappointed, Charlie. What is it? You thought they had horns and tails?'

Private Charles Weller, now in d'Alembord's Light Company, was staring in awe at a small group of men who, a good half mile away from where Weller stood, struggled uphill with buckets of water to their rock-embrasured trenches at the hill's top. 'They're French?'

'The real article, Charlie. Old Trousers, frogs, me-sewers, whatever you want to call the buggers. And just like us.'

'Like us?' Weller had been raised in a country that spoke of Frenchmen as monkeys, as devils, as anything but humans.

'Just like us.' Harper sipped his tea and thought about it. 'Bit slower with their muskets and a bit nippier on their feet, but that's all. Christ, it's cold!'

It was November in the mountains. The Prince of Wales' Own Volunteers had marched through high, rocky passes, shrouded in sudden fogs, the moss-grown precipices dripping with water that soaked the thin, spongy turf of the high valleys. Goats and eagles shared the rocks, wolves howled in the darkness. A storm had greeted the Battalion one night, the lightning slashing down to whiten the cliffs and crack at rocks like the whip of doom.

Somewhere in that land of fogs and rains and lightning and night-howling cold, they had crossed into France. No one was certain exactly where. One moment they were in Spain, and ths next the word went through the ranks that they had entered the land of the enemy. No one cheered. They were in an army that had fought and struggled since 1793 to cross this frontier, but they were too tired to raise a cheer. The straps of their packs had chafed through the wet uniforms, their boots were filled with water, and the sergeants had threatened to crucify any man who let his powder get wet.

'Remember one thing, Charlie.' Harper tossed the dregs of his tea away. 'Get yourself a French pack soon as you bloody can. More comfortable.' It was possible to tell the veterans of the Regiment, not just by their faded uniforms that were patched with brown Spanish cloth, but by their good French packs. Weller grinned. His red coat, which had been so bright in Chelmsford, had turned a strange pink, the cheap dye washed by the rain to drip onto his grey trousers which were now reddened about the thighs. 'Will we fight today?'

'That's what we're here for.' Harper stared down at the French-held hills. The British held the higher ground, but between them and the southern plains of France was this last range of enemy-held hills, hills protected by fortifications, trenches, and marshy, treacherous ground in the valleys. Wellington, whose men had prised the French from the higher peaks in weeks of hard, confused fighting, wanted to be out of these hills before the snows came. No army could winter here.

If the forts that had been hacked out of the rocks on the last foothills were not taken, then the British would have to slink back into Spain. Harper turned round. 'Private Clayton!'

'Sarge?'

'Look after this little bugger.' Harper cuffed Weller. 'Don't want him dying in his first battle. And, Charlie?'

'Sarge?'

'Keep your bloody dog away from the Portuguese. They eat them when they get hungry.'

Weller, landing at Pasajes in early October, had adopted the first stray dog that he found. It was a mongrel of startling ugliness, with one ear missing and a tail shortened by a fight. It proved to be a coward against all other dogs, but devoted to its new master, who had tried to christen it Buttons. The name did not stick. The rest of the Light Company, because of its ugliness and cowardice, called the dog Boney.

Major Richard Sharpe had let it be known throughout the Battalion that dogs would make suitable pets for soldiers. As a result of Sharpe's encouragement, the Prince of Wales' Own Volunteers looked, at times, as if they had collected every stray mongrel and flighty bitch in Europe.

Major General Nairn had greeted Sharpe like a long lost friend. During the three weeks that the Battalion was given to re-order its Companies and train the new men to fight in the way of the veterans, Nairn often rode over to share an evening meal with Sharpe and listen to the stories brought from England. He met Lieutenant Colonel Girdwood briefly. 'Is he mad, Sharpe?' They were sitting in the wine-shop that was the officers' Mess.

'He just keeps himself to himself, sir.'

'He's mad!' Nairn stared reverently into his glass of whisky. Sharpe had brought two cases from London and presented them to the General. 'Mad!' Nairn said. 'Reminds me of a

Minister I knew in Kirkcaldy. The Reverend Robert MacTeague. Ate nothing but vegetables! Can you credit that? Thought his wife was pregnant of a moonbeam. She probably was, I doubt if he knew his business in that area, and all those cabbages? Must sap a man, Sharpe. He didn't drink, either, not a drop! Said it was the devil's brew.' He turned and stared towards the door of Girdwood's room. Light showed beneath the door which had remained closed all evening. 'What does he do in there?'

'Writes poetry, sir.'

'Christ!' Nairn stared at Sharpe, then drank a good swallow of whisky. 'You're not serious?'

'I am, sir.'

The old Scotsman shook his head sadly. 'Why doesn't the bugger resign?'

'I really couldn't say, sir.' Sharpe did not know whether his request to Lawford had borne fruit and that the threat of court-martial and disgrace had forced Girdwood to Spain, or whether the man, from his tortuous dreams of glory, simply wanted to fight his battle against the French. 'He's here, sir, that's all I know.'

'While you,' a finger stabbed at Sharpe, 'are commanding this Battalion, yes? You're a clever bastard, Mr Sharpe, and when you've driven that poor fool mad I'll make sure you get a real bastard of a colonel to run you ragged.'

Major General Nairn was right in his surmise that Sharpe had arranged for Girdwood to command the Battalion because it enabled Sharpe to be the real commander. Girdwood, shamed and humbled by Sharpe in England, could not compete with him in Spain. The Lieutenant Colonel had tried. On their first formal parade, when the Battalion, strengthened and filled by the men from Foulness, had formed up before the storehouses of Pasajes, Lieutenant Colonel Girdwood had publicly reprimanded Major Sharpe. It was his attempt to assert his authority, to make, as he had said in private to Sharpe, a new beginning with old things forgotten.

The parade had been a formal affair, the Companies lined in their proper order, with Captains in front and Sergeants behind. Before the hoisted Colours, facing the whole parade, Lieutenant Colonel Girdwood sat his horse. Four paces behind the Colours, in the allotted place of the senior major, Sharpe stood.

'Major Sharpe!' Lieutenant Colonel Girdwood, surveying his command, shouted over the heads of the Colour party.

'Sir!'

'Retire two paces, if you please!' The manual of drill did, indeed, stipulate that the senior major should be six paces behind the rear ranks.

Every man in the Battalion, not just those from Foulness, but the veterans too, recognised this as a trial of strength. A small thing, no doubt; but if Major Sharpe, so publicly reprimanded for his lack of military precision, took the two backward paces then Girdwood would have succeeded in asserting his formal authority over all these men. The Colonel, recognising the moment, chose to speak in a clipped, loud voice. 'Now, if you please, Major!'

'Sir!' Major Sharpe said. He filled his lungs. ''Talion! ''Talion will march two paces forward on my word of command! 'Talion, move!'

Since that moment, which had brought a smile to every face in the Battalion, Sharpe had commanded. From that moment on he paraded beside Girdwood, in the front of the Battalion, and, though he was careful to be seen consulting with the Lieutenant Colonel, and though Girdwood still presided silently in the Mess, there was not a man in the Prince of Wales' Own Volunteers who did not know who truly gave the Battalion its orders.

Major General Nairn, on his last visit to Sharpe before the Battalion was ordered forward through the mountains, had stared astonished at the still closed door. 'You're not being a bit hard on him, Sharpe?'

'Yes, sir. I am.' Sharpe admitted. 'At Foulness, sir, that bugger gave orders that deserters were to be shot out of hand. I saw one killed. Guessing from the books I'd say he had about a dozen others shot. No trial, no nothing. Just bang. He also hunted men in the marshland as if they were rats. He stole a lot of money.' Sharpe frowned. 'So have I, in my time, but only from the enemy. I don't steal from my men. Besides, he wants to see a battle, so I'm doing him a favour.'

'A favour?'

'I'll fight his bloody battle for him, which means we stand a chance of winning.' Sharpe laughed at his own immodesty.

'Any other enemies here, Major Sharpe?' Nairn asked with mock innocence.

Sharpe smiled, thought of Sergeant Lynch, and lied. 'No, sir.'

'Doesn't look any different to Spain, does it?' Harper, with a fresh mug of tea, stood beside Sharpe on the great hill and looked down on the enemy's last fortresses before the open country.

Sharpe propped a broken mirror above a bowl of water and stropped his razor on the side of his right boot. 'Buggers didn't have trenches in Spain.' He had searched the French positions with his telescope. He did not much like what he saw. The French had made the great hump of hill beneath him into a remarkable fortress. They had built dry-stone walls that connected their small forts, dug trenches, and at the very end of the hill, that lay like a ridge among lesser hills, there was a series of concentric walls that surrounded a pinnacle of rock. The rock was crowned with embrasures, packed, doubtless, with muskets that could not be reached by British cannon, for no cannon could be placed in a position to reach the pinnacle. This, Sharpe knew, would be an infantryman's job. An attack uphill, against stone and trenches, against an enemy fanatical to protect their homeland.

The Battalion's orders, given to Girdwood, but taken by Sharpe, instructed the Prince of Wales' Own Volunteers to attack behind two other Battalions. The first two Battalions would take the out-works, clear the first trenches, and let the Prince of Wales' Own Volunteers go through them for the task of finishing the job. Sharpe's men were to scour the last defences and take the pinnacle, the last fortress. To the right and left of the enemy hill were others, crowned by similar works, to be screened or attacked by other Battalions. By nightfall, if all went well, the road out of the mountains would be cleared and France, with its full barns and winter pastures, would be at Wellington's disposal.

Sharpe scraped the razor over his skin without benefit of hot water. He flinched, then stolidly scraped on. 'I'm giving you a special squad, Patrick.'

'Special, sir?'

Sharpe dipped the blade into the icy, dirty water that had already been used by nine other officers. 'We can't make a formal bloody assault on that place. Too many god-damn rocks.' It would be like threading through a maze of ditches and walls that would tear a tight formation into ruin. 'We're going in two columns, Light and Grenadier Companies leading, but I'm giving you your own squad. Go in the centre, and if you see either column in trouble, go in on their flank. Don't wait for my orders, just keep going.'

'Yes, sir,' Harper grinned happily. He liked such independence. 'Can I pick my men, sir?'

'I've already done it.' Sharpe wiped his face on his officer's sash. 'O'Grady, Kelleher, Rourke, Callaghan, Joyce, Donnell,

341

the Pearce brothers, O'Toole, Fitzpatrick, and Halloran.' He looked at Harper's wide grin. 'And I thought perhaps you ought to take an extra sergeant. Just to help you.'

'And who might that be, sir?'

'I don't know.' Sharpe pulled on his old jacket and began to button it. 'Lynch, perhaps?'

'I think the boys would be happy with that, sir.'

Sharpe gave an atrocious imitation of Harper's Donegal accent. 'Grand, Patrick, just grand. And would you be minding if I finished your tea?'

'Whatever you want, sir.' Harper laughed. 'Christ, but it's good to be back.'

At eight o'clock the Battalion was ordered down to the valley. They left the thin sunshine, going into shadow. The tracks, made by goats, forced the Companies to go in single file. Servants led their officers' horses. Sharpe, like most of the veteran officers, had left his horse with the baggage.

He had bought himself a fine seven-year-old mare in England, replacing the cheap saddle horse he had bought on his second journey to Foulness. Jane Gibbons had named the mare Sycorax.

'I can't even spell it!' Sharpe had growled,

'I suppose you'd call her Florence, or Peggotty.' Jane stroked the mare's nose. 'Sycorax she is.'

'Why Sycorax?'

'She was a nasty witch with a pretty name. She was Caliban's mother, and this is your horse.' She laughed at him. 'And it is a pretty name, Richard.'

So Sycorax she stayed, a sturdy, dependable beast with a witch's name, bought with the proceeds of the diamonds.

Maggie Joyce was pouring the money from the diamonds into St Alban's Street where it was converted into four per cent stock. Sharpe had taken some of the jewels back. Jane had necklaces, ear-rings, and bracelets that had once been worn by a Spanish Queen. Sharpe had also taken a second necklace, the fragile, beautiful piece of filgreed gold hung with pearls and diamonds, which he had wrapped, cased, and sent by special messenger to a London address.

The reply reached him the day before the Battalion sailed from Portsmouth. 'Dear Major Sharpe, How can I possibly accept such a splendid Gift? With Gratitude and astonishment, of course. You are too Generous a man. Be lucky. Anne, Countess Camoynes.' There was a post-script. 'You may see from the Public Papers that Lord Fenner has resigned. He no Longer has the Wealth to Sustain his position. For all Your Services, I will Remember you fondly, as I trust you will me for mine.'

The Battalion formed up in the valley. From above them, dulled by distance and the convex hill slope that hid the events from the waiting men, came the sound of muskets. Sharpe ordered the Colours uncased, the Colours of the First Battalion that were stained and shredded by war. He had been commanded to add the insignia of the three white feathers onto the Battalion's badge, but there had not yet been time to put them on the flags. A wind, that carried the musket smoke into the upper air, rippled the heavy silks and stirred the yellow tassels. Cannon sounded, not British, but French mountain guns that guarded the rock fortresses. The new men looked nervously upwards, the veterans waited, and to Lieutenant Colonel Girdwood, who had dreamed so often of this moment when he would go into proper battle, the sounds seemed like a cacophony of hell and glory and trembling and death. He waited.

The horses were left with the servants in the valley. Sharpe, no longer pretending to consult Girdwood, gave the orders. The

Battalion would advance in two columns. The Grenadier Company would lead the right-hand column, the Light Company the left, while RSM Harper and his detail would go in the centre, ahead of Sharpe and the Colour party. 'I don't want any god-damned foolishness. We're not on a parade ground. You can't keep the ranks dressed up there, so just keep going! Listen for orders, but if you can't hear any then you won't do anything wrong if you just attack to the front. Attack! All the time!' He looked round the faces, staring especially at the new men like Captain Smith and Captain Carline. 'And don't let your men settle into safe holes, understand? They like to do that, so keep them moving! Roust them out, take them forward.' He described what he had seen through his telescope; the nightmare landscape of trenches and walls, of blank culverts where men could be trapped with French sharp-shooters above them, a jumbled, rocky landscape designed for defence. 'It has to be fast work! If they drive us into the ground, we're done for! So tell your men to fire on sight, not to wait for orders, and warn them there'll be sticking work.' Captain Smith looked worried at the thought of bayonets. 'We go in fast. Tell them the French are more scared than we are.'

'They must be bloody terrified then,' Lieutenant Price said, and raised a smile from the officers.

'They are,' Sharpe said, 'because they know they're fighting us.' And oddly, even the new men who had never fought, and who had been given a new lease on their shabby careers, suddenly knew that they could win. They followed a soldier, and they went to a fight.

It took more than two hours to climb the hill and catch up with the first attacking Battalions. Charlie Weller, pushed into the back file of the Light Company, saw his first enemy dead;

a man crumpled on the rocks, his blood congealed by the cold. Another dead Frenchman's beard was frosted white.

He saw British dead, one with an arm seemingly torn from the socket, another blown apart by a cannon-ball with his guts blue on the rocks. More terrible than the dead were the wounded. Charlie passed groups of Frenchmen, one sobbing because his eyes were gone, another gasping out his life in terrible, huge, clouding breaths. His belly had been laid open by a sword. A British private gave him wine to sip, but the man could not take it.

A British sergeant whose left thigh was torn open to the bone and whose blood, despite the leather belt twisted into his groin, pulsed onto the ground, grinned at Weller. 'Go on, lad! Give 'em hell.' Weller thought he was more likely to vomit. He stumbled on, following the pack of men in front, wondering if he would remember to clear the ramrod from his musket before he fired. Ahead, seemingly closer all the while, was the sound of the guns.

Lieutenant Colonel Girdwood walked beside Sharpe. Without the pitch in his moustache he seemed punier. His small, black eyes darted about the unfamiliar scenery. He too saw the dead, but he had seen men torn by bullets before. Yet never in Ireland had he seen men struck by artillery fire. Somehow the gobbets of flesh, like the work of a demented, drunken butcher, seemed unreal. He shied away once as a dog ran across his front.

The sun was fitful between clouds. The smoke of the French mountain guns was like a thin skein above the Battalion, bringing its filthy smell of powder smoke. Somewhere a man screamed, the scream rising and falling in a dreadful cadence. It was silenced suddenly and Girdwood shuddered.

The Lieutenant Colonel could not make sense of what he saw. He could not tell where the enemy positions were, or how far the leading Battalions had reached in their attack. He could see, at the ridge's northern end, the steep pinnacle of rock, wreathed in smoke, but dead ground lay before the pinnacle and Girdwood was confused. Once, through a shifting mist of smoke, he saw red uniforms running forward, a loose knot of men not in any proper order, and he wondered if he heard a cheer, but was not sure. He watched Sergeant John Lynch, plodding ahead of him, and thought that if Lynch showed no fear, then nor need he.

Sergeant Lynch was terrified. He had sensed that there was some purpose to his attachment to this band of Irishmen, and it was a purpose he did not like. He had let his accent flower for them, sounding more Irish than they, but he felt their scorn and he was scared.

He had never been in a group like this. He knew how many Irish fought in this army, but he had thought of them merely as rank-fillers, peasants who could be pushed around and forced into obedience. He had never seen their pride. These men were sure that Major Sharpe had grouped them together because he wanted the best in front, and who were better than they? They spoke filthily of England's King, despised the officers whom Lynch admired, but went to this fight, beneath a flag not their own, with a relish that was almost contagious. 'You know why God made Ireland so small?' one of them, sharpening his bayonet with long strokes of a stone, asked Lynch.

'No.' Lynch was nervous of their confidence, their grim assurance.

'Otherwise we'd have conquered the whole bloody world and there'd be no fights left, eh?' The man laughed, and held the blade up to inspect its edge. 'And what would a man do then?'

Some of them spoke in Gaelic, laughing with Harper, and Lynch felt sure the laughter was aimed at him. He remembered the death of Marriott in the river among the Essex marshes, knew it was still unpunished, and was fearful.

D'Alembord, at the head of the left column, was going into his second battle. He was aware of Harper's Irish group on his right and was determined that his Light Company would prove better. He considered that he had the best men, the fastest, most spirited men, but he wished Harper was back as his Sergeant. He drew his sword and, in the wan, winter light, the slim steel seemed a fragile weapon to take into this land of rock and musket fire and sudden death. Huckfield, a studious and careful man from the north of England who had been promoted to the new rank of Company Sergeant Major, shouted forward to d'Alembord. 'Major's calling a halt, sir!'

The Battalion stopped. Sharpe, standing in front of the Colours that told the French who their new enemies were, drew his sword. The steel, carefully sharpened before dawn, rang scrapingly on the scabbard throat. 'Fix bayonets!'

The seventeen-inch blades were drawn, slotted onto muzzles, while the few Riflemen still in d'Alembord's ranks pushed their longer sword-bayonets onto their weapons. Among the Riflemen was a young Spaniard, Angel, who had never been formally sworn into the Battalion but was one of its best marksmen. The other men of the Light Company, knowing how fanatically he fought, swore that he could not live long.

They were at the edge of the fight, facing the chaos and confusion of the attack, and a Brigade Major, sweating despite the cold after his long scramble towards the new Battalion, gave Sharpe what little news of the battle that he could, then ordered them forward. Sharpe raised his sword and his voice. 'The Battalion will rendezvous at the pinnacle!' Each man knew his task and the sword pointed the way. 'Forward!'

At Pasajes Sharpe had broken up the four Companies he had formed in Essex. He split the men among the existing

Companies, mixing experience with inexperience. Yet, even so, he knew that half of this Battalion had never fought. If he could have chosen an ideal battle for their baptism, he would have liked to fight a defensive action, his men secure in the knowledge that so long as they reloaded their muskets quickly no harm could come to them. Instead he was committing them to a frontal attack on positions that were firmly held and savagely fortified. There could be no flank attack here, the valley bottoms were sodden with bogs, and the road northwards ran along the side of the hill and was barred by the French forts.

The right-hand column, led by the Grenadier Company, disappeared in a maze of trenches and walls that had been taken by the first attackers. The left-hand column, with less cover, became a target for the French gunners. Cannon-balls, smaller than a man's fist, whipped horror through the files.

'Close up! Close up!' The Sergeants shouted. Lieutenant Colonel Girdwood stared in shock at four men lying on the ground, all struck by the same plunging cannon-ball. One, coughing and bleeding, tried to rejoin his file.

Muskets blazed from ahead, the flames stabbing through the smoke that blossomed from a stone wall. Balls plucked at the Colours, thrummed the air over Sharpe's head, and he watched approvingly as d'Alembord inclined right to flank the threat. The Irish squad fired a volley at the wall, charged it with blood-chilling screams, but the French were gone, back to the next barrier, and Sharpe knew that the Battalion was committed now, that it must press on into the heart of this defensive tangle. 'Cheer, you buggers! Let them hear you!'

He jumped the wall behind the Irish. A shallow trench angled forward, its sides heightened by stone walls. A Frenchman was dying in the puddles of the trench bed, his clothes torn where Harper's squad had searched him for money. A musket sounded ahead of Sharpe, a man screamed, and Sharpe climbed out of the trench to search to his right for a sign of his easternmost column.

The Colours halted behind him. He could hear d'Alembord's Company firing, the sharper crack of the rifles distinctive in the constant noise of musketry that filled the air. Bullets were striking the rock beside him, whistling up in ricochets, humming and throbbing about him, and still he could not see the right-hand column. He heard the crash of musketry from their direction, a cheer, and then the cough of explosions that sounded like small artillery shells breaking apart. 'Sergeant Major! Right! Right!'

Someone shouted the order on to Harper. Sharpe was already crossing the open rock, looking for the Grenadiers. He went through a bank of musket smoke and saw them, crouching in a rock gully, their advance held up by two Companies of French troops who lined a stone wall above them and poured musketry into the packed ranks and rolled the shells, fuses lit and smoking, down to the stalled attack where, in gouts of dark red and dirty smoke, the shells exploded to drive the Grenadier Company back. 'Forward, you bastards! Forward!' He went forward himself, coming towards the flank of the French line, and he saw the muskets moving towards him, knew that a volley would tear him ragged in just seconds, but then he heard the shouts to his left and, from the smoke, with bayonets reaching and shining, Harper's men came like furies onto the right of the French line.

The enemy line broke. Harper's men were using bayonets, grunting and shouting, the blood splashing their grey trousers.

'Forward! Move! Move!' Sharpe watched the Grenadiers climb the wall. Sergeant Lynch, his bayonet unbloodied, was walking behind Harper's men and Sharpe shouted at him to catch up.

The ensign holding the King's Colour was shot, the banner

fell and was caught by a sergeant, and Sharpe saw that the next barrier was thick with musket smoke. Harper's men were reloading, crouching behind a wall, and Sharpe bellowed at the Grenadiers to attack fast. The Frenchmen who had fled to the new position were still settling in. They were nervous, and this was the time to strike.

'Forward! Forward!' He had lost sight of the left-hand column now, but he had known the fight would be like this. 'Come on, you buggers! Cheer!'

They cheered. They ran with him, their bayonets bright, and Harper's men put a volley in front of them, driving stone splinters into the faces of the defenders, then Sharpe heard the coughing bellow of the French muskets, saw the billow of dirty smoke, greyer than the British, and felt the balls whip past him to strike into men behind, but he was safe, the sword was in his hand, and he shouted for the sheer splendour of it as he jumped the wall and hacked down with the sword.

A Frenchman tried to parry the blow with his musket, succeedingly only in deflecting it so that the huge sword cut into his forearm, smashing the bone and shearing to the elbow joint. The man screamed, Sharpe was past him, and a French officer, slim sword bright, challenged him. The man was shouting at his own men, whether to go back or counter-attack Sharpe could not tell. He screamed his war-scream, saw the fear in the Frenchman, and lunged forward with his sword, his hand already twisting so that the blade, as it stabbed the enemy's stomach, would not be trapped by the suction of flesh. He ripped the blade free, backhanded the Frenchman's feeble, dying riposte, and stepped over the fallen man and bellowed at his men to keep going. Speed was everything here, speed that would drive the attack through the successive walls before the defenders could settle and aim.

Beside him now, screaming and shouting like men possessed of devils, the Grenadier Company was sweeping forward. Their blood was up now. They had endured the first blow, found they had survived, and now they were racing ahead of him, oblivious of the death which, just minutes before, had terrified them. The air was humming with musket balls, screams, the smoke thick as fog. The new men, Sharpe saw, their first terror conquered, were in the front ranks of the attack. The veterans, more cautious because more knowledgeable, let them lead.

Sharpe went left. The Colour party, trying to stay with him, followed. He heard the rifles again, then saw men busy with bayonets, driving the blades down into a trench while, beyond them, number three Company had outflanked d'Alembord to the left and supported his attack from that flank. That was what the supporting Companies were supposed to do, but three Company was led by Carline, and Sharpe chalked up a good mark to the new officer.

Another stone wall, then another. The French lined them, but the attacks came first from the left, then the right, and the French reeled backwards. A splinter of stone hit Sharpe's cheekbone, a bayonet grazed his thigh, and a musket ball snatched and shattered his canteen. They were the moments that he would remember with terror later, but for now he kept the Battalion moving even closer towards the last defences, the walls that ringed the pinnacle. His men were fighting in deep trenches now, cornering the enemy in rock traps, driving on in the strange exultation of battle that will not let a man feel fear or mercy or anything but the anger to kill and survive.

He saw redcoats with white facings on his right, and knew that men from the other Battalions were following through the gap that had been punched in the hill's defences. No one had told them to come, no officers organised them, but this was Wellington's army and this was how they fought. The South Essex, Sharpe thought, could have held this hill against the legions of hell themselves, and then a crash spun him round and his hand flew to his face which had been punched by the air of a passing cannon-ball. The mountain guns, at the foot of the pinnacle, hammered a volley at the attackers and drove Sharpe, with his Colour party, into a trench. There was no sign of Lieutenant Colonel Girdwood.

He stepped over the dead and dying. He saw a British musket abandoned, its bayonet bent almost double by the force of a lunge that had struck rock. There were puddles of slippery blood. A dog licked at one, then ran on to catch up with its master. The French musket balls were thick overhead, the sound of the volleys like a raging fire among thorns, the crashes of the mountain guns deafening.

The attack was stalled. The trenches led to the pinnacle, zig-zagging through the walls and were blocked, where they crossed the outer defences, by transverse stone barriers. As the French had been driven back their defences were thickened and strengthened by the fugitives from the captured positions. 'Move! Move!' Sharpe forced his way to the front where men, kneeling in the trench, fired uselessly at the obstacles. Three bodies lay further up the trench, showing that the French, hidden by the upper walls, had the approach blanketed by guns.

The men seemed to be shivering, not with fear but impatience. They stared at him from eyes rimmed with powder stains, blood-smeared, and Sharpe knew they were still keen to attack, but that no man could go through the trench and live while the mountain guns, firing from the heart of the enemy position, made the upper ground a death trap. Sharpe heaved himself to the trench parapet to look right. The ground dropped precipitately away towards the road. There could be no outflanking that way. He wondered where d'Alembord's men were and was ashamed because he detected in himself a hope that the other column might lever the enemy out of this position and save him the necessity of attacking.

'Load!' He waited as those men who had empty muskets loaded. 'We're going up there!' He pointed to the left of the trench. 'Then straight at the buggers! One effort, lads, just one bloody effort.' They grinned. Their knuckles were white where they gripped their weapons.

There was no point in waiting. Hesitation just gave the mind time to imagine what waited in that place where the musket balls juddered the air and the smoke rolled thick from the battery of guns. So thick, Sharpe suddenly noticed, that the enemy would be looking into a fog of their own making. 'Come on! Let them hear you! Let them hear you! Let them hear you!' He was shouting it as a war cry as he scrambled up the trench's side.

He thought he was alone for a few seconds. He feared to stand up on the trench's parapet, fearing to lose the happiness that he had found, but he made himself do it, and he ran forward, shouting, hearing his voice alone in the din of guns, and then he heard the cheers behind him and saw, to his left, more men rising from the shelter of walls and trenches and heard their wild cheers.

Patrick Harper, in the centre of the line, saw Sharpe taking the right column forward and he screamed his own group at the wall. There was a boulder outside the enemy line, its flanks chipped white where bullets had struck it, and he ran for it, unslinging the vicious seven-barrelled gun as he drove himself forward, his voice keening in a strange, curdling chant of his own devising as he jumped, steadied himself on the boulder's summit, a huge target for every French musket in their rock citadel, and fired.

The seven bullets smashed outwards, clearing a stretch of the wall by flinging three enemy backwards and Harper jumped, gun flailing like a club, and his men were beside him, screaming like banshees from hell, their blades ripping and gouging and the wall was taken. Sharpe was across it to the right and the trench was outflanked: he shouted the Companies forward to the next wall that was shrouded in the fog of the battery. 'Come on! Come on! Come on!' Speed was all. There was no time to form line, or dress ranks, only time to carry the bloodstained bayonets up to the next defence and kill again. A British corporal, his jaw blown away by a mountain gun, wept into his bloodsoaked hands. A dog, shot in the rump, yelped helplessly for its dead master.

Charlie Weller, in his first fight, listened to the screams and the noise and he thought that he would never be able to go forward. He did, somehow. It helped to be at the back of the Company, following the man in front, not certain what terrible things caused the screams that came from the leading ranks. Once, through a shifting curtain of smoke, he saw a French flag flying on the pinnacle, and somehow this battle did not seem anything like he had imagined. He could hear the enemy's shouts, louder than he had ever thought they would be, and he had already seen what they had done to men bigger than he, yet he went forward, listening to the sergeants but not truly hearing them. Boney, whimpering because of the noise, stayed loyally close. A musket ball struck Weller's shako, knocking it over his left eye, and he nervously straightened it. He crouched when his squad stopped, stared at his unbloodied bayonet inches before his eyes and thought that he would never make a soldier.

'Mr Price!' A voice shouted from the front of the column. 'Take your squad right!'

'That's us, Charlie.' Private Clayton, a fly rogue whose wife was the envy of the rest of the Battalion, grinned at Weller. 'Say your prayers and don't piss yourself. Ready?'

A crash of musketry sounded at the column's front, then Lieutenant Price, his sword clumsy in his hand, was shrieking at his men to follow him. 'Come on, lads! This is what they pay us for!' Weller, thinking that he would be dead within seconds, and thinking of his mother who had told him he would come to a miserable end if he went for a soldier, found his legs moving in obedience to the officer's shout. He held the musket ahead of him, copying the other men, and then he heard them shout, tried to shout himself, though it came out more like a child's whimper of terror, and suddenly, in a trench behind a low parapet of piled rocks, he saw moustached men who aimed their huge muskets right at him.

The muskets fired. He screamed in sheer terror, and somehow the scream turned into anger, and he saw Clayton jumping into the trench, bayonet searing down on one of the enemy. They seemed huge to Charlie, who suddenly felt very young, and then he was at the trench's edge himself and a Frenchman, a great brute of a man who reminded Charlie of the blacksmith at home, lunged up with his bayonet.

Desperately, as though it was a pitchfork, Weller parried the blow. The crack of the two muskets meeting was satisfyingly loud and, even more satisfying, Weller's farm-bred strength drove the enemy's weapon to one side and he suddenly heard Clayton shrieking at him. 'Kill the bugger, Charlie! Kill him!'

He drove the bayonet down, screaming in fear as much as anger, and the blade went into the enemy's neck. The man turned, wrenching Weller off balance, and he fell onto the wounded man. The Frenchman hit him, and Weller pounded his fist into the moustached face, and then a blade came over his shoulder and into the Frenchman's chest. The man heaved once beneath Weller, choked, and was suddenly still. 'Not bad, Charlie, but hang onto your gun.' Clayton pulled him up. 'Get the bugger's pack. Quick!'

'His pack?' Charlie had entirely forgotten Harper's advice.

'That's what you killed him for, isn't it?'

355

Weller unstrapped the pack, lugged it off the corpse's back, and did not mind that it was slick with blood. He shook the contents out, abandoning the spare clothes, but splitting a length of sausage with Boney, then he buckled his trophy to his belt. When this was over he would transfer his own belongings to his new pack. He looked at it proudly.

'On! On! On!' Captain d'Alembord was shouting at them. 'Move!' Angel, screaming with rage, was trying to count the Frenchmen he had killed while he killed yet more. Beside him, silent as ever, Daniel Hagman, his wounded shoulder healed, fired his rifle with murderous precision.

'Come on, Charlie.' Clayton pushed him on. The Light Company was coming to the pinnacle's defences and Weller, with his bayonet blooded, and his hands sticky with enemy blood, was beginning to think that he might yet make a soldier.

Lieutenant Colonel Bartholomew Girdwood was singing. He was sitting in an abandoned trench, the dead lying like broken things about him, and he sang.

'We're in battle's noise,
And all for victory, boys,
We're fighting for our flag,
Hurrah!'

He sang it again. The tears running down his face gathered at the corners of his untarred moustache. He heard one of the mountain guns fire, and he shuddered. The shudder drew new tears. He looked at one of the dead man, a Welsh corporal who lay with a bullet hole in his throat, and Lieutenant Colonel Girdwood explained to the man that, in truth, this was not a battle. Not a battle at all. Battles, he said, were fought on plains.

Always on plains. Not on hills. The corporal did not reply and Lieutenant Colonel Girdwood screamed at the man that he would be on a charge if he did not respond. 'Speak, you bastard! Speak!' Another gun made him whimper. He looked up at the sky. 'Twenty-four inches is the proper interval between men for attack. Form up.' He laughed. He thought he might get out of the trench and bring some order to this place. He looked at the corporal. 'Her skin is white, you know. Did you know that? He cut it with the cane. White, white.' He looked at his feet. 'Two feet.' He sang his verse of poetry again.

Then, from around the corner of the trench, one of the many dogs that plagued his Battalion trotted towards the Lieutenant Colonel. It looked at Girdwood, smelled the blood of the dead men, then began worrying at the throat of the Welsh corporal.

'No! No!' Girdwood screamed at the dog. He pulled out his pistol, aimed it, but the flint fell on an empty pan. His hands were shaking too much for him to reload the gun. The dog looked at him, its jowls redly wet, wagged its tail, and Lieutenant Colonel Girdwood, who had wanted nothing more than to fight in a real battle, screamed and screamed and screamed and screamed.

'Christ!' D'Alembord, who thought it a miracle that he still lived, flinched from a ricochet that slapped the rock next to him. He heard the shouts from the right, knew that the Grenadier Company must be attacking the wall, and though part of him felt an unworthy temptation to let them finish this job, he knew, too, that he could not live with himself if he did. 'Are you loaded?'

'Yes, sir!' the voices chorused at him.

'One more time, lads! Once more unto the breach and we must be bloody mad. Go!'

He was laughing in hysteria as he led them. He saw the

French stand behind the wall, he screamed the order to fire, and his own men's volley hammered past his ears as he jumped to the wall's top, swung his sword at empty air, then his men were scrambling over the stones and he led them forward towards the embrasures of the mountain guns that were thick with smoke. A French officer was hurling stones from the top of the makeshift rampart, great hunks of rock that bounced and crashed down towards the British attack.

Charlie Weller had not fired when d'Alembord had given the order. He had fumbled with his musket, then been startled by the crash of the guns about his ears. His musket was still loaded. Back in Lincolnshire, on the farm where his father was a labourer, he was sometimes allowed out with the farmer to shoot rabbits. The farmer liked to boast about young Weller. 'Can knock their bloody eyes out!'

He aimed at the French officer who threw the great stones. Weller suddenly did not have to think about it, the gun seemed a part of him, he fired, felt the burning powder sting his cheek, and the officer went backwards. He had killed at last. He screamed with delight and achievement and charged with the other men of his Company. He was a soldier. Angel slapped his back. 'Well done!'

Captain Smith, whose Company had come onto the right flank of d'Alembord's, was shaking with terror. A dead French officer lay at his feet, killed by Smith's sword. He had just done what Charlie Weller had done; become a soldier. 'After me!' The shout sounded feeble to him, but the men followed him. He watched them clear the last trenches, heard their shouts, and did not notice that the French fire was slackening.

Charlie Weller, his dog shaking at his side, could find no more enemy on this side of the pinnacle. He was watching the other attack, seeing Sharpe and Harper together, amazed suddenly that for eight days he had shared a tent with the two men who, instinctively seeking each other in battle, now carved a path through the last defences. The Irish group were with them, shouting their own challenges, but the French were running. Everywhere there seemed to be shouting, a sound of victory, but there were still some men crouching in rock holes, muskets loaded, and, like clearing vermin from a field, Harper attacked them. His men's blades were reddened to the hilts. He had his own rifle and bayonet in his hands, but now, as he saw the French running down the reverse slope of the hill he shouted for his men to cease fighting. 'Take prisoners! Prisoners!'

Sharpe heard the shout. He had killed again, sweeping the sword about one of the gunpits, but now he saw what Harper had seen, the enemy retreating in panicked confusion. He looked upwards. The pinnacle, that could be climbed by rough, natural steps weathered in the rock, was flying, instead of its tricolour, a white shirt. A man, waving a dirty handkerchief, peered cautiously over the edge. Sharpe beckoned him down. It was over; the last barrier of the border mountains was broken apart.

He climbed onto the hot barrel of a mountain gun, bracing one foot on its sturdy wheel, and he stared northwards. He saw a wide, rolling countryside, oddly green after these winter mountains, dotted with small villages, and thick with trees that still had their last leaves of autumn. Like spilt and molten silver, reflecting the sunlight, he saw the rivers and lakes of a fertile land. France. Tonight, when the dead were buried, they would march down into that heartland of the enemy. Behind him, heavy in the breeze, were the silken flags that he had fought to bring to this place. They were in France, and they had a victory.

'He's babbling of green fields,' d'Alembord said. 'Or rather of white skins, which is not nearly so poetic. He's gone mad.'

'He can't have!'

'Lost his topsails completely.' D'Alembord was wiping his sword blade. 'He's weeping, reciting poetry that I daren't repeat to you, and gibbering like an idiot. If he was in Bedlam you'd pay tuppence to see him. Sergeant Major Harper is keeping the curious at bay, but I think he needs your attention, sir.'

'What the hell am I supposed to do with him?'

'If I were you, sir, I'd tie him up, turn him round, and send him to brigade. They're used to mad colonels.'

Sharpe smiled. 'Find out the bill for me, Dally, I'll look at Girdwood.'

Bartholomew Girdwood was just as d'Alembord had described. He was piling shards of rock onto his thigh, sitting with tears running down his face, sometimes laughing, sometimes singing sad snatches of heroic poetry into the cold air.

'Lieutenant Mattingley!'

'Sir?'

'You'll need two men. Take him to brigade.'

'Me, sir?'

'You.' Sharpe looked again at the Lieutenant Colonel who had persecuted the recruits at Foulness, who had believed himself a soldier among soldiers, a warrior who had craved the chance of one fight against the French. 'You don't need to tie him up. Treat him gently.'

'Yes, sir.'

Sharpe walked back towards the pinnacle, crowned now by his own Colours in the afternoon sun. The air still smelt of powder smoke and blood, the sobs of the wounded still sounded. He thanked Smith, Carline, and other officers. He stopped by wounded men and told them they would recover. He shouted for the bandsmen to hurry with their stretchers. D'Alembord, by the time Sharpe reached the pinnacle again, had come back with the butcher's bill. Sharpe saw that the tall Captain looked unhappy. 'Tell me, Dally.'

'Eleven dead, sir, forty-three wounded.'

'Badly wounded?'

'Twenty or so, sir.'

'Officers?'

'Captain Thomas is dead, sir,' d'Alembord shrugged, 'which means Harry gets his Company, yes?'

'Yes.' Price would be pleased, even though the promotion was because of a death. Sharpe was thinking that the bill was light. 'Did we lose any sergeants?'

'Just Lynch, sir.' D'Alembord's voice was disapproving.

'Lynch?'

'Torn apart, sir.' D'Alembord's eyes seemed to accuse Sharpe. 'He must have been trapped by a dozen of the bastards, sir. He's not a very fetching sight.'

'He did deserve it, Dally.'

'I was under the misapprehension that there were military courts, sir.'

Sharpe looked at the tall Captain, knowing he had deserved d'Alembord's reproof. 'Yes, you're right.'

D'Alembord was embarrassed by Sharpe's contrition. 'But the Battalion fought well, sir, they fought damned well.'

'Didn't they?' Sharpe was pleased at the compliment. 'How did Weller do?'

D'Alembord smiled, relieved that the moment had passed. 'Damned well, sir. He'll make a fine soldier. And well done, sir.'

'Thank you, Dally.'

Sharpe stood under the pinnacle, staring at the groups of men who moved about the scarred rock landscape and who cleared the dead and wounded before the carrion eaters flew from the winter skies. 'Regimental Sergeant Major!'

'Sir?' Harper scrambled towards him.

'Thank you for your efforts.'

'It was nothing, sir.'

Sharpe had found an abandoned French canteen, filled with wine, and he took a mouthful. 'The Colonel's gone mad.' He handed the canteen to Harper. 'And I hear you lost Lynch?'

'Yes, sir.' Harper did not smile. 'So it's all over?'

'And forgotten, Patrick. Tell your men they fought well.'

'I will, sir.'

The army was already moving along the road that flanked the side of the hill. Sharpe could hear the thunder of the gun wheels going into France. He stared the other way, towards the distant peaks of Spain which, now that the sun had been shrouded by clouds, were darkly shadowed. He had a daughter there. He had fought more than five years in that country, in mountains and river valleys, in fortresses and city streets. Now he was leaving.

'Sir!'

He looked left. Captain Smith was smiling idiotically, looking pleased with himself. Sharpe ran his cleaned sword into its scabbard.

He could see, where the road skirted the hillside, a group of four women whose horses' bridles were held by Spanish servants. The women were wives of Sharpe's officers. Closer, smiling at him, and walking up the hill with the unnecessary attention and help of two dozen men, came his own wife.

They had been married two months. She had insisted, against his direct orders, that she would come with him. 'I've always wanted to travel. Besides, it will be good for my sketching.'

'Sketching?'

'I sketch and paint; didn't you know that?'

'No.'

Isabella, who had decided that London was a strange and fearful place, had insisted on returning as Jane's servant. Harper, who had ordered his pregnant wife to remain in London, had, like Sharpe, been flagrantly disobeyed.

'Richard!' Jane wore a dark red cloak over her dress.

'My love.' He felt awkward saying it in front of so many men.

She smiled, striking her beauty into his soul like a sword. 'I met Lieutenant Colonel Girdwood. Poor man.'

'Poor man.'

She turned and looked at the battlefield. The British dead were gone, but the French dead, stripped naked, still lay among the rocks. 'Have I got time for one drawing?'

'It's hardly suitable, is it?'

'Don't be pompous.' She smiled at him, put Rascal on the ground, and took from her bag a large pad and a box of pencils.

They had been married two months, and Sharpe had not regretted a moment of them. He had not guessed at this kind of happiness, he was even frightened that one day it would be taken from him, and he did not even mind that men laughed at him because of his sudden uxoriousness. The laughter was not cruel, and he was happy. He thought she was happy too. He was astonished how important to him her happiness was. He watched her pencil, amazed at her skill. 'I have to go and form the Battalion.'

'That's because you're important and pompous. Don't forget I'm here.'

'I'll try not to, but you're easily overlooked.' He smiled at her, thinking he was the luckiest man in the world.

They were ordered away from the hill an hour later. The Battalion was formed in parade order on the roadside, ready to march, its baggage somewhere behind it. Captain Harry Price stood at the head of a Company. The flags were cased again. They were marching into France.

Sharpe sat on Sycorax. Jane was beside him on her own mare. It was beginning to rain, the drops huge as pennies where they splashed on the rocks. 'Sergeant Major!'

'Sir!'

'The Battalion will march in line of Companies.'

'Where to, sir?'

Sharpe grinned. 'Into France!'

But suddenly, before the order to march was given, and to Sharpe's embarrassment and his wife's delight, someone cheered. They cheered themselves and their victory. The noise spread, until the Prince of Wales' Own Volunteers were filling the valley with their sound of delight. Sharpe had taken broken, persecuted men and made them into soldiers.

'That's enough, Sergeant Major!'

'Sir! 'Talion!'

Girdwood was mad, so these men, until another colonel was appointed, belonged to Sharpe now. He watched them march, listened to the singing that had already begun, and he thought how they had fought among the rocks to victory. They were, he considered, as good as any troops he had known and, for the moment at least, they were his men, his responsibility, and his pride. Jane watched him. She saw on his hard, striking face the glint of water that was not rain. He was staring at the men for whom he had fought against all the bastards who despised them because they were mere common soldiers. They were his men, his soldiers, Sharpe's Regiment.

HISTORICAL NOTE

The Battle of Vitoria (described in *Sharpe's Honour*) finished French hopes in Spain. A handful of garrisons clung to their fortresses, but the French field armies, trounced by Wellington, fled northwards across the Pyrenees. No one expected their return. It was thought that the rest of 1813 would be spent in mopping up the French garrisons and preparing (from the new Pasajes supply-base) the invasion of France. A good time, then, for a man to return to England.

Yet Sharpe and Harper, by returning to Britain, missed some hard and confused fighting. Marshal Soult, sent by Napoleon to shore up the crumbling defences on the Spanish border, surprised Wellington by attacking instead of passively waiting to be attacked. Armies marched, countermarched, and fought in the mists of the Pyrenees, but by autumn's end the French thrusts had all been defeated, the last fortresses in Spain had fallen (the fall of San Sebastian being particularly horrific), and Wellington could at last advance into France. Sharpe and Harper were back in time for the end of the Pyrenean fighting that cleared the foothills.

The action described in the epilogue of the novel is based on the famous description by Sir William Napier of the part played by the 43rd during the battle of Nivelle (10th November, 1813). Napier described the battle in Volume V of his *History of the War in the Peninsula.* It is an unusually authoritative account, for Sir William Napier had been the 43rd's commanding officer during their attack on the Lesser Rhune.

Sharpe's battles with the hierarchy of the army in England are equally historical. The command of Britain's army during the Napoleonic wars was a shambolic arrangement, split jealously between the War Office and the Horse Guards, with various other bureaucracies ever eager to hold onto their own shares. It was a venal system, open to abuses, of which the most famous was the scandal of 1809 when it was discovered that Mary Anne Clarke, when mistress of the Duke of York, Commander in Chief, had been selling promotions to officers. They had paid her, and she persuaded her lover to make the appointments. Sometimes, when he forgot, she would leave reminders pinned to the curtains of his bed. The Duke, King George III's second son, though it was proved that he had taken no money himself, was forced to resign for two years.

The Duke of York has had a bad press. Every child knows about the Grand Old Duke of York, who had ten thousand men, who marched them up to the top of the hill, then marched them down again. He was every bit as bad and indecisive a field general as that nursery rhyme indicates (it was written after his disastrous Flanders campaign of 1794 in which Private Richard Sharpe, aged 16, fought in his first action), but in truth, bed-curtains aside, he was a highly efficient administrator who brought many much needed and sensible reforms to the army. Employing the younger sons of monarchs has always been one of mankind's lesser problems, but Frederick, Duke of York and Albany, was well matched to his task.

Yet there was little he could do, or anyone else, to curb the venality of the recruiting system. Sergeant Horatio Havercamp, I suspect, reveals most of the trade's tricks, though I like to think Horatio would not have stooped as low as some recruiting parties who equipped their hired prostitutes with manacles to pinion the reluctant volunteers in bed. The brothels where such public-spirited ladies worked were known as Crimping Houses. There was no conscription, of course, and every man (even the prisoners illegally handed to the recruiters) was a 'volunteer'. The army would have dearly liked a press-gang system like the navy, but lacking it, they depended on the wiles of their recruiters and on the depths of their purse. The bounties were extravagant, though the recruit was almost always cheated out of all or most of it, and many colonels added their own monetary rewards to successful recruiters. Crimping existed quite legally. Contractors, independent civilian businessmen, would be offered so much money a head by the War Office, and their profit lay in keeping their bounty low and their promises high. It was much used in Ireland, where poverty drove so many men into the ranks of Britain's army. In the early years of the war senior commissions would be given to a man who brought the army enough recruits; indeed, that is how Sir Henry Simmerson achieved his Lieutenant Colonelcy in the novel that opened this series: *Sharpe's Eagle*. Such shifts were desperately needed for, with the exception of a few prime Regiments like the Rifles and the Guards, most units were chronically short of recruits; a shortage not helped by the existence of the home-bound militia that drained good men from the regular army.

The Prince Regent was fond of victory parades in Hyde Park, especially when enemy trophies were laid before him. The Royal family of the Regency period did not enjoy the affection that the present British Royal family receives from the public. It was not an attractive family. King George III had lost his sanity because of illness and his eldest son was a lavish wastrel who hated his father. Indeed, so unpopular was the Royal family, that the valet of the King's youngest son was roundly applauded by the populace when he laid his master's scalp open with a sabre stroke. The parades in Hyde Park, as well as indulging the Prince Regent's soldiering fantasies, unusually allowed him to appear in public to adulation rather than jeers. The British public, though never very fond of the army, was proud of what it was doing under Wellington's command, and would turn out to cheer dutifully in Hyde Park or to watch the patriotic pageants mounted in London's theatres.

The Prince Regent, after he had become King, did publicly express his fantasies that he had been present at battlefields during the late war. He would embarrass Wellington by claiming, at dinner, to have led a charge at Waterloo. The Duke kept a politic silence.

A politic silence is also best kept about Foulness. It was not a secret military camp in 1813; it is now.

So Sharpe and Harper are back with the army. They, like so many officers and men of that army, now have their wives with them, and they have, at last, breached the defences of France. Wellington is the first foreign General to invade French soil since the very beginning of the Revolutionary War twenty years earlier. There was a feeling, that winter of 1813, that Napoleon would surely sue for peace soon. He was assailed in the north and his beloved France was invaded from the south. But there are battles yet to be fought, and campaigns to be won, so Sharpe and Harper will march again.

SHARPE'S STORY

I'm often asked where Sharpe came from; whether I modelled him on some real person whose memoirs I had found, or whether he is based on a friend of mine, but the truth is that he is entirely fictional. I do recall writing an early story about him, though he was not called Sharpe then. I was producing television then which I liked, but I had always wanted to be a novelist, and ever since reading Hornblower as a child I had tried to find a series of books which did for Wellington's army what C.S. Forester had done for Nelson's navy. No one wrote the series, so one wet day in Belfast I made a start. It went nowhere.

Then, in 1979, I met Judy, an American. Cupid's arrow struck me with the accuracy of a rifle bullet fired by Daniel Hagman. Judy, for all sorts of good reasons, could not move from the States, so I decided I would abandon television, give up Belfast and go to America. The trouble was that the US government, in its wisdom, refused me a work permit, so I airily promised Judy that I would earn a living as a writer, and the only thing I wanted to write was that Hornblower-as-a-soldier series. So I put a typewriter on a kitchen table in New Jersey and started again. This time, unlike my first effort in Belfast, things were more desperate. If Sharpe failed me or, more likely, if I failed Sharpe, then the course of true love would hit a massive roadblock. What little money I possessed would not last long, so speed was of the essence and *Sharpe's Eagle* was written in a hurry. What did I know of my hero? I knew he would be a rifleman, because the rifle was unique to Wellington's troops and that would give him an edge over the enemy. I knew he could not stay with his beloved 95th Rifles because then I would be limited to describing only those actions in which the 95th fought and I wanted the freedom for him to be at every possible action. I knew he was an officer who had come up from the ranks, because that would give him some problems in his own army, but beyond that, not much. I described him at the beginning of the book as tall and black-haired, which was fine till Sean Bean came along, after which I tried not to mention his hair colour ever again. I gave him a scarred cheek, though for the life of me I can never remember which cheek has the scar and I suspect it changes from book to book. What I did not give him was a name because I was looking for something as memorable and quirky as Horatio Hornblower. Day after day passed, more pages piled up in the kitchen, and still he was called Lieutenant XXX. I made lists of names, none of which worked, and it began to annoy me, even hold up the writing, so I decided to give this rifleman a temporary name. I called him Richard Sharpe after the great Cornwall and England rugby player, Richard Sharp, and thought I would change it when the right name came along. But of course the new name stuck. Within a day or two I was already thinking of him as Sharpe, and so he has remained.

Patrick Harper was easier to name. I had been living in Belfast in the years immediately prior to writing Sharpe and had acquired a fondness for Ireland which has never abated. I had a friend in Belfast called Charlie Harper who had a son named Patrick. The problem was that the Harper family were not fond of the British, nor did they have cause to be, and I worried they would be offended if I named a soldier in Britain's army after their son. I asked their permission which was gladly given and so Harper has marched with Sharpe ever since.

The book was finished in about six months, and I had no idea whether it was any good, but I found a London literary agent and he found a publisher, and so *Sharpe's Eagle* was issued in 1981. I have never re-read it but not so long ago a reader told me his reaction to that first Sharpe book. 'I thought it would be like every other book,' he said, 'but when Sharpe killed Berry I knew it was different. Other heroes would never have done that. They're all officers and gentlemen, but not Sharpe.' So right from the beginning Sharpe was a rogue. Berry was a fellow-British officer who managed to upset Sharpe, which is never a wise thing to do, perhaps because Sharpe is so fuelled by anger. It is the anger of an unhappy childhood, of a man who has been forced to fight for every advantage that others were given, and that rage has always driven Sharpe. It makes him very different from Hornblower who is so fair-minded and honourable. Sharpe is a rogue, and a dangerous one, but he is a rogue on our side.

'He could never carry that sword,' an expert told me after *Sharpe's Eagle* was published. 'That sword' was the 1796 pattern Heavy Cavalry sword, a beast of a blade, ill-balanced and ineffective, but I liked the idea of Sharpe, a tall man, carrying such a butcher's weapon. I spent some money I could not afford on buying a trooper's sword (I was assured by the vendor that it was carried at Waterloo, and I like to think that is true) and I discovered that it could be carried. I slung it from a belt and it hung just fine, so that was all right, and Sharpe carried the sword from that day on.

The story of the siege of Badajoz in 1812 is one of the great tales of the war. It was the story I really wanted to tell in the first

Sharpe book, but I reckoned I might not have the skills to do it as a first-time author, and so I began Sharpe in 1809. The story of Badajoz with all its horror and heroism comes in the third Sharpe book, *Sharpe's Company*. That book also introduces the malevolent Sergeant Obadiah Hakeswill. I have no idea where he came from. I was driving one day and the name simply popped into my head. Hakeswill. It's a marvellously villainous name, and he proved to be a terrific villain. But why was Hakeswill's neck 'obscenely mutilated'? Because he had survived a judicial hanging. I remember writing that and pausing. Would anyone believe me? Was I stretching, not just Obadiah's neck, but credulity? I almost cut it out, thinking I would receive scornful letters, but somehow it seemed absolutely right for Obadiah to have been hanged and to have survived it, and so I left it in. Then, months later, I discovered that so many folk survived judicial hangings that the Royal College of Surgeons had a by-law dealing with how such survivors were to be treated by their members. The bodies of hanged felons were sold to the surgeons for dissection, and enough proved to be alive when they reached the hospitals to make the by-law necessary (they were resuscitated, and then, mostly, sent off to Australia). Far from being unlikely it seemed that Obadiah's history was almost commonplace. Obadiah, who was so marvellously portrayed by Pete Postlethwaite in the TV series, was one of those characters who come out of nowhere to enliven a book, and another was Lucille, the Frenchwoman with whom Sharpe will spend the rest of his life, and of all the things Sharpe has ever done, settling in France surprised me the most! I knew his marriage to Jane Gibbons was well on the rocks, but I assumed he would find himself some other woman and settle down to a life in the English countryside. I always intended Lucille to be a consolation prize for Sharpe's close friend, William Frederickson, who had endured a lot for Sharpe, but had never been fortunate in love. I thought Lucille Castineau would be perfect for 'Sweet William', but, perversely, Sharpe fell in love with her. I tried to prevent it, but when a character takes off on their own like that, there's very little a writer can do, and so Sharpe and Lucille fall hopelessly in love, and poor Frederickson is both offended and jilted.

It astonished me that Sharpe went to live in France, yet now it seems inescapable. Sharpe was always an outsider and he could never have been content in Britain after the war. But as a British soldier living among the erstwhile enemy he is as happy as when he was a man from the ranks surviving in the officers' mess. He likes being the square peg. And he loves Lucille. Lucky Sharpe, though I doubt he believed he was lucky when, out of the blue, the Emperor escaped from Elba and Sharpe finds himself thrust unexpectedly into the campaign of Waterloo. The drama of that campaign is such that no fictional plot can live beside it. Not just the drama of the day itself when, till the very last moment, it seemed the French must win, but the human drama of the two greatest soldiers of the age at last meeting on a battlefield.

No one would dispute Napoleon's place in the pantheon of great military leaders, but Wellington, to my mind, is a much greater battlefield general. Wellington, of course, was never a 'war leader' like Napoleon. He did not play dice with nations. He operated at a more modest level, as the leader of an army, and it is remarkable that, unlike the Emperor, he never suffered a battlefield defeat. He had a great talent for soldiering, a clear eye, a decisive mind, and a comprehensive grasp of what his men were capable of doing. His men liked him. They did not love him as the French soldiers loved Napoleon, but the Emperor was a politician who knew how to tweak men's affections. In return they worshipped him. But Wellington? He did not want to be worshipped. He had, he said, no small talk. He did not know how to talk to common soldiers, indeed he was an unashamed snob, yet his men liked him because they knew he did not risk their lives unnecessarily. In battle he protected them, usually by placing them on a reverse slope where they were out of sight of the enemy, and the soldiers in his army knew that he did not throw away their lives lightly. After Austerlitz a French general lamented the vast number of French dead on the battlefield and received a scornful look from Napoleon. 'The women of Paris,' the Emperor said, 'can replace those men in one night.' Wellington would never have said that.

It was only in sieges that Wellington lost his ability to keep casualties to a minimum, but he was never at his best besieging fortresses. In battle, because he knew how difficult it was to replace the dead and wounded, he did his best to keep his men safe until the moment came to expose them. He was once asked what was the greatest compliment he had ever received, and he told how he had visited the wounded after the battle of Albuera. That was a dreadful battle in which the British were commanded by General Beresford and it nearly ended in disaster. British casualties were horribly high. 'The enemy,' the French commander said, 'was beaten, but did not know it.' The battle was won, but at an awful price and two days later Wellington visited the wounded. As usual he was tongue-tied when he had to speak to the common soldiery. He came to a large room in the convent where scores of redcoats were lying in pain. He claimed he did not know what to say, so cleared his throat and, rather lamely, said that he was sorry to see so many of them there. 'My lord,' a corporal spoke up from among the injured, 'if you had been at the battle then not so many of us would be here.' It was, indeed, a great compliment.

Behind almost all the Sharpe books is the relationship between Wellington and Sharpe. They are not men who would instinctively like each other. The Duke, as he became, is cold and taciturn. He did not approve of men like Sharpe. He did not like seeing officers promoted from the ranks; 'they always take to drink,' he said dismissively. Sharpe, on the other hand, is scornful of men like Wellington who were born with the privileges of rank, money and connections. Sharpe cannot buy his way up the army's ladder, yet that is how Wellington gained his first promotions. Yet the two men are inextricably tied because Sharpe once saved Wellington's life. The general is aware that he ought to be grateful, and is, in a grudging way. Sharpe, who ought to dislike the general, admires him instead. He knows a good soldier when he sees one. Birth and privilege have nothing to do with it, efficiency is all. They will never be friends, they will always be distant, but they need each other. They even, I think, like each other, but neither knows how to bridge the gap to express that liking. And Sharpe is always doing over-dramatic things, of which the Duke disapproves. He liked steady officers, unflashy, who quietly did their duty, and he was quite right to approve of such good men. Sharpe is anything but quietly dutiful. He is the odd man out, but still a very useful man on the battlefield.

I always thought Waterloo would mark the end of the Sharpe series. I had written eleven novels, the same number as in Forester's Hornblower series, and I had taken Sharpe from Talavera to Waterloo, and now his world was at peace. Sharpe could go back to Normandy and to Lucille, while I would try my hand at other books. Sharpe was finished.

Then things grew complicated. Actually they had grown complicated a couple of years earlier when a television production company had announced that they wanted to make a series about Sharpe. I was, of course, delighted even though I did not believe that any such films would ever be made. But there was a chance that a Spanish production company would invest in the project. What the producers needed, therefore, was a new story set at the beginning of Sharpe's career which would include a Spanish hero. I still did not think the project would get anywhere, but it was foolish to ignore the chance that it might, so I wrote *Sharpe's Rifles* with Blas Vivar as the Spaniard who could provoke the desired cheque. The book was published and I heard no more about any television series and I deduced that the proposed films had been a flash in the pan. A flash in the pan is when a musket flint fires the priming powder in the lock, but doesn't set off the main charge in the barrel. But I was wrong, the films were to be made, a crew was in the Ukraine, actors were there, and then, just as suddenly, it was all over again. The actor playing Sharpe had a dreadful accident while playing football against the Ukrainian extras, and he was not going to be able to walk for six months, and the whole project seemed doomed. Somehow they rescued it, but they now needed a new actor to play Sharpe, and they needed him on very short notice. There was no time for auditions, and the only actor available was Sean Bean who unexpectedly found himself on a plane to Simferopol (known to all the film crew as Simply-Awful). That was a lucky accident because I cannot imagine Sharpe as anyone else; I hear Sean's voice when I write Sharpe. It is a wonderful coincidence of actor and character.

Before this, having abandoned any hope of seeing the television series, I had started the Starbuck books, the tale of a young northerner who finds himself fighting for the Confederacy in the American Civil War. I was enjoying those books but once the Sharpe filming was underway it became clear that I should go back to writing Sharpe, and that meant taking Sharpe all the way back to India.

* * *

India had always been a part of Sharpe's 'back-story'. Even in the very first book, *Sharpe's Eagle*, India is mentioned. It helped explain much about Sharpe; how he had learned to read and, crucially, how he had saved Wellington's life and was thus rewarded with a commission. So India had been useful to me, but I never had any intention of telling the Indian stories. I knew very little about India, and sources for the Indian campaigns of Sir Arthur Wellesley (as Wellington was then called) were very skimpy compared with the vast amount written about his Peninsular and Waterloo campaigns. I also had a conviction that I could not write convincingly about any battle unless I had visited the place, and I had never been to India and was wary of going because I expected the battlefields to have changed beyond recognition. Yet those Indian battlefields turned out to be the least altered sites I have ever visited. Seringapatam, where *Sharpe's Tiger* is set, was a considerable town when the British laid siege to it in 1799. I suspected that I would have to scratch around in back alleys to find even a remnant of the town Sharpe knew, but discovered that Seringapatam had shrunk to a village so that the impressive ramparts surround a great area of vacant land. It is a marvellous place.

One of the joys of writing historical novels is to 'explain' the small dark inexplicable corners of real history. One of those mysteries is what caused the terrible explosion at Almeida, described in *Sharpe's Gold*, and another is how the Tippoo Sultan died at Seringapatam. We know he was shot in the Watergate, a tunnel leading through the ramparts, but the British soldier who killed him was never discovered. He would have been rewarded, but he never volunteered his action, probably because the Tippoo, when he died, was festooned with jewels. That unknown soldier became very rich that day and he undoubtedly feared that his ill-gotten plunder would be confiscated. So Sharpe takes his place.

Sharpe begins *Sharpe's Tiger* as a private and ends it as a sergeant. He has also learned to read in the Tippoo's dungeons, so now has two of the necessary qualifications to be promoted from the ranks. That promotion occurs in the second Indian adventure, *Sharpe's Triumph*, which tells the extraordinary story of the battle of Assaye and at the heart of that battle is another of those small mysteries. We know that Sir Arthur Wellesley, while galloping across the field from one wing of his army to the other, was stranded in the enemy gun line. His horse, Diomed, had been piked in the chest, the general slid from the saddle and was surrounded by his Mahratta enemies. He survived, yet he was ever reluctant to describe exactly what happened. In a career that was remarkable for his frequent proximity to mortal danger and his avoidance of anything other than the most trifling wounds, that survival was the Duke of Wellington's closest brush with death. Yet what happened? He would not say, but I needed an event that would catapult Sharpe into the officers' mess. That event had to be a display of extraordinary bravery and Wellesley's miraculous survival gave me the perfect opportunity. In all Sharpe's career that is the crucial moment. It brings him to Wellesley's notice, it makes him an officer and it begins his reputation.

Sharpe, of course, had to return from India, and it occurred to me, somewhat mischievously, that his homeward voyage must inevitably take him not far from Cape Trafalgar and, as his last fight in India was in 1804 and because the battle of Trafalgar was fought in 1805, it seemed an irresistible mischief. Hornblower, after all, never got to Trafalgar, but why should not Sharpe fight there? So he did, one of the few men (I have discovered two others) present at both Trafalgar and Waterloo.

I am frequently asked how many more Sharpe novels will be written and I always answer five. I said that when there were only five novels in print, again when there were six, and keep saying it. I say five because it is an easier answer than trying to work out the real answer, which is that I do not know. I only know there will be more stories, and some, like the twenty-first in the series, will surprise me. Judy and I were invited to a wedding in Jerez de la Frontera, a town not far from Cadiz in southern Spain, and a long way from any place where Wellington fought. But close to Cadiz is Barrosa, a small seaside resort, and it was at Barrosa that the British, under the leadership of Sir Thomas Graham, captured the first of the many French eagles they were to take in the wars. I thought it would be interesting to see the battlefield, even though it had nothing whatever to do with Sharpe or Wellington, and so, under the influence of a massive hangover (Spanish weddings are spectacular), we drove to Barrosa. There is almost nothing left of the battlefield now, but I stood on the hill where Major Browne's makeshift battalion marched to certain death and I looked past the construction cranes on the lower ground where Major Gough's Irish took the eagle of the French 8th and I thought Sharpe has to be here. I had no idea how to get him to Cadiz, but the thought of writing Barrosa was irresistible, and so *Sharpe's Fury* was born.

There will be more Sharpe books (five more, perhaps?). I do not know now what stories they will tell, but I do know they will be a tribute to the heroism of the British soldier. There is an odd idea (I heard it being trotted out by a professor on Radio Four not long ago) that Wellington's army was a mass of gutterborn scum commanded by aristocrats and disciplined by brutality. That is glib rubbish. You cannot win wars with such an instrument. There were very few aristocrats, most of the officers were what we would call middle-class, and by the war's end many, like Sharpe, had been promoted from the ranks. The army's morale was high and memoir after memoir reveals the mutual respect between officers and men. They joked, they survived, they did endure terrible punishments, but they fought like devils and they won battle after battle. Sharpe is one of them. I have always thought of him as a rogue, but that may not be a bad thing. I once talked with a retired Warrant Officer who was running a programme for teenaged drug addicts and he told me that 'a soldier fights battles for those who cannot fight for themselves.' I think that is the most brilliant summation of a soldier's purpose that I have ever heard, and I have used it in the Sharpe books more than once. Sharpe fights for those who cannot fight for themselves, and he fights dirty, which is why he is so effective. It's also why I like him, and one day Sharpe and Harper will march again.

Bernard Cornwell

The SHARPE Series
(in chronological order)

Sharpe's Tiger (1799)
Sharpe's Triumph (1803)
Sharpe's Fortress (1803)
Sharpe's Trafalgar (1805)
Sharpe's Prey (1807)
Sharpe's Rifles (1809)
Sharpe's Havoc (1809)
Sharpe's Eagle (1809)
Sharpe's Gold (1810)
Sharpe's Escape (1810)
Sharpe's Fury (1811)
Sharpe's Battle (1811)
Sharpe's Company (1812)
Sharpe's Sword (1812)
Sharpe's Enemy (1812)
Sharpe's Honour (1813)
Sharpe's Regiment (1813)
Sharpe's Siege (1814)
Sharpe's Revenge (1814)
Sharpe's Waterloo (1815)
Sharpe's Devil (1820–21)

The SHARPE Series
(in order of publication)

Also by Bernard Cornwell

The MAKING OF ENGLAND Series
The Last Kingdom
The Pale Horseman
The Lords of the North
Sword Song
The Burning Land
Death of Kings

The GRAIL QUEST Series
Harlequin
Vagabond
Heretic

Azincourt

Stonehenge: a novel of 2000 BC

The Fort

By Bernard Cornwell and Susannah Kells

Fed